I0831370

THE REFLECTION OF INNOCENCE

John Tolliver

ISBN: 0692772707
ISBN 13: 9780692772706

Dedicated to Nancy and Nannie
Who believed there was no
limit on knowledge or imagination.

Thank You to Natalie and Steven West
For their collaborative talents
In Writing & Editing,
And their patience in helping me learn.

1

I've been told that at police academies, they teach officers-in-training that the least credible evidence is an eyewitness. One onlooker will swear the stoplight had gone red before the Mercedes ever entered the intersection while another says she heard the squeal of tires before the light had even flicked to yellow. No one at the scene can agree on the exact length of the light sequence, though if they wanted to figure it out all they'd have to do is look back up to where the wires cross and count.

Memory, famously, is a tricky thing—*differently* tricky, it seems, for every one of us. For some, memories are lost much sooner than we'd like. For others, the scenes won't fade away fast enough. We can try, but there's no guarantee we'll archive the material of our choosing. There are the songs we hate and still find ourselves humming, the lost phone numbers and addresses. There are the usual traumas that haunt us—the shootings, the robberies. The things we know at the time will become memories we'd rather escape.

And then there's a different class, the things we never suspect we'll eventually clench over. There's the shame of youthful arrogance when revisited by a newer, more mature version of you; the deadeyed sigh of a disappointed family member; the painfully earnest smile of a girl who's fallen for you, when you know you don't love her back. Pictures that stream into our mind's eye, always with questions attached: what was I thinking? Where did I go off the rails? What did I do to deserve this?

If we wanted to figure it out, all we'd have to do is look back.

We laud memory as a gift—a privilege to be used responsibly. "Those who do not remember the past," the amateur historians say, "are doomed to repeat it." I've always wondered if they find it ironic how they've chosen to repeat a timeworn cliché to denounce the fate of repetition. If we can't choose our memories or wish them away, and if each memory comes with a responsibility—a burden—then you might also call memory a curse.

Trust me, I would know.

For all I know, I carry more memories than anyone I've ever known. Or, at the very least, I think I might be tied.

What we remember can take us in wild directions.

There are, to be fair, also the happy surprises of memory: the long-lost shell collection you'd squirrelled away. Your mother's special recipe for grilled cheese, the way she stood over the pan flicking packets of sugar to sprinkle over the bread. The special parallel universes a kid could make out of any partitioned area.

Ψ

"John, get out of the clothes rack," I remember her calling.

The first voice to separate itself from the hum was nearly always the one that meant I was in trouble. I peeked out just the tiniest tip of my nose.

Mom stood there, hands on her hips, with a less-than-indulgent look on her face. She'd clearly been flagged down by the four or five inconveniently-startled women who'd already uncovered my hiding place amid the winter coats. Indeed, she was flanked by the familiar faces of two crimson-faced women in horn-rimmed glasses, who had discovered me.

My older brother Jim took in the scene like he would any TV sitcom: smirking.

The predictable propriety lecture began—and had blurred—before I'd even climbed out. The women then marched righteously away, stomping their heels against the linoleum like war drums. Mom trailed off mid-sentence. I looked up at her, and I think she might have winked.

"I love each of you equally as complete packages—the good and the bad as well," she'd always said. But deep down, I always suspected that I might be the favorite.

Like most middle children, I wasn't much like my other brothers. They were sports stars, smashers of bugs, jungle gym gladiators. Mom didn't treat me much like them. No one did.

No, I was the poet, the collector of memories. I was an astronaut of imagination…*a black sheep.* As such, I was beloved. Everyone knew I was special: Johnny the Dreamer.

Mom and Nannie had built me up as such, and I lived for them forever after.

After all, they introduced me to entire worlds.

At four, I memorized every bedtime story I'd ever been told, the first time I'd hear it. Any story. That was all Mom's doing—the greatest storyteller around. Years later, I discovered that she'd always neglected to mention she had a one forty-five IQ, although we kids and the larger community had certainly suspected it all along.

The traits we were most familiar with were her patience and kindness. I'd never be content with simple answers to simple questions, so every question spiraled into a million more. Mom celebrated that inquisitiveness—even when it stretched to excess—as the first sparks of a creative life. Within that childish analytical framework, I generated dozens at a time, sometimes extending into accidentally existential lines of inquiry. Why are there so few primary colors? Why so many shades of red? How come orange isn't red?

Mom had inherited the presence, equipoise, and elegance of her own Mother (my Grandmother); so you always felt like you were the only one in the room whenever either woman spoke to you. They never talked down to children, but instead treated them the way they expected to be treated: respectfully, with an emphasis on dignity. Humanity was a foundational virtue for both. In spite of being an aristocratic gem cut from Old Virginia, my Grandmother would only respond to the name "Nannie," "Grandma" seeming somehow too formal.

My rack antics were bound to end in a trip to Nannie's anyhow, so Mom might finish her errands in peace. She'd hug me when I arrived, sit me up quite straight on a high stool, and demand, "Well now, what'll it be, John? How are things?"

Nannie lived in an enormous house in Garden City, which had an entirely different degree of formality than ours. A different sort of quality and longevity was at work there with huge, thickly lacquered wood furniture, long slick hallways, and an elegant staircase. Time had refined the whole place. It was magical, a place of dreams. (There was also a television the size of a bathtub, which for once I didn't have to share with my brother.) But it was in silence, or in conversations—strolling around with Nannie—that the house really came alive. I loved wandering through the four poster beds upstairs imagining conversations with ghosts, secretly peeking through drawers full of shells and combs, or staring from the high windows. Seated in her fine paneled library surrounded by innumerable novels, history, myths, and poetry, I'd sit and draw for hours. Nannie always feigned amazement, as if every sheet presented to her was a masterpiece. Sometimes I just stared at the books, running my finger across the spines, taking in all the colors and designs. She had so many wonderful books in that library. Although I couldn't quite read, I never tired of looking at images and elaborate typesets, the shapes different paragraphs made, hunting for the few words I knew. Nannie loved to share those books, and would spend hours reading them aloud from her favorite chair.

I'd commit them all to memory, reciting them back to my brother late at night when I couldn't sleep, in goofy orations that echoed off the corners of our shared room, torturing my hardworking Father who was trying to sleep just beyond our wall.

A World War Two veteran, my overworked Father was the type who'd always limited his wartime travel stories to remembered snippets of the men he'd served with. He would never talk about his role, or how he'd earned the Purple Heart we'd discover years later in his room.. In many ways, he was the opposite of me. He always deliberated before he spoke, while I would think things out while I spoke. He never minced words, and never had a chat without some message to send. But he could express a million words merely with his big brown eyes. You knew it immediately when you'd said something wrong at the dinner table. But you knew just as quickly if a joke or story you told was really funny, because Dad's eyes would sparkle like nobody else's.

Even in the case of my late-night declamations, Dad had maintained enough discipline upon his reentry to Long Island civilian life that his responses to my incessant chatter would never be too salty. He'd just bark the number representing the hour at which he'd have to awake for work the next morning.

"FOUR, JOHN. FOUR. GOODNIGHT!"

The special child, every family has one. It's not that the parents love them *more*, but *differently*. You could tell by the side-glancing smiles when you'd been caught in the act. The ginger hold they'd take of your hand as they pulled you from behind the clothes rack into the flickering fluorescent lights and festive holiday music of Christmastime. Everywhere, USA.

This was Mineola, New York. But mostly it's the same things you'd expect anywhere…

Chaos, frenzy, terror, and manic euphoria.

It was all over their faces. Everyone! Every single person. Personally, I'd always had a hard time with something one could call an "oversensitivity" to extremes of emotion. I liked to be in control of those states, but I'd always had a hard time tuning out other people's emotional signals. I found myself staring, slack jawed at the scenes, over-receptive to anything, no matter how slight.

I was somehow programmed for people, moved to really zoom in on them. It'd been that way as long as I could remember. At the time, I was too young for it to be considered rude, but without some kind of intervention, I think I'd have been bound for heartache in later years.

Expressions, gestures, the tiniest nuances: together they represented this terrible magnet I felt powerless to escape from. They would overtake me, and then I became this bizarre floating library of all these fleeting moods and feelings belonging to other people.

It never brought me anything but trouble. So I'd sometimes improvise solutions like coat racks to avoid worse things. Things like my recently retired—much tried, much regretted strategy of asking lots of probing questions to agitated strangers who seemed distraught while shopping. That had never gone well.

Daydreaming, I evaded my brother's impatient hand and skipped halfway back to my mom's side—but panicked upon remembering my glasses. I darted back to my Coat Cave to grab them, but unfortunately went sprawling forward while attempting reentry and—yep. A sharp sound from under my knee. Broken glasses, once again. My Dad was going to kill me. I vaguely considered staying in my cave. Maybe my Mom would forget me. There was a peace to be found in that muffled cocoon, buried between heavy cloth. Lulled into a false sense of security by the constant Doppler effect of shopping carts moving past, until all at once, with a horrific metal shriek, the clothes hangers would be shoved aside and the jig was up. Emotional stress made me absentminded as a kid. I had a hard time staying on task, chasing whichever seemed the brightest light around. Jim's disembodied head parted the coats. "What just broke, John? Better not have been those new glasses. Dad will kill you."

Ψ

Nannie and I strutted up to the Woolworth's counter, dressed to the nines in full formal regalia. We took our seats at the high counter, the store chatter floating all around us. As was custom, I rigidly policed my leg-swinging, for fear of being perceived as some sort of child. But it never seemed difficult to be cool and mature when I was out on the town with Nannie. I was always proud as could be.

Just like that, I was suddenly grown. I swiveled to watch people from my perch. Tall, serene, impassive—

"Well, what'll it be, John?" Nannie indulgently began.

"Well Nannie, I'd like the grilled cheese and bacon with a strawberry shake."

"Don't you want to try something else this time, John?"

"No thanks, grilled cheese please! The way Mom makes it."

"Don't you want to try something else this time, John?"

"Really, John, you're probably half cheese and sugar by this point. But you just get whatever you'd like honey, and then we'll go see about some shopping."

I'd laugh and drop hints about our upcoming shopping trip, leaning forward precociously into exaggerated winks, wobbling terribly while I did so. (We never, never addressed the fact that I was always sitting atop two phone books to reach the counter. This would have been horribly taboo.)

In those days, Nannie had a wonderful strategy to keep her house filled with toys for our weekly visits. She insisted on stealing us away, one at a time, so as to give each of us some unique attention. In a family as busy as mine, that one-on-one time meant the world. We'd look forward to it at least as much as going to the seashore or getting a birthday cake.

Naturally, bribery was often involved. She knew each of us was in the process of developing our own miniature sized personalities, aesthetics, and preferences, but at home the law of the land often drifted towards primogeniture, and all the degradation of equal privileges inherent in the hand-me-down system.

To remedy this injustice, Nannie would slowly build up unique toy sets for each of us, cumulatively compiled from our individual Woolworth lunch outings. It had become a sacred tradition.

My brothers Jim, Richard, and Rob were three peas in a pod—fanatics about sports and scouts. Their spaces resembled armories of sports-craft.

I, on the other hand, was the family collector. I poured over collections of things with a religious sort of fervor. Coins, stamps, miniature models, and famous autographs were an obsession. As effusive as I could be in the outside world, the chatterbox persona would immediately fall away the moment I was left to my own devices, alone with these nostalgic collections. Suddenly I would transform into the archivist, the sacred keeper of memories. I became a Zen master of concentrated quietude. For days on end, I could fuss over model boats or planes.

Nannie kept shrines of these pristine models around her huge City home. Never one to rush changes, she'd preserved the bedrooms of her now-grown children as time capsules of their vanished childhoods.

And now, she carried on that tradition with us. In a spare closet under the staircase, entire battle squadrons of my meticulously crafted land and sea vehicles sat poised and ready. They were flawlessly painted in raucously colored patterns I'd spent days determining from the books in her den, immaculately sanded with perfectly fitted joints—expertly glued under a lamp so bright that the glue nearly boiled. To the eternal chagrin of my parents, many sets of my glasses had been sacrificed to this "closet artistry," broken beneath my knees as I toiled away.

Most importantly, ornate wooden boxes were filled with obscure relics of the past: arcane coins from far flung quarters, unreadable maps, feathers of every stripe, transparent gemstones, polished rocks carved with what appeared to be runes, Asian fans, an extremely dull but wicked-looking Arabic dagger, and a piece of parchment printed in ancient Greek symbols. (It now lived locked in a special box, after Jim and Richard damaged it while recklessly tumbling through the corridors in an impromptu tennis match.)

There were ornate inkwells, scrolled magnifying glasses, hunting horns made of antlers, innumerable walking sticks, and animal skin hats. When Nannie discovered how I'd marvel at anything from the past (like the travel detritus from her journeys with my Grandfather), she'd hidden ticket stubs amid the corner floorboards of the closet, in the recesses of a lost shoe—all for me to discover when alone, to puzzle over. I could still find seating-cards to blimps, planes, trains from the other side of the world in my old glasses cases.

Nannie took great pains to alchemically transform my adolescent imagination into something wonderful, something that would sustain me for life. She was an undisputed master of childhoods and magic.

Three hours passed like a flash; I'd barely noticed it was our normal time to go. I felt myself lifted, carried. Suddenly, the roar of Nannie's big blue Cadillac pulled us into the hair salon where Mom was enjoying her final moments of peace.

Ψ

"Well, John—I suppose we should go in and find you a wife now, yes? Let's get started," Nannie crooned.

We gazed through the window upon half the women of Mineola—their heads transformed into strange hatching eggs by hard-plastic perm machines.

"Not just yet, Nannie. I'll still have to finish my support group, if those aircraft carriers want half a chance of safety in open waters."

Nannie smiled. "I see your point. A wife will wait."

We walked in and Mom turned around, looking like a movie star. She was clearly in her element, attending to several conversations at once. All her melodic tangents fired off towards the four corners of the world, immediately answered by peals of laughter echoing off the walls. All who saw her could immediately recognize a community matriarch. People had always adored her for her counsel and compassion. The lady could talk, but she could also listen and help like nobody else. She was the kind of woman that left everyone smiling around her. Including me.

"Hey there, kid." She beamed as I walked closer. "How was Nannie's?"

Mom knew very well that our long-established rules of grownup life conventions formally barred me from proper elaboration of Nannie-Time, but she never gave up asking. Nannie's visits were sacred; they were a world apart, magical in part by their distance from the outside.

I couldn't get out of the salon soon enough, though I didn't yet recognize that my aversion was something more than a dislike of the heat and the acrid smell of nail polish remover and hair products. It was more than the strange effect of Naugahyde seats, which tried to absorb you like quicksand, or the loud Formica patterning materials favored at that time, stretching from floor to ceiling like a monster's magical cave.

It was more, too, than Nannie's constant gag threat of prematurely ending my pristine childhood by marrying me off to one of the town matrons. No, something about the intensely emotional nature back as far as I could recall, gradually increasing with every visit of that claustrophobic congregation space supersaturated my senses. It almost suffocated me. This place served as "temple" for a rare kind of sincerity and the unearthing of unspoken baggage—a very good thing. So I never could quite understand why I always reacted so intensely against it.

Each time I'd walk inside, I'd get "the spins." It had stretched

"Why look, it's Johnny the Boy Wonder!"

As a sweet middle aged schoolteacher patted me absentmindedly on the shoulder, I shuttered and succumbed to the spins yet again.

Each time these ladies laid a hand on my shoulder as they sorted through their emotional travelogues, I felt faint.

Why? I hadn't the slightest idea.

Each time, the hair on the back of my neck stood up, my heart first fluttering before bottoming out in a thud. My mouth always salivated with an almost metallic taste, and lights abruptly intensified. Finally, I always imagined a very peculiar sound. The closest way I could describe it would be very dry, crackling sound—like leaves getting whipped up by a sudden whirling breeze into a slow crescendo that approached something deafening, an obliterating roar.

Something was very unusual here. Something was changing.

And the changes were speeding up.

Shivering on the way to the Mom's car to drive home, I caught a glimpse of myself in a passing window.

My pupils were enormous and my face had gone tomato-paste red.

What *was happening* to me?

2

Looking back, I can still feel the churn in my stomach as Nannie's heirloom crystal bowl shattered. (I'd stepped on my poor glasses again, as usual, and as I over-corrected to try and save them, I'd bumped into a pedestal.) I experienced the rest of the scene in slow motion.

It wobbled twice, then almost seemed like it might steady itself. (It didn't.)

One piece of the potpourri Nannie kept inside wobbled into view, free-falling in the open air. And then a second. Then a dozen. And then I watched the full rotating tilt as the top rolled over the base. Imagine tragic opera music as I watched the swansong dive of the magic bowl, with time itself finally standing completely still.

And then the huge explosion shook the house, as a million shards found new living situations lodged in every corner of the carpeted hallway, every lampshade, in every hand-towel.

It wasn't long before Nannie herself appeared as well, racing down the long hallway towards me. By this time—in spite of my need to be a Grown Up—I was inconsolable.

I'd stared at this very same bowl for years, imagining it being used exclusively for magic potions and/or seeing into the future. It was devastating to think I'd been the one behind its untimely destruction. The sound itself was also earth shattering, and it'd be remiss to now downplay how close I'd been to either actually peeing or having a minor heart-attack.

I think the tears I produced at that moment might have actually been tiny cartoon fountains, arching airborne away from my head.

"Aw, honey, it's okay. You didn't mean to do anything wrong—" Nannie began.

"I'm so-o sor-ry I broo-ooo-oke ittttt!" I shrieked, punctuated by hysterical hiccups and sobs. I was halfway into that process of actually dissolving into a liquid that only children can do, and only while weeping for an audience.

"I know, honey, but that doesn't matter! We can always get another bowl, bowls are just *things*. Are you okay? C'mon over here, Johnny."

Nannie cradled me like a baby, rocking me back and forth. And for once, I didn't mind not being an adult. She held both my hands in her soft fingertips and kissed my forehead a million times while quietly murmuring "There, there…It's okay darling, everything is fine…" on repeat. I began to calm down, staring at her beautiful opal ring that had always centered me.

But then something extraordinary happened. It felt familiar, at least at first.

The hair on the back of my neck stood up. My heart first fluttered and then thudded, and the ground seemed like it was falling out beneath me. My mouth salivated with an almost metallic taste, and all the lights in the room seemed abruptly intensify—

My eyes became huge black orbs. My eardrums trembled and throbbed.

Finally, I heard the same peculiar sound—the same sound I'd always remembered from Mom's beauty salon, crescendoing up into an obliterating roar.

But then without warning, something completely new happened.

The world around me paled and dulled to a strange sepia haze that tumbled and rolled over Nannie and me, like someone had blown up several huge bags of dyed flour over the house. Everything slowed and froze. Through a mist, I discerned Nannie's hand still resting against my own, but that world already seemed light years away and still receding. The roar suddenly cut to absolute silence, and it was a silence like I'd never known. The air itself seemed to vibrate, like there was some sort of living ether quivering in the air, rather than the breathable stuff I needed. And finally, something within it squirmed.

Indistinguishable at first, a writhing dark smudge quivered some distance from me. It seemed to stretch in the gloom, and then sprung to life.

In the strange half light, the bizarre ink creature elongated into one bending line, and then another and another—eventually joining together, crosshatching and blurring, brightening and pooling, changing in values and shade until the smudge I'd been horrified by had become a full image. It continued to clarify itself as my jaw fell wide open. Then suddenly, it snapped to something perfectly clear.

Somehow—floating between me and my Nannie—was the perfect image of a young girl, a stranger who I had never seen.

The image hovered a moment, and the lights seemed to flash. A huge *whooshing* sound crescendoed until it resolved into an inaudible squeal beyond my hearing range, so high it made my eardrums throb. My hands rose involuntarily to my head.

Finally, with a noise like the universe itself getting vacuumed down a garbage disposal, the image of the strange girl melted. In its place, several half images careened past fluidly, like Polaroids running out of a camera, one after another, until they melted back into compounds of hissing chemicals and shadow. Even as I tried to squeeze my eyes shut—and although my hands were bolted over my eardrums—I saw new images and even heard voices.

What was this?! What was happening to me?!

The world looked like somebody was watercolor-painting atop a rippling bowl of water with India ink, but at a rocket's speed, with all the regular world boiling furiously miles beneath.

I was only able to pick out a few meaningless details from the slipstreams of images and sound, before I felt a tiny trickle of blood spurt from my right ear. My mouth fell open—to speak, to scream? I didn't know. Then all the images lurched back together and exploded into light and chaotic white noise. My head felt like it was crumpling in.

I let go of the world, let myself fall into the mess of ink and light.

Then I blacked out completely.

Ψ

I came to, lying in a hospital bed, with a clear plastic tube poked through my wrist. As I considered retching into a plastic bin on my chest that seemed to be tailor-made for such an occasion, a young nurse breezed into the room.

"Awake at last! How's my favorite patient doing today?"

Somewhere in the back of my throat I gurgled like my dog Frosty after eating too much grass. A bit of drool pooled at my bottom lip; my arms were dead limp. I wore a thin frock covered in cartoon dinosaurs.

Oh dear god…

"Where am I?" I mumbled weakly.

"Nassau Hospital. Somehow you hurt yourself pretty bad last night. Do you remember anything about your eardrums? Or your hand?" The pretty nurse seemed quite concerned.

I tried to muster all my gallantry and charm, lifting myself up on my elbows. "Oh, it was nothing. I actually don't remember anything about my hand."

"We pulled some nasty glass out of your left palm there, mister. You were still clutching a broken glasses-frame when you came in here…"

I was halfway through playing it cool again with the injury when I finally became aware of a horrible feeling in my right ear. I remembered something about shooting pain, but not really anything specific. Did Alfred the cat get me again? It seemed a little extreme, even for him…

"Um, what happened to my ear?"

"I was hoping you could tell me that, Johnny. You've got some cuts all around the ear canal, which would normally be a cause for alarm for us, if we thought somebody had tried to hurt you."

I blinked. Processing, or trying to. So far, nothing. "It's just…the cuts on your ear seem like they came from your own fingers, John. Exactly the same size and everything. Your fingertips are all torn up, too. Can you try to tell me what happened?" She leaned on her clipboard against the side of the bed, hoping for something simple, something she could help fix.

"I have no idea," I mumbled incoherently. "I don't remember. I'm sorry. I think I need my Mom—"

I slumped after seeing she was clearly disappointed by my answer. I was trying!

"Sure." She smiled sweetly. "But you'll give me a call here at the hospital if you ever need help with anything, right? My name and number will be right here in your discharge file when your Mom gets back."

She slipped a card into a manila folder full of papers, pulled my IV tube out to clean and bandage the site, and made as if she was about to leave.

An obvious thought occurred to me for the first time and sent my sluggish mind spinning.

What would *Mom* make of all this?

"Is she here?" I asked quickly. "Does she know?"

"Sure, honey. She just stepped out into the hallway to grab a coffee." She tossed me a lollipop and left.

The car ride back home was polluted with a tense, unfamiliar silence. Mom kept her eyes very steady on the road, only rarely stealing glances back at me in the rear view mirror. Usually she'd used the mirror when she was halfway through making a joke and wanted to monitor my reaction to the punchline. Today, it was different.

"John, what happened over there? I just don't understand. I just—" She drew in a quick breath but then changed her mind, letting out a long sigh.

"I think I broke my glasses, Mom. I'm sorry. They hurt my hand."

I tried to keep myself together, sensing that things would somehow only be made worse if I started to cry.

"It isn't your glasses I'm concerned with." She paused, then continued after some reflection. "It's the fact that you put your fingers through your eardrums."

Ψ

It wasn't long until the memories crept back into my mind. The noise, the impossible lights, the images I saw, and the abstract terror that stretched across it all. It was all bound together in a strange amber solidity of terror: a picture frozen together and divided off from the outside world. My attempts to explain it to family…were not going so well.

"John, you know you can talk to me. If something is going on, you have to be honest. No more stories…"

Mom was at her wits' end. It had been nearly a week, and she was still convinced I must have gone histrionic on her, albeit with a level of dedication entirely inappropriate for a child. Something about the self-mutilation side of things must have thrown her. She had to know what had happened, but couldn't escape the vague sense that I was telling tall-tales somehow, in spite of my best efforts to be honest.

For his part, Jim also took me aside and let me have a piece of his mind. "Look, John. Take a look at Mom. You think that's any way to treat her? If you got in a fight, you've gotta just be straight with her, and with me. If somebody hit you, you tell me and I'll take care of it. Me and Greg and Mikey, we'll make sure nobody hurts you again…"

"Nobody hurt me, Jim," I interrupted. "I already told you."

"Yeah, right," Jim mumbled disgustedly. "Some kinda ViewMaster toy bit you or something."

"Jim, that's not fair, I already told you what happened, and…"

The closest thing I'd gotten to any sort of empathetic understanding was my cartoon-loving eight-year-old brother Richard, who seemed certain that I'd most likely experienced what he called my *Spidey-Sense.*

My Father was just glad I was home in one piece. He rarely brought out displays of emotion, and this was no exception.

"John, nobody is going to get angry with you. There is nothing wrong with getting hurt, nothing wrong with getting scared. But sooner or later, you've got to *tell the truth* about what happened. Your Mother is worried, and I'm worried. You are my second oldest son, and you'll have responsibilities to your little brothers soon. I want to know that you're serious enough to—"

"Dad, I'm not lying to you, I promise. I don't know how to say it differently. Nobody will listen to me; what do you want me to say? I wish that—"

I stopped just before crying, but Dad had a resigned, stern tone to his voice.

"This has gone on long enough, John. You need to be more careful. It isn't just your body at risk, but your mom's emotions, your family's … And you nearly scared your Nannie to death."

He got his tools together and began working on a loose doorknob. Whenever emotions got thrown around too much, he retreated to something a bit more practical—something reasonable. It usually involved metaphorically-realized tasks, like Home Repair.

"But Dad, I—"

"If you can't get past this picture story to tell us what actually happened, at very least you bury all that storytelling right here. Understand?"

And so I did. I didn't mention the pictures to anyone for months.

But that didn't mean they stopped. Not hardly.

It was just the calm before a storm.

3

Dead stop. The world lurched from one crazy night's slipstream to a dead stop.

My family was still in denial that anything unusual had occurred. Exasperated, they eventually had to formally forbid me from further mention of the phrase "the pictures." After a few weeks of pretending, it almost seemed like the whole bizarre event hadn't happened. My ears healed, as did my palm. Life returned back to normal.

But how does a human memory move on from something so enormous, something entirely outside everyday life? I was just a kid, after all.

I felt like a veteran astronaut—banned from discussing space. Moreover, I felt like I would never again feel safe. After all, what had caused this? I hadn't chosen any of it, not like an astronaut would have! I'd never elected to fly to space. I'd never trained, never studied advanced physics. All I understood was that I had touched a loved one, somebody I trusted, and then somehow…something in my brain had exploded. And now it was all a dark secret!

But if the people around me had to keep it a secret, then a secret it would stay.

I learned to go through the motions—to smile, play along. I learned to keep things easy. Eventually, my constructed smile even became a real one again, albeit a slightly more complex one. Kids are pretty elastic, right?

It helped that immediately after The Event, we weren't just sedentarily stuck in the awkwardness. Every winter my grandparents headed someplace warm to escape the cold New York chill. That year, they headed to the Tampa area, and they suggested to my parents that since I was bored and off from school they should put me on a plane at JFK. My grandparents would then meet me at the airport in Tampa to join them for a week in the Florida sun.

Everyone was thrilled with the idea, myself included.

My parents drove me to the airport, walked me into the terminal, and introduced me to the Eastern Airlines stewardess who would be taking me on-board. She brought me into the cockpit and introduced me to the Captain, who was very impressed that I was making the trip alone. The man sitting next to me on the flight encouraged me to sit down and shook my hand.

"Hello John! They told me we'll be traveling together today." He grinned kindly.

Having been born a Lutheran, but growing up in a town that was almost exclusively Catholic, I knew the man sitting next to me was a Catholic priest. He wore a gold cross so large that I fixated on it immediately and could hardly make eye contact with him. I just said, "Hi" and sat down.

When the stewardess walked over later to ask me if I needed anything, I murmured a quiet, "No, thank you." But she said something that caught my ear when she spoke to the man next to me, asking, "Can I get you get anything, your Excellency?" He murmured that he was fine, and she walked away. I immediately turned to him, staring in awe.

"Why did she just call you *Excellent*?"

He laughed and tried to explain to me that he was like a priest, but one that worked at more than a single church. I nodded silently, utterly mesmerized by his cross and the large gold and purple ring on his finger. I was later to find out the man sitting next to me was Bishop Fulton Sheen, a famous man who served millions in his flock.

When the plane lurched forward, he covered my small hand with his in an automatic protective gesture. That's when the pictures spiraled into my head. I nervously pulled away, but this time, the images looked different. They didn't scare me; they entranced me. This time, there were also words and music but with no sound. I felt the noise in my head, but I couldn't hear it. It was the strangest sensation.

I looked up at him and smiled, and he smiled back down at me.

There were so many pictures. I saw children, bells, sunsets, sunrises, people singing, people laughing, people in funny clothes dancing, and old people crying with happiness. There was no sadness, just soothing pictures that made me smile. The pictures seemed endless, until what seemed like hours later, they stopped.

But when I opened my eyes, we were still on the runway.

The plane gently took off and landed, and the priest kept me engaged the entire flight with questions about me and my family. I was proud to share my recitation of The Lord's Prayer, and tell him about what we'd learned at Sunday School at St. John's Lutheran Church. I knew he must be impressed by my years of wisdom in all matters religious, and in truth, he seemed delighted.

We landed safely and on time, walking off the plane together and laughing like old friends. He had an impressive number of people waiting for him, as well as local media. I saw my Grandmother and Grandfather in the crowd, and ran to my Grandmother's arms for a big hug. Her eyes were fixed on Bishop Sheen.

He walked over to greet my Grandparents. Gramps was Catholic and Nannie was Episcopalian, and meeting the legendary figure was perhaps the first time I ever recall seeing them both speechless. He told them that they were lucky to have such a nice polite grandson who was so knowledgeable on Christian beliefs. He smiled and walked away after shaking their hands. After a long moment, my Grandmother regained her composure.

"Johnny, do you know who that was?"

"Yeah. He's an Excellent Priest. One that talks a lot."

My stories of the trip made me seem crazier than ever. But nobody could deny the man, himself. For the next few months, there was a limbo balance between a consensus that I was finally nuts and that something bizarre was going on. Nobody could be quite sure.

But then, it was finally summer! And for my family, summer was always a massive ritual, a convergence.

Those days, the long days of summer always meant Cape Cod.

Ψ

Our cars always celebrated arrival with a long honking commotion at the seaside driveway, waving to the people on the boardwalks and waving hats and any fairly portable children out the windows.

Dad especially transformed for these trips. This was the great payoff from all his absurdly long hours at work: he lived then for the summers as much as any of us did. Dad would be in great spirits—from the first sighting of distance signs for our arrival point. Thus, we were all considered "on duty," spotting from our back seat crow's nest from the moment we pulled out of the Mineola traffic.

On arrival in Cape Cod he'd break character, transforming into vacation mode. Before we arrived at the house, he'd pull over and park by the beach. We four boys always darted from the car, teared off our shoes, and threw them into the back seat, sprinting down what seemed like miles of beach—the wet sand sticking to our feet. Mom would be in that same spirit, drinking in the open feeling of the ocean. Dad stood by the car and watched, with the most beautiful look of serenity on his face.

Then it was on to the beach house.

First thing out of the car, we'd disappear in a cartoon puff of smoke. We'd all try to strip off most of our clothes and race back into the dunes, beyond which we'd surely live lives of freedom, living as Kings. (We'd then always get dragged back to help Dad unload the car.) But with perfect timing, the hordes of extended family relations always swarmed over the sandy grass like wild ants, and we'd be innocently swept away.

Only poor Jim remained to help Dad unpack; it had become something of a tradition. Jim was a few years older than me and most of my cousins, so that was the price he paid for almost-adulthood.

Mom strictly adhered to certain lifelong rituals on the Cape. She had to spend the first three minutes after arrival in a hammock—otherwise, heaven forbid! Surely she'd get no rest for the whole trip. Thus, even she always mischievously smiled from far away atop the porch, swinging in and out of sight with a quiet cackle as baggage made its way inside, floating atop conversational bubbles of grunts, complaints, and assorted salty language.

"You're doing great, guys! Use those knees!" she'd snicker. This was my only memory of my Mom ever shirking a chore. Years later, the playfulness of this image is still a prized relic of her amazing personality.

But like myself, Mom never really mastered indolence; so within a few minutes she was always up, off to find her own Mother. Every time they got together it was as if they hadn't talked for decades, though in fact, they usually talked several times a day. Where you found one, you generally found the other. They were on exactly the same wavelength, and they could practically finish each other's sentences.

Of course, the second all suitcases and heavy luggage had been deposited indoors, we younger siblings would miraculously reappear in the sprawling beach-side house, seeking cold drinks.

Now commenced the famous Bickering Bedside Bazaar.

With this many extended family members congregated in such a small space, we'd have to accelerate all our social-role antics into an incredibly compressed, catch-up procedure. This was serious business! Social totem poles would have to be established and cemented, bunks measured and spatted over. The youngest cousins and I crammed into the narrow doorway like sardines, just in time to watch the spectacle of bigger boys battling for the inner sanctum bunks. For now, we would leave the blood sport to them. Our time would come.

"Gentlemen," Andrew began, as he was shoved by Matthew, "I'm sure you all know why we're here." By this time all the boys had congregated around the favored bunk, jostling and jockeying in a crude sort of rugby scrum.

"Aw buzz off Andrew, you got it last year," Craig piped in. But he was the smallest…so really, he had no say. His hat was immediately smashed down over his eyes by all present.

Jim cut in. "Fellas—while I'm glad to see you, and I know we'll have a great time this summer, I do see a certain obligation to stand up for my family rights here. Much as you all did last year. I'm sure you'll understand that?

Some of the congregated boys shifted uncomfortably. This did seem a fairly reasonable proposition and fairly elegantly put.

Cousin Matthew simply bristled and spat out the word "Hell." (He'd always been sort of feral. His interests mostly included stomping on things, living or dead.)

Andrew pushed forward again, past snarling Matthew. "Well Jim, I hear what you're saying and I think I understand where you're coming from. But you also know that I've been accepted early into the magnet program for the high school running team, before even finishing junior high. I've also gotten perfect grades this term. I got a kiss from Kathy Summers, and everyone saw." (Scattered nods, moderate levels of impressed looks from the assembled cousins.) "AND I caught more fish than you last year. I believe we all remember how that went down…So I'd say it's time to face the music. I'm faster, I'm smarter, and I'm ready to take what's mine! There is, of course, a natural order of things: nature finds a leader. Nature has a plan, Jim. Sorry." He attempted to move towards the bed with his head held high, walking with a lordly gait.

Hugh laughed. Unburdened of lordly scruples himself, he tripped Andrew's feet from beneath his body. His own clambering climb into the bunk was only slowed by Cousin David attempting to scramble over his back.

Jim leapt upon the pile of bodies, screaming, "I said it's MINE!" Cousin David gave way immediately, retroactively remembering and honoring the sensed nobility behind Jim's claim to the bunk. He held up his hands in surrender and stepped back onto Andrew's face.

Hugh struggled on. Matthew had gone in search of some sort of weapon. Jim stretched one finger and then a second onto the bunk mattress. moaned from the floor. We watched, rapt and breathless.

Craig was the only boy to break the boys' cardinal rule of noninterference. A maverick—tiny Craig tried a new tack: screaming.

"MOM!" His pipsqueak voice echoed down the halls.

We scattered. Jim snuck back into the room a second later and tossed a shoe onto the desired mattress. The deed was done! None could challenge the time-hallowed claim now: no boy with *honor.*

The law was the law.

However, the second we heard the definitive cadence of an adult's footstep approaching up the hall, everyone took to the hills.

These were the hours that each of us would whisper about the toys we'd secretly brought along for the trip (despite the remonstrations of Mom and Dad). These forbidden toys would inevitably come out for admiration and elaborate trades once the lights were out. This was the time when we'd hack out plans of exactly how many hours we would spend beach-side, and how we'd pool our resources to secure adequate rations of sugary liquids and candy. We'd commence all the necessary wagers and boasts on both the quantity and diversity of sea life we'd find. We'd then speculate as to who would triumph over the others in terms of scavenger hunts, foot races, swimming, sailing, animal sounds, jokes, and storytelling.

In short, it was the best time of our young lives.

Tradition held that older boys would then draft Jim, and arm-overarm together they'd troop off into the underbrush, into the morbid surveillance tasks that make boys, "boys." This mostly centered on seeking and attempting to capture the reclusive hog-nosed snakes that were the recurrent villains of our campfire stories. They'd seek the legendary monsters in the back extremes of the grassy dunes, where legend had them preying on Fowler's toads—and surely also occasionally picking off the weakest, smallest boys...

Ψ

"Hi, John."

A tiny framed figure was backlit at the top of the dune. She descended carefully, stepping over sea wrack, watching for hermit crabs, stopping to sniff at patches of hydrangea, watching the clouds move.

Elizabeth's arrival was always the most wonderful part of the summer. My eyes immediately lit up, and the sky itself almost seemed to as well.

She was tiny but only a few years younger than me and wise for her age. Pink-faced from the hot car trip and exhausted from an early wake-up call, she nonetheless already wore a huge smile. Something about the smell of the place, the way the Cape Cod breeze carried the sea up to you, immediately revitalized everyone.

"Elizabeth! Great! Hey, I have so much to show you!"

As always, I grabbed her hand and started lurching forward into a dead sprint towards the seashore.

"But wait, I just have to tell my Mom that I—" she protested, her feet already flying off the ground.

"THERE'S NO TIME!" I cried, and we ran over the bluffs towards the endless blue.

The summer annually melted, from that moment on, into a blur. Elizabeth and I tracked down every monarch butterfly amid the goldenrod flowers and breeze. We peeked into every clump of beach heather and dusty miller hoping to spot ground-nesting birds like an eternal Easter-egg hunt. I grossed her out with the broken husks of horseshoe crab shells slippery with seaweed; she'd laugh and cringe. Sometimes I'd solemnly present her with an odd skate-egg case. She was perfectly the type to reply without missing a beat, "John! At last, a mermaid purse! We must return to the sea at once!"

We flew into the shallow shoals, the vernal pools, the marshes and the dunes, year after year after year.

By every summer's end, we knew each secret of every new tidal flat. We named all the beach grass patches and the salt marsh hay and dug "roads" between them. We then brainstormed the habits and traditions of the animal inhabitants, populating each vegetative shadow with imaginary armies of English-speaking birds, crustaceans and insects—all eager to do our bidding. We developed a strange reputation of sorts, after being continually spotted hunched over some flower bush somewhere solemnly intoning, "Arise, arise!" together, arms in the air at dawn.

We then ducked down and hit the sand whenever our noisy voices started attracting the older cousins, who always jealously called out,

"Guys…? Guys? Did you see a dead bird?!"

Ψ

A moment even arrived when the innocence of childhood transitioned into the coldblooded, ruthless capitalism of two business-savvy adults ready to take on the world.

Well, maybe not adults. But sage souls, to say the least.

One day, while eying the massive beachside candy-shack after exhausting our daily sweets budget, Elizabeth and I got wise to the system…

"There is nothing holding us back now, but ourselves," Elizabeth mused. "That candy should be ours."

All cultural activities pertaining to crenellating sandcastles, poking sea squirts, or decorating half buried picket fences with sea rocket blossoms abruptly came to an end. Elizabeth and I prematurely entered the world of high finance.

We knew what we were doing. We did our homework.

We had the market cornered before we even began.

From that moment on, nearly half our summer was spent in the procurement of valuable gems, which we arranged into priceless heirlooms and sold at an enormous profit margin. Well, we didn't have many gems. Elizabeth and I therefore substituted with every marvel we came across on the beach or in the woods behind the house. The collection process was pretty intense, as we'd long subscribed to a local legend that the old spooky cabin hidden in those woods was haunted. Therefore, we'd have to balance our rigorous collection procedures against a regular program of fleeing, shaking with laughter and absolute, abject terror.

When we'd get home, we'd spill our gathered loot, and together arrange masterpieces out of the various relics. Each scallop formed the base of an elaborate mosaic in shell combinations: with glinting cockle shells linked to razor clam stripes, angel wings flying overhead, moon shells in an arc, with a permanent marker copyright providing artists' names and creation dates. We'd normally scrawl something nostalgic like TREASURE THE MEMORIES in a large, wobbling script. We were proud to include our names on them, in case there was any doubt who had crafted these Van Goghs of the Sea. We meticulously arranged these miraculous works with Elmer's glue on old shingles piled up in front of an old culvert we had spotted under the roadside. (Endless. Profit.)

When business waned, we had an emergency meeting after which we transformed our act. Elizabeth innovated, adding floral-accent improvisations from our seashore experiences in acrylic paints, while I learned to orate all the pertinent nostalgic stories from index-card notes. When pressed, we further expanded our skill-sets: crafting wind-chimes with some knotted old twine and jingle shells. We made elaborate picture frames and decorated whelk shells with sharpied googly eyes and glued seagrass "hair." We arranged shells into fake flowers that could hold tea-light candles or loose change. We did it all.

After going to a local museum we claimed "our aesthetic" was mostly "working in homage" to the old Sailor's Valentine art we'd seen there. And, being business-people, we asked a reasonable fair market price for these avant-garde creations.

Do you want to guess who refused the hard-sell tactics after our presentation? Nobody.

Elizabeth's quiet whisper of a voice endeared her still further, as she would conclude with, "and who might be interested in patronizing local arts and crafts today…?" while eying a room full of family relations.

Unfortunately, we also discovered the candy stomach ache; and it was right amid our revels of triumph.

But business acumen, ladies and gentlemen…You can't ever take that away.

Ψ

Nighttime remained a world apart. Nighttime: all games deflated, the fun rested. At night, headaches set in.

Every night we all returned to the bustling beach house for endless talking, laughing, storytelling, and playing cards. It was wonderful while it lasted, and the boisterous hours sometimes even stretched into the early morning. No curfews, no television, no school—just laughter, cards, fun, food, and the beach.

But sooner or later, everyone fell asleep. Even the older cousins eventually did, after the wild wars fizzled out. And then it was pure quiet.

All day long I was safe. The chatter and the sights, the warmth and the bustle combined to flood out any other thoughts. I knew daytime was my salvation, with no quiet there to undermine me.

"If every moment, every day of my life could just be exactly like this," I'd murmur, "I'd be fine."

But there were always thoughts that flooded back in with alarming regularity as I climbed into bed, into the quiet space of snores and dreams.

Somehow, I hadn't yet quite managed to forget the rocky transitions of the last few years. Nor did I succeed at dulling the intensity of images burned into my memory from that night at Nannie's. Quite the contrary, actually.

Every night the pictures seeped back into my brain, more and more emotionally charged, more otherworldly. They seemed all the more so, as I had no idea what they were supposed to mean, or why it was happening. Was I broken?

Every night, I remembered that I couldn't tell anyone anymore, that I must surely be crazy, and that I was driving other people crazy with my attempted honesty. So every night, I unbottled the stress of that cognitive dissonance, once the lights were off. I rocked back and forth in my bed, willing the images to be forgotten with all my might—squeezing my fists, breathlessly wishing to be normal. I'd taken to smashing the pillow again and again into my face, trying to mash any trace of confused tears back into my eye sockets.

The nights were still and calm, and nobody really seemed to notice, besides Jim's long established deep-sleep autopilot-exclamation, "John! Stop rocking!"

And then every morning, I bottled it back up again before the crack of dawn. I washed and dressed, and emerged, and acted like it was all fine: like the world was normal. And really, it almost was. The day and the night became two completely distinct versions of *me*: an internal and an external one, both pure and uncompromising. But I had to wonder how long life could last like that. I had a whole life stretched in front of me, keeping Mr. Hyde buried in Dr. Jekyll. And these pillows weren't going to last much longer with such harsh treatment.

I remember staring into a whelk's shell, thinking that the *nautilus' life* was the one for me.

Deep beneath water, everything predictable and procedural, clean and simple.

Safe within my shell.

4

"Wake up, John—you're going to be late for school!" Mom called up the stairway.

Summer was gone, school returned. Life moved along the gears of a clock once more.

Saying goodbye to Elizabeth and golden Cape Cod life was always horrible. But additionally, exchanging those things for an absurdly oversized backpack full of heavy books and homework seemed like a cosmic injustice. The town slid across the car windows, and we drove sleepily onward, to Jackson Avenue Elementary.

Great waves of undersized humans washed up against the rocky school grounds. I watched safely from the car. Innumerable, they were! They splintered away into gossiping circles, games of keep-away with all the scrawniest sprinters shouting, "HEY GIVE THAT BACK!" Some sickly few lay slumped, staring up slack-jawed from the grass, others coolly leaning against walls, greeting friends with slight upward jerks of their chins. Mom kissed me, and she escaped.

After so many isolated days of summer amid only familiar friendly faces, the schoolyard felt more like Mom's dreadful salon than anything I'd ever yet experienced. An electric feeling filled the air, and I picked it up like I was a four-hundred-foot-tall antenna. Every trace of nervous energy and anticipation written across the faces of these strangers hit me like diesel trucks. This was going to be interesting…

The school year began simply enough. Assigned seating, group projects, hand raising, and preferential treatment for the smart kids. Nothing new. Kids grouped themselves into cliques, sorting themselves by personality phases and consumer affectations. But that's where the familiarity stopped. Because the first time somebody touched me, the whole world fell away.

"What's he *doing*?!" the kid acting as crossing guard screamed—pointing straight at me.

When he had tapped me on the forearm just moments before, my eyes had bulged out of my head, dilated to the size of apples. I'd gone through something like a mild seizure. I went down, immediately.

"The Pictures" I'd been living in terror of for months had just returned with a vengeance. But this time they looked different. They looked faster and clearer. The burning sensation felt as strong as ever, but most of the sickness was gone this time. There remained just an indescribable feeling of cartoonish vertigo, like I'd somehow forgotten that I'd just walked off a cliff, so now I had to fall.

Images fell into place in my mind's eye within an instant, one after another. Discolored, rippling images of a baseball breaking a window, of a present getting unwrapped, a yellow-faced old woman lying in-state in a coffin, and a scoop of ice cream falling on the ground. A strange hum suffused them all.

There was no sense or logic to the images, nothing tying them together. But for each one, an overwhelming emotional charge accompanied the images: horror, joy, frustration, terrible sadness and loss, and all the petty devastation moments of early childhood. The visceral feelings accompanying the images were absolutely pure, and absolutely confounding…

These were memories, that much was clear. But they were not *my* memories.

Clearly, I was merely going mad.

As I struggled to pull myself up off the white paint of the crosswalk in one piece, a second crossing guard grabbed my bare elbow to help me to my feet. Another set of images flooded in and sent me sprawling. As I jerked upright, he was thrown over, toppling into a group of small girls crossing the road. Their drinks flipped into the air, and the liquids glinted in sunlight as they soaked a meathead looking football player with a lady-friend on his arm. I was dead. This was clearly the end. In the corner of my eye, another stranger moved to help me.

"DON'T TOUCH ME!" I screamed in panic.

By now a small crowd had gathered, assuredly wondering what in the world was wrong with me. Images of other lives whirled through my head, like a swarm of bees. I couldn't help swinging my hands fruitlessly in the air, as if to fight them off. People stared. And no wonder!

"Are yooou okaaaaaaaaay?" said a disembodied voice in slow motion, the sound stretching like a long yawn. Right about that moment I realized that "in real life" I was hyperventilating, wheeling about, and loudly groaning in the middle of a crowd. And drooling, drenched in sweat. I pulled my raincoat over all my exposed and reddening skin…and ran.

I found an apt hiding place in a utility closet, where I waited out the day.

Later that afternoon, after discovery and capture, I experienced my first parent/teacher conference. It was to become quite a tradition.

"Go ahead, have a seat," Mrs. Ramses snapped, absorbed in her reading. Then she looked up. "Oh! Hello, Johnny! Why might I be seeing *you* in here, today?"

I stared at my feet in silent horror. Mrs. Ramses had always been kind to me, glad I was an easier charge than my enormously overenergized brother, Jim. As I tried to shrink myself down into my seat, she began going through a manila folder with my surname on it. She periodically eyed me over the papers as she read them, seeming confused.

"Well this certainly seems strange, Johnny. You don't strike me as a disruptive boy, and moreover truancy doesn't exactly become you. Would you like to talk about what's going on here…?"

I was silent as the grave. I watched leaves falling outside, watched my palms, and watched the pens on the desk (they didn't do much). I felt horrified.

"Your Mother should be along shortly to pick you up. But I need to ask: are things going okay at home? Trouble with your brothers? Is your Father doing okay at work? How are your grandparents doing?"

She seemed at least as lost as me, grasping at straws.

"No, ma'am. Everything at home is fine. I'm sorry to be trouble, ma'am. It won't happen again."

"I just don't understand what's happened here...Isn't there some way I can help you?"

"No. Err, I don't think so. I'll be fine. I'm sorry. I don't know what came over me..."

I shuffled uncomfortably. I felt worse for her than I did for myself. Nothing could be worse than watching this woman worry about me.

Nope...I was wrong.

In walked Mom, her eyes deep red. She clutched her purse—looking like she'd been lost in the subway system or perhaps like her dog had just died. She seemed completely disoriented, somehow smaller than usual. She didn't look at me but just sat rigidly upright and stared straight ahead. Now typically, with Jim, she would have understood an office visit; but this was not *my* style. This was unprecedented. Mom was mystified, mortified.

With her purse on her knees, she sat down on the child-sized chair. When Mrs. Ramses handed the manila folder with my name on it across the table to Mom, I watched her eyes widen.

I wished then that I lived in some deep dark sea, curled up in a forgotten shell.

What had I become? What was I doing to my Mom?

The faculty consensus was eventually hammered out. The armchair psychologist, my teacher, and the guidance counselor determined that I was suffering from panic attacks based on an acute "fear of germs."

As you'd expect, the news spread across the schoolyard like wildfire. Soon I was the "resident circus freak," until the bullies had found some new novelty. I started wearing long coats and over-enforcing personal space boundaries. Mom and Dad were at wits' end.

It was going to be a long year.

Ψ

Nannie's famous chicken crackled in the pan as music played softly from a record player. Mom had dropped me off, hoping out loud that "Nannie might make heads or tails of this, because I sure know I can't." She whispered with Nannie a few moments before driving away and gave her the gist of my situation. When Nannie walked back inside she didn't say a word about it, just offered me some hot chocolate and then some chicken, acting as if everything was fine.

"I just don't know what's happening to me," I began, with no prelude.

Nannie put the kettle on again, her soft house slippers scraping quietly across the tile. "Well?"

There was really no way to relate what I wanted to say. I'd wanted to say something similarly open to Elizabeth over the summer, some glimmer of *the truth*. And now once again, words were failing me—with Nannie.

How do you confess to stealing someone's memories? Was that even what was happening? I didn't know, myself. But no matter what triumph or tragedy I would ever experience, Nannie always knew the words that would provide the most comfort.

She looked up at me quietly, for a long time. "Just know I love you, John. That's all that matters."

Ψ

Weeks went by. Years went by.

It almost seemed like my containment policy might do the trick: so long as nobody was allowed near me at all, I might be able to pretend to be remotely normal. After all, school years were repetitive, kids' changes were always awkward and bizarre, and I wasn't exactly popular. Suffice to say, people didn't quite understand *what* was strange about me, but they sensed irregularity at the core. I was usually given a pretty wide berth, and I was honestly pretty thrilled with that state of affairs.

However, one day I came to school and found my teacher crying. She tried to gather herself, and eventually managed to raise her head and even out her voice enough for a few sentences.

"Class, I have some terrible news to share," she began and then paused for a very long time before restarting with slow and deliberate words. "Today our president, President Kennedy, has been shot and killed. So this...this is a national tragedy. I'm sorry I don't have any more news. School has been canceled for the day. You will all be going home to spend the day with your families."

There was a huge silence in the room. Nearly none of us had any concrete idea what *death* was. All we knew was that an *adult*, our very own Ms. Polasky, was crying at school. This was highly irregular. Everyone paused awhile, trying to determine the appropriate course of action for this scenario. In the back rows of the class, there was a low murmur as a few of the less-motivated students put two-and-two together (realizing this meant no school and thus a great triumph). Ms. Polasky adjusted her scarf while staring vacantly out the classroom window, as the rows of kids quietly began to file out the open door, dumbfounded both at our luck—and our complete incomprehension of *why*.

As I waited in line I began to feel terrible, watching Ms. Polasky shyly try to suppress her sobs. My Dad had taught us that *good boys* aspire only to be polite and strong young men, that we basically existed to support and protect "the women" when they were sad.

Therefore, I marched up to Ms. Polasky, grimaced, and quietly wrapped her in a determined hug.

As I'd feared, the pictures immediately emerged. I held on tight, clenching my teeth.

But it was completely unnecessary this time. These pictures glittered, warm and gentle. A tremendously pleasant feeling pervaded all of them. I saw a pretty lady with a big hat, a handsome man in a sailor uniform, a little boy and his dog, and a big castle.

Nothing at all that was related to the sadness rocking her now.

Stepping back, I simply couldn't understand how she could feel so sad when all of these images of people (ostensibly oozing from her) seemed nothing but happy.

"Oh, thank you John. Run along now, your Mother will be wanting to spend this time with you," she sniffed.

She smiled wanly down at me, touched, and I marched out into the world a better person.

Ψ

Any "good-person points" earned might have been lessened by the state in which I found myself within mere days. I was asleep, head halfway into a cardboard box in a mostly empty room in Garden City.

It had come to this.

One eye peeked open. A very valuable vintage baseball card of Gramps' was stuck to my forehead, a tag along from the massive stacks I'd been sorting through and lately dreaming about. A massive picture frame corner's deep impression traced a right angle across my cheek, where the cardboard box hadn't managed to fully support sleeping-me. Nannie had given me a candy-bar as a "thank-you gift" for helping with the move, and it had both melted to my hand and bonded some crumpled newspaper to my pants leg.

"Make sure you pack those health insurance documents with the ones in the file cabinet!" a shout echoed up the stairs. I awoke with a start.

Good lord, *I'd had one job*!

I bolted upright and aimed to look busy as somebody passed the open doorway.

Gramps and Nannie had lately decided that the time had come to leave the "rat race" of work in NYC behind. They would be relocating from Garden City to a sleepy seaside village with simpler pace of life: Sag Harbor. I'd spent most of my morning trying to wrap my head around what life would be like without Nannie right down the road, as Sag Harbor was at least a two-hour drive across Long Island. We'd jumped at the chance to be their packing crew, knowing that sorting through their maze of artifacts would be more fun than anything brothers and I could devise ourselves.

The house had already seemed a time capsule for years, where each new decade had to war against several previous ones to stretch out its legs. All the shrines to my grandparents' children had already been packed up into stacked boxes in the hallway. For the first time in my life, I saw what the childhood bedrooms of my now-adult Uncle and two Aunts looked like empty—and it was otherworldly. I'd spent years staring at each airplane diorama and toy chest, my Uncle's bugles and conscription posters, my Aunt's matching libraries and dolls. Now there was just some threadbare shelving, and some scuffed, permanently creased wallpaper coming off the wall in strips to carry on the story of our family, to tell it to the world.

"Hey John, be careful with Nannie's Lladro figures. Let me know if you need more newspaper," Gramps called from a room down the hall. He couldn't know that I'd already found mountains of newspaper, evidently enough crumpled paper to quite comfortably fall asleep upon.

I'd been tasked with collecting the last items out of Nannie's spare closet and making sure they would survive the long truck trek east to Sag Harbor. I'd been bursting with pride at the responsibility, eager as ever to prove I was a grownup, and eager to overcome any weirdness my strange visions had been casting over my family relationships. So far, I'd fallen asleep…so I doubled speed and started anew.

Handling the super delicate Spanish porcelain was easy enough: I basically just stopped breathing. I was way more careful than could possibly have been necessary, and I reveled in my maturity as I did so. The portraits provided a different problem. Most of the frames were bigger than both my arms and body, so I'd have to lean them against the bed frame and wrap from top to bottom or I'd never get anywhere. I worked quickly, mummifying the sepia images of my Aunts and Uncles as children in layer after layer of protective padding.

There was my Uncle John in his Military School uniform just before my Aunt Mary looking like a glamor model in her New York City apartment. My Aunt Caroline and Uncle Bob, and then Uncle John and Aunt Joan, all looking like movie-stars in their wedding photos. I remember thinking what *beautiful* Aunts and Uncles I had. There were dozens there, plus several of my Mom and Dad, of my cousins and brothers, and me. My reflection wrinkled its nose at my younger face beneath the glass, as I wrapped it all up.

Then I found it—the picture that startled me.

Buried under all the familiar family portraits were three older black and white pictures with a very different style of framing. All were the same person: a pretty little girl with curly hair in different poses. The clarity of her bright features, the striking pale eyes beyond the frame, immediately translated in my mind to the bright blue eye color that I remembered so clearly.

I instantly recognized the girl I'd seen in my first terrifying vision, almost a decade earlier, in this very house.

I sat there and stared at the picture for a good half hour, knowing without a doubt that this was the face that I'd seen that day. It was like overlaying one picture onto the next.

Eventually, I ran downstairs with the pictures in hand and found my Grandmother. "Johnny, you've got melted chocolate all over your hands. Here, let me help you," Nannie murmured distractedly as I approached her.

Squirming away from the frog-march to the sink, I faced her and interrupted—

"Who is this?" She squinted at the picture frame, and a big smile lit up her face. "Why, that's me darling, back when I was a little girl."

At that point I noticed my Grandmother had the grandest, brightest blue eyes: just like the girl I'd seen on that bizarre night. All at once, a rush of details poured out of my memory about those visions; fortunately none had faded.

Without pause, I began the inquisition.

"You had a doll, didn't you? A doll with a blue ribbon in its hair, and another on its dress?"

"I…what?" Nannie seemed considerably taken back by the randomness of the question, and my insistence. "Well I suppose I had a lot of dolls. That was a long time ago John, I don't really remember now, honey."

"But you did live in a long house, which had the letters E-A-S painted across the fence, right over here to the left…" I tried to mime the rippling sepia scene in my head, amid the blue-green florescent light of her kitchen.

She looked at me blankly. "No, John. I didn't have E-A-S on my fence, growing up. Now how about those picture frames upstairs? Is it coming along okay? Do you need any—" But she paused in midsentence with a suddenly spacey look over her face. She considered the countertop in front of her while arranging her hair, and slowly strolled back towards the stove.

"*Did you*?! Did you live at a house with E-A-S on the fence, like this?" I mimed a house on one side, with a very specific fence adjacent, a crazy look in my eye.

She looked right into my eyes, and spoke very slowly. "John, I didn't have E-A-S printed alone, but our family house in

Fredericksburg was called EASTWOOD. The name would have been printed quite large on the gate, right next the house. But how…how could you have known that?"

"Wait. Did you also have a pony, a terribly behaved pony with spots like a Dalmatian would have?"

Unconsciously, I gestured with my hands up in front of my face, as if trying to sort through the images—like referencing files from a card file box. My mind raced with the vivid images I'd been trying so long to repress, and I wanted to know about each of them. My words couldn't keep up with the pictures in my head, so many of my sentences seemed fractured. Everything was still there—not a single scene had faded.

Finally, something was happening!

Her eyes suddenly looked very glassy. She seemed far away, and her hands clutched at the countertop for support. "Yes, John. Why yes, I did. He went by the name of Murdock. I don't believe I've ever talked about my old pony with your parents, or with anyone else now for almost half a century. Did you…? Did you find a diary or something up there?" She seemed very concerned.

"AND THE PONY BIT YOU, didn't it?! But you bit it right back!" I screamed, grabbing my hair.

She stopped cold. "My Father would have killed that pony if he'd ever known such a thing. Nobody knew, I made sure of that. I hid the marks, I iced them myself in the basement. I told nobody, not ever…"

She staggered clumsily over to a stool in the corner, walking into things en-route as if in a trance. She plopped herself down. She was so far into her own head, she didn't hear the tea-kettle screaming atop the stove. I wandered over with a footstool, clambered up and turned it off myself. She didn't look up. Several moments passed as she silently shook her head back and forth, considering past and future.

When she spoke, she did so very softly, choosing her words with care.

"John, there's something very special at work here, with you… I've…I believe I have seen something like this before."

Her words jolted through me as if I'd been struck by lightning. I stared up, breathless.

"WHAT?"

"I'm so sorry I didn't see it sooner, that I couldn't have helped somehow..."

She stared straight ahead into her hands.

"John, we have a lot to talk about."

5

"A long, long time ago…I had to make some promises I didn't believe in: then or now. I've spent many years wondering if those decisions were necessary or worth it, if I should have acted differently. It was a very different time back then."

She paused reflectively, one foot struck in the past.

I was a block of wood: purely in the present and clearly not understanding.

"I was not born an only child, honey."

I wobbled in my seat. We'd been told than Nannie had been an only child all our lives. All our favorite back-stories on her history had centered on her playing with cousins, and constantly joining clubs specifically because her family life *was so lonely for an only child.* It'd actually come up for discussion pretty often between my brothers and I: we were glad to be such a big family, so we'd never run out of things to do…

"But I thought—" I began cautiously.

"I know, and I'm sorry. We were told that all evidence of my brother's life would have to disappear after he was taken." She paused, and corrected herself, "After he chose to go."

Her whole body was slumped in a way I'd never seen. She looked exhausted.

"*Taken*? By *who*? Why would anybody want to hide your brother?" I exclaimed. "And why would you all go along with it?"

"Very powerful people, John, and for many reasons. It was my brother, himself, who pleaded with us to do it, to go along with it. He thought secrecy and silence was the only way to ensure that we'd have safety and privacy, that we could live long and normal lives."

I had begun to get over-agitated. Nannie was an only child, always had been…

"I don't understand. I don't understand any of this. Who did this? Who is this brother? And why did anything so serious happen to him? Where is he? How long has this been going on?"

I was stomping back and forth in the kitchen, nodding manically, slapping the countertop to punctuate my words, trying not to explode. My head was in a million places at once.

To be honest, she almost didn't look like she had it in her, to relate the story. A sickly look I'd never seen had come over her, like some dark illness that had long been safely cocooned in isolation somewhere had suddenly reentered the main systems of the body, starting a war of attrition—of exhaustion. Gone were the pink rosy cheeks I knew; her face was instead pale with the anxiety of answering my questions. Even her breathing seemed labored.

"John, give me a moment. I know you're excited, and you have every right to be. But I need to think of where to start. Nobody knows about this—not your Grandfather, nor anyone alive. I promised him my silence…I'd always intended to take this information to the grave. That's the way he wanted it."

"Start anywhere. Anywhere will work for me. Just tell me Nannie! I *have* to know."

Nannie absentmindedly sat on her famously pristine table surface, in a complete break of character. I followed, dumbfounded. We both sat and watched each-other, wide-eyed, as she gathered her thoughts and worked up her strength.

You could have heard a pin drop in that kitchen…

Ψ

"His name was John, like you."

"Okay, well, like me. And Gramps, Uncle John and—"

"Major John Grey, eventually—" she continued insistently, "—was his full name. Until they took him. Until they erased him."

"Who?"

"We'll have to slow down, Johnny. There is too much to say, and I don't want to mess it up. One thing at a time, okay?"

She settled herself a moment, and began.

"In those days, knowing something you couldn't, or shouldn't, would draw a lot of eyes onto you. It was wartime. Even at home as a civilian, he was developing a reputation of having some sort of abstract mental weirdness: some sort of 'otherness.' The sharecroppers and workers at my family's home whispered about *spirits* and *possessions,* though no one took them seriously. He just had a way of knowing things, things that he couldn't have really learned logistically. He played it off as simple intuition but the man could see things no one else would know, clear as day long before they would happen."

"So I have a Great Uncle, and he was somehow kidnapped, even though he could see the future?"

"I didn't say he could see the future, exactly. I don't even fully know how much he could see. Usually, he just saw fragments, little glimpses. He saw pieces of people, which they didn't want him to see. He said when it started he would see things blurred, like he was squinting through amber. When the visions came over him he'd sloop over involuntarily, like he had some kind of narcolepsy. I barely understood it myself, and he was terrified to ever talk about it. He was the sort of man who grew up holding his cards firmly to his chest, even though we were very close. There was no way to be safe without some secrecy, and so he lived for privacy."

I was barely breathing. "I don't understand. Why was he so worried about getting caught? What were the…risks?"

Nannie sighed. "Like I said, it was wartime. Everyone was on the lookout for people who seemed different, desperate to label outsiders. Desperate to root out spies. At that time, in that climate, people would over-police any irregularities here on the home-front. There were panics going on, 'witch hunts' for all sorts of people who seemed socially scary at the time. It didn't seem implausible to worry that he would get snatched up as an assumed-foreign agent, or even forced into a dark role as some sort of exploitable tool."

She paused, sorted her thoughts, and recommenced.

"Sometimes my brother would just see nothing. Sure, there were never any guarantees. But sometimes, Johnny, he'd see incredible things. Selling newspapers outside a closed door, outside a hotel, bar, or something like that—he'd see a certain man going in—who was going to cause trouble, or was going to celebrate his upcoming wedding, or a spectacular fishing trip...and he just knew. He'd tell me minutes before the trouble began, or the news broke. I always thought he could somehow just tell because he knew the person from selling to them before, but they were always complete strangers. He was very interested in doors and gates, they always seemed to agitate his... his gift."

"His gift," I repeated automatically, in a flat voice.

I sat quietly and considered. So I was not alone? Not that it sounded like this man, this Major John Grey, had the same sort of gift as me. I had long lost family, disappeared or dead. *Check*. Was I splitting hairs? Should I call his gift "a gift?" And mine? What was the point of it? All the little analytical wheels in my head were spinning.

The little wheels' conclusion was that I should not feel comfortable. How could I take any pleasure from the fact that a relative's existence was so oriented by this "gift" that he'd volunteered to have all traces of his life and legacy erased, to keep his family and secrets safe—by distancing them forever?

My head started to hurt, and my stomach rumbled.

Was this to be my life? Would I even grow up—live my own life? Or would I just be taken, too?

I imagined disappearing in plain sight, a grain of sand hidden atop an open countertop.

Ψ

Nannie knelt down in the old second story bathroom: a room I'd probably taken one million baths in. This time, however, she took out a flat screwdriver and did something quite strange. She pried the baseboard off a narrow span in a corner and gently teased out a perfectly sized, moldy bit of plaster that looked like it had suffered a very rough life.

This little ruse had evidently been in place for a while.

She then stopped to sweep up the mess, and I couldn't hold in my impatience any longer.

"What are you doing!? Don't you feel like we're dealing with something important? Leave the wall, Nannie! Tell me more!"

I paced in circles before the bathtub, pulling my own hair.

She made an exasperated face at me as she pulled a long, narrow tin box out from the shadows beyond the plaster plug.

"Oh, it's a...What's that, Nannie?" I huffed in confusion.

The outside of the box looked disgusting from the moisture beneath the baseboard. It had a tinny hollow sound when it hit against the plaster wall and a tortoise-shell look, with spots of rust and a grid of dents across the lid.

Nannie was now using an unwound wire curtain to pry open the lock, a skill set that I'd certainly never seen out of her. Then again, there was never any knowing what sort of skillsets Nannie might have; she was an endless source of surprises. She stopped momentarily, and with a mischievous smile, murmured, "*What*?"

Laughing, she finally succeeded in jimmying the lock. The lid snapped open, and dim light poured onto some strange and sundry things inside.

"This all has to be between just *you and me*, Johnny. Nobody else must know about it."

It almost seemed like she was messing with me. We were huddled in the bathroom, staring at a tin full of junk, covered in dust. I'd had so much anticipation building, that there was an inevitable disappointment when she uncovered some tattered black and white photographs, something rusting, a cigarette case, and some broken sunglasses.

"Patience, Johnny; you'll soon understand. First and foremost, I'd like you to meet your Great Uncle John." She held up a photo of a very tall man with an arm around a beautiful girl who I immediately recognized as young Nannie—the girl of my vision. "He was real, he was good, and he deserved a better life than the one he got." She looked at the picture for a long time, before carefully propping it up in a place of honor on the tin lid and riffling through the other objects.

"I know we haven't much discussed the specifics of your apparent gift yet, Johnny. But I do know that your Great Uncle had some pretty dramatic trouble with his eyes, when he'd start seeing something which he shouldn't have been able to see. His eyes ballooned up like bowling balls. I don't know if you've ever had this problem, but if you ever do, maybe these will come in handy."

As she pulled them out, I realized that the broken sunglasses were actually quite fancy. They were the old original editions of the wayfarer sunglasses from the early 1950s.

"I'll have them repaired, if you're interested. It might be nice to have some privacy, when your eyes do something like that."

Without confirming or denying anything, I grinned and grabbed the sunglasses.

She continued, holding up a strange box. "My brother was never a smoker. But he knew *people*, and he knew the world. He had to spend a lot of time playing 'catch-up' due to the downsides of an irregular experience of life. One thing he realized early on was that he could accelerate the process of making new friends and acquaintances by conscious efforts, gaining a simple warning buffer, a protective circle. These folks often taught him more about the world and about how to behave and appear 'normal,' both more quickly and thoroughly than he could ever hope to do on his own." She mused while holding out an object at arm's length.

"So he was always the approachable, always prepared guy who could offer a light, a cigarette, a pen, spare paper, change for the bus, or offer to buy coffee on a whim. Always listening, always open. Although strange, he was well liked, and eventually quite socially agile. Moreover he often got his glimmers of future insight while out in elaborate social situations, the kind where he couldn't afford to pull out a notebook and write notes to himself. So he'd keep small scraps of paper hidden behind the line of cigarettes, and track any details he might need to remember of *his futures* by hand there, scrawled in jagged shards of pencil lead."

She stopped and fixed a wary, stern eye on me, before continuing—

"I give this to you only on condition of a firm promise: you will never be stupid enough to become a damned smoker. Your Mother would never forgive me, nor would I, myself."

Fortunately none of the decades-old, yellowing cigarettes inside enticed me much.

I pocketed the case, wondering if this part was mostly symbolic. Now she scrubbed something vigorously, and then she turned and held it out into the light.

The most enormous, ornate golden ring I'd ever seen flashed into the light. A purple red color glinted and blurred the light around it, flashing amid the shadows in the corner. It was certainly not the slight rusting thing I'd thought it to be—it was amazing.

"Your Great Uncle was attached to this ring more than anything. He received it when he was quite young, and I remember the day he got it in an unmarked box with no explanation. One of the only things he ever said about his gift was that without this ring, he'd have felt helpless. He always felt like the ring centered and calmed him. He said it balanced him somehow, but he never could explain to me what that meant. I was young…and so terribly confused by his whole situation, but he saw how much I admired the ring as well; he wasn't blind. So he gave me this one, as a consolation prize of sorts." She held up her own wonderful ring, the one that had fascinated me my entire childhood, stroking it admiringly. It had never occurred to me that this ring wasn't on her wedding band finger.

She paused again, watching me very closely, as she handed me her brother's ring.

"I don't know very much about it. I've never dared spend the time to study it, for fear somebody would interrupt me and ask questions I knew I couldn't answer. I've read up a bit on it over the years and I know some bare-bone facts, but nothing profound. I believe it's called a cabochon, and it's quite old. The gem itself was engraved as an "intaglio seal" for some big ol' somebody. I don't know anything more. Some of the symbols on it seem like maybe they are religious."

She watched as I turned the ring in the light, observing the ornate band decorations.

"Actually, I know exactly what it is," I said quietly. "But I don't know why *he* had it, or how in the world he got it. It makes no sense."

"What is that supposed to mean? What is it, then? And how would you know?" Nannie demanded dubiously, clearly thinking I was joking.

"It is a Bishop's ring, Nannie." I paused while turning it over and over in my palm, daydreaming. Eventually, I murmured, "It's strange, too…because I met someone who has an almost identical one.

6

Everything had changed. The fundamental feeling of panic and terror, the horrifying sense of isolation—they'd all col- lapsed as soon as I knew I wasn't *alone.* Walking through my last days of childhood, I'd regularly clasp the new relics in my coat pockets, thrilled knowing I was connected to something, that I wasn't simply an alien or a freak.

That realization made all the difference, because the way the pictures affected me shifted as well. As soon as I understood what was happening, I felt calmer. I developed more confidence and an increasing sense of control. Whenever someone touched me and the inevitable rush of images moved too jarringly, I'd stroke the soft surface of the ring in my pocket until I'd regained my sense of balance and center.

The pictures also shifted not just in speed and intensity, but also in their *quantity.*

For a long time now, I'd been sensing them as if they were strange, unconnected images. Whereas early in life I'd sensed merely emotions, and later got images with confusingly abstract emotional static, I was now starting to understand the relevance of the emotions accompanying the images. As I learned to move away from a chaoticpanic mindset, I was slowly gaining the presence of mind to "steer" my gift. I was also increasing my receptivity to an exponential degree. Soon, rather than receiving a few images, I'd get droves of them. It became exhilarating.

I was still strangely incapable of forgetting images, so I'd begun trying to see how much I could sort through at once. I was stretching my limits. It took time, but I was finally awaking to the idea that my curse was in fact something wonderful.

Still, I had my blind spots. After one inexplicable exception with Nannie, the gift never again seemed to work on *family* in any way. Instead there was just a massive blank, a shuddering feeling when I'd try to read them. The tragedy of this mostly manifested itself in our card games, where a little illumination could have been quite helpful: Gramps was killing us as usual.

He'd taught every child in our family how to play card games like poker, gin rummy, and bridge by the time we were four years old. If you didn't know how to open seven card stud—deuces wild (with jacks or better) by that age—you were already "behind the eight ball."

Only in playing cards did the self made businessman emerge, complete with a galloping sense of competition. Eventually, Nannie would have to come out and flash her bright blue eyes at him—as a warning. If he absentmindedly tried to ignore her along his clear path to triumph, one slight "John!" was all it took. He'd abruptly backpedal towards letting us children win. It became one of our many traditions: leaving the house with more money than we'd arrived with.

Every night, Gramps fell asleep in his favorite chair, snoring gently, his hand grasping a glass of Dewar's water with ice. A consummate gentleman through and through, even asleep, his hand never permitted a drop to spill from the glass.

I hadn't attained his technical mastery yet, but I'd taken away a few functional pointers.

At school, I'd quietly begun to fleece the town with card games. I'd bet with the snack foods in my lunches, trying to win answer copies to the boring math assignments I didn't feel like doing. It didn't take long to attract the attention of the school bullies with my newfound prowess.

Shane and Mark looked like the robbers out of an old vaudeville sketch. Massive heads that were nearly square—these were hulking, sinister guys. They'd come to believe that I was making *money* in these games and evidently felt they held some claim it. So began a long campaign of threats and pushing, and more threats and more pushing. Always, an eventual threat of further violence hung in the air. Wherever I found myself on the school grounds, there they would be, yearning to have some imaginary money, yearning to intimidate, all the while seeming like absurd vaudeville villains, but nonetheless terrifying.

But a distinction must be made. If it was even possible, Mark might have been the "more stupid" of the two. He just sort of vacantly-mimed whichever violence Shane thought up. Shane was the ringleader. Yet his greed and sense of entitlement couldn't block out the rest of his thoughts when he would try to intimidate me. The second he'd make physical contact and shout some threat of, "You'd better give me that money, or else!" I'd see all sorts of images of his turbulent life at home. So one day, I impulsively blurted out something about it.

And perhaps I got carried away...

"Your brother Willie killed your fish." I said, immediately wishing I could swallow back the words.

"What did you just say to me?" Shane paused mid-push, twisting and glaring into my eyes, whispering with a hiss of his horrible breath.

Mark was dumbfounded. "He said something about your brother Willie!"

Shane tipped his head sideways in a vicious sneer. "What would you know about Willie?"

I gulped, wondering what I'd gotten myself into. Well, I'd come this far...

"You went to a carnival. Willie wanted to go, but couldn't. You snuck out..."

My eyes blackened like huge holes now. The images surged in like a waterfall.

"Your Dad was blacked out on the couch again. He's hardly ever sober anymore. He comes and goes but doesn't care about anything or anybody. He only cares about showing everyone who's *the boss*. He uses his belt to help: on you, on your Mom, or your brother Willie. Well, that day he heard you had snuck out. But he held Willie responsible, because he was older. So he took his belt—"

By this point Shane had seemingly lost his footing and was reeling, staggering backwards, touching his face confusedly as if he'd lost a piece. He didn't look up.

Mark had absolutely no idea what was going on. He stood slack-jawed, taking in the spectacle, his huge arms nearly dragging on the ground like two hogs sitting alongside him. A small crowd had begun to form, but I continued as if in a trance, mesmerized by the speed and cohesion of the images. I spat them out as soon as they entered my vision.

"You came home and Willie didn't say anything. But when he crept into your room that night and saw the bag with that fish, well the rage took the better of him. You watched it happen, you couldn't stop it."

Shane recovered momentarily, and in a last-ditch effort at keeping up appearances, shouted, "None of that is true, you little freak. You just wait, I'm gonna—"

There was no way to stop it now, everything was spinning. I wobbled a little as the images coursed through me—every memory, every rage, every terror and lonely moment. For the first time, they'd managed to sort themselves, to stitch themselves into chains, like ringed card file boxes, scrolling through every theme and emotion. All his fears and insecurities were tearing out as if in one tangled mass, squelching and clattering all around him into the cement courtyard.

"Your Mom tries to pretend everything is okay, but she always has to make up a new story of 'how she got hurt.' She spends all her money on makeup to cover up bruises and black eyes, and trying to keep the fridge stocked with more and more beers. But it's never enough to please him.... So she walks down to Mr. Heller's grocery store, alone, for more. It always takes a few hours and then she slowly creeps back in. She never makes eye contact when she comes back with the beers, she just—"

I get peripherally aware that Shane is losing it, but by this time, I'm somewhat out of control too. I've forgotten that I need to center, that I need to be calm. As my voice rises to a semi hysterical pitch, I speed up the pace, half shrieking, wobbling on my feet.

"You're worried that you'll never be anything after school, because you can't concentrate here, you can't learn. You head doesn't see anything but fists, sources of shame, shadows. No, you're too worried somebody will catch on to what your life is like at home. You lie awake thinking of ways to impress Mark with your cruelty and violence—because you're afraid if he gets bored, he'll go and you'll be left alone in the world…Too dumb to learn in school, you're afraid you'll be like your Dad: never be able to hold a real job. You're terrified at the thought of surviving your own family: the violence of your brother, the viciousness of your Father, and of a lifetime being ashamed and afraid for your Mother. You have this feeling like you have to defend the honor of a family you don't believe in yourself, by being tough and abrasive and strong on the exterior. But inside, you've never known respect or kindness. You've never been loved, and that's left you alone, and scared, and small, and…"

But Shane was no longer there. He had run away. Literally turned and fled.

The crowd vibrated, bewildered.

Mark looked stupidly at me, and back towards where Shane had just disappeared, clearly perplexed. After several moments' mute consideration of the situation, he'd resolved to just punch me when an older boy stepped between his fist and myself, clapping slowly.

I heaved a bit, lurching back to reality, slowly comprehending all I had just said.

"You are going to have to tell me *how the hell* you just did that."

I looked up in a daze, unable to come to terms with what just happened. "I'm sorry…" I muttered, "…what? Who are you?"

The boy extended a hand, followed by a huge grin.

"Bryan Walker."

7

Years later, kids still talked about the epic takedown of Shane the Tyrant. The episode had already passed into mythology, helped by the fact that Shane ended up transferring out, moving to live with an Aunt in Connecticut days after the incident. Conjectures had flown as to how I had done it, ranging from simple eavesdropping—to occult powers. But Shane's bullying had not been a limited affair; he'd been an equal opportunity assailant across the schoolyard. Left to his own devices, Mark the Secondary Bully had basically just gone mute. He now lived the life of a confused, contemplative monk, standing pensively at the edges of games wondering about all the ways ol' Shane would've once suggested they interrupt them. He'd become frozen in inaction, his violence rendered impotent by indecision and stupidity.

As Shane's legacy faded, the power dynamics of the school shifted. Short of an apex predator, the next rung of hierarchy took over and started running amok. The power vacuum sucked me into a new role alongside the formerly bullied nomads, now crested and laureled.

Together we reigned as enlightened despots, ensuring peace and tranquility. However, unfortunately every group thrives by identifying and labeling an outsider, who gets condemned.

At our school—this ended up being a boy named Eric.

Eric was not all well. There was some sort of congenital issue at work with the poor guy, and his parents couldn't really afford a proper diagnosis. However that didn't stop the rest of us from guiltily-pleasuring in mimicking his gait, in parroting his speaking impediments, or in using him as the butt of our jokes about 'who will marry Eric?' I had become a real boy: half-golden, half-cruel monster, running alongside the rest of the pack. It wasn't intentional viciousness; it was absentminded herd-mind.

It never occurred to me how dramatic it was until one day I saw Eric sitting on some steps beneath the auditorium doors, staring into his feet. He was nestled behind shrubberies between the nearby sidewalks full of students. He knew he was hidden from their gazes; I assume he thought he was free from all observation. Just then, somebody passing by made a noisy joke about Eric and did the most perfect exaggeration of his voice ever, twisting it into an animalistic moan. Someone else said, "Oh my god, that's a perfect Eric!" To my horror, I turned back towards him just in time to watch one silent tear slide down his left cheekbone, as he kicked his left foot with his right and crumpled into a ball.

As he swayed on the steps, it occurred to me that we were absolutely alike—he and I. No amount of social acceptance or play-acting normalcy would change the fact that I was not like these other kids, nor they like me. I was wired differently. I would hide my true self all my life, the different world I saw, the steady torrent of stolen, secret sights. I was that poor kid on the steps, just pretending I was different.

Something about it didn't sit right with me. I guess I was at that pivotal moment of childhood where a kid's internal awareness of external injustices expands into an awareness of external injustices they'd participated in themselves. Call it empathy—call it a developing conscious—it set up shop in me. I felt awful, like my stomach was full of baby snakes.

Later that day at home, looking into the kitchen, I saw a woman with the same expression of discomfort that I was going through. My Mom was being respectful and gentle, carefully asking her to elaborate, and letting her guide the conversation along to progress towards an obvious conclusion—but at her own speed. It only took a moment's eavesdropping to realize that the woman was considering an affair, and had basically come only to get talked out of it. She knew it was a bad idea, and knew it was indicative of other problems and bigger conflicts, but she didn't seem willing to face those other questions yet.

Mom never pushed her, just patiently let her 'soundboard' her own conscious out. Eventually, I heard a long sigh, after which the woman started softly crying and admitted she couldn't face the idea of getting old, that she was afraid of vulnerability and excessive familiarity, and a whole host of other generic ills of long-term relationships and adulthood. She was redirecting those fears into more manageable short-term solutions, which would inevitably derail her life, but nonetheless force the same bigger questions amid new heightened tensions.

She started talking about reconnecting with her birth Mother, and tracking down her therapist, and finally about getting relationship counseling or considering a divorce, rather than leaping into an affair. Mom didn't jump into any sort of judgment; instead she just quietly and calmly encouraged her to seek out situations where she'd feel like she was respecting herself, rigorously thinking through her decisions instead of acting on impulse, and striving to keep all her passions and connections as sincerely overt as possible. As she did so, Mom made the woman some tea and helped her straighten up her hair.

By the time the two emerged from the kitchen, both were laughing and leaning into each other. I spent the evening thinking about what I'd seen. Sincerity, warmth, and intentional decision-making. I'd heard these themes looped in my Mother's conversations a million times: these were the subtle pillars of my family life. One derived a calm sense of self-respect with which to help the world—by first being real to one's self. Mom encouraged us to never play-act cruel roles because of peer pressure, never to take easy routes out of simple laziness. We were good people, who naturally strained and strived towards goodness. I tried to never forget that.

Eventually I made an effort to apologize to Eric, on behalf of all of us. It wasn't much, but it alleviated the shameful feelings I'd had of betraying my Mother and Grandmother's moral example. It felt good. I felt human.

Ψ

So the seasons blended into each other: bells and binders, bad fashions and height variations. I settled into a fairly apathetic routine with school. I wasn't unintelligent, but I was having trouble motivating myself to concentrate with all the changes that kept rolling in. Everything I'd grasp through the snail's pace lectures seemed so distant compared to the things I would learn through my gift: things that were practical, actionable. I'd started learning to see straight to the heart of somebody while talking to them, to see the core of their emotional decision-making processes by assembling long lines of precedent decisions and the emotional states behind them. My intuition itself was getting trained, because none of these memories ever faded in the slightest, but instead were tucked away into the dark recesses of my skull. They were always summonable at a moment's notice—and as the thousands stretched into millions into hundreds of millions of exemplars of precedent emotional choices, I started to be a very strong gauge of how people would respond to scenarios, long before they'd considered them themselves.

But the slightest tiny tear of doubt had begun to unwind the edges of my confidence. For one reason: I was an anomaly. As springtime set it, everywhere I looked there was the same oblivious magnetism at work amid the returning sunshine and blossoming flowers in that all creatures great and small were pairing up, two by twos. It wasn't a question of whether they were tremendously good at it or somehow deserved it—not at all. Some of them seemed like monsters. But there they were, monsters and their mates. I don't know where it came from, the sudden springtime flush wherein we all got struck and corrupted by hormones and cupid's arrows, but it certainly happened—and it happened hard.

Where was I to find myself in all this, in the quiet baroque of small talk? Would I marvel at the way somebody "really seems to understand just everything about me," if I could actually literally do just that, beyond the limerence? Would I ever be sincere, or would every attempt at well-adjusted life just see me feigning ignorance of every cumulative thought process, every unmentioned fear and fantasy, every precedent stumbling block to avoid or uncover? Would I just be toying with people? Was that to be my life—a predator to unknowing prey?

As my arms and legs grew, some yet-unused part of my brain began to stretch as well. The part of me that had once striven to compete for the attention of Mom or Nannie now instead looked out into the wide world—as an answer to all the eternal questions about loneliness, comprehension, and meaning. The second I'd considered the idea, the second the magic of confirmation-bias set in, everywhere around me I saw couples and pairs—joined at the hands, the mouth, the waist, the heart. It became a question of progressive immersion: in that the more I found myself steeped in the imagery of couples, the more I found myself wondering absentmindedly at the concept of otherness and togetherness. The slow springtime defrost of the long winter was taking with it my latent phase, just as the world was springing back to life.

Jim had started going on dates—tucking in his shirt and combing back his hair in a preposterous way. He'd taken pains in his presentation that I'd never had imagined out of the Jim who I grew up with. Something was in the water. About the millionth time I'd lingered– asking romantic questions beyond the doorway as he prepared himself to leave, he'd realized I was utterly flustered by an early onset preoccupation with *dating*. A viciously meticulous teasing campaign thus blossomed in all his hours at home, where he'd come courting Rob "as me," carrying flowers, Rob wrapping a pillowcase over his hair, speaking in a high pitched voice and batting his eyelids. The two were insufferable, until the sports season distracted them.

Certain places in the city began to be saturated with meaning, a meaning as-yet barred to me: reserved for those in a pair. They were *places for couples,* places to be properly experienced only as a couple. I'd been forced to break these rules constantly by trips with my family, and I took careful note of them. Such places meant for couples included diners, roller-skating rinks, park benches, study groups, field trips, dances, and public pools. I had no idea how it was that somebody found themselves in such a pair, but was very intrigued with the results and lifestyle that seemed to ensue. I found myself passing an impressive and embarrassing amount of time daydreaming about double-strawed strawberry milkshakes like on the television shows, or laughing-scenes helping some pretty person up from the slippery ground of a roller-rink, stretching my arm behind someone glad for the warmth on a city bench.

What were these sudden yearnings? Something deeply human and jarring permeated them, something completely alien to the long lectures that now comprised my school hours. School had lately become something to be endured: a frustration mitigated by a newfound fascination with other human forms.

Ψ

Bryan Walker lived in an impressively large home near Nannie's old place in Garden City, alongside a massive country club. While my friends and I lived in modest homes on 50x100 sized lots, Bryan's family had acres upon acres of land. Though I'd been invited over that very afternoon, the man at the door seemed deeply distrustful after watching me walk up the driveway rather than being dropped off by some sort of suitable chariot.

Bryan sauntered out from behind the house, sighing, "George, leave it, he's fine. Come on inside, John!"

Bryan Walker's house was the biggest house I'd ever seen. His lethargic devil-may-care veneer couldn't hide the fact that he was pleased by my thinly-veiled intimidation at the scale and excess of the place. One section of the house had been done up like Teddy Roosevelt's house in Oyster Bay: complete with mounted beasts on the walls, lined up according to their power and position.

"My Father works in politics, and has a lot of his meetings here. So he likes to project the values he cares about: strength and capability, ambition and virility. I couldn't tell you how many times I've suffered through his whole character-values speech…I know it by heart now," Bryan said, laughing and weighing my response to his carefully scripted words.

My response might have been underwhelming as I stared at a lamp-base made completely out of antlers—with a shade of stretched animal skin. As I listened to sneering Bryan talk and talk, it occurred to me that this was the first time I'd ever shown up at a friend's house to play where they didn't immediately seem like a better, more approachable person the moment we sat down to play, and to relax. Usually, the effect was more human. Bryan simply seemed robotic, as if programmed to be conniving. He seemed more on guard than ever—tense and histrionic, orating in a high, artificial voice. It seemed like we were playing an understated game of cops and robbers, and he wanted to be a villainous kingpin—with me acting as an innocent bystander. So far, he was playing the role "to a T." I found myself absentmindedly glancing at my watch.

We walked outside, and Bryan sat nonchalantly by a massive pool on a reclining lounge chair. He talked about himself a whole lot and told me about all the people at school he didn't think much of. I hadn't realized how much of a snob he was.

When he finally sauntered inside to complain about nobody bringing us drinks and snacks, I head other voices approaching from the back of the house. Two young girls walked around the corner, arguing. They sat down on the chairs by the poolside, one taking careful pains to appear bored by the presence of a stranger—yawning and stretching in the sun.

The other grinned up merrily at me. "Oh, hello! You don't look like anyone I know here."

"That's because he doesn't live here, Megan." The rude girl had a strong family resemblance to Bryan; I supposed she must be a younger sister.

"Oh, that makes sense. My name's Megan," she said, reaching her hand past her friend, who simply rolled her eyes. She tried to slurp through her straw loud enough to drown out our conversation.

"John, John Calabrace. Nice to meet you, Megan," I managed to stutter. (Genuine kindness, at the Walker house! The stars themselves threatened to fall from the sky!)

"Do you know Colleen then?" Megan asked, gesturing at Bryan's little sister.

"Of course not, Megan," Colleen interrupted. "If *he* was worth knowing, I'd know; and I'd have told you about him already."

I couldn't believe my ears. This girl couldn't be fifteen but had evidently already moved into full expression of the woeful Walker family genes.

"Apparently, you'll have to excuse my sweet friend Colleen, here," Megan said slowly, her shadow blocking out the simpering child below. "She isn't quite housebroken yet…I tutor her, but they can barely bribe me enough to stand her manners." She laughed, leaning forward and flashing white teeth.

Colleen wasn't amused, hissing, "Oh really, Megan? Really?" She stormed away.

"Anyhow, I'll hope to see you again sometime, John Calabrace. Sorry about Colleen…you know how they are." She ran back inside after Colleen, just as Bryan returned. He turned to watch her leaving.

"Did you see the ass on that one? Whew!" Bryan whistled, as she disappeared inside.

"Megan McConnell. One of the most connected families around, and yet she still looks like that. Not a bad catch, as far as they come."

"Is she your…girlfriend?" I carefully hazarded, still trying to figure out the rules and ropes of Bryan's social life.

He laughed, eyeing me carefully. "I wouldn't see the point. I'm not made out for all that chocolate buying, ice skating stuff. Still, she's put together pretty nicely, right?"

I laughed uncomfortably, and he led me inside.

"One day, my Father and everyone like him are going to realize that they've gotten old and irrelevant, and then we'll take their places. I aim to have a pretty good hold on things by that point," Bryan boasted.

"What is it you want to do exactly?" I wondered aloud. "Politics?"

"I want to do whatever it takes, John. I want to live a better life than this. I want it all. I'll do whatever I have to—to get it."

I looked at the pool and sipped my iced tea, as Bryan ground his knuckles together with a faraway look.

Ψ

Holding my tongue had become a brilliant campaign management strategy. Suddenly, I was a front-runner in the games of school age social life…and the only substantive difference was that I was letting people sermonize at me constantly, and withholding my responses afterwards. I listened to a lot of tales of mad ambition and took a lot of quiet sips of iced tea. But now I was getting invited to all sorts of strange outings, and rarely hugging the shadows I'd trained myself to expect, and to seek.

One day I got a strange phone call from an unfamiliar voice. It was Megan, who'd found my number through a mutual friend— inviting me to go to the Mineola Public Pool with her. I'd never even been there! I was a decent swimmer from my childhood summers at the Cape and South Shore, but this was something new. This was the world of peacocks, the art of strutting about and being seen and judged, all the while with a smile on your face. This was stranger than anything so far.

So I went. I experienced for the first time in my life the hilarity of taking too long to prep *myself* before the bathroom mirror, with Jim, Rich, and Rob banging on the door.

How the tables had turned!

I knew I was still an awkward sparrow; there was no changing that. Let's not romanticize too much the glorious blossom of life— the transition between preteens and teenagers was a bumpy ride for all of us. Sometimes it seemed like one limb would grow at a time, half my face would spring growth, etc. But we were growing into our social selves in spite of the lurches. Despite our awkward forms we were together as a generation, scampering around in our new swimming suits, the frontrunners of a new era.

All at once, all the transitions out of childhood caught up with me. I spun around and around in that pool in the bright sunlight, admiring all the lithe forms nature had sprung up around me in the splashing water, the sparkling skin that flashed and gleamed around me in every direction. A laughing circle of other young strangers trailed around Megan, and we'd immediately become friends simply by virtue of our shared ages and wet swimsuits, with the ancient courtship rituals of chase, splash, and various water sports applying as if we were the oldest of friends. I felt more alive than I had for years. I also became aware of certain stirrings which will doubtless be familiar to the lot of you, while staring around me in a wide arc at the beautiful forms our awkward childhood bodies were blossoming into. I felt some dizziness, and I won't lie—my dreams became racier.

Months went by, and I lost no time in aspiring to be an outward being. I finagled my way into a roller-skating rink, and like everyone else, spent half the time falling, laughing up a storm and shoring up solidarity. I sat on the park benches in threes, still wondering about the magic of twos but thrilled to be appreciated among friends. I went to study-groups and felt what it was like to play-act being in someone else's family, with sleepovers and sibling bickering showing a strange vantage point of inner intimacy from outside. I attempted dances and quickly learned they were not for me for obvious reasons—the nerves, the terror, the anticipation. The past traumas felt just too palpable: etched on the faces of even the most well-adjusted folk there. But the important thing was that I had tried. There was an entirely new spirit of openness to new experiences, and to an expanding sense of self in relation to the exterior world. I was suddenly a person among people, and volunteering to be so. This was a strange state of affairs, but I was blossoming.

All that got shaken up in late October, when a friend of mine suggested we sneak into a party some distance outside Mineola, in a girls' school held inside the former Woolworth's Estate. We both knew friends there and knew that the indulgent groundskeepers and chaperones often cast a blind eye to unexpected guests as long as their behavior and comportment was kept within bounds. Of course, Mom and Dad would have had their own thoughts on the wisdom of this endeavor…so in one of my less intelligent plans to date, I didn't tell them. Instead, I climbed out my window after claiming to be unwell and retiring early. I ran down the block and caught a ride with my friends. My heart was beating faster than ever before as I watched the streetlights rush past the car windows, knowing life would never be the same. I was a fugitive, wild and free.

We were sure we'd already gotten hopelessly lost, twice, before we finally pulled onto Crescent Beach Road. We parked some distance away from the main twisting access lane and walked the rest on foot, peering through the endless perimeter fencing at the flickering shadows stretching from the main building. As we approached, we carefully arranged our masks and hoods to pass unmolested and invisible. Fortunately, it was just crazy enough it worked—and we waltzed through the open iron gates of the estate unquestioned.

Within minutes, from across the endless lawns, Megan recognized me skulking among the Linden trees, as I had promised. She recklessly shouted my name, leaping, waving, and bounding towards us. She gave me a huge hug and hugged my friends as well; though we hissed and protested, reminding her that we'd need girls' names and obscurity tonight, or we'd all be doomed. She scoffed and laughed and smiled, and together we were all dragged towards the incredible corridors of Winfield Hall.

A tremendous golden light spilled down the steps and out all doors and windows as we approached, as did an unimaginably loud white noise and sound vibration of the partying within. We stepped through the doors and into the strangest B-movie ever seen. Groups of costumed monsters, bees, astronauts, vampires, and skeletons were bunched in tight clusters around every inch of the elaborate Great Hall, laughing and gobbling down ice cream, candies, drinks, and ghoulish-themed food. Every step of the way from here on out was a marvel, and everything I encountered was ground zero of the completely unknown.

The central staircase itself was a bizarrely overwrought mass of every sort of marble the world had ever known, twisting and writhing a few million dollars' worth of material into the realized, arrogant visions of a short lived, egomaniac multi-millionaire. The ceilings were gilded, elaborately carved and loudly lined in unmistakable gold leaf. An enormous fireplace loomed over the whole room, fourteen feet tall crackling with a blazing fire. It was lined in fake spiders' webs, black gems, and jack 'o lanterns. The whole place glowed, like we were dancing through a golden goblet.

And dancing we were! From the second we'd walked in, great surges of dance steps had exploded through the place, as an enormous pipe organ in an adjacent room shook the walls half down with spooky strains and old medieval dance music. Wild ripples of girls spun in tangled tessellations, laughing and swaying, spiraling through the few folk not dancing until nearly everyone had gotten wrapped into the clutches of the dance steps. When we were swept into the music room, the whole scene changed, and the lights themselves varied with the melody strains, huge red, blue, and yellow bulbs transforming the room every few seconds. We saw the silhouette of the mad genius pumping at the keys behind some elaborate sliding walnut paneling. A few bored chaperones sipped green juice from champagne flutes, but mostly, the place was plain pandemonium left unto itself.

My face hurt from laughing and smiling so much. A slow ache formed in the back of my jaw. The room felt about a million degrees, with next to zero air circulation. My arms were wrapped around Megan, or rather hers around me she'd been galloping me back and forth across the dance floor in a mock epic, tango style. About the hundredth time I'd mentioned needing some air, shouting the words silently over the obliterating noise of the pipe organ, she mouthed the words LET'S GO OUTSIDE while miming two of her fingers walking away.

"It's haunted, you know," she cooed playfully, as we passed under an elaborate coat of arms. "This whole place! See that big crack up there?" She gestured to the tiny stone images of several women on the family crest, one traversed by a huge crack. "They say that appeared there the night one of the daughters of this household, Edna, committed suicide in New York City, and the image fractured at exactly the same time. They say she still walks here." She skipped ahead, smiling, thrilled to see all over my face how unsettled I was. She grasped my hand and pulled me out towards the manicured gardens, towards some fountains beyond the light. I found myself looking around warily in spite of myself, oblivious to how I'd gotten here. I felt completely terrified of any expectations of me that I'd be unaware of, wondering where my friends were, wondering if word would get to my brother Jim that I'd been spotted out at a party and he'd blackmail me…Or worse, Bryan Walker would hear and get even more insecure and bitter than before— that I hadn't invited him—that I'd somehow pierced his golden circle…Assuredly he'd rage on and on that I was aspiring beyond my means…Or that I—

Megan suddenly turned and kissed me hard on the mouth.

I blinked. It was so sudden! She'd half bitten me, excited and effusive and reckless, something halfway between a laugh and a kiss. Before I'd even managed to construct some sort of reply, she'd already hopped up and was walking around the edge of the fountain, chattering.

"I'm so glad you came out John, it was so sweet of you! We never get to see anyone from outside the same circle, it's always exactly the same faces here. Every holiday, every outing, it's always these girls, or Bryan's country club, or the Saratoga races, or the Hamptons—

I was momentarily numb as my brain melted. I had never experienced such an incredible dizzying array before, and there had never been any force like the onslaught of images that the simple kiss had brought.

The ring did nothing, though. I fingered it desperately in my coat pocket like it was a magic lamp. I saw it all: the life of a lonely, somewhat-spoiled only child, the exquisite luxuries and expected privileges, surely; but I also saw through all that, to her own experience of all those things. It was bleak. Megan was completely alone. Her parents were represented by thousands of images of their shoulders hunched busily over their work, her friends and extended family distractible and distant, already forming plans of world domination like Bryan. The thrills and novelty of economic circles perhaps unfamiliar to me were utterly moot to her, being everyday sights. She was just thrilled by the momentary escape. What I marveled at most were exactly how many images I saw of windows, like this poor girl was just constantly living for something different, for something unknown, something new.

She danced absentmindedly around the fountain ledge, slashing water at the boy and Roman statues, and smiling over at me. "Well now. What do you think of me, John Calabrace?"

I stared at her, smiling. I searched for anything substantive to say, from beyond the waterfall of images still pounding my eyes half out of my head. I had to protect this one, almost every image I saw was of a little girl being driven past a world she didn't ever get to be included in. Tonight would be a good night, if I had anything to do with it.

"I think I like you, Megan."

She said nothing, but quietly touched her index fingers to the dimples of her reddening cheeks and hastily parted her bangs and looked down, and up, and turned momentarily towards me with an impish grin. She then turned again, and began to prance back around the far ledge of the fountain—smiling straight up into the sky.

"I like you, too, John Calabrace. I think I like you too."

Ψ

The boys had gotten squirrely. We'd promised to meet up at the same spot we'd met Megan beneath the trees, but they were nowhere to be seen. The late hours came and passed, and the party began to wind down. Finally, they were escorted to the main doors and booted into the night, with an unseen person's outstretched arm pointing them the way back to the road.

They saw me beneath the trees, and we raced like the wind together, howling with laughter and a flood of stories, towards the arch entranceway. The gate was closed! So one after another, we boosted each-other up, and howled with laughter at how utterly incapable we were of getting over. One or two disapproving chaperones who had given chase after the boys looked towards us with disapproval but didn't bother with further pursuit. After nearly twenty minutes, the three of us were still occupied with getting down the far side. We finally toppled over and then waited for Matthew, our resident climber. He propelled himself over instantly, clearly with the aid of some superpower of his own.

And then we were alone, back in the world we knew. Changed and familiar, our buzzing heads whirling along an extraordinarily empty black street, in the middle of the night, in middle of nowhere.

We found the car, set our sights on Mineola, and drove towards home in silence.

8

Well, all good things come to an end.

We'd all said our goodbyes a bit down the road from my parents' house, laughing and clapping one another on the back and shushing one another, then splitting off towards our separate destinations in the four a.m. darkness.

I'd been smiling to myself, half sleepwalking and absentmindedly considering how much everything had begun to change. I fell headlong over the curb obscured in the shadows, laughed and continued. What a different world I seemed to be living in! A different life was beginning. Things were changing. Things were getting better. I could get used to this…

Then I froze on the lawn like a deer in the headlights.

My bedroom lights upstairs were all up, bright, illuminating the tree in the front yard. I had definitely turned those off when creeping out the window.

The front door to our house suddenly slammed open, and bright yellow light spilled out: a long slanting diagonal across the garden hedge and lawn, illuminating me up to my knees. Of all the images that might have rushed to my mind, the one thing that seemed appropriate was an enormous guillotine…

"John, you get in here NOW. You've got a lot of explaining to do."

Ψ

Really, it almost sounds too stupid to describe how I'd been caught. You see, there had been a kitten…

There was a low slung tree outside my bedroom window, and the cat had been meowing up at me all week from the top branch. I'd finally taken the initiative to climb out the window, collect the cat, and bring it back into my room. We'd both been thrilled by the adventure and novelty, and as I'd finalized my plans for sneaking out, she had taken to exploring all the corners of the room, pouncing at my bunched socks, hunting through the trash. In the total ten minutes she'd been inside the house, she had already managed to get locked in a drawer and in my closet, both times wailing loud enough that I'd had to make cover stories for my suspicious siblings about the weird sounds emanating from my room.

Not wanting to take any chances on my big night, I had finally set the kitten back outside on the tree branch and watched her scamper down the road happily, before I'd set out my clothes, gone down to dinner, feigned illness, and prepped myself for the escape caper and the party.

A few hours later, with all lights out—I'd inched open the window and somehow missed the same kitten batting at me playfully from the far edge of the windowsill. Focused on my ninja stealth, I'd scrambled past her completely unaware. Some ninja. Before I managed to shut the window again, she was blissfully back in the bedroom, ready to recommence her own torrid adventures.

However when she realized she was locked in without any playmate, she'd immediately decided to awaken everyone within a half mile radius with her wailing.

I'd probably been found out before I'd even reached my friends at the car.

Betrayed—betrayed by kittens.

So once again, I became the pariah. I got to see life from the vantage point of the cheaters, criminals, and juvenile delinquents; I got to be grounded. I'd even half-convinced my classmates that I was the new class rebel, as nearly all my oblivious friends had received one a.m. calls from Mom, asking if they knew where I'd run off to. It hadn't taken the community phone-tree long to activate, and my coconspirators absences had been similarly identified. What this actually meant substantively was that I never got to answer the phone, nor go out and visit my friends. And it also meant that anyone who hadn't been invited nor informed beforehand of the plot—now knew.

Drama on that point mostly circled around the person of Bryan Walker, who was wildly bitter. Fortunately, all his attempts to call and berate me for it were thwarted by Mom, who'd say something along the lines of, "John can't talk with friends right now, he's working on his morality," which would only enflame Bryan more: via his implied exclusion from the circle of friends 'in the know.' He hadn't yet worked out where or with whom I had been, though, or he would have been even more furious.

Not all the phone calls were from Bryan, however. Megan herself had begun calling regularly, all sunshine and wildflowers. She never seemed the least bit daunted by Mom's juvenile delinquent inferences over the phone, but rather just happily apologized and mentioned that she'd try calling again later.

Mom had been visibly taken aback by a girl's voice, and later by her perseverance, as if the possibility hadn't occurred to her yet that there might have been girls at the party, or that another child's dreaded sexual awakening era might have defrosted sooner than expected.

That night, there'd been a long interrogation at the white table where Mom was known to give community counselling sessions, and I'd huddled miserably on the small white chair listening to an especially potent sermon on responsibility and honesty. Themes of girls, puberty, temptation, safety, and morality circled up the staircase to the eager ears of my eavesdropping brothers, who then spent weeks gleefully parroting back their favorite lines at me as we'd brushed our teeth.

Ψ

I'd evidently lost all my luck. I'd known it was going to happen long before it did, but I was still taken back by the intensity and ferocity with which Bryan Walker laid into me for excluding him. One day he finally found me at an abandoned corner of the locker room after school. He was hiding behind a column supporting a drinking fountain, waiting for me to be alone.

"Who the hell do you think you are, John?" he'd began, seething with rage.

"What…?"

"Yeah, I found out you went to Winfield Hall. And I know exactly who you saw there. It didn't make sense to me at first why you'd have tried to keep the whole thing such a secret, but of course you thought you'd just slink in and try to key off my connections…As if Megan would ever have wanted anything to do with you if she hadn't thought you were connected to my family? She probably just hoped we'd arrive together, and that"

"Bryan, Megan invited me. She's really into me, I guess. We were at the pool a few weeks ago, and she said—"

It caught me completely off guard when he hit me with a wild, clumsy, cartoonish punch.

He leapt over me when I hit the ground, crouching over my chest, screaming and howling like a feral animal. The words were indistinguishable, but not the punches.

But then, something much stranger happened…

His face began rapidly shifting through conflicting emotions— and in between his wild punches, he kept grasping at me—clutching desperately at my jacket collar, as if begging for forgiveness even while he continued assaulting me. Tears, saliva, and mucous coursed down his face as one—as if he'd turned completely into a wounded animal. At one moment, he stopped the violence completely and collapsed into sobbing over me, pressing his cheek against mine and shuddering—trying to wrap me in a hug.

The guy had clearly gone completely mad—I didn't even know where to start.

I pushed him away, but it barely made a difference. I finally had to literally pry him off of me and roll him to the side, where he rolled, at first seeming sad—then immediately purple with rage. Even his eyes were blood red, sweat pouring down his face.

"THIS ISN'T OVER, CALABRACE!" he roared. "Don't think you've won! Nobody betrays me! You had to ruin everything, but don't think I'll ever forget! You'll get yours, you little freak! You don't fool anyone! You won't get away with this!"

What could I even say to that? He'd clearly gone drunk on maniacal super-villain fantasies. How had I ever betrayed him? I could get exactly zero read on his thoughts, beyond a wounded, animalistic vulnerability. He groaned as I wiped blood off my face, scooped up my backpack, and moved to rejoin the world outside the dim locker room—in total shock.

"Fuck you, Bryan," I mumbled towards the deranged boy—still whimpering in a fetal position in the corner. But I limped out of the room, a free man.

Ψ

Mom held a towel with ice to my eye, after she'd received a call from the school. She'd taken the rare step of calling in sick to her job, so that we might talk uninterruptedly. I could see from her face that she'd had enough surprises about my life.

"We're going to talk this out, John, and figure out what's been going on with you lately. First of all, I want to know where this black eye came from," she said, brushing my hair back from where it was sticking to the ice pack.

"It was an accident…" I started, lamely. "A friend—"

"Some friend, John! You don't need friends who would ever treat you like that." She wiped the moisture off my forehead, sat back, and looked at me a long while. "I honestly don't understand what's gotten into you lately, but I'd like you to try to remember something that I know and that I'll never doubt—*you are a good person.* I don't know what it is you're going through lately, but this stuff just isn't *you.* You don't sneak around, you don't lie to people. You don't get into fights. You're better than all that, and you know it. I'm your Mother, John, and of course I'm going to worry about you; because I love you. But I also expect better. And I know you can do better."

"I know," I muttered softly. "I'm sorry. I don't know…"

The mumble tapered off into the quiet room.

"Alright, alright, that's enough of all that. Go get yourself cleaned up, and then come back and help me set the table. And no more getting punched in the eye, John. Nobody has the right to make my beautiful boys look like raccoons. You have any questions on that score, you talk to your brother Jim. That's what big brothers are for." She laughed and watched me slipping away, while smoothing her dishtowel and wistfully picturing a simpler life, all of us all back as babies, inevitably.

Ψ

As I had before, once again I healed and moved on. My relationship with Bryan—if ever there was one—was destroyed. I never pointed a finger at him when the school had demanded the name of my attacker. Nonetheless, he never again passed me without glaring. Whenever I'd see groups of gossiping people staring at me, he'd always be in the shadows, whispering something or other! So now I had my first nemesis. Life was developing quickly!

Time passed and my parents lifted the solitary confinement sentence. Megan continued to call, and I finally answered. I wanted to explain how horrible Bryan had been and how angry he was, but I couldn't find the words.

It also quickly became clear that Megan was pretty eager for a relationship status that I wasn't ready for: one that would never have occurred to me. I tried to make that clear once or twice, but words continued to fail me. We went to a diner in Mineola, and as I tried to explain to her that I just wanted to be friends, who should waltz in and see us together in a booth—but Bryan Walker. He threw a plastic glass at the floor that bounced around impotently for a few seconds, and he stormed out the door. I tipped the waiter with all my spending money as a disturbance apology, apologized to Megan, and took her home. She didn't understand at all and didn't stop calling. But to the horror of my Mother, who had always trained us that sincerity and kindness were the keys to good living, I asked everyone to always say that "I was out."

9

Things had gotten out of control. For a long time, it had seemed like the ring was centering me enough that I could become a regular person: one who went outside, who spoke to strangers. But that period had passed. Somehow the sheer quantity of images I'd retained had begun to gum up the works of me. My brain was not well.

I'd finally taken to affecting my Great Uncle's sunglasses; it was the only way to stop all the questions about how dilated my pupils always seemed to be. (I guess folk must have just thought I'd developed a bit more of a stylish spirit, or at least I hoped so.) Nothing seemed to be moving as easily anymore. I was losing my grip, and losing the wherewithal to tell how normal is seemed from the outside.

Part of the problem was that the images I'd received and cataloged had begun to overwhelm me. It was like a broken copier, printing infinite pages that you couldn't get rid of. I had an endless catalog that kept growing and growing every time somebody touched me.

While I was typically pretty comfortable amid familiar routine, novelty normally threw me a bit. So when we learned that we'd have a mandatory field trip to the site of Meig's Raid in Sag Harbor for my history class, I was horrified. Not that I didn't know the town—Nannie and Gramps had moved there some time before and had already settled in, so I knew the town quite well. But this wouldn't be that sort of visit. I couldn't just sneak off to their house. It'd be a million kids crammed in a bus, jostling about for hours on the rides there and back—clapping each other on the back, tapping each other on the shoulders, slapping each other on the knees while laughing. And I knew I couldn't take even one more image. What would I do?

Nothing. My strategy ended up being nothing. I didn't plan quickly enough; I didn't improvise. Looking back, I think I sort of wanted to wallow in my misery. So I sat on the bus and basically went nuts. By the time we got to Sag Harbor I was panting with horror; all the sights and sounds around me were overwhelmed by a sea of my classmate's memories, jostling amid every other memory that I'd ever absorbed. I had to get away, to get some peace. Out of the corner of my eye, I caught sight of an acquaintance sneaking sips from an oldfashioned flask. Without any further consideration, I opened my wallet and offered him everything I had. It was a small fortune in high school terms. I spit the words, impulsively.

"Thomas, I'll give you forty-three dollars if you give me that flask."

"Why, what flask, officer?" he said grinning.

"C'mon man, the steel flask. You have no idea how much I need it right now."

He paused. "For forty-three dollars? You got it. But if you get caught, you didn't get it from me!" In a motion entirely too effortless for any novice, he bumped my outside jacket pocket and it suddenly contained a flask. Meanwhile with the same sleight of hand, he'd somehow slipped all my dollars into his sleeve; in one fluid motion he'd already turned his back, rejoining the group without any eye contact.

I melted into the dunes of the Hamptons, and disappeared. I drank in the smell of the sea and all the nameless booze in five minutes flat. Within ten minutes after leaving the bus, I was sick as a dog. I found a dune overlooking Nannie and Gramps' house, and laid down to rest inside an old canal bed where my cousin Elizabeth and I had been stacking shingles each summer to reprise our childhood Cape Cod glory years.

I couldn't go inside the house, and I couldn't go back into the past, so I'd sleep. I was drunk and sick, I was quickly racing out of childhood, and I was drowning in emotional memories nobody knew I had access to. As the world swam away from me, a blurred vision of Elizabeth's face floated into my mind.

"John…?"

I laid down my head and flew away to dreamland…

Ψ

Except it wasn't a dream. Elizabeth sat watching me for a moment, perplexed, until I began to snore. She then shook my shoulder.

"John? What are you doing here? Do you know you're sleeping in a canal? Anyway, isn't it a school day for you?"

Her questions weren't strung together in abnormally quick succession; it just took a while for my head to climb out of the fogbank and register the meaning of the words.

I blinked stupidly for a moment, and mumbled weakly, "Me? What about you? I thought you'd be in Massachusetts?"

"Dad's old business partner is getting married here this weekend. Mom called us all in sick and got us a three day weekend," she said, eying me, waiting for my story.

"That doesn't sound much like your mom," I dodged the question with a one-liner.

"Nope, it's a one-time thing. So really, John, what's going on with you?"

"Class trip! We're learning about Meig's Raid, the kings of Long Island espionage, the true marvels of New York's past. Our dreams are shimmering…"

In the middle of my beautiful soliloquy I wobbled, worried I mightthrow up.

"Ah, I see," she said, very unimpressed. "Well, is there a reason you smell like a dead fish on this trip?"

"Oh, that. That'd be the booze." I sat up, casually lifting cobwebs out of my hair, and kicking mud off my Keds.

"And the reason for THE BOOZE would be…?"

"It's been a rough couple of years, Elizabeth." I intentionally avoided eye contact, looking into the distance instead.

"Am I supposed to just leave it at that, John?"

I was silent for a moment, considering what to say. "I'm just having a hard time connecting together all the parts of my life. My head is all over the place, and sometimes I panic. A bit."

She picked up the small flask and held it gingerly at arm's length. "You think this will help you in your struggle? You don't think this is a bad habit to start off this early?"

I slowly turned and faced the favorite figure of my childhood. She was dead right, of course. "No, I know it's a terrible idea. I suppose I didn't really think it through, completely…exactly."

"No, I wouldn't say so, either. C'mon John. We'll walk into town and find you some coffee and food; get you fixed up."

"Look, Elizabeth…I appreciate all you're doing and I'm both horrified and sorry you had to get involved with this in any way; but I'd really rather that Nannie didn't hear anything about this unless it's absolutely necessary…"

"Of course not, John! You know any secret you have will always be safe with me; what do you think family is for?" She supported my arm and lurched me to my feet, and together, we stumbled into town.

Ψ

Within an hour and a half and several cups of coffee, Elizabeth had rebuilt my spirits and courage. The liquid devils had also lost most of their power over me. So I regretfully said goodbye, and attempted to melt back into the ubiquitous herds of my classmates as they roved around the Umbrella House. I'd heard my Uncle's lecture on this place a million times, so when a chaperone glancing over the group posed a question directly at me (exactly as I rejoined them), I managed to appear like I'd been listening the whole time while wandering: "A British cannon ball hit it, you can still see the damage." I'd wildly hoped that this answer matched the question.

"Exactly," she said, continuing in her lecture without a hitch.

My head had begun to reel as our walk continued across town. But I still considered myself ready to fire off a pre-arranged answer when an inevitable question was posed about the church steeple at the Old Whalers Church. In my peripheral vision, above the blur of faces I saw the teacher turn away from the building and gesture at me, and immediately, I was ready.

"John…?"

I snapped back to reality and responded in rapid-fire. "Yes, it blew off during the Great Hurricane."

She laughed. "No, John, I just said it looks like you've got some mud on your pants. Just there, see?"

I looked where she was gesturing and noticed the perfect print of the canal pipes edged in black mud across both my calves. Perfect. I reddened.

"Oh. Thanks."

Ψ

Nobody ever knew about the horrible trip. It got lost amid all the words people keep to themselves: alongside all the petty internal dramas and scheduling bustle. Stories never came home about the boy in a canal bed. I managed to frantically elbow-grease the worst of the mud and rust stains out of the pants, before leaving them soaked in the empty washer. If anybody ever wondered, they never said anything.

What was really causing trouble was my sleeping. Or rather—my *never* sleeping.

Mom had gotten wise to it after I'd started becoming forgetful about turning off lights and cleaning up the kitchen. It was cool and quiet there, so I'd usually wander in and let all the images defragment themselves against the blank white walls of the empty room. Hours would go by with nothing but the dim light (I'd only use the small light above the oven, to avoid attracting my light-sleeping Dad). I'd make myself a bland sandwich on autopilot (which I'd often forget to eat), and then just stare at the walls as my mind tried to make heads or tails out of the huge amounts of information that had climbed out of strangers' heads to set up a home in mine...For me, that meant school, relationships, and the capacity to achieve a generic perception of sanity were all fairly complicated.

After a few attempts trying to indulgently nudge me back into normalcy, Mom changed tacks and tried to get me to take chamomile tea. She implored me to avoid fluorescent lights after a certain time of day, to exercise more in the late afternoons, to drink more water, to get a better diet, and to express my feelings more. All for naught, of course. I could tell her intent was good, but taking advice was never a strong suit of mine. As she had no idea what was going on and couldn't be expected to magically find a brilliant solution, she tried a terrible idea instead. Monday morning, I found myself scheduled to see the school counselor.

"Hello Matthew, what seems to be the problem today?"

"John…"

"Sure, you can call me John. Being casual is fine…My name is John Filch, Matt—and I'm very glad to meet you."

"No, sorry to be unclear. My first name is John."

John Filch frowned over his paperwork. "So you are. What's bothering you, other John?"

I tried very hard to shake off the notion that this idea didn't have a prayer, that this poor man couldn't do anything for me whatsoever. I tried to give him a shot. But all my high hopes dissolved when he remembered he'd been remiss in politeness as I'd entered, so he flashed me a broad white grin, loomed across the table, and vigorously shook my hand.

"Well I, you see…I—" But the second I started talking to this massive red-faced white-toothed man, all his thoughts and emotions poured into me. I tried to achieve the impossible: to tune it all out and just talk to somebody authoritative, force myself to believe there might be some benefit from this absurd situation. I did try. For a minute.

"I'm having trouble sleeping."

"Ah, sleeping…. That one is difficult, Ma—, uh, John." He continued. "Have you considered adding some sports into your schedule? Running might be good. Perhaps you're just bored with your routines."

As he said the words, he craned his neck momentarily to the left to glance at the legs of an unseen woman passing by. I tracked slowly back from the receding footsteps of the woman passing, and abruptly noticed that his brow was even redder than before, speckled with perspiration.

"You've got to find a way to involve yourself in the system, John. To really motivate yourself to excel—"

As he continued to talk, his flood of memories and emotions drowned out the words. I saw image after image of young Mrs.

Winters; the same professional in an awkward parka now walking down the hall. Here she was reaching forward far across a table, or crouching way down to throw paper cups into the trash and lurching back her hips for lack of balance. There she was, slowly picking a pencil off the floor, or sighing while adjusting a run in her stockings, stepping her long legs out of a car door, or jogging languidly out to help line kids up for the bus ride home. I didn't make much of the images themselves; it was the accompanying *emotional* component that was harrowing. For though I could see his lips weren't moving the whole time Filch stared at me, I could still sense overwhelming sounds, low, wounded animal sounds made by his psyche—suffusing all of these images. I'd stepped into a circus mirror maze of asymmetrical lust, and I did not want to be there any longer than I had to. Had there been an affair? It didn't seem so…instead this was just one man, trapped alone amid his own longings for a stranger. I lost the capacity to look at him and his horrifying forehead still beaded with sweat. However he, none the wiser, recommenced…

"It's all about your attitude, John. Winners have to choose to win." I gathered myself and my things as he paused, but it was evidently just for effect. Were we done here? No; he re began with gusto. "Take golf. I've been working on my golf drive for—"

As he was well into delivering a stock inspirational speech he'd clearly long ago prepared for general use, I allowed myself to plunge away from the present. If I was going to witness one corner of horror in an authority figure, why not go all in? I dove headfirst into the composite slipstream of all assembled images of the life of one professional guidance counselor, the less than legendary John Filch.

I saw John Filch, adolescent: wandering into a large campus, seeming none-too-certain about his choice to be there. I saw even younger John Filch, failing to decide between competing scholarship offers, and throwing a dart to choose. I saw older John Filch regularly failing early morning tests after discovering late night booze escapades.

The more images I saw, the less I worried about impressing the Authoritative Adult: John Fitch. Also, the less I worried about making absolutely perfect choices to survive. This guy was a mess…But even he had a job, tacky gold jewelry, potentially fake hair, and even those teeth had had some serious work done since childhood. He had stability, and an endless supply of silver pens which he'd been playing with absentmindedly throughout his generic lecture. I made a mental note that if everything else in my life fell through, I'd have to strenuously avoid falling for a young geography teacher. Short of that, it seemed like I'd probably make it. If he could, anyone could.

Ψ

With a lot of work (and a lot of speeches to myself in the mirror), I managed to pull myself together for the outside world. My sleep didn't improve, though, so we eventually even tried psychiatrists. I visited the stately Dr. Stoller about half a dozen times, and ultimately, he determined my issue was high anxiety. He tried to drown any symptoms in prescription antidepressants, antianxiety medications, and beta blockers, and though the results were underwhelming, he sent me on my way with a CURED stamp on my folder.

So by the time my high school experience was wrapping up, I was a new man. Board certified, shrink approved: enabled, ennobled, and ameliorated. Nannie and I found ourselves together at a Woolworth's counter for the first time in a good while, and I marveled at my effortless scale relative to the lunch counter and stool. Childhood had flown by, and here we were again, like nothing had ever changed.

"Well, what'll it be, John?" Nannie indulgently began.

"*Well* Nannie, I'd like the grilled cheese and bacon with a strawberry shake."

"Don't you want to try something else this time, John?"

"Actually, I think I'd like to hang onto the past a bit more these days, Nannie."

She reached out quietly and stroked my hair while smiling up at me. "I know the feeling, John. You're doing fine, you know…this isn't an easy time in life. We're terribly proud of you."

I drank in the simplicity of the scene and hoped the moment would never change.

10

"John, you are the only person I've ever met that makes even me look normal," Mark sighed.

He squeaked open our shared dorm-room door and immediately tripped over my as-yet unwrapped math textbooks. He crossed the room and ripped the mangy curtains open, flooding the dark room in afternoon sunlight. I jerked up my head. By opening our one small window, all New York City was symbolically welcomed to climb the stone walls from the park into our small apartment. And so it did: a million car horns, a million lovers, a million pigeons, a million buses, garbage trucks and muggings all entered at once, in a riotous cacophony.

"What's that supposed to mean?" I mumbled, wincing while unscrewing an aspirin bottle. I'd fallen asleep while studying, and the old pen I'd been writing with had leaked a pool of ink between my arm and my face, staining my temple and forehead with large dark ink smudges.

"Well, to start, your face looks like a leopard's. It's also two p.m. You've been in exactly that position for ages. Several ages, I think."

"It's been maybe a few minutes, Mark! I just fell asleep while studying!"

"It's been sixteen hours, John. And that's the same chapter and page you were on when I left." He flashed me a concerned face and tossed a package of breath mints in my direction.

"Oh." I found a mirror and quietly scrubbed away my jungle-cat facial markings.

He stepped across the mess of clothes and papers that had formed a semi-circling moat several feet thick around me. "So, you've started going to classes again?"

"Of course!" I murmured, adding, "Well, some of them."

"Well, at least the drinking has lessened a bit. Things had gotten a bit out of control there, buddy. I didn't want to say anything…"

I quietly kneed-closed the desk drawer to my right, with an incriminating fifth of whiskey in it propped up by crumpled balls of paper. Bad timing!

"So anyway, how is…what's her name you've been staying with… Carol? Amy?" I muttered, changing the subject.

"Jonathan? He's fine. That's not…a problem for you, right? Maybe I should have said something? Been clearer about—?"

"No, not at all! All the more power to you. At least you seem happy." I sighed, leaning back in the wooden chair. In two months of school, I'd made precisely two friends: one was my roommate, and one an alcoholic beverage in a drawer.

"Sometimes I wonder if I should call Megan…" I murmured, feeling a bit sorry for myself.

"Not that again. You said straight out—you didn't like her romantically: there wasn't any spark or overwhelming attraction. She *did* feel all those things for you, it seems. Now what would calling her and rekindling a façade achieve besides leading her on, or giving her some hope you'd somehow changed your mind? Look around, there are all kinds of people here. Whatever it is you're into, apart from the booze…Why not just find some nice person you're actually interested in?"

"Yeah, I guess…" I sighed, staring out the window at the coursing crowds on Washington Square, "…there sure are a lot of them!"

There was nothing stranger than the absolute lack of supervision out here. The freedom and sense of social liberation was a double-edged sword, because there was never any safety net. Everything was unfamiliar. Every person was a stranger. Thus every trip outside was a world-ravaging flood of images—without any protection or respite. There was no sense of relevancy, no learning-curve, I could never choose to turn on or off being wildly oversensitive or receiving everything around me. I longed for some sense of normalcy, for some cap on novelties; but found no such luck. Hence the retreat.

"This isn't the easiest city for anybody to adjust to, John. You'll figure it out. Now come on, you need some real food in you, my treat! First you march off to the shower, and meet me back here in five. I refuse to live alongside Charles Bukowski."

I laughed and obliged. Twenty minutes later we were bundled and scarved, and together we forayed out into the apocalyptic wonderland of 1973 New York City.

Ψ

Lately I'd found myself thinking a lot about Bryan Walker, now that I was finally free of him. To be in such traumatic proximity to somebody so dysfunctional, for so long, sort of impresses their influence all your perceptions of your own world. It takes time to fade. Every time somebody stopped me on the square or in the hallways—even when kindly, earnestly, and genuinely interested in bonding with me—I couldn't help but imagine Bryan and shiver. I always visualized the way he'd have jealously guarded them, and me, and himself, all at once. Perpetually hoarding. Every time, my mind flashed back to the bizarre scene in the locker room, one that I never fully understood and basically just compartmentalized for years.

While I still feared him and regretted the lost time I'd wasted trying to maintain a dysfunctional friendship, I pitied him nonetheless...He was a man who would never be happy, who would never really know what it was to connect to a person and know real warmth. He could access nothing beyond manipulation, immediate gratification, and a self-limiting lust for power. As Gramps would always say "learn from other peoples' mistakes, and learn how to avoid making the same."

If I knew anything now, it was that despite all the risks and heartache, *connection* meant everything. My life's work would have to be avoiding the easy route, avoiding closing off, avoiding manipulating people for the sake of my own convenience. But that sort of abstract goal is easier said than done. And sometimes, shortcuts don't seem that bad until they malfunction.

School was a prime example. I'd stopped going. What could possibly go wrong, there?

Before college, I'd already crudely experimented with a few purely-academic shortcuts. I'd always wanted to speak a foreign language but didn't seem to have any gift for it. Eventually I got the idea that perhaps I could cut a few corners if I just bumped into teachers who already knew the languages, hoping my brain would magically *sort through* the details. I hoped that faced with the novel jumble of bulk sounds, my hungry synapses would somehow "solve for x," and just like that—I'd absorb a second language. Unfortunately it didn't, and I didn't.

I mostly saw a bunch of memories, with language itself barely registering any impact. Specific foreign language memories were few and far between, and usually so unpleasantly oversaturated in the pungent emotional stress of trying to teach them to utterly unreceptive students, that I preferred to avoid them altogether. Moreover, I hadn't gambled on the remarkable feelings of nausea that often accompanied them.

Instead of effortlessly mastering foreign languages, I'd learned details I would rather never have known about my teachers: the opera songs Mr. Freiberg bellowed while inexplicably re-sorting his underwear drawer every morning by color, or the fact that Mme. Delpy's substantial marital problems were pushing her into an ominously accelerating eating disorder. I learned with horror their favorite sites on campus to get sick, a feature I found to be universal amid all my overstressed teachers. Far from helping me academically, I think I became even more distracted in classes as I worried about their unraveling lives and sanity. In seeking shortcuts, empathy now weighed me down as heavily as any ball and chain.

In college, it was different. I'd been struggling to find an academic emphasis route to appease my parents and the counseling office, and I'd been coming up empty every time. Suddenly, History hit me like a freight train. It happened after a chance contact with the longbearded department chair, Dr. Michelson, who tapped me on the shoulder to ask me about a late paper. This was a man who lived for *nothing* but history. The absolute stereotype of an Ivy League, absentminded professor; he was to leave a huge mark on my life and the way I saw the world. Though he probably couldn't have had any idea of it, because I nearly never attended his lectures. Why bother? I couldn't have gotten his thoughts out of my head if I tried, so I figured I might as well sort through them at my leisure. So I tried. In bed.

Dr. Michelson had spent thirty years dragging his family to the sites of every historical event he could find within flying distance, though he preferred to drive or take trains so he could sort through maps of the trips beforehand and scrawl notes along the route. (He collected and itemized "historical photos and travel detritus/artifacts" for his lectures, and thus used the trips as substantial tax write-offs.) At the end of every semester he'd fill the doldrums—while proctoring exam weeks—with a rigorous routine of speech preparation for his family: a truly captive audience.

He lived for those trips. All the webs of his emotional overinvestment bound the lectures together into one intensity saturated blob, making what would—normally—be scattered fragments into something nearly whole, and visible to me.

It was like digesting a message via a language which I'd never learned, one purely accessed by my emotional circuitry. He'd practice elaborately lectured speeches in the mirror for weeks: drenched in sweat and flailing his arms for effect, making sound effects and leaping about. He was a perfectionist, one who felt he'd clearly missed his true calling as some sort of Thespian. Something about the level of animation and intensity with which he rehearsed and delivered them meant the chained images of his memories were more cohesively intact than anything I'd ever yet seen out of a stranger (short of childhood traumas or sexual embarrassments). It was like a pointillism portrait on cheese cloth: you could still see a fairly coherent image by squinting.

So just like that, I became a history buff. I suddenly felt like I was half-way to a PhD myself!

The thing was, I loved it. I'd long ago given up on resisting my brain's ceaseless gallop into a drowning pool of sights and emotion. Something about my mind had already been slowly rewiring for years, to accept the broad swaths of diverse storylines, (seemingly unrelated), to try to sort them into some sense. It always seemed to be thirsting for more.

History seemed to be all about that: small, subtle webs of past exploits that linked and informed everything, anchoring it all together in invisible chains of connection and coincidence which normally seemed too slight to sense. My brain ate it up, like Dr. Michelson was a master chef who'd crafted a multi-course masterpiece just for me.

Suddenly the world I knew was populated with even more ghosts than before. More and more, "pasts" were conceptually redrawn into a sort of vaguely glowing present-tense physicality whenever I'd walk around, suffused with their own drama and significance. I'd sit on Washington Square, watching the kids with guitars and chessboards shriek and laugh, but now I'd know they were sitting blissfully unaware atop the twenty thousand bodies of a former potter's field, with birds chirping and a cheerfully bubbling fountain alongside, to boot! I daydreamed about the sleepy shopping mall back home where I'd furtively smoked pot as a kid that had been built atop an airfield that had seen the launch of both Charles Lindberg and Amelia Earhart's famous airships. The whole width and length of my mental picture of Long Island now rocked and writhed with the images of Dr. Michelson's lectures on British espionage rings, of missiles being tested on the wharves of Nannie's sleepy Sag Harbor, of famous whaler's barroom brawls and the owners' dramas amid the Gilded Age mansions up North which I'd never bothered to think about.

My comprehended world had effectively expanded by a power of two in a matter of minutes. So no wonder I was locked in a dorm—I was in recovery! Life had gotten crowded again. Somehow, I'd stumbled into post-traumatic stress for the millionth time in my young life.

Ψ

Somehow, Mark managed to push and shove me through the worst of it. I started going to more classes, although huge lecture halls were barely worth the effort. (I'd always get touched and distracted by some apologizing stranger's life story right at the crux of the lecture, and professors would complain that I looked high whenever my eyes were still dilated at the close of class.) Fortunately, my academic advisors started laying off me when my history test scores rose dramatically, and Mark recommended a friend who would trade tutoring in Math for my help with History. College started to pull itself together, at least in an academic sense.

Personally and interpersonally, it was "back to the drawing board."

Ψ

"Well? Did you call her?" Mark clapped his hands together, thrilled at his matchmaking.

"Yes," I snapped in a clipped voice. Kassandra. "Yes, I did call her. We went out this evening."

"And? Go on, how did it go?" He'd missed any implied hints in my voice, to lay off.

"I…she…it didn't go that well, really. I don't think she really liked me that much."

"Oh, that's terrible! I thought you'd really like each other, you have so much in common! I'm so sorry, John. Keep at it. When at first you don't succeed, try and try again, right?"

"Right…Goodnight Mark," I mumbled, already buried beneath my pillow and blanket.

Ψ

"WHAT DID YOU SAY TO HER?!" Mark yelled, banging open the door.

I had just returned from the showers and hadn't yet dressed. I was wearing a ridiculous towel and halfway through brushing my teeth before the mirror as he yelled the question.

"Mrftfph? Tschthyg pgthylf?" I replied.

"John, you told me you were lonely. You said you wanted to spend some time with someone nice, to start up a real relationship. Explain to me why when I ran into Kassandra after she spent one day with you, she was crying, and called you, 'that cruel-spirited bastard?' "

"Mrfthlsoph Kwylft!" I made desperate face and noisily spat out the window. Someone yelled out in protest below as I shut the glass.

Mark stared at me, tapping his foot. "I'll wait!"

I finished wiping off my chin and pulled on my old bathrobe. "She came onto me!"

"Okay…so how did that translate into her considering you to be a 'cruel-spirited bastard?' I must be missing part of the story here, John."

"I thought she was nice.

"I thought she was really nice. And we did have a lot in common. For one, evidently, we both really like to drink. She drank a ton, and asked me back to her apartment to see her record collection."

Mark was exasperated immediately and interrupted me. "You do know about grownups and grownup conventions, right John? You know what *come back to my apartment* means?"

"Sure. I guess I just thought I would…I don't know, want it more."

"The two of you didn't work out some sort of rapport? There was no vibe measurement beforehand, no discussion of whether you were into it or not? Into her in any way?!"

"No! We just sort of…went! It was cold outside. I tried to just walk her home, but she asked me in. I thought it'd be harmless, she said she could make some coffee…"

"Jesus, John, it's like I'm talking to a toddler. Well, at least you didn't do anything? She just got her feelings hurt by a misunderstanding, and nothing more? Right?"

I paused, looking elsewhere.

"*Right* John? You didn't sleep with the poor girl for pity's sake?" He waited. "Right?"

"I might have—"

"Good lord, John. So you didn't care much for one of my oldest friends, fine. You didn't reciprocate her boozy advances, fine. Except you did, evidently, and all the while knowing you didn't care less. I believe I understand perfectly so far. Please, do go on, you may continue. Pray tell, what happened next, once you'd had your fill of poor Kassandra's performance?

I muttered something quietly, ashamed.

"I'm sorry, I didn't quite catch that."

"I panicked! I grabbed my shoes and coat and said 'Thank you Kassandra,' and ran down the stairs into the street!"

Mark stared at me, concretely bewildered. " *'Thank you, Kassandra!'* Well, aren't you the gentleman?! I was wondering how you'd planned to explain these, but I suppose that explanation was sufficient after all!" He held up some pants, covered in frost. "Anyhow, Kassandra said she threw these out the window after you but you were already halfway down the Mews, clutching newspapers to hide your ass as you ran. Is that true?"

I threw myself at my bed groaning, horrified and ashamed. I'd probably just lost my only friend, I'd hurt a sweet girl who'd only meant well, and I'd surely gained a nickname or two on the campus grounds. This would be a very long year.

He laughed in spite of his anger. "One thing is for sure, John. You do appear to know how to make an impression." He snickered, looking out the window. "I may never again connect you with anyone I care about…ever, EVER again…" He paused, still seething a bit. "But, as your roommate and friend, I nonetheless must…congratulate you, sir."

I lifted my head slightly out of the mattress where I'd been groaning. "What?…Why?!"

"You might not give a shit about any of your classes, and succumb to trivial expressions of meaninglessness—and perhaps even suffer a premature lapse into alcoholism; but at least you'll absolutely *ace* the age-old collegiate Walk of Shame. So far as I can imagine, nobody will ever top you there, for style."

I threw my face back at the mattress. The pants landed atop my head with a muffled thud.

11

As always, a liberal application of time cured all ills. Moments and seasons blurred, and suddenly winter gave way to summer, somehow skipping straight over spring. I'd begun making an effort to creep back into the world in spite of the entropy. I still mostly avoided Washington Square and anywhere I'd be known, opting for anonymous crowds and long walks. I especially enjoyed walking in the early evening, when the fluorescent lights glowed across the puddles and pool amid the setts. All my life I'd been warned of the violence risks of recession-era NYC, but that was nearly never my experience. I loved the place.

While the vast majority of my classmates would have been at home studying, I was strolling every sight from lower Manhattan through Midtown, memorizing every street corner. I'd probably named all the stray cats from Central Park down to the sea by the time I left.

Looking back, it's still bizarre to recognize the transformation that the recession had inflicted on the city. I'd visited NYC every few years of my childhood, since my Grandfather had been a powerful force around Midtown: where he was considered a marketing guru. A self-made man, he understood the power of connections, work-ethic, and self-presentation. He had taught me all about always trying to look as sharp as possible: always dressing for success. However, suffice to say, with the 1973 oil embargo shocking the entire economy, New York had lost its appreciation of those critical life lessons. Central Park had dried up. The Belvedere Castle, housing meteorological equipment for measuring temperature fluctuations, had gotten to a point where scientists were considering moving away somewhere else—after repetitive thefts from the ramshackle, graffiti-covered building. But there was still a magic in the place, in spite of the grit and grime. There was motion and vitality, granted sometimes of a vaguely insane bent. And for a family boy from the burbs, there was an entirely unfamiliar sense of adventure, a thrill to the insanity of it all. I found myself walking places I knew I shouldn't be, trying to tell my way by the texture of the place: a braille of brickwork, telephone wires, iron fire escapes, and paper litter on the ground. Sometimes it seemed there had to be some schizophrenic sense to the randomness of it all, and I pretended to try to decipher it like a lunatic's Rosetta stone.

I was never able to erase Mark's story from my mind of why he wore a whistle around his neck after getting ambushed by a street gang in late night SoHo. I'd even wandered past ominous alleys where I'd seen fresh blood on rusty, dented trashcans myself: I'd come away with the sensation that I'd opened some gristly cautionary tale on the last few pages of the epilogue and missed the majority of the story.

I, however, seemed to live a charmed life, where nobody bothered to hassle me beyond a periodic bum or some angry street-corner drunk longing for the validation of a midnight fight, yelling, "Hey! Hey you!" but immediately giving up if never engaged. I'd continue on to Dave's Corner on Canal Street and Broadway for a four a.m. breakfast, with only the barking dogs, yowling cats, distant echoes of the barfing barflies, and the screeching tires and horns of fire trucks for company. I loved the solitude and intensity of the place, especially after a rainy night when the moon would cross over the wet street and set the whole place aglow. Nobody touched me, nobody interrupted me, and the greatest city in the world was all mine.

So yes, my experience of several NYU years gradually resolved itself into a truant, werewolf-like existence. I'd watch the checkerboard of lights flicker on and off on the new World Trade Center towers from Battery Park, tuning out the growls and potential threats around me. Blind luck was clearly the only possible reason I'd thus far escaped outright physical harm, mugging, murder, and all the other fears I'd been warned about. But I continued to trust in the protection of providence, wandering farther and farther into the late nights.

I certainly didn't avoid dangerous places. I'd wander across the Brooklyn Bridge itself sometimes, just to clear my mind of voices. To the million voices already fighting it out in my head, I'd now add the luminaries from whatever class textbooks I'd half-engaged that week: literary and historical figures populating the dim streets of Brooklyn where I'd grab a coffee and head back towards home, towards a bed I couldn't stand to sleep in. *Bed*, I'd finally come to understand, was just the megaphone where all the specters in my mind yelled out their impossible demands upon my waking life. So, rather than lying awake rocking trapped in migraines, I became a consummate wanderer.

And when that didn't work, I switched to the harder stuff.

Nothing too fancy, mind you. Following the great tradition of all hungry heartsick romantics, I turned to alcohol to answer life's great unanswerables. While the reach of my wanderings decreased when sloshed, my solitude increased commensurately with each splash of liquor. This was my first glimpse of quiet respite since childhood from the constant, competitive chatter of memories that weren't mine. I loved the hazy hush that would fall over the world as I staggered along the piers, or watched through barred windows of bars and taverns that some called Home, with the neon lights stretching half blocks toward me like great unfurled welcome mats.

Eventually, I'd cataloged all the other midnight souls claiming the streets as their own. Old folk slept on vents, and desolate folk wandered roadsides and loitered around the diners or circled quietly around rosy flames spurting from trash cans, warming their hands. There were lost-looking folk-singers who'd evidently missed the great wave, and salts of a bygone era. They looked nervously around in the dark near old beat haunts like The White Horse Tavern or the Lion's Head, shivering atop their guitar cases, flipping through Port Authority bus schedules—and hoping to find their futures within. Hungry-looking, lonely men lined up chatting in the dark lanes along the empty shipping trucks of the meatpacking district; and I was still young and naive enough to wonder if they were a labor union. (I was too shy and wary of strangers to ask; I just hurried by smiling politely as they sang songs and danced in the half-light.)

A few diners stayed open, and side by side one could encounter every variation of soul the massive city could produce. They sat there in various shades of makeup and lipstick, shapes of hat, age, race, and sex—and eagerness to talk. Usually, around those late hours, folk seemed to keep to themselves, quietly nursing whatever grudges or hauntings had forced them out into the night in the first place. There were also cops—some good and some bad—who loved to pose very direct questions for which they hoped to receive impossible, concrete answers. More than once I found myself obliged to improvise nonsense scenarios to explain my otherwise perfectly legal late-night ramblings, when interrupted at an abandoned street with:

"Hey! You! What are you doing out here tonight?!"

To which I certainly couldn't reply, "I'm running from the ghosts of memories; though they're not my own." So I tried to keep quiet.

There would be an entirely dehumanizing process of sizing-up and cross-examination, after which I'd be sternly informed that good people shouldn't be out in dangerous streets so late. He'd bark to me to head home—not to spend the midnight hours on "his streets," insomnia or not.

Ψ

Somehow, I never failed out of school completely. My vampiric life continued unabated, though I realized I'd have to work harder in my general education courses. I was sneaking by in my classes with the help of a whole lot of tutoring in cafes in the late afternoons and an arm's length policy with lectures themselves. Mark's periodic interventions roped me back into reality when my excesses got out of control. I'd inflict periodic sobriety where I'd basically chain myself to my desk for three days at a time and cram just long enough to get enough financial aid for another semester's loop of the dysfunctional cycle, then retake to the streets and the night. I held myself together after a fashion, with alcohol and secluded rambling standing in as my fairly effective ostracization and self-medication regime.

It never occurred to me that I was lonely. I was too afraid of the over-stimulation chaos I'd experienced with Megan's kiss to ever seek out a regular relationship for its own sake. There was nothing there for me...It didn't hurt that in moments of stress I still visualized cartoonishly awful interpersonal moments like Bryan sweatily tackling me, and so terror regularly overtook attachment: if I attached surely I would just be hurt. It never occurred to me that I needed that sincerity factor, or that in fleeing scenarios of prematurely perceived skeletons in the closet of every other stranger, I was stockpiling skeletons of my own. I was becoming an unknown, a nonexistent person in the daylight hours. My professors didn't know me, my neighborhood didn't know me, the beautifully smiling girls strolling Bleeker Street didn't know me; and a mere twenty-five miles away my own parents would barely recognize me, at least in my current state.

Only the night owls.

All that depersonalization came to a head, literally, one late night in September. I was a little worse for the wear, watching the moon rise over some stray planks of an abandoned pier, with the quiet sounds of water farther on. Suddenly, for the first time I could remember, a whisper from deep in the darkness addressed me and invited me into the shadows. I knew better, but for some unknown reason, I walked in anyway.

Stooping under the boards, I could see next to nothing. The quiet sound of a steady drip somewhere in the darkness reverberated around the wooden structure, the salty smell of the sea, and a shadowy darkness in one corner that congregated in a tall shape that must have been a person. The same husky whisper merely whispered the words, "Come here," and for some reason I did.

The next thing I knew, I sensed a sudden surge of motion and somebody was right there before me, with their fingers grasping through my hair, kissing me hard on the mouth, breathing hard and hot on my neck and shoulder. I froze, shocked in place, more surprised at myself for showing up than eager to go, though I was terrified and excited all at once and completely at a loss for what I'd stumbled into. I felt unknown hands slide down my chest and side, and the pressure of practiced knees settling alongside my feet. Inches away in the dark, someone fumbled with my shirt through my open jacket, and unclasped my belt and pants in an instant, while my brain failed completely to deliver some idea to me of what was going on. As I struggled with grasping the moment to moment reality, my partner in the darkness had no such trouble, and I felt the most historically solitary part of my body taken quietly into the hands and mouth of a stranger. I nearly fainted at the transition; all the blood draining from my head, my knees shaking, my mouth dry, my heart hammering like a war drum. A strong hand wrapped around my right thigh and clawed at my buttock, pulling me off balance further and further forward, more and more forcefully. My head spun and brain melted, as sweat, confusion, and the consternation of the ambiguity of this unexpected encounter exploded into the darkness as an age-old mechanical process progressively silenced all my other thoughts, apart from an oncoming train-headlight effect. For the first time in my life in the presence of another person, I felt my climax coming fast and hard, inevitable, with the surging sensations at my waist each paired with simultaneous worries posed in ceaseless inner monolog as my head spun…

What was this? Where was I again? Who was this person? (The stranger did seem fairly friendly, all said…) *But how had I gotten here? How did I feel about this? Why had I walked into this darkness after a whispered invitation? Was this real? Didn't I know better? Should I ask for a phone number? Buy flowers? Would I be pressed for money? Would I be robbed? Might I be killed? Was this the end?* Some illogical reversion to childhood whispered from the back of my subconscious: *hadn't I been warned to never talk to strangers?!* Panic and pleasure mingled in the darkness, and greatly sped along the process.

I tried to grasp hold of the situation and slow it down, to concentrate, by focusing my attention on a roving flashlight beam moving quietly towards us along the roof, until I realized with a start—it was real. A strange voice shattered the silence as a third human shape outside our structure trained the flashlight beam directly on my face and barked an order. "HEY! YOU GET THE HELL OUT HERE, RIGHT NOW!"

The noise shattered the silence, awaking droves of roosting pigeons all who exploded into flight. My unseen partner vanished with a resounding rhythm of decrescendoing footfalls into the cobalt darkness of the opposite direction.

And just like that, I was alone. I hid into shadows, pulled my pants up and hastily buttoned my jacket over my still open waist, while the clouds of my breath shot illuminated in the single firm spotlight. Terrified and horrified, I emerged into the light alone.

"Well, if it isn't my midnight poet!"

I immediately recognized with horror the familiar face of a beat cop I'd passed a million times, who'd always encouraged me towards a better bedtime and a warm glass of milk to mitigate my insomnia.

"What brings you this far out tonight? Everything okay? Was someone hassling you down there? It's an awfully unsafe place, to loiter this late!" He was toying with me, clearly.

I stared at him, completely unsure what I should expect. By now, my faceless partner was blocks from here. I had no idea what this cop had seen. More than me, certainly! I thought a moment, at a loss.

"Well, I was walking down this path and someone grabbed me. I think they were going for my wallet, officer. I, uh, I feared for my life! Thank god you came along just in the nick of time!"

He stared at me, with a slight sneer in his face. "You know, this place has a pretty rough reputation at night. I'll bet it will look pretty bad, on paper…Technically though, I do have to call this incident in—and make a formal report. Rules are rules, you know." He smirked.

I swallowed hard, halfway to hyperventilating. I had no words, just terror and shame. My legs felt like they could give out any moment, even worse than a few moments before.

"If you'd like, I'm sure we could find some way just to keep this between ourselves?" His right hand raised softly through the night air, and hung flat at a ninety degree angle alongside his chest.

I sat there blinking for a moment, not even understanding what he was implying. The sea breeze blew across the path with a noisy *whoosh*. Finally comprehending, I dizzily pulled my wallet from my pocket and stared at it. I silently pulled out a twenty dollar bill, and felt time suspend in slow motion as I reached across the chasm between us to lay it on his hand. He stayed completely still, only his head jerked a little to the left and he winced his smile into a half shrug. He wanted more. We repeated the process twice more, until my entire food budget for the month was gone, my wallet empty. I stared at him hard, unsure where this was going. I half expected him to punch me, to shoot me down.

"You have a wonderful evening, kid. I advise you to get right home now. You never know, these streets just aren't safe anymore."

He took three steps backwards, maintaining constant eye contact, tapping his eye socket while pointing straight at me. He then spun on his heel to stroll easily into the late night gloom, whistling as he went.

12

For the first time in ages, I engaged the world in the bright light of the day. I blinked at the doorway and forced myself out into the noisy city. Earth tones, greenery, and gusts of exhaust circled all the bright cars, replacing my normal nocturnal world of deep blues and greys. I wandered past the rows of brownstones to the murky Hudson River, hoping a breath of air would clear my mind. There, who should I run into but Mark and Jonathan? They were sunbathing at the Morton St. Pier amid a circle of friends, flattened onto long benches. They were as thrilled and surprised to see me as I was them. We had a long superficial conversation about my quirkiness, troubles with academia, and the weather…I was just as astonished as anyone at how casual it felt to be back out in the world, talking like I was the most-well adjusted guy around.

After a point, auto-pilot took over and I just let my mouth move while my mind wandered elsewhere. Deep in my head I still poured over all the strangeness the last few years had thrown my way, puzzling over how few images I'd gotten from the stranger in the darkness the night before. The rare blank reads always threw me for a loop—but it wasn't like I could ask anyone for advice.

It wasn't the first time I'd pulled a blank in a moment of emotional stress…At least it was nice to know it was theoretically possible, if perhaps difficult, to replicate the circumstances. Freedom! Sometimes, this gift or whatever was willing to say, "Huh, seems enough is enough" and just give me a rare moment of silence. (It nearly never happened.)

But how I wish I'd had my wits about me when facing that cop! That scene was as bad as any mugging, just with a tidier uniform. "Monday morning quarterbacking" is always easy, but I've always suspected that I could (and should) have scared the crap out of the cop with his own memories, had my own mind been centered and ready.

After a time I flashed back to reality, suddenly aware that I was still talking out loud, on subjects I wasn't keeping track of. Jonathan's mouth was hanging open, and when I zoomed back into control of my own body I became aware that I was authoritatively lecturing on violence stats and social policies of New York City to Jonathan, who worked in social services and was an expert on the very same. These were his favorite subjects to ramble through (boring Mark to tears), and I hadn't even been aware that I'd been prying around his brain after he'd jabbed me in the ribs while telling a dirty joke. He was thrilled, and Mark was thrilled to see me seeming so well adjusted. Everyone seemed so happy! For another half hour I hammered away only on themes that I knew would thrill the both of them, and I basked in both the attention and the validation that was quickly forthcoming. This was *way* easier than I had remembered. And fun!

So a new era was born, an era of daylight hours. I had one year left of school, and a new defensive mechanism: chameleon-like powers of redirecting conversations to easy places where I'd look best. To each audience-preference that presented itself, my scales and stripes shifted into a perfect match, and in no time at all we'd all be laughing and smiling together like the oldest of friends. I was abruptly known as a jack of-all-trades, a mildly precocious eccentric with a heart of gold. What could be better? The cursed gift had become a golden touch. I imagined an easy life that stretched on this way for years.

I even got the school off my case and into their good graces, by volunteering and helping out at a few Alumni Dinners. Perhaps one could even say, I got a little cocky. After so long secluding myself, the magnetism at play in feeding people just what they wanted to hear was pretty fun. During the meet and greet I was finally feeling like an artist, instead of a passive observer of the mundane stillness of lives I shunned. It was like alchemy, assembling only the minimum words that would give them optimum joy, and make me appear the perfect, missing the capstone of every new construction that could be assembled.

I was introduced by Jonathan to an old oil magnate who had a penchant for art collecting, and I was able to speak of art like I myself was a lifelong collector. He was completely charmed and thrilled. We roved through the crucial masterwork contexts of Turner, Klee, Pizarro, and Kandinsky. He laughed and gushed that he felt like he was always halfway on the ropes, thrilled to be challenged by someone so passionate. With another group, I rhapsodized on the vagaries and caprices of Wall Street, the oil bust, and the speculative real estate market. Everyone was left stomping their feet with enthusiasm, staining their jackets with emphatic cigar ash while cheering that I was really on to something, that I would be a rising star in their worlds. Everyone I met fueled a firestorm of ego just behind my cranium front, with drink and atmosphere conspiring together to pull down my defenses and let the information fly out without filter. With each sentence I cut to their emotional centers, and nobody sensed arrogance or trickiness, just brightness and charisma. (Their own.) Nobody questioned where *I'd* acquired such insights. It was a marvel to behold. I watched their eyes transfix on every sentence, every word I said. I felt something not unlike greed seep into the center of me.

And then it all ended. With a few final congratulatory pats on the shoulder—I was thanked for my chameleon act, and one by one they all shuffled out of the room. And there I was, alone. I'd talked myself hoarse with a bunch of lies, a bunch of nonsense I didn't care a whit about. There was a bizarre moment of reckoning, of realization that I'd basically just spent six-odd hours betraying every basic trait my family had spent decades working to instill in me, to "be who you are, and never try to be someone you are not." I watched janitors locking up the doors, and I wondered what the hell I was doing there.

There was an enormous ache of emptiness as silence rushed back into the deserted lane. For no reason the streetlights flicked off, temperamentally. It had never seemed so clear that I hadn't become anything, that I'd worked towards nothing, that I was coasting, and barely so.

Meanwhile, by some magic, I'd been granted incredible insight into any stranger. Half the secrets of the world were immediately apparent to me from the second someone lightly touched my arm: but I hadn't ever managed to do anything with the gift. Far from it, I'd managed to turn this power into a blight, from which I'd retreated for three years, and then I further sullied it with some tricks PT Barnum would have been proud of, just to get attention. I hadn't felt quite so small and lost in a long time. I had to sort out my feelings and face this realization like an adult, and get my life in order! Or rather, I should have.

Instead, I found a bar.

Ψ

Three hours later, I leaned on the doorframe on my way back out into the cold. This wasn't the answer. There was a long pause between every out-of-place memory and ricocheting synapse, but my brain certainly hadn't been healed or effectively medicated. Basically, the only symptom I'd treated was the steadiness of my legs, which I'd effectively cured. I wobbled out into the night, pulling my jacket into my neck. Cats fought on a fire escape, and for a moment, their sound masked the human screams accompanying them.

"Somebody help me!" screamed an old man, chased by two muggers.

It was closing time, which meant the masses wandered down several main lanes in an exodus from the bars. This was not a private place; everyone saw what was happening. But it was New York. Several clusters of burly sports fans ignored the scene, singing their drunken ballads and blithely lurching into the night. Two large men had cornered the screaming old man in an alleyway, and with one punch to the nose, the old man had gone down in a corner, whimpering and crying out for aide. He hadn't even tried to put up a fight.

As I approached the entry to the alley, I couldn't help but be aware that I didn't have a prayer against two much larger men, but I impulsively shouted out anyway, "Hey, leave him alone!"

One of the man absentmindedly glanced over his shoulder, sized me up, and turned back to the task at hand. I was evidently less than intimidating, especially with the audible hiccups.

At that moment, a side door in the alley slammed open and a small shadow roared noisily into the reverberating darkness, backlit by the blindingly bright open door frame. The two muggers swore loudly, caught completely off guard, as one was stunned by a large metal trashcan that hit him square in the face. The other leaped forward and slashed wildly with a knife towards the stranger, but was broadsided a punch to the groin that brought him to his knees, and then a sturdy punch that hit him square on the temple. He fell back a few feet and wobbled as he stood. His shamefaced friend ripped him up by his blood-spattered coat lapels, and the two of them raced out of the alley and fled, blindly knocking me to the ground in the process.

"Are you okay?!" I called out to the shadow at the end of the alley who had intervened.

"Yes I'm alright," the old man who had been being mugged mumbled weakly, believing my question had been addressed to him.

"I'm glad to hear it," I barked, looking past the old man. "Sir, in the doorway, are you okay? Do you need help?"

"Oh, it's nothing, I'm fine…just glad he's okay," the stranger said in a quiet, strangely pinched voice. But then there was a muffled sound of something slipping, and the splash of a man falling facedown into a puddle. As I approached the freely bleeding body, I realized the man had no legs. He smiled weakly up at me, and glanced at his now broken wheelchair and shrugged. "Okay, well—he got me a bit."

Ψ

None of the taxis would stop. He'd directed me into his kitchen where I found some rags and he guided me through heating one and gently cleaning the surface, then pressurizing the wound with an old belt. Though I was close to passing out, the evenness of his voice and his steady demeanor kept us both calm.

And so, on the strangest of nights I'd ever experienced, I found myself dragging a perfectly calm stabbing victim down Broadway in the middle of the night, as his reassuring voice got softer and softer.

Eventually, I found myself making conversation, just to be sure the blood loss hadn't doomed him.

"So tell me, how does an amputee like yourself feel comfortable fighting in the alleys of New York?"

He laughed quietly. "I've never been one to have the sense to run from a fight. Besides, those men were cowards. And nobody else seemed to be in a hurry to help, besides you. It's the third mugging in my alley this month, but the landlord refuses to put in a light, or even a gate. Typical, huh?" He made no mention of his legs, I noted.

"So, uh, where'd you learn to fight like that?"

"I've had to protect myself and my friends most of my life. I came from a rough neighborhood, and all my brothers were the neighborhood instigators…Vietnam was no different, after that." Finally he looked down at his legs, pointedly, "I know, I know, it's a real sob story, right?" He laughed, but a cough interrupted it. He spat blood on the ground, and made a slight smile. "I've had worse. What's your story kid?"

Good lord, was he making conversation in this state? My arms and legs ached but I certainly wasn't in any position to complain. Fortunately the booze remaining in my system took the edge off the work, and some very confused adrenaline filled out the rest of the job. My mind raced between the scenes I'd just witnessed, the complete air of casual fraternity projected by the man before me, and the horrific scenes his body emitted of his past: the draft, the butchery, the trauma, the night terrors that had followed…I wanted to stop and run so bad, but instead I swallowed down all that info and played dumb, playing casually along with this polite banter as I dragged a knife victim down the streets…

So I tried, best as I could. What choice did I have? I made conversation.

"Oh, you know, I'm just your average Friday night college kid, right? I should be studying for quarter finals…I really should reconsider my life priorities, one of these days. You aren't gonna lecture me on life goals, right? Not while you're bleeding. What can I say, it's New York?"

He laughed reflectively, appreciating my effort to keep the ominous mood light. "Yup, it's New York! Next time, stay home and do your homework, boy!" The sound of his cackle mingled with muffled thuds as I dragged him over the last sidewalk cracks into the hospital lobby, flooded in fluorescent light.

"Thanks, kid," he murmured simply, as he was lifted into a gurney by the frantic hospital staff. He finally let himself pass out as they carried him away. I fell immediately into oblivious snores atop an overstuffed waiting room chair in an abandoned side room, to be awakened a few hours later, by an exhausted-looking man in teal scrubs.

"Your friend is going to be fine. The knife missed doing any permanent damage. We're going to keep him here awhile to make sure there's no risk of infection, but he won't lose the arm. He' sleeping quite peacefully now. You did well to clean and cover the wound so well."

I shuffled awkwardly at being congratulated for frantically following the clear instructions of a stabbing victim who'd calmly directed me while bleeding out in a puddle.

"Next time, tell him to consider calling the police." He paused, reflecting. "Or perhaps carrying a gun. One thing is for sure, a man in his condition shouldn't be jumping into fistfights."

"I dunno, doc. He did alright," I stated as I left the lobby. "I'll mention it at my next mugging."

As I walked towards home, all the images from the stranger swarmed through my head, things heroic, and things grim and awful. Horrible sights and nightmares. Followed by more of the same. I never knew life could be so dark; but I also saw act after act of selflessness and self-sacrifice. Scenes of confusion and feelings of colossal betrayal at the things he'd seen and been asked to do—things that had wreaked havoc on his simple sense of patriotism...But he had an absolute willingness to do whatever it took to protect his friends and loved ones until they were all home safe. He was a good man who'd been put through the ringer.

More than anything else, I saw the post-traumatic stress from war—the anguished scenes awaking from nightmares that had blurred with reality, the muscle memory terrors that set in automatically at the sounds of backfires and fireworks. All at once I understood the seamlessness with which adrenaline had coursed into action with this man—legs or no legs. He lived to serve people, to protect people; never considering himself. He used that protective instinct thoughtlessly, without thought of compensation or rationalization: he considered it a strength, almost as a gift. It motivated and energized him to complete the tasks he believed in, to finish the jobs he needed to finish. And he always did them, where stronger, bigger men passed by and blithely ignored the scene.

Something about that lingered with me, stuck in my brain on a loop, throbbing increasingly noisily in my thoughts. I never made it home. Preoccupied, overstimulated, tired of closed loping cycles that never changed, I broke my routine. I found the train station and determined to face some questions that had been plaguing me for years.

As the sun rose, I hopped on board a train towards Sag Harbor.

Ψ

The Long Island train shook and shuttered as we pulled into Bridgehampton. There I got out and walked the Seventy-Nine up towards Sag Harbor. My heart had not stopped pounding an instant, nor had my teeth stopped chattering. There was a five mile walk on my map, but I barely noticed. The tall trees and white horse fences seemed to lean in over me, and I followed the power lines into town. Clouds pulled away towards the horizon, and the sun began to shine feebly, growing in intensity moment by moment.

From the far end of the lane I saw a hunched figure gardening before a grand house, and I knew it must be Nannie. I jogged the last leg of the journey with an inexplicable spurt of energy, and she was absolutely bewildered to recognize me after being startled by loping footfalls passing the garden gate.

"John!? Why hello honey, what in the world are you doing here?" She held back a big floppy sunhat with her forearm, squinting through the bright morning sun. "You're drenched!"

"I needed to talk to you. Is Gramps here?" His station wagon was nowhere to be seen. "No, he's off on a fishing trip with your Uncle for the weekend. Did you just come from school…?" She looked down the street, confused to see no vehicle or explanation.

"Great. I need to talk to you, and don't know how I'd do it guardedly. I…I need to know more about your brother, Nannie. I need to know absolutely everything."

"My brother?! You came all the way here to talk about him again?"

"Yes," I said, exasperated, "because I need to know how he survived this."

She looked at me for a long moment and then pulled me into a hug. I was a lot bigger now than the last time, so she really had to reach. "How are you dealing with it all, John? Did something go wrong? Did you have a rough semester final or something?"

"Nannie, it's a bit more than that. Can we talk, please? Now?"

"Of course John, tell me everything. I'll tell you all I know, though you know I don't like digging through the ashes of the past like this with your poor Great Uncle. Come on inside I guess, I'll put a kettle on…"

For the first time in my adult life, I was upfront with Nannie about what a hard time I'd had adjusting to life since "the gift" had entered my life. She never spoke, nor appeared to judge, but took it all in quietly. She'd never posed the question directly since we'd had our only conversation on the subject, half a decade before. Our discussion on the subject was constrained mostly to furtive looks of preoccupied concern she'd shoot me at family events, or her constant attempts to find the two of us alone in isolated rooms during visits, in case I should want to discuss things. So far as she knew so far, everything was going great—I was well adjusted, amiable, and marginally gifted with a subtle intuition for images from the past. She had no idea how extreme things had gotten, or how unraveled my life had become amid coping mechanisms.

"But I don't understand, what happened exactly, John? Why are you acting like the sky is falling? Did something change? Are you seeing something new?" She couldn't know how silly the words sounded to me. She resisted really listening, it seemed.

"YES! I'm not sure what's happening. I see impossible things, constant things! It never goes away… Everything I've ever seen, things that others see; they're all still right here in my head, swarming—competing for attention."

For the next three hours, I brought her up to speed on exactly rough my world had become. She held her opinions, suspended judgment, and treated me like a human, my first completely sincere, unguarded human contact in ages. Finally, after I'd poured out my heart and she'd taken pains to reassure me that I was a good person, that I'd be okay and time would cure all ills, she finally sighed and leaned back in her chair.

"But what can I do about any of this—with my old memories, John? I don't know anything too special. I don't have all the answers…"

"We have to be missing something, then, Nannie. I need you to tell me everything about him you know. No matter how big or small. I need to know, Nannie."

"John, this is pointless. I don't know what sort of things you're getting mixed up in at college, John. If you want to mention using drugs or something, you need to just let me know now and we'll move on from there…"

"I'm not using drugs! I know how strange it sounds, already! I have no explanation for why I've seen or what I've done, I'm human and imperfect like everyone else…And how are we pretending to know what are the lines between unreasonable and unreasonable, reality and unreality? Is it reasonable that I see the pasts of strangers? Is it reasonable that I can learn whole subjects without opening books? That nobody around me has secrets? To start with, we both know I'm not even the first! Your brother had something unusual about him, and now I do too. I need to understand more about him to figure out what on earth I'm missing about me, about how to live, about how to stay sane. Don't you understand? This is important!"

I'd become oblivious to the fact that I was raising my voice at one of my favorite people in the world. I stopped and stared at her with tears in my eyes.

"What am I missing? Why do I know nothing about the one person whose life might contain all the answers I need? How am I supposed to figure any of this out without your help? Please Nannie, understand how much I need this to happen!"

Nannie sat quietly for a moment, tears in her eyes as well. "I don't know where I should begin with him. I don't know what will help. But I'll tell you everything I remember."

We sat face to face in the quiet house until about one a.m., sorting through every life event and insignificant anecdote she could recall. Nothing seemed especially relevant. She talked about his struggles to hold friends and his absentmindedness as a child. She thought it was all to do with the distraction factor. Once he got more confident in his skills, he also became much more guarded, and limited his exposure to company entirely once he knew his skills to be both a professional asset and social liability. She spoke of his increasing awareness of far-flung events, and his attempts to figure out how to deal with that insight. She meandered through the first times his intuition was noted by high-level schools, where his personality testing regularly pushed off the charts.

But where everything got pretty murky was his military service. He'd made the decision early on that he wanted to do something with his gift, and he believed that his skills would benefit his country, which he supported unilaterally. Nannie didn't remember exact details of the time and place of his recruitment, just that he took to his new work like a fish in water. He loved the gravity of the job, the builtin sense of purpose and prestige. It didn't seem to hurt that America's enemy at the time was indisputably evil, so there was an uncompromised moral clarity to the decision to relinquish his capacity to make his own choices in favor of becoming a cog in *something greater.*

She described his job as if he was James Bond. Everywhere he went he'd been trained to project unflinching confidence and situational awareness, and the difference she saw during his leave periods was tremendous. He was suddenly the go to guy that everyone loved and leaned-upon, always ready and capable of giving and completing any task. Wherever he went, everyone knew they could put all their confidence and faith in him to do just about anything. But by this point, Nannie had basically run out of ideas, and was grasping at straws…people would ask him for a cigarette just for the chance to be nearer to his winning personality, talk to him…They'd borrow a pen just to mingle with—

My brain locked up and cartwheeled a few times. Of course, why hadn't I thought of it?

"When did you get his ring?" I asked, with all my blood superheating my face.

"A few weeks before he disappeared…Why?"

"And the other things? The sunglasses, the cigarette case…?"

"I suppose they were shipped back over a few weeks after we lost contact with him."

There was a roaring as blood rushed and reverberated through my ears.

"And did you check the cigarette case, Nannie?"

"What?" She looked up, suddenly panicked.

"Did you check the case?" I insisted.

Her face whitened. "No…now that you mention it, it never occurred to me to check."

Ten minutes later we were on the road, racing into the afternoon. We arrived in my dorm-room in NYC within record time, both hyperventilating after sprinting up the stairs. I fished through the textbooks stacked in the corner to find the one fake book with a carved-out chamber inside, where I'd hidden the cigarette case. It fell out with a clank just as the door-knob jiggled, and in walked Mark.

"John, I thought you were dead and so I oh, I beg your pardon—hello Ma'am!"

Nannie and I acted like two preteens caught in a bank heist attempt—we could not have been any more obvious. After some strained introductions and less than convincing belabored explanations that Nannie was here for some big-city tourism, Mark subtly shrugged at me, less-than-curiously, and excused himself, saying he wouldn't be back for a few days and that he "hoped we had a grand family visit…" As he closed the door we both expelled huge sighs of relief and continued with our work.

I found the cigarette case where I'd furtively kicked it under the edge of the bed. I wiped it off and then gingerly pried open the little clasps along the side. I opened it and saw the same yellowed cigarettes in a tidy row, with one missing as before. I carefully observed along all the edges of the case, trying to find some way to open some unseen compartment. There was nothing! I tried again and again for several minutes, beside myself with exasperation. I tried hitting it along the side of the bed, and stomping on it, and was quite close to tears when Nannie suddenly froze, and sat bolt upright, shouting, "WAIT!"

"What is it, Nannie? Do you remember something? Anything?"

"Yes I do. Until his training had wiped it out of him, my brother had certain nervous ticks he'd constantly cycle through. He used to absentmindedly pinch at his fingertips for ages, his hands coming together and separating a million times whenever he'd get really reflective. It became an emblematic gesture for him." She stared ahead reflectively for a moment, and then looked at the case in my hand. "Try pinching together there, at the brackets that would have held that missing cigarette in place, John."

As my quivering fingers pulled together the clasps, I heard a quiet click. The back of the cigarette case fell to the floor with a clatter. I was left holding the row of cigarettes clasped to a thin aluminum panel, with the very slightest of hidden chambers just visible behind it. Something was barely visible, sticking out in the most subtle way imaginable. Something nobody would have seen in a million years without looking for it.

"Pull it out, John! Here, use this."

Nannie pulled a nail file out of her purse, as my fingers had failed to extract the object. I pushed from one side, and a small, tattered paper slipped onto the floor. We both stared. I stooped and picked it up, slowly unwrapping its creased edges.

"What's it say?" Nannie said, scooting closer along the bedframe. I cleared my throat softly, feeling suddenly subdued, and began to read…

Dear Nancy,

My time has come. I must say goodbye. There is no way for me to act on the information I've uncovered, without alerting the enemy to crucial vulnerabilities we're now exploiting: secrets that are right now saving the lives of thousands. I've uncovered a spy ring and managed to determine their ultimate goals, but I've unfortunately realized that I am under constant surveillance as well. I've managed to get notice to my superiors of the plan and all exploitable weaknesses, but if I disappear or stray off course at all they'll surely change their plans—and all those people and opportunities will be lost. If I do nothing now, as I intend to, my small sacrifice will allow many more to live. We'll be closer than ever to a place where we can end this thing, once and for all.

I intend to sacrifice myself, and do so knowingly, with full control over my faculties. I have never been so sure of an action in my life. I'm at peace knowing that my death will save countless others and help end this war. I am not afraid to die. I believe what I'm doing is right, and I hope to live on in your heart; I wish I could hug you one more time little sister, but have no doubt that even after my physical body is gone, I'll be in your heart forever, and you'll be in mine…

All my love, my dearest sister,
JOHN

13

Nannie and I arrived back in Sag Harbor in trances, fairly dumbstruck. What could you say to any of that? There was no reasonable response. We quietly prepared dinner while waiting for our brains to send some words to our mouths, but it was slow going. Suddenly, Gramps surprised us both returning early. He was thrilled and perplexed to see me, and I stumbled through some half-baked story of having a hard time at school, and needing to just get away and clear my head. As I sat, he didn't press me, just hugged me and kissed my head instead, and reminded me that I was always welcome in his home, and that we'd figure it all out.

As we cleared the dishes after eating, I found myself robotically asking questions I hadn't yet fully formulated in my head. As Gramps was closest at hand, I started by addressing them to him.

"Have you ever felt like you've worked as hard as possible to back yourself into the wrong corner, somewhere you never wanted to be?" I mused openly, keeping all my metaphorical cards to my chest.

"Sure, that's part of life, John! That's what being a man is all about: persevering and rebuilding, doing the good work. We work to be better, more thoughtful, and to try to make each job come out better than the last; sure, but also to redirect through the storms and keep our bearing true with our values. Nobody is perfect, and long-term plans are always flimsy in the moment. I've changed course in life more times than you'd believe, but like a river, sometimes you have to go where life takes you rather than charting a new course. What matters is that you believe in what you're doing, and that you keep your priorities straight. For me, that always meant providing for family and making a comfortable life, and recently, it meant being home as often as I could be with my family," he said, kissing Nannie on the forehead as he reached past her to put away a salad strainer.

"Yeah."

"Are you having a hard time with those kinds of questions already, John? Why, you've got your whole life ahead of you! If you still want to be a professor one day at an Ivy League School, you could not be better situated than you are right now. As an NYU grad, the world will be your oyster, and Nannie and I would be happy to call in a few favors for you if you need, and—"

"I don't think I believe in any of that, though. That's the problem. I don't want to teach classes at a college, and I don't care to spend my life looking backwards at history. At least, I don't think I do. I don't know what I want. I've never really even given it much thought, it just seemed easier to accept it, than to plan it," I sighed, exasperated.

He absorbed this thoughtfully. "Well…it's not easy, John, that's a tough call that only you can make. Sometimes we do really find ourselves places we never meant to be, in the wrong places at the wrong times. But what's important is working with what you've got, and finding a route that takes advantage of your talents and passion—extends the benefits to the widest circle possible. This is how we serve and live the good life, buddy."

My skull felt like it was full of cement. I decided to lay down and think things through for a while. I'd made too many habits out of recklessness lately. What I needed to do now was think for a while. Nannie made me up a guest bed, kissed me, and left.

I lay awake for a while in the dark room, listening to the ticking clock and the screech of the weather vane above the ceiling I slept beneath, bending with the sea breeze. For some inexplicable reason, an old Bible verse came to mind from a Shakespeare course I'd spent weeks studying for. It came from Corinthians: "When I was a child, I used to speak like a child, think like a child, reason like a child; when I became a man, I did away with childish things." I thought of my books and my dorm, accounts of past turbulence. I imagined them all as so many children's toys.

I fell asleep dreaming of changes and futures of action. I awoke with a jolt from a dream about the steady sea breeze pushing the weather vane pushing it, guiding it, and symbolically providing me all the direction I needed. I thought about my Great Uncle's letter, his legacy, his trueness of self and willingness to self-sacrifice.

And before anybody awoke, I tiptoed down the stairs, and hitchhiked down to the Navy Recruitment Center.

I kept it a secret during several weeks of tests and bureaucratic delays—claiming to be staying with a friend—but my mind was made up. I stayed in a grimy budget motel alongside the recruitment office, where I saw and thought of nothing other than what came next. I only announced it to my family once the ink was dry on my recruitment paperwork, and everything was in order to go. I remember Mom had dropped her fork mid-bite.

Ψ

Once again, I found myself on a rumbling train. They'd told me to bring minimal personal effects, as everything I needed would be provided by Uncle Sam. To a completely new life, I was bringing a few pairs of underwear and socks and a toothbrush. That part certainly felt bizarre. It would be a completely fresh start.

This time, a few dozen other fresh-faced men accompanied me, wild eyed and cheerful. We celebrated our last few hours of freedom. There was little rhyme or reason to the cross-section of society we represented: rich and poor, good neighborhoods and bad, lucky in love and the not-so-lucky alike. There were folk like me fleeing life routes that seemed meaningless, and folk fleeing crime, court ordered to serve voluntarily or be subjected to even fewer liberties than a Spartan military life offered. We were alike only in our youth, in our awareness that we had fewer than a few days left on the train down. With each mile the train moved out of New York towards Florida, we moved closer and closer to eight weeks of boot camp.

Ψ

The new names and faces were mostly a blur. Most familiarity dissipated in the sheer exhaustion of the grueling weeks following our arrival, once we'd gotten through the turnstiles of several days mostly taken up by medical, dental, and administration screenings, inoculations, bad haircuts, and uniforms. We were split up, arranged into anonymous bunks, addressed in barked coarse scripts, and referred to by new titles. Every aspect of life became an exacting inspection of our attention to detail: our conformity to directions and our capacity and willingness to push through every excuse and restraint towards any demands.

But in the solidarity of common suffering, we all considered ourselves a family in no time. We were the fresh meat ground through the works. We had to help each other or nobody else would. And so, in every aspect of this mundane life, we came to accept the replacement of privacies and luxuries with the existentially-realized motto, "All for one, and one for all."

There weren't really any limits to the areas in which we were tested. There were mental and academic capacity tests as well as physical ones: stamina, dexterity, alertness, and strength and conditioning work. There were endless teamwork-building exercises. We were carefully gauged on problem-solving, cooperating on the fly, and our improvised responses to panic-inducing disasters. Every situation was drilled, drilled, and drilled again, with ceaseless, meticulous notetaking by mysterious observers (who we in the trenches were all too exhausted and preoccupied to maintain much notice of). Even in our sleep, we had dreams in unrelenting verbatim about "saluting all officers, colors and standards not cased" with our bunks buzzing at lights out with murmured memorization of the chains of command, Uniform Code of Military Justice, and Naval regulations.

Of course, waking up was at least as jarring as sleeping had seemed welcome. The screamed sounds of "reveille" had found some saltier supplements of invective through the decades, as well as a charming soundscape achieved during the wakeup call by banging a hammer against a brushed aluminum "shit-can." After just a few days, anyone who wasn't already numb to swearing and aggravation, became so. Our minds hardened up and our concentration narrowed. But the physical tests brought up at least as much challenge as the mental ones. I'd never been much of an athlete beyond swimming, and so the endurance activities and standardization of brute strength took work, dedication, and the assistance of a good number of former strangers who'd become best friends simply by proximity and common situation. When I couldn't reach the minimum number of PT pull-ups, there wasn't a moment's pause or consideration; rather, all my barrack mates pitched in and improvised slow dead-weight drop repetition drills and elastic bands to mitigate the practice of partiallifts as we hastily augmented my upper body strength. I learned what it was to strain past a point where I had to yell to keep going—we all did. We reached the qualification threshold just in the nick of time. Similarly, I found myself helping bunkmates with exactly the opposite challenges, spending late nights explaining logical reasoning and core concepts of science to struggling teammates, rapid-firing Q&As while we practiced drills, and repped reflexes and endurance work. We learned about attentiveness, discerning slight variations intentionally devised to throw us off. We were growing, and we had nobody to thank but each other. We took pride in our company's organization, sure, but every night we also fell asleep like stones.

The diversity of information to absorb was a challenge unlike anything I'd ever known. The sheer number of customs and courtesies, vehicles, uniforms, ranks, weapons, protocols, codes, regulations…it all left my head spinning. But we pulled each other through all the hurdles. Every new mockup and themed test: firefighting scenarios, marksmanship, and water survival drill forced some of us to become leaders and some to work on learning new skills leaning on their neighbor. Everyone pulled and pushed as one, with a sense of community I'd never have imagined possible in high school or college. Most importantly, for once I was too exhausted and overstimulated to fixate on the images that surged around amid the constant physical contact. I even managed to tune most out as white noise until I'd freed up more brain-space as familiarity and routine set in.

Ψ

And then, as abruptly as it began, two month had passed.

With great pomp and circumstance we graduated, and that was that. All of the questions that I might have considered if I'd had an ounce of extraneous energy a few weeks before now flooded in: what was next? How would my life proceed? I'd never had a very clear picture of long-term strategy, beyond a vague idea that I liked the idea of what life as a photographer might look like. Well, somehow I'd forgotten I'd volunteered myself to be a cog in a wheel, not the wheel itself. I now sat on a low rung of the ladder, and my considerations didn't weigh too heavy in the balance of things. The men responsible for making decisions tended to do that, and the rest of us would say, "Yes, sir!"

So, that's exactly what happened. I was marched into a room, same as any of a million other qual and eval and interpretive occasions. I was asked about my plans and muttered something about being a Naval photographer, and two men holding my tests results raised their eyebrows dismissively in unison.

"Photography! Look at these scores, son. You're destined for more than that. Is photography really all think you can do?" He stared at me, impatiently.

"Well, I suppose that I—" I began warily.

"Nonsense!" he interrupted. "What the Navy needs now, is engineers. If I was a betting man, I'd say you're up for the challenge—you just need something to really sink your teeth into. Anybody can take a picture, right? This way, you'd be serving your country where it really needs it. You do love your country, right Calabrace?"

"Well, yes, it's just that I—"

"Well splendid! I think in the route that we have planned for you, you could do great things, truly wonderful things. Sign here, Calabrace."

He pushed a small stack of papers across the table, and as my vision spun I felt my fingers wiggling the pen.

"Ah yes, the Naval Nuclear Power School is where it's all happening today. You're going to love the challenges. Congratulations. Next!"

Ψ

Over the next few days, I had the opportunity to ask around about the role I'd just stumbled into, and I found it was one of the most challenging, competitive, impossibly difficult programs around. The reputation it did have, beyond all the hush-hush, was for breakdowns and burnout. I was told failures ended up in the "armpit" duty stations, or even in the past, on gun boats off the Vietnam coast. I'd decided in an instant—or rather, I'd bumbled my way into signing on. So there it was! Game on, whether I liked it or not.

I completed machinist mate's training in an A-School, while trying to figure out what strange life I'd just signed on for. What a relief it was when I received word that evening that my billet wouldn't be free for a while, and instead I'd be temporarily join the crew of a Destroyer! I didn't even bother to ask which, just being thrilled for a buffer period before the impending Nuclear Power School scare. (In my head, I could hardly contain my excitement, failing to suppress an emotional regression to quaint vistas of my childhood toys in Nannie's Garden City closet.) But that all changed when I saw the ship.

We had just spent months going over exactly what constituted a seaworthy ship; so I knew at once that *this wasn't one of those.* The William R Rush DD-714 was the oldest ship in the Navy fleet, after limping on from the 1950s. I met her on her last legs, before her gift transfer to the Korean Navy. She hadn't aged well, but was homeported beneath the Throgs Neck Bridge in the Bronx: close enough that I was able to see how proud my family was of my Navy decision while on daytime or weekend liberty, and unfortunately also close enough that the high of pride I'd said goodbye with was still was fresh enough to be wounded by the situation of the ship. It was to be an exercise in humility.

The ship was literally falling apart from the inside out. Fortunately, I'd recently been pushed into a life course of engineering, so I attuned to be the go-to guy to fix everything, every system and old valve and bracing and latch. If nothing else, it would be great practice and a good confidence builder in myself, if not the ship: I was to be a machinist mate, why not start at a run?

On a weekend trip to Newport, RI, we were instructed to carry out a mock sea battle. We had to repair leaks after a hand grenade was thrown well away from the ship, but pierced the hull like a dart into a balloon. I shuttered to think of entering dangerous waters onboard the flimsy relic. They used it to train the reserve forces, some of which (I cringed to imagine), once served on her—albeit when she was new…However, human nature is human nature. Like anybody would, I eventually became attached to the quirks of the ship and put in whatever extra efforts were necessary to help coaxing her slow limp through a few more years of service.

I loved the closed environment of being onboard, I must admit. I felt safe and isolated from the world. I was finally doing something, and that made all the difference. I was proud of the work I'd done to get here, proud of the discipline we maintained, and the quick attachments inevitably followed in the close quarters. With every handshake accompanying an introduction, each slap on the back, I was given insights on the small crew onboard. We were underpopulated enough to be unintimidating, with familiarity taking the place of fear as my sensitivity to images increased alongside autopilot-tracked routine.

But just when I was getting comfortable, it was over. Go figure.

News arrived, and off I went towards a new life.

My space was free, so Johnny went back to school.

14

Byzantine Iconography?" The section advisor raised an eyebrow while mumbling his way through my NYU transcripts. "Well fuck me…Revolutionary War I, II, and III, mmm-hmm…"

I shifted uncomfortably from foot to foot as he ticked through my academic experience, looking for anything remotely applicable to Navy life. There was a biology course or two, some basic math, and a whole lot of holes where I hadn't applied myself enough. I hadn't seen this coming, clearly.

"Are you sure you're even in the right place, son? This looks like the resume of someone from the National Geographic, not some potential nuke grease monkey. Are you sure you're geared for the nuclear Navy?"

I tried to make a joke. "Dr. Leakey, I presume?" I looked back at him with a stupid grin. Maybe I'd make a new friend?

He didn't smile in the slightest degree. I re-straightened and leveled back up my eyes onto the far wall, near the ceiling. Shit. "Well, yes sir, this does seem to be the right place."

"Seems to be, indeed. Very well, Petty Officer Calabrace. It seems you've got some climbing to do, and perhaps a hard wake-up call as well…These papers have in no way convinced me that you're fully aware of what you're in for, here. This place is no picnic in the park, and it's certainly not gonna fly—to waltz in here with some fancy college references hoping to find any kind of special treatment waiting for you. If anything, you'll find yourself working twice as hard as the others."

I started to try to reassure him of my seriousness, but he silenced me with a glance.

"You'll be starting out this month with a mandatory study pattern, do you know what that means?"

I gulped, but he interrupted to answer his own question.

"It means you'll have to clock in and out of additional study sessions. I'm requiring thirty-five hours supplementary study, weekly. You'll be in class forty-five more hours, weekly."

As I raced to do the math on what free time I might have for my night-owl habit, he continued.

"A lot of people get kind of stupid about their health when they're in the adjustment phases of entering here and starting out baby steps into a nuke lifestyle. It can be a pretty challenging element—I want to neither understate nor over-celebrate that. Some folk forget there is a physical imperative beyond the book smarts. I don't want to see you falling into any of the common vices that cause us to lose people here, do you understand?"

I started to respond, and again, he interjected before I could.

"Let me make myself perfectly clear, Calabrace. I don't want to see your physical readiness degrade just because you're memorizing some books here and there. This is the Navy: sailors do both. I want to see you stretching and running first thing every morning, *and* with a smile on your face. I want your uniform and appearance spotless. I want your physical presentation to be indicative of the fine standards we abide by here: because the way you present yourself reflects on me too—and everyone else here. I want the Duty Officer to wet himself with joy when he sees you speed-walking between classes, racing to be the first to raise your hand with all the right answers."

He held up my NYU transcripts dismissively. "Books are nonsense if you aren't always on your toes reaching for excellence, Calabrace. Furthermore, let there be no illusions here: I don't do drunks, degenerates, or slobs on my watch. No pranks, no whiners, no dicking the dog. I simply won't take it, you'll be out. Is that clear? Do you have any questions?"

I started to answer, and for one final time, he interrupted me.

"You're dismissed, Calabrace. Welcome to school. I recommend the pizza, it's great. A bit frozen sometimes." He gestured to the door, and that was that. It all began.

Ψ

I sometimes wondered how much research work had been done analyzing the changes in the normal parsing of human expressivity and lifestyle during moments of severe strain.

Actually, this might well be one of the only subjects which I was never made to study during my time at the Naval Nuclear Power School. We were trained on compartmentalization and getting things done. We rose to the occasion, no matter what. We moved to clocks; we became gears. Life became a mad machine, impossibly well-oiled and utilitarian, like the slide-rules they gave us to help with math. All frills and side-stories collapsed alongside the sheer complexity and intensity of simultaneous demands on my concentration. I became a machine.

How did one describe an institution like NNPS? Could I?

The first thing I was given was a secret security clearance, so maybe I should just hold my tongue. But it was just too big, just too much to be merely a location. It would be misguiding to describe it as just another background setting of my life, where some interesting things happened to me. No, NNPS was at least as influential as any active character in my life. To be fair, NNPS literally crowded out all the real active characters in my life. It became my closest association, my biggest influence and preoccupation by default—an elephant in the room carrying a megaphone. There was just no time, no discretionary energy to spend on socializing. It took up emotional and spiritual space, wormed its way into my dreams, and changed the way my mind made correlations.

The part of my mind that lived to chum, to cast wide nets and gobble everything, to swell and expand with no limits in sight jumped for joy. Because from the ground up, I was unwired, broken down and recast in the squat institutional buildings, like a forged sword repeatedly plunged into water, tempered and hammered again and again until the result was some shimmering thing: utterly unlike any of the initial ingredients.

How hard could it be to become a nuclear engineer? I entered hoping it was pretty easy: Drag in some water to cool off a little clump of radioactive rock (and maybe poke it with a magic stick to speed up and slow down reaction). Cycle those fluids through in a loop again and again, and they'll heat up as they cool the radioactive lump. Gather up the resulting steam to spin turbines, generate some power, create oxygen from seawater for fresh air, keep the lights on, and spin a fancy ultra-quiet propeller. Easy, right?

Well, it turns out it was a bit more complicated than that.

If ever I came to deeply and intuitively understand that my brain was different than other brains, it was here. My brain longed to expand and explore and leaped at the chance to stretch around anything, the more complex and stimulating the better. I could almost hear the raindrops splattering as my synapses flooded their way over the textbook pages, roping all the new novelty information together. This was a side I'd never known at NYU, a frantic compulsion to acquire, a hunger. I needed to secure it, and to do it in six months. I was absolutely determined it should happen.

Before, I'd never considered myself to be abnormally, excessively intelligent—I was perhaps above-average, but certainly not genius. Not the way some of these kids were: they'd prepped for this stuff all their lives, they breathed it. I'd barely squeaked through the rigorous admission quals. My meticulous reference letters detailing a brilliant work ethic and personal sense of responsibility didn't make a dent, nor did my "almost Bachelors of Arts degree" from NYU. No, this was something completely different. This was a league I had never encountered, and I was thrown in right between the bulls and the matadors.

But eventually, I managed to close the distance and somehow swim alongside the strongest swimmers. Maybe it was initially a gift of abnormal cognitive elasticity that made it possible, or just a sheer determination not to be one of the first pins to fall down. But it was only by impossible amounts of work that I made it happen. I covered the distance myself through sweat and mad perseverance. In the process, I nearly wrecked my own sanity. Too much! Too fast! I traced the ring surface in my pocket in these moments, and I reminded myself why I was there. With every barely-passing score and each slow progress, I kept slogging on through the rough seas.

Monday through Friday classes ran from 7:30 a.m. through 4:05 p.m., with several additional study hours mandated daily. The pace was grueling. The attrition rate was brutal. However the world outside ceased to exist while school was in session, as did other individuals. It was a world of pages, of messy pencil marks scrawled over crumpled sheets of paper accumulated into desperate, four foot tall pyramids of crumpled paper balls where the trash can used to be. It was a lifestyle limited to parroting formulas and models, ceaselessly striving to understand and retain fundamentals that could be extended into vital applied fields, and trusting in authorities guiding me towards pristine, assuredly correct answers that one quoted verbatim.

Nothing was taken from the building "for security purposes," including me. Studying and repeating. As soon as this was mastered, the tablecloth was pulled out beneath us, and scenarios then shifted to "what would you do" situations that supplanted the tidy routines we'd previously studied. Now we analyzed occasions where breakdown crises had forced quick thinking and problem solving drills. We were abruptly back at the drawing board, using different parts of the brain in simulations where desperate decisions either saved or doomed lives.

The after-hour instructors who were on duty each night were my saviors, and I clung to them like barnacles to a whale. When the studying was done, I studied some more. I ate and studied, did pushups and studied, studied on the toilet and in the shower. I hit my rack without thoughts or dreams, and I woke up just in time for more. Breakfast was merely more propulsion. It was a hurricane of new information, unrelentingly themed, constant.

If ever there was a universe built-up from a tempest in a teapot, this was it. Existing in isolation from the sundry dramas of normal everyday humanity, I was in a closed-system, a box. Here in this box, I lived in a world of probability analysis, special relativity, and attenuation factors. While I read about how much shielding was needed to hold volatility in isolation, I lived the same reality. I'd mastered the formula. Voices had fallen silent: I lived for the school, in the school, in absolute isolation. The systems of the normal world fell away: with its stored awareness of maps, of social skills, of pop songs, and bus schedules. Memories were gone. Sometimes I yearned to be one of the few that didn't need to study and didn't face those mandated hours: the gilded princelings of the nuclear Power School that never seemed to need to expend much energy to achieve success. But instead, I was pared away into a vessel of information: sciences and math, design and troubleshooting, systems and responses, micro minutia and macro patterns.

I became an engineer facing a pretty broad problem. Quite broad, actually: I was training to move the Navy, and anything the Navy threw at me as a wannabe nuclear propulsion expert. For that reason, I was learning absolutely everything from the ground up: electrical systems, reactor plants, operations, reactor dynamics, and core characteristics. At the start, I couldn't even understand the syllabus. Within a few mere months, I learned to embody the Albert Einstein mantra that you didn't really know anything 'til you could explain it to your Grandmother. I was circulating anonymously in a world where mealtimes buzzed with banter, whose punchlines ended up being things like, "Nil Ductility Phenomenon, haha!" It was an alien and strange world that we ruled over like astronauts. We broke every huge insurmountable system into the comprehendible baby steps that constituted it, and moved from there. Fortunately this meant that the math, physics, and chemistry could be applied piecemeal and spoon-fed to us only in practical applications. But I won't say there was any sense of reasonableness to the pace. One way or another it eventually became a violent force-feeding for everyone, and we all gorged right up to the breaking point. The whole school was set to be just twenty-four weeks: just enough time to achieve full-on brain aneurism.

Nighttime's became interesting tests to see how one could empathize with the feeling of the bends without diving; submerging from such intensity too quickly into the quiet space amid a pillow. The brain tried to leap back out of the thinner air, having grown accustomed to pressure. Something in me had shifted, and I'd been geared differently; geared for exactly this sort of work. So I dove in headfirst and thrived in the madness.

It felt just like the performance anxiety at boot camp, where the folk failing swimming exams had their elbows hooked by supervisors' long poles, pulled from the pool and sent off packing. People were dropping like flies. We'd watch the stress take them: the pranksters blowing off steam with some stupid antics bound to get them kicked out. Sometimes people were desperate for an excuse to get switched out of nuclear, after realizing too late they'd made a terrible decision. Technically it was "dereliction of duty" by this point, to get failing scores out of personal negligence. You were contractually bound to give up whatever you had to make success happen. To thrive, or at least survive (That part, they never really mentioned in the brochure.)

Usually there wasn't much art involved once you wanted out. Alcohol eventually did the trick, once citations for contraband got the ball rolling in the endless room inspections. Depravity and disorder were reliable stand-ins in a pinch, as long as it made an impression. Go out with a bang! Nearly nobody used ominous phrases like Bad Conduct Discharge or even Captain's Mast; instead there was an element of much-needed levity inserted: Ricky was headed straight "for a Big Chicken Dinner!" We got to know the warning signs, too, even those of us trying to keep our heads low to the grindstone. In a mere six months we witnessed every possible expression of human desperation: whether less than dignified depravities on the walk of shame away from any of a million strip bars encircling the grounds on the notorious Orange Blossom Trail (including more than one half corpse so inebriated that they were found cold-out, leaned against structures by the morning joggers), or ransacking the cheap bars where one hoped to avoid contact with Senior Officers who would ask difficult questions about drinking on school nights. There was something profound about the breakdowns that happened—nobody wanted to do them halfway when the time came. So when they determined to fail they went all out: streaking and trying to startle the fire patrols, throwing lockers from the balconies of the roach motel, trying to kidnap alligators and transport them back towards barracks. There were endless kids who disappeared after their third or fourth violation for drunk driving, or showing up late to inspections and getting caught after whatever bender had detained them. We'd heard every cover story, usually having to do with getting trapped by snakes or gators near the docks, or intervening to help an old lady with a broken hip who was mugged near Rosie O'Grady's (and that's how he got that black eye and he still reeks of beer…sure!).

After a point we'd hear the desperate last excuses and melodramatic pleas and they'd all just fade into background noise: these were shades who weren't going to make it. A strange impulsion on towards, "save yourself!" mentality set in, and we shored ourselves up in the study hall desks with built-in blinders to block peripheral vision. Machines, we unloaded ballast and moved on.

Ψ

Then it was over! Except in my case, I'd passed. My mantra had been 2.5 and survive, and in the end, I survived with a 2.54 GPA. By the slimmest margin imaginable, I'd passed.

I had never been more proud. I'd never worked so hard for something before, nor started with such an expectation of impossibility and beaten it with pure determination. The last few hours before the comprehensive exam were pure shock. I leaned somewhere between woozy euphoria and sleep paralysis as the last few classes that would ever play with slide rules imitating Star Wars lightsaber duels on their way out of the halls. I felt glorious, and as proud as I could possibly be at graduation.

And then in came the Nuclear Power Training Unit for another six months, just in time to ruin the party. It was a dry run of all the work I'd do on the sub, on a land-based nuclear plant prototype facility. It was just what it sounded like: the intimacy of engineering on a sub minus all the intimacy and the sub. Instead, there was a strange proxy upon which we tested our new book-smart competencies, and a demanding structure of shifts and challenges guaranteed to weed out whoever hadn't already fled before actually being assigned to a boat. I ducked down my head and worked as hard as I could to learn the ropes, wondering all the time if I'd made a huge mistake. It was hard to see the picture from this place: "the good" I would do, the people I could help. It seemed insular and cold, but I held out hope for the future and tried to make a good impression, working myself to the bone all the while.

But the first day I had to discuss my future plans with my superior officers, I found reason to be thrown completely off balance. There, loitering off in a doorway behind the man sorting through my paperwork and asking me questions, was a young officer evidently a few ranks above me.

A man who I'd long hoped never to see again.

Ψ

There was a delay of a day or so, and then I got the order to report back to the same room as before. However this time, there was just one man there, where before he'd been flanked by other officers. The room seemed quietly stark and cold by comparison.

"Come on in, Calabrace. Please, be seated," he said distractedly, piecing through papers on his desk. "I'm going to need your help today to understand something that's been bothering me."

"Anything I can do, sir," I chirped, though I was confused. Why was I back here again?

"I've gotten tons of commendations for your work ethic far, for the efforts you've put in at the plant and the nuclear power school. Your instructors at A-school had nothing but good things to say, and even your roommate wrote that your constant assistance helped him pass electrical systems."

"Thank you sir, I—"

"Not so fast, Calabrace. I called you in because I also got one extremely disturbing report that didn't fit in at all with the others. Granted, the reporter has a bit of a reputation for overzealousness, almost to a fault. I've been looking over the things he wrote, and—"

"Bryan Walker."

He abruptly looked up at me over the forms he held, gave me a hard glance, and sighed. "Well yes, actually, Calabrace. Lieutenant Walker, made this complaint, though I wonder how you could know that?" He scanned through the forms as he paced the room. "This will be a bit unorthodox, and I apologize. We try to take complaints very seriously, but also get a bit wary of serial complaint filers. While this one is evidently no longer anonymous, we still give officers' statements an awful lot of credence in consideration. It says here that you guys come from the same area…which might at least help explain things if I can flesh it out." He paced, and as he did so mechanically brushed off his embroidered sleeve.

"Is there some sort of bad blood between you two that I should know about? I like to give these sorts of critiques the benefit of the doubt, but this particular one just seems scathing beyond all bounds, and I just want to be sure whatever I'm dealing with here is fully within the realm of professionalism, not some petty grudge. I'll be frank, I don't know what to make of the strange level of hostility: as the attacks against your character seem to be pretty broad, including some attacks that just don't line up with reports I've been hearing from your Chain of Command. Petty Officer Calabrace, I need you to be absolutely honest now…Did you…I don't know…have you made a play at this man's wife or something?"

I'd gone completely pale. This was an area of protocol I knew nothing about, the whole interview. How do you answer questions like this from beneath the rank system? I proceeded as cautiously as possible.

"I haven't seen the Lieutenant since we were kids in Mineola. We didn't really get on much….It's been almost ten years since I've seen or spoken to…Lieutenant Walker, sir. I have no idea what was said about me, but I'll do whatever it takes to clear any doubts relating to my service record or character. I hope that my actions will speak to—"

"That'll do, Calabrace. Just wanted to be sure you didn't kill the man's dog, or screw his wife or something. I'll continue my due diligence at this end, and try to see if I can find any more reports calling your qualifications or psychological well-being into question… Simultaneously, (and this is officially off the record now, son): if it ends up appearing like there's nothing here—then I'm going to get to the bottom of this hissy fit. It's beneath the dignity of an Officer, and this wouldn't be the first time exaggeration has entered into readiness-appraisals in a way I disapprove of. I won't have witch hunts under my watch."

He stood before the window and ground his knuckles into the sill, before continuing. "For now, I want to see you on your best behavior until this investigation is carried out. Furthermore, I want you to do some serious reflection on your future options. Rank is tricky, and ships are small. You are both scheduled to be quartered at pretty close contact aboard the USS Enterprise, short some sort of immediate intervention. We'd have to burn that bridge when we get there," he muttered with a sigh.

A tense silence floated in the room before, suddenly, he cleared his throat and popped all the knuckles in his hands, swinging back around towards me.

"Well, enough of that. We'll look into things on our end. I'll be in touch Calabrace, excuse the cross examination. Any further questions you'll be contacted. Dismissed."

15

"I'm going to make things as clear and simple as possible for you, Calabrace. We need submariners. The pay is more, but so are the responsibilities. The crew is tighter knit. You seem to be the right kind of guy for the job. Looking into your scores and performance evals: I definitely feel you would be a better fit than most on a sub: your patience and versatility will serve you well in the cramped confines undersea. The thing is, I can't make this decision for you alone, it's voluntary. Well…technically, at least. Many consider the submarine force more stressful, and luxuries onboard are few and far between. But everything you do right will be noticed, and lauded. You'll have more challenges, but less of the military pomp of the surface fleet. What do you say, Calabrace? You in?"

I sat quietly for a moment, my mind racing. I'd been intentionally bumping into superiors all week, trying to scheme out how I'd arrange an escape from the same ship Bryan Walker was on, trying to arrange glimmers of talking points and strategy, weak points and ways to convince. And now this fell straight into my lap…

"If you're worried you'll be on some ancient submarine, let me put your mind at rest. You'd be commissioning the newest sub in the fleet. It's so new, it's just starting to be built, down in Groton, Connecticut."

This time, I didn't wait. "I will always do whatever I can to help my country, Master Chief. Tell me where to sign."

Ψ

When I arrived, I was directed towards the massive ribcage of a beached whale. Or at least, that's what it looked like. There was an enormous steel scaffolding stretching across the shipyard construction hanger, with workmen scrambling over the site like so many ants, swinging on pulleys and bosons chairs. I reported early as part of the Pre-Commissioning Unit, here to familiarize ourselves with our nuclear crew of officers and command, and with the boat we would run together. The familiarity came fast, as there was little else to do the first few weeks after we arrived, apart from training. Initially, we only had a dozen men. A Captain with decades at sea, and experienced in command of other submarines. An Engineer, three junior engineering officers, and eight enlisted men—of which some were senior. There were also some officers and enlisted men who were so junior (like myself), we were simply referred to as NUBs— Nuclear Unqualified Body (or Non-Useful Body), as we were not yet fully qualified, so we couldn't stand watches. We were considered dead weight to our respective departments, during the transition.

Much of what was happening was steeped in Navy tradition and ceremony. As per tradition, we'd long missed the ceremony where a stranger's name was inscribed by a welder in the keel-laying ceremony back in 1976, yet this commissioning period was all ours. It made real the submarine that was rapidly materializing before our eyes, and the reality of the changes: that the sub was near completion, near delivery and launch, and then a new life was beginning for all of us. The steel skeleton became our home, and we watched her blossom into a miniature-sized fortress.

It was a strange transition from life with a crew of twelve, through all the stages that would take this steel skeleton into the sea, manned with one hundred and twenty souls. Over time, rooms and halls and mechanics multiplied across the steel frames, and a real submarine started to take form. The precision demanded was legendary, so there were no shortcuts taken: every measurement taken in triplicate, every system checked again and again, and initialed on clip boards by both the Electric Boat Company and a Navy crewmember. At every stage, updates and construction accounting were demanded by an Admiral with a vice-like grasp over all affairs of the nuclear submarine fleet. At every step of the way, he'd want to be involved in logistics of the S6G nuclear reactor, as well as the weapons systems, the labyrinthine hydraulic and electric systems, the galley, the berthing specifications…He considered all these boats his babies and didn't like leaving the responsibilities to anybody else. So our lives became a series of iterated reports and tests, with nonstop training scenarios, testing our abilities to think "outside the box." Life changed fundamentally when the new USS Jacksonville was floated out of dry dock, and we began her sea trials.

How do I present our lifestyle in this era? Different, completely different from any perspective any boy or man might imagine. Our lives took on a strange cubist tilt as we took the boat through her paces—verifying that she could excel in even the most extreme exaggerations of evasive maneuvers. Everything about our lives at that period was about intentionally upsetting all the easy order and making sure we'd built something sustainable, stable, and safe—a home cut off from light, air, cities, and countries. Every kitchen utensil had to be safely stowed, and each bolt tightened enough that nobody would get a concussion, nor an enemy a sonar read on us, should we be forced to make extreme motions in the pursuit of normal duty at sea.

As the nuclear crew of a brand new submarine, we hadn't been mandated to attend the generic theoretical lectures of a typical "sub school." Instead we learned them straight from the source, flying from the seats of our pants. The youngest and greenest were always tested on Dive and Drive skills first, literally putting the safety of all in the hands of novices to drive home the All for one and One for All motto we lived for here. However, nobody was going to miss any points on safety codes and best practices with the Admiral and his merry men lurking around…we were on our best behavior. Rather, everything was done to the textbook, and then tested some more, and then double-checked again. No stone was left unturned, and every single process the JAX would be expected to perform as a fully functional sub was exhaustively tested in the littoral waters. We ran through lectures and drills on escape, flooding and seawater leaks, on minimizing sound pollution, on the importance of isolating our mechanics from our hull with shock absorption features everywhere one could imagine. We exhaustively covered the importance of electrolysis function: providing all the oxygen generated to breathe and facilitating desalination plants for water to drink, shit, shower and shave, etc. We had backups for everything, in some case backups to the backups. We exhaustively covered all the business I'd just spent six months covering at the Prototype facility all over again: nuclear safety and shielding, best practices and regular testing, neutron poisoning and control rods, life under emergency conditions and responses. Someone helpfully pasted up a cartoon drawing of several contorted stick figure bodies screaming silently while being irradiated with a bright green glow, and had scrawled NO! over the image to help all us baby nukes "remember best practices."

Of course, everything we learned *was* actually crucially important now and vitally relevant because with our furtive, pressurized intensity lifestyle we might as well have been swimming in space. We couldn't just pop up for a soda while cat-and-mouse chasing Soviet Alpha-class subs around in radio silence.

And so we were to become creatures of the deep, leaving all the rest behind.

Ψ

Commissioning day finally came and went, full of pageantry, speechmaking, confetti, and Naval brides' tears. Then, the first orders were given and the first watch begun. One voice hung in the breeze, ordering, "Man this ship men, and bring her to life!" And just like that, we were a real sub with a real course. We cut out to sea; the men lined at attention topside beneath the sail, as the waving families faded into horizon. Nobody spoke; everyone prepared their heads and hearts for the dive. Then, as the choppier waters were reached, the last men climbed the sail like ants retreating into an anthill, and the adventure began. They sealed the hatch from the blue sky above, and the deep beckoned. The orders were given and confirmed, the ballast tanks flooded. Water jets fizzled into steam as all remaining air was expressed, and we became an undersea thing again. Finally the diving planes moved quietly, the as-yet barely familiar groans and creaks of pressure on a new hull protested, and we slowly made our first proper dive at full capacity.

My first impression was marveling at the multiplying the call and response of each order by an impressive multiplier now that we were fully manned. The eerie quiet of the first days was gone. The sea was now ours, and we hers. But what an empty sea it seemed to be!

We learned to lean into each other and fill voids with new fraternity. Brothers in arms.

The galley helped. Morale was intimately tied to the otherwise mundane conditions of grooming, resting, and eating onboard a sub. Getting enough food onto the darned thing for a long tour was a struggle all of its own, due to the construction of submarines. Everything became a question of team work, of chain-gang-like cooperation. Everything always seemed easy and great at the beginning of a tour when everyone was in high spirits and ready for adventure. But within a few mere weeks, food prep meant much more. It became a vital component of morale: since the fresh milk, fruits and vegetables would by then be gone. Creative, and sometimes frightening, substitutes were used in the kitchen, but they always found a way to make it happen.

The men lived in cramped racks, with inches of storage space, endless shifts, with no privacy. Plus, the normal mundane strains of rank and file drudgery. Food and feeding was the human element, the one guaranteed luxury. Any degradation of any of those conditions would thus result in far wider ramifications, ultimately leading to fantasies of mania, mutiny, and widespread social collapse. We didn't want that! So we sought to establish regular routines that worked and cheered up the men, and then we stuck to them. For many, meal traditions were the sole reminder of calendar days actually concretely rotating in the outside world: curry meant Friday, like red glowing lights delineated nights in the control rooms from day, etc. We all ate together, everyone eating the same level of food, side by side.

For someone accustomed to isolation, this was a novelty. Thirty of us dined at once in a room the size of a living room, along a series of eight tables. There were no wild personal boundaries or pretensions; there was just no space for it. So instead, we became as close as any bunch of brothers before us, a bunch of humans sat in a cylindrical bathtub—hurtling through the depths.

I was a Petty Officer, but in the eyes of naval tradition, I was a "nub" yet. Was the term Sophomoric? Perhaps. But that peer-pressure raced us towards the ultimate goal: familiarity with all quarters of the boat, all tasks done there, all needs and stresses. Well rounded sailors; Useful Bodies. We all aspired after the old seafaring adage that had persevered for hundreds of year: to be an Able-Bodied Seamen, ones who had crossed the doldrums, survived encounters with enemies, fought down storms, grown lithe in salt and sunburns.

But in our era, a young submariner lived a different life than atop a wooden ship with sails. He not only had his job to do, but also had to work on his overall knowledge of the submarine himself, to earn a coveted silver badge of honor called "dolphins." It was an earned honor, as you had to learn not only the systems that encompassed your job function, but *every* system on board from weapons, navigation, operations, propulsion, sonar, radio, mechanical electrical, reactor, hydraulics fresh water, seawater, and the list went on and on.

But first, we had to do the busy work and the grueling stuff: we mastered every mundane task relating to measuring and recording of temperature, pressure, and every conceivable mechanical reading onto clipboards and data sheets, working every stripe of conceivable bilges and bellows, the elaborate arts of cleaning spills, and of course, drilling and drilling some more: fire response, disaster response, protocol responses, evasive maneuvers. More than anything, we mastered the art of standing watch. Anytime, anywhere, we'd valiantly arrive and relieve people for break and then:

...We...would...stand...there.

We were "doing our dues" with these skim shifts, but not too eager to stay in the low rungs for too long—adventure called!

So every moment off-shift was spent racing to learn every new system onboard the sub. Everyone had Navy submarine qualification cards issued that checked off each new task and system along the way, waiting for the coveted signatures of system experts, towards eventual total mastery, Dolphin qualifications, and the (SS) designation as fully qualified submariners. Until reaching this point, the jobs mandated for us were dramatically less glamorous, as were the sleeping conditions.

If we fell short in our qualification progress, we were deemed as DINQs (Delinquent In Quals), which was not a moniker anyone wanted to bear. It almost always meant the few hours of sleep you were getting a night was henceforth going to be spent studying harder and longer—until you caught up,

As a nuke, I was lucky to have at least entered through an elevated rank, but even I barely avoided being on a "hot rack" arrangement. Due to space constriction, hot racks are one of those charming relics of sociology wherein one might have to share a bunk with the man whose watch they relieved, thus with every shift's end one would crawl into a bed already hot from someone else's sleep. You would only pray that the person who proceeded you hadn't spent his shift playing with hydraulic oil or something similar, now embedded in the sheets. Others would get a makeshift mattress atop the torpedoes they'd spent all day maintaining. What could be more relaxing? All I could think of when watching the politics behind "bed attribution" were the tooth-and-nail battles I'd watched between my cousins way back in Cape Cod. But it turns out I had indeed finally triumphed, as I'd hoped I would way back then: because I was part of the pre-commissioning crew, I was a "plank owner" forever after. I would have symbolic pride of place in the bed that I'd first claimed aboard the sub: because it had been mine first. (Eat your heart out, Jim.)

Not everyone was so lucky. I went to rouse a young enlisted man named Bob to take his watch, and as he sleepily scrambled out of bed he suddenly reached back into the few free inches of free space and carefully extracted three glossy precious somethings, which he wrapped in a soft cloth and bolted into his storage locker.

"What have you got there, Bob?" I wondered aloud, just making conversation.

Bob was thrilled to share, positively bursting with joy. "This is my daughter, Mina." He sidled alongside me, instantly the oldest of friends. "Here she is at summer camp, riding a horse. She's seven! Imagine riding a horse at seven? And here she is at soccer practice. And this one," he mumbled reflectively, staring and soaring far away from the sub in his mind, "this was her second birthday party. Look at all the cake on her face!" His eyes trembled a few times, and abruptly he began to stiffen into role-play. "Huh, this tape isn't going to take much more of this."

I laid a hand upon his shoulder. "That's a beautiful girl you've got there, Bob. Never you worry about the tape, I'll figure something out. You will never have to worry about that. You get ready for your watch, I'll see what I can do."

His face said all that needed be said, as he collected himself. Somebody entered the berthing, exhausted, and stumbled into the only momentarily vacated bunk, instantaneously snoring. "Jeez. I'd better get ready, then. Thanks again." Bob scrambled out to wash and shave, worlds away already. I wasn't so lucky. I instantaneously knew everything Bob hadn't said about his family leave-taking. It had been rancorous. His wife had begged him to stay, screamed at him for not being there for the family, threatened to leave him, and even made intimations that if any infidelities accrued while he was gone it probably wouldn't be the first, and that he—and he alone—would be solely to blame. Poor old Bob, he only saw Mina: at summer camp, at soccer camp. He worked his butt off to buy her things on a sailor's pay, and missed them all, and now it was all up in the air. He was breathing dreams.

I quietly wiped a tear from the corner of my eye and made a mental note to do anything I could to make his berth easy and gentle as possible, while the dream lingered…

Three weeks later, Bob cried on my shoulder when he got the dreaded Family-Gram.

But this wasn't an isolated incident; it was an intimate place. We lived, worked, slept, ate, and dreamed our lives away at less than an arm's-length, all of us. There was a sense of camaraderie on board that I never had experienced in my life. It softened the blow: the family feeling. It mattered less that the days were long, the work challenging and difficult. It's true: you were pushed in your knowledge, your skills, and you were constantly challenged to give it your all. But the collective spirit was something to behold, as we grew into both a proper functional team and a family as well.

There were mentorships in place, wherein all we green folk onboard would be under the wing of old timers trained by eons at sea. Sea-Dads, they were called, had normally been out to sea countless times; all this new launching business was old hat to them. They could do everything demanded of them in their sleep. One ship was the same as another after serving long enough; there was an intuition that developed, muscle memory, flawless timing, and reflex responses. But in addition to a level of virtuosity and confidence transferred by these mentorships, they were also fiercely protective of their Sea Pups, and would keep a wary eye out at all times over their charges while we learned the ropes. I'll never know exactly what was preemptively whispered between my mentor and the men tacking on my Crows insignia as a Petty Officer, but there had never been such a gentle, reverent procedure realized in practice. He barely pressed them on the collar of my coveralls, with a fearful look over my shoulder at my mentor, who quietly nodded with a satisfied grin under his heavy black beard. We younger guys had all heard horror stories of crows and dolphins "tacked-on" in a much less civil, more painful fashion so I was quite relieved.

Hazing was minimal with that kind of protection, so we learned instead, and were able to throw our backs into fully growing into our roles. The Captain was additionally not the sort of man to go in for any misbehavior or bullying, or allow his crew to remain blind to it: he worked hard to acknowledge and respect everyone's roles in maintaining sub-wide morale, and he expected that example to be widespread. He had little toleration for antics that would be divisive to harmony between decks. When that expectation wasn't met, retribution was as predictable as any textbook.

One day, we all got to remember exactly how stringent were the clockwork demands we'd run the sub by: because the Admiral had returned. Inconvenienced by some catastrophe on shore during his habitual watch over new vessels undergoing sea trials, he'd now returned to finish the job with a supervisory observation crew of mixed military and civilian origins. They were here to check up on the ship performance, and that mostly meant here to check up on us, our performance as sailors: our discipline and efficiency.

Nervous energy overtook every corridor, as we waited to see what new trials we'd have to live through. In a ship of that size, being observed means there is no respite: a steel labyrinth with nowhere to hide. Every inch is easily monitored and every gesture investigated. We became perfect paper cutouts of submariners: flawless, sterile, and creased. But it couldn't last forever.

16

And the mad dash for qualifications began! There's really no overstating how much it sucked to be not qualified in such a precision environment. These men beamed with pride at handling such important equipment; they lived for it. Not to mention, most of the best moments of crew morale-building exercises were barred to folk without their dolphins. While we raced to memorize the jungle of piping schematics and electrical circuit diagrams of systems and structures, we could hear them laughing, watching movies, or playing cards in the galley. No matter the rank, should any nonqualified submariner curiously investigate, we could be turned away and directed back toward our qual cards and procedures: even by a dolphins-wearing sailor who we technically outranked. What it came down to was we were there to *learn.* And once again, we entered the story already behind schedule, racing to catch up.

Why was it so important? What was the big deal about "dolphins?" It wasn't just empty ceremony, fraternity, or rites of passage for the hell of it. We were in a unique situation within the submarine fleet, knowing that—were we to have problems at sea—the odds of a successful rescue mission reaching us were slim to none. Who would come? We had Steinke Hoods, which in theory would allow us to ascend to the surface and breathe, but first our eardrums would be punctured, and the rapid decompression would probably kill us long before we saw the sun at the surface. Furthermore, our standard operating procedure relied entirely on stealth, self-reliance, and isolation. In situations of crisis, therefore, we couldn't suddenly pretend otherwise. In the moments that crisis struck, we knew exactly where chances of rescue lay: with ourselves, and ourselves alone. Each man relied on the next.

We'd all heard dark legends of the Thresher and the Scorpion. The ice that would travel up the spines of every submariner was enough to help us remember: we were on our own. For no reason could we lose control. Everything around us was hostile! The surface was hostile: if we were spotted in any of a million complex situations at sea, we could die. The water was hostile: if we drifted or stalled, or sprung a leak, we would die "crush depth" was an unescapable part of our reality. We had to quickly control fires, or the metal ship would turn into a convection oven and fry us (if it didn't corrupt all our air first). We had to make our own air, power our control systems, and produce sufficient light. If we didn't, we'd first suffocate—then crash and then die tripping around in the dark. Our own CO2 could get us, without constant vigilance and work. Our own nuclear power source could get us. Or our hydrogen. Or our torpedoes. We lived in a reality at least as potentially harsh as outer space.

So how do you deal with that level of environmental hostility? You deal with and master every "given" you can. The number one "given" that can be controlled in our case was the comprehensive education of every man on board. "Casualties," we called them: the catastrophic events that we constantly drilled for, which trained us on quick thinking and quick solutions.

As our world was a simple one—a metal eggshell in the unrelenting pressures of the deep sea—we had to steer perfectly! We had to have perfect control. We had to have perfect propulsion. We had to be sure nobody or no scenarios knocked us off our safe, well considered trajectories, no matter the degree of stress or distractions. And the "given" we could control for, there were "other people" in the deep; we could aspire for quiet! If they couldn't hear us, they couldn't harass us and mess with our navigation, and we'd not raise our risk unnecessarily. We fixated on perfect mechanics: mitigating noise, developing crew awareness, and attention to detail. It was one of many reasons why nobody got to practice bowling or strike gongs at mealtimes on a sub: there was an issue of "transients." Noises like this could transfer through the hull and invite unwelcome attention, by resonating out into the cold water, traversing long distances towards the eager ears of other deep wanderers. We knew we had a secretive sound surveillance system stretched all across the sea floor, looking for the Soviet subs with hydrophones stretched in wild arrays. They were always seeking anything that moved, by triangulation, by hook or by crook…but who was listening for us?

Well, one thing was sure: in our line of work, risks were never wanting. Casualties were never far from mind. So we wanted the best damn team imaginable to face that ceaseless slew of challenges. That's what our entire submarine qualifying culture was all about: everyone knowing every bit of that boat. More importantly, everyone could and would chip in to keep every bit running in a disaster, regardless of their primary competency. Everyone could chip in on crisis response. Everyone would be aware of protocol for dealing with problems, wherever they should arrive on the ship. But that took TIME. And training. And work. And study. But mostly time.

It just so happened we did have that, tons of that. Time was everywhere. We were floating through the deep dark for ages at a time, cycling six hour blocks of life into eighteen hour days. Six hours were designated "watch," but when you were non-qual pukes, what help were you? Six hours were sleep, but who would want a bunch of NUBs crowding up bunk space when they aren't contributing their share towards the collective team pull? The other six hours were spent studying, training, cleaning or maintaining equipment; then we'd repeat the cycle again. There were simple pleasures to be had, if you could sneak them in: eating, sleeping, watching one of the dozen or so movies brought aboard, or checking a book out of the ship's library (no library card required) from a ragtag assortment of shelved paperback books that other learned scholars onboard had contributed. But it was basic pride that motivated us more than anything, the desire to be fully a part of the team. So mostly, we worked.

I had wonderful motivation from my Sea-Dad Rusty, who pushed me at every turn and eventually helped to welcome me into the crew. But that took time, it was still miles away when we were under way! So Johnny went back to school, yet again. This time, on my toes.

Ψ

It was a long process, in which we'd meticulously master the systems of every corner of the ship. It wasn't a question of how we were ranked or what our career pipeline was, nothing like that. It was a small complex boat, and like anything complex, it was prone to challenges. Everyone had to lean on the next man with absolute trust. In learning to trust one another, we needed to know that we could count on every man to identify, maintain, and even repair crucial systems when the need arose. And those qualifications were mandatory for every soul on board. So it became a necessity, every one of us starting the qualification process on a sub was given an elaborate sub qualification card, to be signed off by the resident expert chiefs and officers of each of the zones across that sub: not just propulsion and damage control, but navigation, combat systems, electronics, and auxiliary systems. We needed to know that we could fill in wherever we were needed, at a moment's notice. So we did!

It all started with generic submarine orientation, everything basic we'd need to know about living on a sub. As I was a plank holder, I'd arrived early, and had already received a fair amount of info here from some of the best sources around during pre-commissioning; but any remaining holes were stitched closed as well—doubled, and reinforced, and ironed over. We went over safety (again, all the interesting places to potentially get killed), and introduced fairly straightforward concepts that the nukes among us were used to, but were still Greek to the others: ideas like "dosimetry" and "reactor protection." Words that would in time become everyday features of life. I'd fortunately been exposed to such ominous signs as an everyday fact of life in prototype training and the already mentioned irradiation cartoons left to "help us" in the reactor area, so it was nothing new. This was an era of walkthroughs and introductions, where everyone got too much information at once and everyone wanted to panic and slowdown and freak out and instead...*we just didn't!*

That became the common calling card of the submariner, really. Everywhere we should have panicked and broken down, we sleepily did what we had to do, to finish the job right. We worked our asses off, and when done we aimed our bodies towards our racks on the horizon, and then did it again. The occasional Navy "shrink" unfortunate enough to be selected to monitor the psychiatric effects of life onboard a submarine usually needed more help for himself than for the crew he'd been sent to monitor. He'd be picked on and screwed with for days by a bunch of bored, mischievous submariners who found pleasure in making the job anything but a scientific pursuit.

The next quals were the vital ones, where we moved beyond babysitting in the estuary of intros, into how we could really be of service right away: casualty drills. We spent months learning a love/hate relationship with our damage control equipment, until it fit us better than our own skins. Endless, impromptu drills and inspections on our techniques and cooperation—working through proper responses for every sort of leaks—you name it—radioactive liquids, superheated steam, seawater, oil, but also sites of flooding, problems with electricity and fire; and protocols for clearly communicating needs over the phone system while staying cool under fire, even while wearing an air-fed mask.

Finally, most importantly for our egos, and the most horrible news for our legs, we moved into the dirty work-watchstanding quals. This was really the point at which we'd start influencing our sub mates in positive ways—so finally nobody was racing to hold up our dead weight as much. Until we were ready to stand watch, it wasn't like the position would sit empty. Some poor soul would have to do it—and fair or not, resentment brewed until watches were split more equitably. "Port and Starboard," they called it, when someone arose to take watch at six, had lunch at noon, and then at o-eighteen hours, they were right back out on watch; murderously grumbling that the 'dinks' and 'nubs' better speed things up, OR ELSE.

Whenever the whining got too pushy, an overprotective Sea-Dad or two would step in, and remind the complainers the way the system worked; and there would be a grumbled resignation. Boy, let me tell you though, the second it was my turn, I raced right out, eager to represent my division, eager to serve my country.

I'd been training for this very moment—and...I...well...Truth be told, watches aren't that interesting at the beginning, really.

I filled out pre-made checklists and data records of temperature and pressure readings, as well as other key equipment readouts… and then turned them in at the end of the day to the Engineroom Supervisor or the Engineering Watch Supervisor; and I shared any problems I encountered with the Engineering Officer of the Watch when he made his shiftly rounds. Then I fell dead asleep, and it all repeated. But I even could see a method to this madness—I was becoming a useful part of a bigger machine. I was learning.

I finally began to move a bit more around the boat. We spent a great deal of time focusing on the great water systems that would enable us to dive and surface, and to maintain balance and bearing. Really, once we dove in, it never seemed like we came up again. From that point, there was a never-ending acceleration into learning a huge variety of systems. We transitioned through sea water systems, pure water systems, reactor plant systems, air systems, hydraulic systems, electrical systems and more.

Each time, I had to slow down my head and really tune into what was being said to me the first time, though I was always still halfway stuck in processing the info from last week or the week before, or the one before…As life in a submarine transitioned out of being a charming novelty, into being a full-fledged lifestyle; everyone had to make a tremendous effort to be malleable and pliant in the face of the everyday living challenges. Beyond constant close proximity and an utter lack of privacy, we had to psychologically deal with the lack of any trace of natural sunlight, more so than if we we'd been in space. We had to deal with learning to "rig for red" when the boat was going to be surfaced, or coming to periscope depth at night. (It was the submariner's way of pre adjusting our eyes to be ready for the night so we never wasted a moment while we were visible.) We had to learn to live on that strange eighteen-hour loop, where time didn't seem real without normal circadian rhythms. Instead, we had to inflict patterns with gimmicks: things like mid rats (midnight rations) were out so that meant it was night, or "I know it is Monday because they're serving lasagna again, but we'll have no sliders until Friday."

We learned to push on through those strains anew, like we'd persevered through boot camp getting screamed at, and pushed through nuke school getting an ear chewed of, and being dressed down by the duty officer for skylarking instead of studying—but now it was an endurance marathon mixed with a science Olympiad, with a smattering of seasonal affective disorder tossed into the mix. But for every moment of "low," the men came together and propped one another up.

Every victory was a shared one; every challenge became collective. We were constantly striving to hold this mad boat together, though it would take every one of us to budge her onward. As we began to get into our stride, we finally began really to excel at it. But just when your division officer would tell you how happy he was with your progress, you could almost always count on hearing from your division chief shortly thereafter—how disappointed he was in you—and how you needed to try and concentrate more, and get things done.

Good Cop/Bad Cop, I guess?

I ventured further out into more and more unfamiliar challenges. I had to get signed off on each of the furthest freshwater systems, and it forced me into a first-name basis with more and more of my sub mates. We had to go through systems that would deal with dumping trash and dumping the shit; whereupon everyone had to wait for the laughing to stop to insist on exactly how many horror stories already existed of nubs screwing it up: pulling pressurized tanks and blowing themselves half to hell with pressurized raw sewage.

In an odd harmonic contrast, we then worked on weapons systems, which didn't seem all that different logistically from the weaponized toilets we'd just been warned about. It was while passing through the torpedo bays that I was made aware for the first time exactly how lucky I'd been to have entered with an advanced rank. As we walked into the torpedo room, two poor souls were using unused torpedo shelves as bunks, with narrow mattresses wedged above the steel, atop the bombs. One slept in his skivvies, and one in less: his blanket mostly raised over his eyes to block out the bright lights. Yes, I realized how lucky I was. I hugged the bulkhead and tried to tiptoe, but the CPO didn't seem to notice—he just kept on shouting best practice guidelines.

Eventually, I found myself stretched all the way out, my hands touching a bit of everything, everywhere. One day I'd be checking out sonar, another day something in the control room, and then drills and needs in my own department would attempt to wipe all my mental slates clean, and yet I'd just have to keep going, or I'd have to answer to the XO, and account for being delinquent. What's worse, if I was "dink," my tirelessly crusading Sea-Dad, who was keeping me on target this whole time, would have to muster time out of his personal time to come and mentor me further. That in itself was motivation enough to really push myself for timely advancement and organization.

Nick was an electrician in the same shoes as I was; he'd reported onboard about five months behind me. He was also part of the Engineering department—and had originally come from Long Island, too.

I was in the middle to lower tier of qual progress. I tried like hell, but the information didn't stick well—I was just too distractible. Two of my closest shipmates Chris and Bart were the opposite—one listen and they understood it; with me, it took two or three. With Nick, it took four or five. We desperately tried to help each other study and spent as much free time as we could walking down piping systems together, cramming. Nick was one of the few people whose memories broke through the wall of stability and overstimulation in the sub, so his memories preoccupied me for weeks at a time, as I tried to concentrate on studying.

He'd had a troubled life before the Navy: some he talked about, and some only I could see. His Mother died after the birth of his little sister, and his Dad never told him the cause but would choke up and change the subject anytime it was brought up. His Dad worked long hours making deliveries for a commercial bakery and wasn't around much, so his Aunt would fill in. Nick hated his Aunt, who watched television, smoked cigarettes, and did little else. His Aunt was a monster. She'd pull one liners from the Bible like, "Spare the Rod, Spoil the Child" when it suited her immediate impulse, but Nick learned at Sunday School that the Bible wasn't a manual for being a beast, even if his Aunt acted like one. Nick had often prayed that his Aunt would just disappear from their lives. But instead, it had been left to him to raise his baby sister, from the time he was nine, onwards. If his sister cried too much, Aunt Louise would slap her; so Nick would try to keep her quiet. He could still hear those slaps in his head every day and never forgot the horrible sound.

He'd retained huge stores of guilt in his head for not doing enough for his sister, as they'd grown up together, for not standing up to his Aunt or telling his Dad. He still beat himself up for what he could only guess what had gone on when he was in school, and his Aunt was left alone with the baby. When he joined the Navy at eighteen, his proud sister Maria wrote him letters almost all the time. She was twelve now, happy and well adjusted; but Nick carried that guilt with him every day. He felt as if he wasn't the big brother that he should have been, and he couldn't let that go.

I wanted to reach out to Nick so many times, but how does one say, "Hey Nick, I can see the personal tragedy in your head—and understand the pain you feel about your abusive Aunt, and the guilt you still carry about not standing up more for your sister Maria…I just wanted to know if you want to talk about it?"

I could hear him now, imagining how he would have responded. "Who are you Calabrace, Dr. Joyce Brothers? And how the hell you know about that?" So instead, I said nothing—like Nick did with Maria—wanting to help, but not knowing how.

It was one of many times I hated who I was—I hated seeing the pain of strangers. I hated that those memories were now a part of me; they would never be forgotten. I hated being a peeping Tom into other people's memories and emotions. What I could see, no one else could, and sometimes they couldn't even face these memories themselves. Even if they could let them go, could I? I always hoped someday the door would open and all the pain, anguish, fear, and terror would be wiped away.

Every morning was a new morning, though, so I was determined just to wait it out—and see. I had no choice, really. So I did my best to stem the tide of memories, and cram my mind with the countless tasks already at hand. There was enough of a torrent there to overwhelm anyone that I didn't need any help with that.

But finally, the steady onslaught of novelty specifics of the systems began to taper out. All at once, it became clear that we were coming to that magical point in our training, the point of convergence. We started practicing tying larger systems together, and troubleshooting difficult questions of causation, and considering leadership roles in logical casualty responses. We began to discuss pipes in terms of their long, convoluted routes, and how they stretched across incredibly long stretches the sub, rather than the tidy regions implied by out qualification checkbooks. We digested whole chapters at a time of the Reactor Plant Manuals, Casualty Procedures, and JAX specific learning materials we had laid out for us, in the transition towards full qualification. We learned every complication along the way.

But the tricky thing was, there was never an end to this long uninterrupted expectation of concentration. We had to develop this unflappable sense of perpetual, "Oh, sure, I guess I'm doing this now, no problem…" We all seemed to do it just fine, surprisingly. And that was that. There were always the dreaded field days to interrupt the studying, where the entire ship's company scoured every corner of the boat from the torpedo room to end of shaft alley, where the shaft that turns the ship's propeller leaves the vessel. We spotlessly cleaned every component, panel, turbine, console, railing, table, valve, and anything in between: to be made ready for rigorous cleanliness inspections. Every piece of exposed metal (we called it brightwork) had to shine. It wasn't like college where our primary function was to learn; here it was different. You were required to learn, but also made fully aware that you'd be multitasking, and you could be pulled away at a moment's notice—and that didn't repeal your expected qual. The expectation was DEAL WITH IT, and get it done.

I was thrilled with my own place onboard. The reactor was fascinating, and we had some great people working back there, who made it all bearable and kept us on track. They'd been in the same shoes before.

Bill, our leading first class machinery division Petty Officer, was one of the funniest people I'd ever met, and used his humor as a tool for morale. He helped us all prioritize things, with the simple thought that if he could do it, so could anyone. He tried to make us think that he was a simple guy, but he was brilliant.

Johnny was a Reactor Operator who spent countless hours with me breaking down the reactor and reactor protection systems into short bursts of information for me to digest, since he saw I seemed overwhelmed by it all. He would start with a broad concept, then next time peel back another layer, and then another the next time. Usually, while we talked, he would fiddle with his moustache, and his eyes would tell you when you were on the right track. He loved his job but daydreamed every moment of every day about how lucky he was to be married to the most beautiful, sweetest girl he'd ever met; and he missed their two beautiful girls. He always amazed me with the sheer purity of good memories that he carried.

Rusty was my Sea-Dad: a bit crusty on the outside, with a scraggly black beard like you'd see in a pirate movie. He'd served on two other boats before the JAX, and although he was in Machinery division, he was one of the go-to guys who could fix anything onboard. He was a master machinist, a troubleshooter kind of guy who could always think outside the box. He'd take a component that two other people had already given up on and make it work. He was well respected by every department. He had that Indiana farm-boy type personality, where his brilliance would sneak up on you unexpectedly. He could develop a troubleshooting-plan that was usually successful for any component, never taking credit for the solution, only raising his eyes above his glasses and speaking in a soft voice. Once, it was, "I don't know much about how they do welding in the shipyards, but looks like the x-rays they used to verify these five different welds are all the same X-ray, so you might want to ask the inspector who signed off about that…" He was right of course—and it was a major scandal: that was luckily corrected early-on.

I kept working at it, never flagging, never giving up. I had to go through and learn all the compartments like the back of my hand, until that boat really became something that I felt I was ready to assist with, to provide for. All the last details were squeezed together, and the nets and webs of information were tightened together to encompass everything. After this point it sort of became clear that we were headed down a pipeline towards completion. For a long time, we'd sort of lost all track of time because the strains were new, and so was everything else. But as progressive mastery started to accrue, we started closing holes and replacing phrases like individual response scenarios with "all-ship emergency systems," "all casualty systems," "all damage control equipment" and "all radiation monitoring equipment." It all had to be under my belt—and more and more, it was. I could not only draw piping systems but actually understood their relationship with adjoining and complementary ones.

Finally, the day came when my Sea-Dad Rusty told me to rest up for the next morning, because we'd be doing 'walk-throughs." After so much preparation, it almost seemed all-for-nothing: the questions were routine and reasonable (now, though certainly not when I'd stepped aboard). It had never really occurred to me how much I'd grown, how quickly all the changes had come. But I'd come to understand her in a much more profound way—the sub I'd already felt an emotional attachment to upon boarding—as I'd watched her be built from the ground up. I'd come to understand all the layers: every deck and bulkhead and overhead mapped out in my mind. I could've walked most of those narrow corridors in the dark, and my hand still could've come to rest perfectly at exactly the exact position and height of each port, each table, or the release valve at the head.

I was ready.

The guy walking me through the walk-throughs seemed to think so too. He shrugged his shoulders and mumbled something to the effect of: Huh! Looks like the little nub might be ready!

He booked me for a qualification board appearance to do the final exam component, patted me on the shoulder, and walked away. As I stood there, I realized that all I had left before me was the most dreaded test of all.

I shuffled into the room, and tried to project determination and competency, though I think I might have looked green anyway. No matter, I was ready for this. The board was made up of a Submarine-qualified Officer, a Chief Petty Officer, and a Petty Officer.

During the Board, I was asked to draw and explain most of the systems I'd been checked off on. I was also asked a million practical "what would you do now?" questions on disaster responses, casualties, and subtle moral judgment questions designed to make me think, and possibly trip me up. I thought it was a pretty reasonable setup, until someone asked me about the names of the two dolphins, a question on Navy history and values. It took me a second to realize he was joking, so I could restart my heart. Finally, someone else broke the silence and asked the old textbook riddle question, "You are a molecule of sea-water in the Atlantic Ocean. Describe in a one line diagram how you ultimately make the light above my rack glow, when I turn on the switch."

I knew I had this one, if I didn't trip on my words. The question was relatively simple—a nuclear submarine uses its Main Steam Turbine and propeller to drive it through the ocean. It also uses a ship's Service Turbine Generator to supply its electrical needs. They wanted to see if I understood the *big picture* of how all these components worked together, with the details on how I got there. Main Seawater Valves, Main Seawater pumps, distillation units, the piping flowpaths of how water becomes steam, and how the steam turns the generator. Then I had to lay out how the electricity was generated from the rotating generator, then transferred to electrical panels and buses all the way until the seawater's resulting electrical power was pushed through to its ultimate destination…flowing into the tiny ballast of the fluorescent light fixture above each man's bunk.

I got the impression that all they wanted to see was that I was deliberate, and that I didn't lose my cool. They needed to verify that I was able to take challenges in stride, and do all I could to solve them with the composite skills I'd acquired.

After five or six more questions, I started to feel pretty good. I wasn't doing perfectly, but I knew from the people in the room that I hadn't messed up anything big. As all the blood rushed into my head, they abruptly all moved away, evidently done.

Was that it? The board told me I was dismissed. I suppose they discussed it, and decided I'd done alright.

The next thing I knew, I was told they had recommended me for qualification to the CO. A few days later I was presented my "Dolphins" by the Skipper and designated as "Qualified in Submarines." My Sea-Dad stood behind me the whole time, proud as could be, clearing his throat loudly "and very affected by some fumes from the galley" (as he kept grunting). I have never been as proud as that day when I finally became a full member of the crew—and passed my jacket in for my new designation modifications: MM2 (SS) CALABRACE, glowing and bursting with pride.

17

Life advanced, hermetically sealed away, with time suspended. But hidden away in our submarine, we bustled and blossomed, wildly working weeks into months within a closed tube, hundreds of feet below the surface of the icy sea. How did we do it? How does one thrive in a closed box? We did it because it needed to be done. We stayed sharp for the sake of one another.

An old Russian Submarine Officer once summed it up well: "Submariners are a special brotherhood, either all come to the surface, or no one does." On a submarine, the phrase 'all for one and one for all' is not just a slogan, but reality.

Although the Jacksonville was a new boat, there were still classic traditions to lift us through the monotony. We always ran to watch dolphins race in the bow waves as the boat left port. Everyone treasured the "Ayooogah, Ayooogah," ship's dive alarm, followed by the "Dive! Dive!" announcement every time the vessel submerged. We also had all the same ancient Naval traditions for equator-crossing ceremonies as anybody else, albeit carried out more discretely than on the surface fleets. "The God of the Sea" always attended, usually in the guise of the most-obese member of the crew. The 'green' kids went through some kind of imaginative ordeal and then were considered "initiated." The boredom momentarily abated, and morale raised.

Everyone got involved in guessing of how long milk and eggs would last before we were forced to endure their awful powdered equivalents. We all rushed to enjoy the sliders and pizza available to us before relieving the midnight watchstanders. But nonetheless, we all complained ahead of time about the culinary concoctions set to be offered in a few days' time. We took on the age-old complaints of the sea, swimming with age-old scripts. We complained about the living space onboard since each man had only a six foot by three foot storage space, six inches deep —at best—for all his worldly possessions. We complained about extra errands, and weather, and delays in Family Grams. The 'Kitsch of Complaining' was rigid and formalized. It was always the trivial things, never enough to be interruptive but never too slight to miss points for style. We needed something… Surprises were minimal, and novelty and distractions were tightly controlled. For me, that very arduous repetition and the regular challenges helped minimize redirects into the other sailors' minds. Instead, we all learned everything about everyone "manually," though of course I learned more. We became open books, archetypes, family. But of course, aboard the small boat we also became casually competitive partisans.

No man onboard was less valuable than the next, but there was a loving sort of sibling rivalry between realms. There were three distinct groups of men onboard a submarine. We refereed to them as the "Nukes," the "Coners" and the "O-Gangers." The nukes were the men who operated the back end of the sub: mostly the nuclear reactor. They were the electricians, reactor operators, and machinists like myself. We compromised about one third of the ship.

The "Coners," (a name that was lovingly attached), were the men who handled the cone-shaped forward end of the boat: the helmsman, planesmen, sonar, radio, weapons, supply, and auxiliary operators.

The "O-Gangers" were the ship's officers: usually numbering about a dozen, with a Captain and Executive Officer at the lead. Ten others officers shared both crew and engineering duties onboard and managed their respective departments of five to fifteen men. Looking back, it's funny that we always spoke of the Captain as the "Old Man," when in reality he was only forty years old. However both enlisted and officers' average age was quite young, (around midtwenties), with only a handful of senior department enlisted Chiefs to guide us.

You couldn't explain the submariners' "Brotherhood of the Phin" to anyone that hadn't experienced it. It wasn't mysterious or secretive, but much deeper than that. Every man on that vessel—from the Captain to the newest seaman—was bound to each other's safety and security, like no other vessel. EVERY single man comprised a vital piece of the operation and was given immediate responsibilities—no matter his rate or rank.

Every man onboard volunteered knowing he would be taken away from virtually all communication with his family, and for months at a time. The vast majority of that time—he wouldn't know where he was going, what his submarine was doing, or even if they'd already been successful at doing it, until long after they'd returned...if ever. He and his shipmates patrolled the deep abyss of the sea for months without seeing anyone but each other. You literally become closer than any fraternity, fellowship, or community. You become brothers, connected at the core, and that connection never left.

In my case, I knew the men more than they would ever realize. I almost felt a sense of betrayal with some of the men after peering into their souls...Was this really *all* they'd chosen to share? Perhaps it was already more than typically shared—in shoreside society—but I knew their passions, their loneliness, their joys, their sorrows, and all the hurt and fears that they wouldn't dare show to another man—yet I still had to play dumb. I knew I was privileged to see their positive emotions on the other spectrum: the pride, the empathy, the thrills, the love and sensitivity. I think it's why I understood better than most when an occasional disagreement or scuffle would break out: I knew the backstories behind most of the frays onboard.

One day, I wasn't thinking of any of those lofty things because something was squirting right into my eye. I was standing a watch in the bowels of the boat, fighting leaks of the lubricating oil and the seawater sprays that always seem to appear on a new ship. It looked like a bad slapstick routine, one spout arriving after another in a whack-a-mole routine, as I stretched and raced and tripped all over myself trying to plug them all. Suddenly the silhouette of a stranger interrupted my private war. A loud voice informed me I was to be immediately relieved and ordered to immediately go to the forward part of the ship, for an interview with a representative from Naval Sea Systems Command.

It wasn't an unusual request during the initial trials of the ship, but one everyone hoped to avoid. Big shots boarding ships for "evals" would often request a random cross-section sampling to give a composite picture of the crew, challenging us with tests of knowledge and best reactions to potential scenarios. However, I certainly thought it unusual that five people came back to get me, including the Ship's Executive Officer, Ships Engineer, my Division Officer, my leading Chief Supervisor, and a Navy Captain who I didn't recognize...That definitely seemed unusual.

As they escorted me forward, they rapidly removed the oil-stained clothing I was wearing and replaced it with new clean clothing, and literally washed me off with towels and soap—on the move. There's a certain coordination demanded to move amid the tight spaces of a sub, and it's not something you want to do blindfolded by a halfremoved uniform. Attempting to ease the tension, I tried to make a joke to my division officer. "You have to take me to dinner before you take me back to your place, Lieutenant!" But the men all seemed too tense for levity. I asked them what was so serious, and my division officer was curt in his response.

"Be quiet, Petty Officer Calabrace. You'll find out in a minute."

The Executive Officer cut in, uncharacteristically animated.

"If *he* asks you anything—answer 'yes sir,' 'no sir,' or 'I don't know sir.' Do not ask any questions. Do you understand?" For some reason, he just oozed worry. What was going on here?

I nodded yes, and muttered a confused but obliging, "Yes, sir."

They brought me to the Commanding Officer's stateroom and simply said, "Stay here, the Captain will be here in a minute." They quickly disbursed, moving mechanically away, though clearly trying to present their motions as casual and routine. What was this?

Two minutes later the Captain arrived. "Petty Officer Calabrace, I know you must be confused and nervous, but the Admiral wants to speak to you."

"The *Admiral*—" I began in a half shout, but the Captain shushed me with a finger, shaking his head. He knocked twice on the door, and a scratchy voice said, "Enter." I stood rooted in position in terror, until the Captain made insistent, panicked eyes at me. He motioned frantically that I should enter—quickly. Once I did so, the Captain shut the door behind me and left us alone in the small room.

The Admiral was a legend in his own time. He stood out not only because of his work, but the way he accomplished it. He'd never matched the tried-and-true mold of a Navy officer at that time. When most Annapolis Navy officer candidates were traditional Catholic and Protestant young men—from well to do families—he'd come from first generation Polish Jewish immigrant stock. He'd always famously despised the good old boy club of the academy, and later the Navy, resenting their assumptions about resting easy on privileged laurels. Personally, he worked with an obsessive drive, and transformed the culture and the thinking in a way the world had never seen. He understood "being different" and never saw it as an excuse for failure. Rather he saw it just as an additional challenge to deal with: an obstacle to learn and grow from. Where others might have given up, he'd exceled and broken barriers wide open, leaving others in the wake of his changes.

As I approached, he was still absorbed in his reading, hunched over his paperwork. He was dressed in a suit that seemed just as dated as his age. I guessed he was in his late seventies but feisty, with thinning white hair, bulging eyes, and thick lips. He didn't look up at first, and just rasped and motioned for me to sit. Finally, he finished a page and turned around to look at me. He didn't speak but just stared at me for a long while, mute. He glanced back down and up again from his paper a few times, perhaps comparing notes to reality, calculating divergences.

"Did your Executive Officer tell you *not to ask me anything*?" he mumbled distractedly, abruptly succumbing to a tremendous yawn. I was enormously relieved by the end to the awkward silence.

In a very quiet voice I slowly replied,

"Yes, sir."

"Well, you just ask me whatever you want. I outrank him," he snapped, with a fiery spark in his eye.

I paused, unsure of what to do or say. I'd been ready for a grilling on my work in the engine room, but this exchange surprised me. I was still in a shocked silence, when he cut off any prospect of waiting for me to find words.

"Well, they tell me you read minds. *Do you*?"

I blinked.

Surely…this couldn't be happening. This was one of those dark dreams—run away with me.

Warily, I started to say "Well, sometimes I—" but before I could say another word he cut me off.

"The Navy pursues a systematic strangulation of anything they don't understand, Calabrace. And they don't understand you."

I stared at him in shock. "I don't understand. They don't even know what I—"

He interrupted, with his eyes bulging. "THEY KNOW. When you were in the hospital last year, they told you that you had a pneumonia? You didn't…They just wanted to run tests on you. I found out, and put a stop to it. I got you out—and I've had someone watching over you ever since."

His words hit me like a ton of bricks. My legs suddenly lost their confidence.

"You're getting out of the Navy soon, Calabrace. *They* will try to recruit you, even they aren't sure why they want you, or what they will do with you." He riffled through the Captain's desk looking for a piece of paper, took a pen out from his inside jacket, and scribbled the name 'Dannels' and a telephone number in some quick, barely legible marks. "You call Captain Dannels at this number if anyone in the Navy or Government bothers you again. He knows how to handle problem people." Then he abruptly made direct eye contact again, paused reflectively, and said, "What am I thinking right now?"

"Sir, I don't know. Sometimes, I get—"

But before I could finish the sentence, he cut me off.

"Get the hell out of here, then. We've got a reactor plant to test!"

As I automatically rose, he continued under his breath, almost as an afterthought, "You know—I always felt irregular when I joined the Navy…but to hell with them. Tell anyone who asks that we discussed mistakes you made in the Engine Room, and how you've learned from them. Sigh; sell it. Be penitent. Now get out; and tell your Captain to get in here.

Shocked, I stared at him for a moment too long, grinning with gratitude.

"Now, Calabrace, Move."

"Yes, sir," I barked.

I left quickly, just to then spend about an hour sitting in the officer's wardroom—where the Captain finally returned to debrief me on my conversation with the Admiral. He asked me what we'd talked about, casually balancing a notepad across his knee, acting like today's interview logistics had been completely routine. I told him the Admiral had asked about mistakes I'd made relating to my job and mentioned how he'd inquired about how I felt about life onboard the sub. The Captain pressed for specifics and tangents, but I answered evasively with more banal generalities. Eventually he looked a bit frustrated by our conversational loops. After about twenty-five more long minutes of crafty fishing, he told me to return to work in the engine room.

I trusted the men onboard, especially our Captain, one hundred percent. Among the best the Navy could provide, he was honorable and looked out for his men better than anyone in the submarine force. But at the same time, instinctually I also knew the Admiral's warning was true: the Navy mold didn't account for irregulars. It would probably be best to keep the hand I'd been dealt close to my chest. Through the uniform, the crumbled piece of yellow-lined paper with the name 'Dannels' seemed huge in my mind, as it scratched against my chest. I imagined my Captain staring right at it through my uniform with some sort of x-ray vision, and I felt like a criminal for hiding the note—but knew I had to. If what I'd heard was true, it might be a necessity later on in my life. So I straightened my back and stared ahead during debriefing, then furtively hid it (and all residual worries) in my heirloom cigarette case that night.

Ψ

The years passed, and my skills and rank grew.

Our Captain left for a new duty assignment, and a new Captain arrived in his stead. He may have been good at what he did, but he had tough shoes to fill. No one on board liked him as well.

We had been out to sea for about two months as part of Carrier group in the gulf of Oman, seeking out and tracking Russian Alpha class submarines. One day I was standing the Engine Room Supervisor watch and was called by my superior to report to Maneuvering, in the Engineering Control Room.

The ship's medical officer was waiting for me at the doorway. A no-nonsense man, he simply demanded I turn over my watch station to Chief Morotini and come with him.

"Wait, what? What's this about?" I protested uselessly, as he walked away at a brisk pace.

In as few grunts as possible, he summarized a vague medical issue that needed to be addressed immediately. I turned over my watch station, and jogged after him to his office space—with my mind racing. There, the ship's executive officer was waiting for us. I was very confused. The executive officer looked down and began in a low voice. "It's been determined that you have an anomaly in your blood cell count, Calabrace. We need to quickly get you off the ship to seek medical attention."

"I feel fine!" I rebutted, both startled and a bit confused. I knew I hadn't reported any issues in the months we'd been at sea.

He ignored me. "Gather your belongings. We're going to surface to meet a helicopter, and it will take you off the boat—today. You're headed to a shore facility, for emergency treatment."

As he started to walk away, he brushed against me in the narrow hallway. I knew immediately that the 'medical emergency' yarn had no truth to it. I didn't know yet what the truth was, but I suspected I had some ominous, rare form of cancer. None of it made sense as I hadn't had a blood tests since before we left Norfolk, two months earlier. Was it the bureaucracy of the Navy Medical Service so bad that it took them two months just to look at results? Maybe he just didn't want to be the one to tell me? I shuddered, suddenly feeling half-dead already. Just when my gift would've been a handy tool, I drew a blank. It figures.

In the whirlwind of the next few hours, I packed my seabag, the ship surfaced, and I climbed topside in a daze. It would turn out to be my last time onboard the USS Jacksonville.

I wasn't allotted any time to say goodbye to the people I trusted most in my life, arguably the closest friends I'd ever had. Instead, all my feelings were obscured by the white noise of helicopter blades roaring above, while the team onboard transferred my few belongings and me to the mechanical bird—plucking me from the chaos I felt. The ride was unreal; I couldn't settle on reality. I felt so alone! I was still lost in shock when we arrived a few hours later, on a tiny ring shaped coral reef, south of the equator in the Indian Ocean.

The sign turned my blood cold. *Diego Garcia.*

My whole career in the Navy, I'd heard rumors that this place was the End of the Line for troublemakers and nobodies, the farthest place from anywhere. They described it as a British protectorate the United States leased for its strategic location: formerly *a leper colony.* It was Tatooine, in the flesh. A harsh land that had found its purpose.

The pilot and crew disbursed, and I stood by the helicopter with a dazed look on my face. A chief appeared and introduced himself politely, gesturing for me to follow—and I did my best. He led me to some low-slung barracks nearby and into a room with a full-sized bed and nice furnishings. All things considered, it was much better than I'd ever have expected, especially after life in my sub rack. He didn't say much; he just made sure I was okay with the logistics. I nodded, numb. In any other situation, I'd have been amazed at how kingly the living situation seemed by juxtaposition. At that moment, I felt nothing.

"I hear you'll be flying out tomorrow, so try to get some rest!"

I asked him if there was a hospital on the base. His face fell.

"Yes, why? Do you feel sick?"

"No, I'm fine."

I'd stumbled across a good litmus test question, which now confused me even more. As I mused over my confusing trap, and his complete casual attitude to my purported medical emergency visit, he explained a bit about the base. He blithely explained where I could get food or a beer, and mentioned that there would be a guy staffing the lobby—in case I decided to go out. He intimated that the base could be tricky to maneuver at night. From what I could see it was basically a grid, with bright roads of crushed coral swarming with coconut crabs, but I took him at his word.

"Welcome to Fantasy Island!" he said, smirking as he left.

The whole situation seemed quite odd. The Navy had thought it important enough to airlift me off a nuclear attack submarine— mid-cycle—for a medical emergency, but then after arriving at a base that had hospital and medical staff, no one thought that I should see a doctor? And now I'd literally been told to relax and rest up, and maybe have a beer? It all seemed so strange. But I allowed myself to dream now of less-dire scenarios, less than the initial ones I'd envisioned in my head. If I was going to explode or something, at least they'd take my blood pressure. Right?

With nothing better to do, I looked around. The modular building had two floors and four small wings, with a common lobby for entry and egress. It had office space downstairs, with what looked like guest quarters upstairs, though I didn't see any guests. I went back in and threw myself on the bed. It seemed so regally grand compared to my my submarine sized rack. After a couple hours of fitful rest, I tried halfheartedly looking at news stations on television. Awful. So instead I headed downstairs for a bite to eat.

I met Matt in the lobby. He was the same rank and rate as me. I immediately saw his 'pictures' when I introduced myself and shook his hand, and I could tell he was a stand-up guy. He had a wife and baby at home, and almost all of his pictures were of them, or his Mom. He'd had trouble with the law in his late teens, evidently. But now I could sense how proud he was to be a reliable husband and Father, even when it meant spending all his time on this little hell hole—Diego Garcia.

As we talked, I discovered that he was from Massachusetts, near where my cousin Elizabeth lived. He had actually enlisted in her home town, Norwood. But my stomach's growling interrupted our conversation: still used to a rigid submarine feeding-schedule.

"Well that's embarrassing," I said as my stomach performed some gymnastics. "Where should I go around here to get some food? Things are getting ugly, apparently."

He paused. "Actually, if you can wait a minute, I'll make a quick phone call, and then take you over there myself. Roberts owes me, anyway. The foods not bad, but it's no New York Pizzeria."

Soon, another Petty Officer showed up to take his place. Matt led me to a pub fare place on the corner of the base. I realized right away that I didn't have a dollar in my pocket. With all the chaos, it hadn't even occurred to me that I was landlocked again, with shore rules. And money. I mentioned it to him, a bit embarrassed.

"Never mind that, Calabrace! You're a Diego Gargia celebrity tonight. The food and beers are on me."

"How am I a celebrity?"

"Well, to be honest John, it doesn't take much here. You're new—it's as easy as that."

We exchanged sea stories. I mentioned that they'd pulled me off the JAX by helicopter, and that I was going stateside for medical treatment. He didn't say much, just looked into his drink, nodding. After a few hours and a few more beers, he finally found some liquid courage.

"If it's not too personal, what's so wrong with you, that they would pull you off?"

I told him I didn't know, just that it was something vaguely to do with my blood. He nodded again, clearly not understanding any better than me. We finished off our food and beers and then walked around for a while, looking at limited landscape the lonely base provided, talking about homes that seemed very far away. Then we headed back to the barracks. I told him I was going up to go to sleep and thanked him for the beers and company.

Shortly after I'd returned to my room, Matt knocked at the door.

"They called while we were out eating. A 'Lieutenant Kopchik' will be by in the morning to pick you up. It'll be around 0800 for breakfast. They want to be ready to arrive at the airfield by 1100."

"Who is Lieutenant Kopchik?"

He hiccupped before responding, and laughed. "I can assure you, I haven't a clue. I've never heard the name Kopchik on Diego Garcia; and it's a small flock we have here. But from what you told me it's a safe assumption he's a medical officer."

As always, thoughts raced through my head at a million miles an hour. In the nine hours after Matt left, I probably got two hours of sleep. I couldn't stop wondering what was going on with my blood, and why everyone I talked to was so dodgy with their answers. I was also angry that my Spidey-Sense wasn't helping me when I needed it to. It was completely sporadic, as if responding in shock to the sudden loss of stability the sub had provided.

Morning came and I shit, showered, and shaved. I sat watching television in my room when a knock on the door came at 0740. I opened the door, and in walked Lieutenant Kopchik. As he introduced himself, I noticed right away from his insignia that he wasn't a medical officer. He was wearing a khaki service uniform, neatly pressed, with his tan garrison cap neatly folded into his belt. He had a gentlemanly bearing and impeccable attention to detail in personal presentation—in the Navy we'd say, "squared away." As I'd spent my Navy service years mostly on submarines, I didn't know a lot of iconography for surface fleet or those shoreside, but I could tell he wasn't a submarine officer as he didn't have the gold Dolphins insignia. He had a gold-winged emblem: a gold parachute. He had about twenty ribbons, but the only ones I recognized were the Rifleman medal and the Navy Distinguished Service Medal. The rest—I hadn't a clue.

"What do you say we go over for breakfast, then we'll grab our seabags? We'll head out soon, with Senior Chief Fable joining us for the ride stateside," he boomed.

From the start, he insisted that Diego Garcia was pretty informal, but once we'd leave it'd be even more so: so calling him CJ would be fine. We would be "attached at the hip" the next few days and would have to stay comfortable. He was right about Diego Garcia being informal. As we walked, there was a hardly ever a salute given, or acknowledged. It was similar to the submarine force: the formal pomp and circumstance was minimized, since you were five hundred feet below the ocean anyway. This was no different: as far off the beaten path as you could possibly get. So we went off to breakfast as if we were just a few average civilians. As we walked, he gestured to our day's route along a paperback geography Atlas. He mentioned his home was near San Diego, and how he couldn't wait to return. Strangely, when our fingertips happened to touch in tracing our way on the map, I saw nothing. No thoughts, no feelings, nothing. That nearly never happened! His images remained hidden.

LT Kopchik was a big guy. He was maybe six feet tall, with massive arms and a strong build. He was the kind of guy you wanted on your side if you ever got into a fight. He reminded me a lot of my friend

Mark Ostrander, who'd served on the Jacksonville with me. Mark worked out every day onboard, right between the main engines. He was very focused with his training and meticulous in his consideration of every mundane detail of life.

Similarly, while I babbled away, Kopchik listened—really listened. His green eyes locked on to anyone he was speaking with and didn't lose contact until the person was finished. He never looked up or down, just directly back at your eyes. This made quite an impression, as I still had the attention span of a five-year-old at twenty-four, and I suddenly felt accountable to it. I was nearly distracted enough to forget the trip we were about to take, and the circumstances. I lurched clumsily back into reality, remembering I was on land again.

"Before I forget, nobody mentioned which uniform I should wear while traveling."

"It doesn't really matter. We'll change into civilian clothes in Kenya, when we refuel."

Thrilled at the straight talk and straight answers, I decided to risk pressing my luck.

"Also, do you know where we're going exactly?"

He didn't pause or consider. "Navy Medical Center, in San Diego."

"LT Kopchik, do you know why?"

"That's what our orders say, and I'll get us all there safely," he said simply. "And call me CJ," he added.

After breakfast, we returned to the room. I changed into my salt and peppers, grabbed my seabag, and headed down to meet LT Kopchik at the van. We arrived at the airport in a few minutes time, and I met Chief Fable. Chief Fable had similar insignia as Kopchik, and they seemed to know each other. Chief Fable was a bit grumpier, but everyone would surely cheer up the closer we got stateside. From the terminal building, we were directed where to head next. LT Kopchik handed me my orders to report in to San Diego, and absentmindedly, as I went grab my bag, I inadvertently grabbed his instead. I felt his hand reach over mine and clasp the upper part of the canvas grip.

"Thith one's mine."

"Excuse me?"

Our hands brushed, and for a moment I saw a glimmer inside LT Kopchik—much more than I'd yet seen. He had a slight lisp when he spoke, and I retroactively realized I'd heard "thith" instead of "this." I immediately regretted my response, though polite, as he immediately straightened back up and seemed to retreat into himself.

However, the moment our hands had intersected, I saw a spurt of images about his past. They were choppy but came at me like a bullet train. He was an only child, and grew up in Southern California alone with his Mom. His Dad had been a Navy pilot but was lost at sea. I wasn't sure when, but Kopchik must have been young when it happened. He'd emotionally shut down after the loss, and developed a bad stutter. It got to a point where he hardly ever talked. Eventually he moved in with his grandparents back East, as his Mom didn't know what else to do to bring him out of his shell. His grandparents adored him and eventually coaxed him back into the light. He moved back to his Mom's place as a teen and really took on the man of the house role. He started excelling in sports and even academics, and—

But just as his story had started to unfold, it stopped.

It seemed kind of strange that his story had just stopped dead. But I'd been frustrated like this before. It was rare, but it had happened a few times: the connection would just go blank, with choppy recall of what I had already seen. I knew I would need to reconnect in the future to get the whole story. In his case, I knew we were going to be stuck together for a while, so I figured the connection would be established soon enough.

We were the only passengers on our plane and had the whole bay to ourselves apart from a large array of pallets and wooden crates of supplies. Three rows of seats with four seats across, bolted to the deck. I sat down on one of the end seats to politely give the other men space—but LT Kopchik asked me to move over one—and Chief Fable took the seat directly next to me on the other side. Thus we started our journey home in a tight little bunch, wearing clunky headphones to minimize the noise. I was kind of glad they'd chosen to sit so close to me, because I knew that if I'd really had some monstrously infectious blood disease or something, they wouldn't. Plus it wouldn't be long until I made physical contact with them, and then I'd finally get a better clue to what was really going on.

We landed in Mombasa, Kenya, where the plane refueled at a civilian airport. We were told to be back onboard within three hours, so we headed to an airport bar to kill the time in civvy style. We sat down and each ordered a twenty-four ounce bottle of "White Lager" beer, which I didn't realize had three times the alcohol content of US branded beers. At six feet tall and one hundred and forty-five pounds, it took only three bottles before I was totally ripped. Luckily Chief Fable and LT Kopchik seemed to be in better shape, probably because of their mass compared to mine. They laughed as they slung me back towards the craft.

We returned to the plane on time and headed towards the next stop: an airbase in Italy. The beer had served its purpose; I slept the whole flight. I was only awakened when I felt Chief Fable shaking my shoulder to tell me we were landing. Laughing, he mentioned that after I got wasted, I'd spent ages babbling on about the funniest things. I was mortified...What might I have said? I certainly had zero memories that could explain the pounding in my head.

But as he shook and awoke me I began to see his story, clear as a bell in my head. He was a decorated Vietnam Vet who'd spent most of his time in the Marines. In the mid-seventies, he'd switched over to the Navy after some personal drama. Evidently he still felt lots of animosity for a guy with whom he'd served with in the Marines, who was responsible for the split.

He believed the guy had ruined his first marriage. The marriage had already been in bad shape, but Chief Fable felt angry and betrayed by the Marine superior who made it worse. After he confided some of his problems to the superior, the guy then turned around and talked about the Chief's complaint with his own wife. Eventually, those complaints made their way through the military wives' circle, whereupon his wife only discovered them third-hand. Needless to say, she was furious, and demanded an immediate separation. Feeling their love had already died, he didn't really mind the separation. But he resented the idea that she'd somehow "defeated" him; that part, he couldn't stand. Emotionally I couldn't understand how he could care less about losing his wife, but feel so indignant that she'd "won a fight." None of that conflict was projected outward: externally—he just seemed like a mid-forties, polite kind of red-neck. He seemed calm and self-assured, if a bit of a smart-ass. Who knew?

He had a group of about ten guys that worked under him. He and Lieutenant Kopchik had worked together several times in the past and had a strong mutual respect for each other's abilities. The Chief was a traditional sailor. Yes, Kopchik outranked him and was more than ten years his junior; but the Chief looked out for everyone he worked with, Officer or Enlisted—it didn't matter. The Chief always kept a big picture overview.

I could see from the Chief's pictures that he thought of the guys who worked for him like he thought of his own kids. He worried about them, but knew they were good at what they did. Two were wild cards that gave him a few headaches, but they both reminded him of himself—when he was younger.

Their units weren't based in subs or even ships; they were land based and multitasked as troubleshooters. I thought maybe they were Seabees; but protocol demands a standard uniform, and theirs didn't add up. Eventually I asked him point blank what his assignments were; and he just told me "me and the boys just go where they need us." The pictures in his head didn't match the words he said—he did a lot more than what he was saying. But I didn't push the issue, and just let myself get lifted up and out of the plane. The guys laughed and called me a lightweight, but they did so in fun.

Still hung-over from the last stop, I decided food might be a better choice this time. We departed the plane and were warned about our departure time. We found some food places quickly and sat and talked as we ate. Soon our flight crew found our trio and joined us too.

The airport in Italy included a mixed group of military people from all over the world. I think I counted at least seven or eight nationalities, based on uniforms. It was like the cantina scene in Star Wars: a mixed bag of novelty nationalities and uniforms that were completely new to me. I was fascinated by the mix. I could only identify three or four uniforms. I couldn't figure out the insignia of the two guys sitting next to us; it was complex and obscured by shadows. I asked our pilot if he could identify the uniform from his position, and he told me they were Saudi pilots.

My eyes fixated on the Saudi's green uniform. Suddenly, even though he was about three or four feet away, I started seeing his images—as if we'd just touched. He was raised a Bedouin, in a very large affluent family. He was the second oldest. His Father, Farid, worked as manager to a Saudi royal family member that controlled defense.

His eyes looked glazed, gazing absentmindedly down our direction along the table, when something inexplicable happened. I abruptly zoomed straight into his head, and found myself right there amid his daydreams. He was musing about why he preferred flying the lighting F.53 to the Northrop F-5E. He preferred the capacity for multitasking as you could carry two Firestreak missiles, two Red Top missiles, twin retractable launchers for 50 mm rockets, or a reconnaissance pod fitted with five 70 mm Type 360 Vinten cameras.

Well! I remember thinking. This is an interesting development!

Our pilot turned to our copilot, motioning at the table where the Saudis were sitting.

"Whaddaya think, Jerry? I bet they're flying those Hawker Hunters you love!"

Without thinking I corrected him, interjecting through the lettuce in my sandwich.

"Nope, they fly the Lighting F.53; it's a much more versatile machine. They used to fly the F-5E, but it didn't perform as well. It got better when they fitted it up with a Litton LN-33 inertial navigation system, and inflight refueling capability so they could use those RSAF's KC-130 aerial tankers."

"Friends of yours, huh?" The copilot wondered aloud, his jaw hanging open.

"No, they're based out of No. 17 Squadron at Tabuk/King Faisal AB.

"Wait, WHAT?" Our pilot had finally managed to re-operate his own jaw after his, too, had been locked in an open position. He could barely achieve the syllables.

What I had just said really made no sense to me, but judging from our pilot's face, he knew exactly what I was talking about. Our pilot looked at me square in the eye and said "How do you know that? Do you speak Arabic?"

I mumbled, "No, sir," and carefully avoided turning to face him, locking my eyes on the Saudi pilot instead.

I scrolled through scenes of his past and inexplicably knew that the Saudi pilot would be having a Tagamet for acid reflux right after he ate. He always kept extras in a pill bottle, kept in his upper, right hand pocket. Feeling crazy, I attempted to test this trivia's veracity. (It seemed too easy!) But after about only thirty seconds, I watched him robotically reach across his chest with his left hand and pull out a pill bottle. He excused himself from the table to go get a glass of water from the cafeteria lunch counter. I watched mesmerized, with a huge grin spreading across my face.

"You okay?" our pilot asked slowly, dumbfounded.

"Yes, sir—just feeling a bit strange."

At this point all the rest of the people at our table were staring at me, obviously with good reason. I awkwardly swallowed my crust and stared at my crumb-covered napkin.

Somehow I managed to convince the rest of my tablemates that I must have read something about the Saudi Air Force, to try and explain away my ramblings that afternoon. I made a joke that we had a lot of free time—plotting dots and chasing Alphas—which half worked. Luckily, time was on my side. Blinking back to the present, our co-pilot mentioned we needed to get back to the plane. Saved by the bell! But close, I thought. Entirely too close.

Ψ

This Saudi pilot incident opened up a whole new chapter of things which I'd never expected. On one hand, it scared the shit out of me. It was all new and bizarre, and instinctively I just wanted it to stop. Life on the sub was probably the closest I'd ever been to well-adjusted normalcy, and I wasn't nearly ready to give that all up. I kept hoping all this "would just blow over" somehow.

On the other hand, I was thrilled. I'd wanted to pull more stories and emotions from his head, and I felt thrilled when it worked. I could barely disengage myself from doing so. It was the first time I'd ever connected to another person with only proximity contact—and it was thrilling. It was like a roller coaster ride at an amusement park: the first time a bit scary, but as you learned the nuances of the track, you knew how to ride it—and sometimes to enjoy it. As far as I could remember, every person that I could *read,* we'd always experienced some type of physical contact: a touch, a handshake, a hug. With him, however, there was none of that. He was sitting several feet away, and the ONLY contact we had was when my eyes locked on him.

Apparently, now, this was enough.

I cringed to imagine how much this might change things, remembering how vulnerable and unpredictable I'd felt when adjusting to the gift in the first place.

More and more, from that day going forward, I imagined my brain seeing memories and emotions as if they were several decks of different colored playing cards—all thrown together. Perhaps it was the way my own memory had been colored by Gramps, so many years ago? Emotions stood in for the suits (spades, hearts, diamonds, and clubs) and all the associated memories stretched like numbers in increasing intensity. For example, I'd see a king of hearts as a very high love emotion. A three of diamonds could be a moment of joy, an eight of spades could be pain or loss in someone's life. My mind instantly sorted all these memories, emotions, and their associated impact on a person's life as easy as it could sort a few decks of different colored playing cards. I would simply call it 'pictures' but there was no way to truly describe it to anyone that hadn't experienced it.

It also became easier to put together predicated conclusions based on actions that had happened in a person's past. My mind intuited exactly how to combine things and could analyze the proverbial hand one had been dealt, instantly. Then, based on their emotional and memory reference library, I'd draw a logical conclusion of what would happen, usually long before the person carried through on those actions. It was like their playbooks were pre-drawn in my head, and I only waited to see the performance. It truly fascinated me to watch but also scared the hell out of me.

By the time we left Italy I was totally exhausted. Every drop of energy had left me, and every cell was thrilled to sleep in the cavernous hold of that cargo bay. Our flight lifted into the afternoon sky without incident, and we were on our way to our final stop—San Diego.

As I closed my eyes, I remember thinking, "these guys must think I'm nuts."

In San Diego, I'd find that I wasn't far off.

18

We arrived at Coronado North Island Naval Air Station late in the afternoon, and I was told that we would all be staying in transient housing for the night. It looked like every brick motel ever made, with a tall center block towering over the adjoining wings. A cracked concrete roof sheltered the central lobby entranceway, where a receptionist yawned. A rather anticlimactic end to our long journey.

After the long days of travel fatigue, I was surprised that both LT Kopchik and Chief Fable were spending the night, too. They were both from San Diego, so I'd assumed they'd be anxious to see family and friends or something. On the other hand, I was glad they were staying, since I knew no one in San Diego. We found a crummy pizza place on-base, and then headed to the rooms for the night. Though we had connected rooms, within a few minutes CJ knocked, and asked if he could use the spare bed in my room because of some ventilation/air conditioning issues in his. I told him that would be fine.

That night I had my first clear read of CJ Kopchik. I'd seen bits and pieces of his memories before, but this time it was everything. I saw that it hadn't been mere coincidence but actually his explicit mission to see that I made it to the Naval Medical Center in San Diego. All he'd been told was that I had both physical and psychological issues, so it was imperative that he deliver me quickly and safely to San Diego. He was also told that the Navy considered me a critical asset, without anyone elaborating why. At first I felt somewhat betrayed, but then again he never implied otherwise.

I'd assumed that he was a Seabee for no reason, but in reality he was an Intelligence Officer for the Navy Seals, based out of Coronado Island. Until recently, he'd served aboard the USS Nimitz, and prior to that he'd been involved in Operation Eagle Claw: an unsuccessful attempt to free hostages in Iran. It only took a moment of sorting through his mind to see that his strongest emotions were trust, honesty, and self-confidence. He truly believed there was nothing he couldn't accomplish. My Mother would have loved him.

After only a few days together, he already felt nothing but admiration for me. He'd accepted me into his inner trust circle almost immediately, something even he found a bit odd.

He couldn't piece together why his superiors viewed me as a critical asset. It wasn't until Italy that his interest and curiosity flared up, and he started putting the pieces together. In his mind, he'd already moved beyond believing the narrative about psychological problems that might be dangerous to those around me, and now believed he was witnessing a crucial part of those assets that he'd been entrusted to safeguard. I also learned that there was no ventilation issue in his room; it was just an instinct to protect me further—once he thought he understood what he was protecting.

The next morning we grabbed a quick breakfast and started the trek over to the Naval Regional Medical Center San Diego. I thanked Chief Fable and CJ and climbed into a waiting van. A Hospital Corpsman named Max introduced himself and said he would be facilitating my check in to the hospital. It was a quick ride.

Peering out the window I could see the hospital: a semicircular drive followed by row after row of four-story Spanish Colonial buildings. It looked like a bad dream—some sort of scary Mexican resort gone wrong. I was brought to the San Diego Naval Hospital Surgical Building and checked into a room on the fifth floor. It was a private room with a private bath, telephone, and a television—luxuries any submariner could get used to. Max hastily clarified that the telephone would only work for local calls, and if I needed any long distance calls, I would need to get approval from floor nurse.

The feeling of comfort and safety fell away almost immediately, as fear and loneliness set in. What were they going to tell me about my blood? Was it cancer? Was it worse? I knew it had to be life threatening, or they would never have pulled me off. I also knew every story I'd heard so far had only been shades of the truth, and I couldn't understand why. Since we'd left Diego Garcia I'd let such thoughts go, but now that I was here, I'd have to face them.

I spoke to the floor nurse about calling my parents. She told me she was busy at the moment but would get back to me later and arrange something. I also asked her about when I would be seeing a doctor, and she told me Dr. Peter Van Aiken who would be coordinating my care. He was en-route to see me, so I was advised to return to my room.

I sat on the side of my bed waiting, my mind racing a mile a minute, trying to play out every grisly end scenario that a doctor might throw at me. What kind of cancer? How many months? Kidney disease? Would I be on dialysis forever? If it was an issue of blood flow to my heart, surely I'd need a transplant...What if they don't have a donor? I was trying to think of everything my family members had died from, but drew a blank. They were all healthy and alive! And yet here I was, destined to find out my own demise was near?

All of a sudden a voice interrupted my thoughts, and I jumped ten feet in the air.

"John? Hi I'm Dr. Van Aiken. I'll be your primary care doctor while you're here in San Diego."

He was a bizarre-looking man. He stood at maybe six-two or six-three, and had exceedingly long, thin fingers. Graying brown hair topped a head smaller than the rest of his body. He wore the standard military issue, black plastic glasses.

I slowly reread his name, embroidered in script on his upper pocket, as the moment became real: this was happening. Though strangely, I felt more secure once he stepped inside.

He sat down on a chair next to the bed, his eyes peering up from his glasses. "Okay, I can only imagine what's been going through your head, since you left the—" he looked down at the paperwork in his folder, and then continued, "the, uh....Jacksonville. You had a few strange results on some routine medical tests: a small mass that needs removal—but nothing we can't correct. The Navy just wanted to play it safe and get you here to correct the issue before it became something serious." I felt a short moment's relief hearing that I wasn't going to die anytime soon. But the relief quickly passed as my mind filled with pictures and memories from Dr. Van Aiken's head.

The words he'd said about the Navy were rehearsed and untrue: in fact, nothing about my Navy file was routine. My health, on the other hand? Of that, he was confident and he *was* telling the truth. Evidently I wasn't about to die, but did have some sort of growth in my stomach they needed to remove. Though he projected a confident and secure air, he felt deeply uncomfortable lying to me about why I was there, but felt like he had to.

In spite of his attempted deception, I felt truly empowered by the news, even more so by his sense of protectiveness. I'd already been warned about the military machinations currently at play. Beyond that, this man would be more than capable to provide necessary medical care, and if they did some additional tests, so be it. I think for the first time in my life, I wasn't afraid what was going to happen. I was there truly for one reason: they saw me as a possible asset. They only wanted to learn about, control, and direct whatever ability I might have—for their own ends.

Although what exactly those ends might be, I couldn't see yet…

Hundreds of his pictures and memories raced through my head in fractions of a millisecond, along with his surging emotional accompaniment. He'd been told to absolutely avoid physical contact with me, and more importantly, to help assure me that I'd only been brought in for my own benefit and protection. He didn't believe the Department of Defense reports he'd read on someone who could 'foretell the future' or 'read minds,' but intuited there was a simple scientific answer behind all the hype. He'd actually believed it to be a waste of time and resources to bring me there, but someone above him in the chain of command in Washington had believed otherwise.

He wasn't military but actually an employee of the National Science Foundation: an organization that sounded pretty nonthreatening. He was a psychiatrist, so clearly not the guy who was going to physically remove my appendix—or whatever was brewing inside me. I didn't understand most of what I saw, but I could easily see that he was only telling me partial truths…so I didn't trust him.

He was a graduate of Duke Medical School, and had been recruited right out of his residency by the FBI. He'd made the move to Army about ten years later but despised working under bureaucracy—so he'd taken this position to escape Army life. He liked his job at the National Science Foundation, and he was considered a leader of his field: Neuropsychiatry and Synesthesia.

I grouped the factions I met at NRMCSD into three types: the white hats, the black hats, and the stars and stripes.

The white hats were the ones I knew to be forthright and honest, who I trusted to have my best medical and professional interests at heart. There were three white hats: Dr. Nitzkorski (the surgeon), Dr. Elkarra (the director of Clinical Research at NRMCSD), and Dr. "Mike," a psychologist from Stanford Cognitive Science Lab.

The two black hats were Dr. Van Aiken and Dr. Ann Robinson: a staff neurologist at NRMCSD. She didn't even pretend to be warm and friendly, but walled herself up behind a cold blank stare every time I saw her. Unlike Dr. Van Aiken, she believed whatever my brain could do with its "memory exercises" might be useful for the Department of Defense and thought about me exclusively through a terrifying prism of words like "compulsion" and "involuntary extraction."

The only consistency with the black hats was that they all shared a common confusion in terms of what they thought I could actually accomplish. They'd all been briefed that I had some type of advanced cognitive abilities. These abilities were described as being "enhanced by physical contact with outside subjects." Furthermore, the brief had implied additional talents: for example, that my gift "would potentially allow remote viewing of contacts, even after physical contact had been terminated." Their job was thus to gather data on those abilities and feed it back up the chain of command.

The third faction were the stars and stripes: military men and women, plus intelligence services. For some reason, they were generally the easiest to get a read on, as most were direct and mission oriented. Their heads were very clear—they knew exactly what they wanted. They wanted clear True or False—actionable—facts about my capabilities. They also sought additional testing done, to solidify or challenge all the vague theories then in vogue about the nature of my gift. If they determined that my gifts were truly significant, they hoped to set up a timely plan to exploit them. They wanted reins.

In a way, it felt good to know what they wanted—I felt less threatened. However, I had no idea if I could deliver the outcomes they were hoping for. I had no idea what level of risk I'd be in for if they realized my gifts were incompatible with their wants or needs, and the Admiral's warning rang heavy in my head. The only thing I knew at that point, was that nobody was going to find out about what had happened with the Saudi pilot who loved planes. All those long nights playing bridge with my grandparents had taught me to recognize a trump card when I saw one.

This one, I needed to keep to myself—at least for now.

The first three days in the hospital were a nonstop battery of tests. I can't think of one part of my body that was immune from the mix. Blood, urine, and mouth swabs were taken more times than I could count, followed by every other medical-test acronym ever imagined. They mentioned unfamiliar names in passing: EEG, ENG, PET, MRI, CT and Polysomnograms—like so many exotic birds.

Of course, a second after meeting the nurses and technicians, I shared their technical understanding of what the tests were supposed to accomplish. But I happily played dumb, as they bent over backwards to dumb it all down. A nurse named Margaret wheeled me around for ages, saying things like, "John, this is Dave, he'll be doing your CT scan. It's like a fancy X-Ray, and we look at it on the computer."

She said the words extremely slowly, in a loud Georgia drawl. I found myself wanting to interject, "Like an X-Ray with a 10mm wide beam that takes a transverse section of the skull? Lemme guess: it can see hundreds of different levels of density—it can see internal tissues that are parts of other organs—it uses composite data to develop a 3D cross section visual display? Did I miss anything?" But instead I just kept quiet, laughing inwardly. Shaking my head, I tried to personify the word "gosh," a word I'd heard Joe-Bob on the JAX mutter a few dozen times. I kept intermittently babbling, "Oh yeah, okay, sure," as if I didn't really understand the hows and whys. Other times, my highbrow doctors tried to explain—in detail—what they thought was going on my brain.

"Physiologically, John, the beginning of long-term memory is actually a process of physical changes of neurons in the brain. This series of events commences a process known as "long-term potentiation." (Phrases were pronounced slowly, and in distinct syllables—as if speaking to a disobedient dog.) "Whenever new sights, memories, or emotions are encountered, circuits of neurons in the brain, known as 'the neural network,' are created, altered, or strengthened."

Perhaps getting a bit mischievous in my frustration, I'd nod my head solemnly, with huge eyes, like I wasn't comprehending a word but was terrified to say so.

But it was never over that easily. They'd inevitably continue: "This neural network is composed of neurons that interact with one another through relays or junctions, called 'synapses.' Then, new proteins are created within those neurons, and the strength of certain circuits of neurons in the brain is reinforced! Do you see?"

They'd pause for effect, and I'd hang my mouth open. Sometimes I went to extremes, just to see if they'd discern that I was screwing with them. It never happened. Nonplussed, more wonders followed.

"With repeated use, the efficiency of these synapse connections increases, facilitating the passage of nerve impulses along particular neural circuits, which may involve many connections to the visual cortex, the prefrontal cortex, and medial temporal lobe."

Even *they* yawned.

I'd barely managed to keep my wits about me, struggling to survive the boredom.

Looking deep into the mind of one expert—I saw exactly how much all this information meant to him, how very challenging the struggle had been in university to master those entry-level classes, always dreaming of advancement. Never recognized as an intelligent pupil, the poor young doctor had spent all his student years with a chip on his shoulder, eager to prove his intellect and academic prowess. Thus he'd grown to see the information as pure, sacred, and almost holy. I couldn't resist saying what I did next. I tried to resist, but I…I couldn't.

"So it's like in the Hall & Oates song, 'like the flame that burns the candle, the candle feeds the flame?' "

There was a split second pause.

"What?!"

"What you just started to say about neurons, synapses, and all that *stuff*, 'like the flame that burns the candle—the candle feeds the flame,' and that's what happens in my head, right? The more memories I collect, the faster and more efficiently it all works? Is that what you're saying, Doc?"

"Well, *yeah*. In a way..."

Sweat beading on his face, I watched something spiritual die—deep down in the poor doctor. After that, we spent a whole lot less time going through meticulous explanations.

Soap operas filled a lot of my time. Not on television, just through the increased receptivity I'd been feeling to strangers' thoughts since being exfiltrated from all my normal routines and challenges. My bored brain couldn't help it. It latched onto the world wherever it could. So I wondered about my nurse, and abruptly, had to wonder no longer.

Though she always had the sweetest demeanor with me, nurse Margaret was a deeply frustrated woman. She was one of two sisters, and evidently her younger sister Evelyn always gained all the attention in the family because she was an "artist." She'd never gotten over the injustice, even as an adult. In spite of the fact that she'd graduated Georgia Baptist Nursing College and continued her service for the Navy, her family was never impressed. Her sister still lived at home ten years after graduation and still hadn't sold a picture to anyone other than a family friend. But the artist was the belle of the ball, while poor ol' Margaret was chopped liver.

The trivial soap operas of my hospital stays eventually blurred, competing with days on end of endless meetings with psychologists, psychiatrists, therapists. We exhaustively covered every moment in my childhood, my teen years, and my adult life. Based on their recent memories, most of them had no idea what they were seeking from me—or what to expect. They were just told to record every detail I babbled out, and to look for patterns—and triggers.

Some days were tedious. The same questions were looped again and again, in the hope that intellectual fatigue and boredom might break down any residual resistance, so they would get perfect honesty. They almost seemed disappointed that I'd come from a simple, loving, hardworking family. We finally addressed the bowl at my Grandmother's house, and how the floodgates had opened. Every grade-school incident felt like they were trying to set up a trap. Their minds were racing with difficult questions they'd been ordered to press, though they tried to come across as easygoing—and work them in naturally.

Seeing the taboo questions highlighted surprised me, as I'd rarely, if ever, discussed these scenarios with anyone. Somehow, they knew certain stories existed nonetheless. Somebody had been doing their homework.

Weeks became months, a whirlwind of tests, doctors, trial and error.

Nobody really knew what they expected to find, or what was there. They brought in professors from universities, brought in an NSA psychiatrist, and some furtive-looking CIA and the Defense Intelligence Agency psychologists. Eventually a broad array of Navy and Army neurological experts marched through to see the show. Even a famous Two Star Army General who was an outspoken advocate of psychic warfare peered in at me for a while.

They moved me from the hospital to some rather nice guest quarters on the base, but mostly my interactions would still be the hospital staff—and CJ. He'd been reassigned to help me during my stay in San Diego. Having CJ stay on during the tests was purely a goodwill gesture on their part, for me, as I had absolute trust that he'd have my back in any situation.

At first, they routinely fed me false information about the people I was meeting. But seeing through to the core of people was what I did best. Eventually my smirks gave me away. After the first week and a few whispered conversations, they dropped that tactic. Even if someone was watching me from one way glass or via a camera, I somehow intuit it. I'd mention it to them, knowing it would spook my concentration. They were at wits' end for getting around "my intuition." You'd think with all these brilliant minds around me, someone would put two and two together: to conclude that if I could sense people that I couldn't see or touch, I probably didn't need the physical contact I still strenuously insisted I did to make a mental connection.

There were only a few hospital people who I felt comfortable confiding in: the surgeon who removed my tumor and the clinical research director. They believed that the other doctors/professionals were pushing too hard, while both felt their sole interest was their patient....me. They knew that sometimes I was scared of what was ahead, so they did their best to try to help me. They offered constant suggestions and prescriptions to help "turn off my brain," so I might finally achieve a few hours of sleep at night. Since I'd been brought to San Diego, my mind just wouldn't ever shut off. It almost seemed dependent on finding new memories to capture, regardless of me or what I needed.

The testing continued for months, with constantly-added variables. Mostly meetings were one on one and they'd lineup an impossible spectrum of people for me to meet. They'd make the introductions, then watch from a different room via a camera—or one-way glass.

One day, while going through my things, I came across a forgotten piece of paper marked Dannels with a number scribbled beneath. If ever it might be useful to me, now was the time.

So one day, while no one was really paying me any attention, I called him up. I was surprised that he even knew who I was. He didn't mince words, but just told me he would be in contact with me soon.

They finally got it in mind to stop beating around the bush and start testing my abilities. At first, the testing was limited to use on "vetted people" whom I encountered on the hospital floor, but later it broadened to other patients in the hospital. When they tested my ability to read patients who were suffering from post-traumatic stress, I discovered some of the worst emotional pain I've ever known. In my easy experiences up until this point, things had gotten to a point where it was almost like a game—my mind innocently wanted more and more access to strangers' minds. I was fascinated by the memories that people had and always hungered to access more. But that wasn't the case with these new people. It was torment: plain and simple.

There was so much anger, fear, numbness, guilt, and depression! These interruptive feelings would snap sharply on and off— without warning. I couldn't take looking for more than a few minutes at a time, as the intensity burned me out completely. These were the deepest, darkest memories I would ever see. All their normal memories and emotions seemed completely suppressed by the feelings of guilt, pain, worry, and sadness. It was impossibly difficult to access the deeper, better memories…so I could only imagine the pain these people felt themselves on a daily basis. Dr. Robinson and Van Aiken always insisted I try more and more, though of course, they were aloof—distanced behind their clipboards. But after a few minutes I always ignored their requests out of self-preservation— just to save my own sanity. I'd lurch my focus onto someone else, some passing stranger, some bystander—anyone. My heart raced to a point where it pounded through my chest. My hands shook to a point where only clasping them together kept my composure. Eventually, I reported that only minimal contact could be made, that fuller access was effectively blocked by the memories of pain and suffering. Luckily they accepted that, and we moved on. I wondered for years what would've happened if I'd had the courage to force myself in deeper.

I noticed that as they grew more confident in my abilities, they spent dramatically more time and energy trying to shield themselves…from me: from those same abilities they sought. Whoever came to get me for appointments generally only knew that they were to bring me to a location. They'd never be told 'why' or 'with whom.' I'd then be handed off to a second or third party. The more they attempted to shield their developing plans for me, the less physical contact I was permitted with the higher authority figures. I guess they hoped that by shielding me from information, they might keep my awareness at bay.

One day, my nurse suggested a trip to Point Loma Sub base where I'd have a small reunion of some of my old shipmates recently reassigned there. Team morale being exceptionally low amid the post-traumatic stress experiments, the scientists reluctantly agreed to release me for a day. Once we arrived, I had lunch with two old friends, Steve and Ray, who were now assigned to the local Submarine Squadron. Steve was one of the best electricians on JAX, and Ray was one of the best mechanics I had ever met. Both were looking forward to their new roles in the civilian world.

We caught up on old shipmate gossip for a few hours and had a great exchange of sea stories. However, by this point, I'd already been meticulously warned about which things I should be revealing to people, outside the closed group in the hospital. The story was to be simple: I suffered from an irregular pattern of seizures, one that the medical community hadn't seen before. They weren't sure of the cause but were frantically studying it—hence all the tests and the urgency. Because it was a medical anomaly, they were working with interested parties at the Stanford University School of Medicine, developing clinical research trial to eventually obliterate it. I implied that I would only be under their care for a year or two. I'd used this same story when talking with my family over the past few months. There was more truth in it than not—so it was easily spoken and believed.

We spent the afternoon walking along the beach. My friends brought me up to a clearing on top the base, where you could see the submarines below—in their cove. I saw a few super-sized Aircraft Carriers across the bay, through the mists of the Pacific, over on the San Diego side. It was a wonderful afternoon, and wonderful to feel a bit of that lost laughter and comradery. But by around four p.m., CJ mentioned that we had to get going soon; so we said our goodbyes and parted company. At first everything seemed normal, but after only a few moments in the vehicle, I sensed a change. I could clearly see within CJ's head that he'd been ordered to bring me to a different part of the base before we returned "home."

As we drove off, we abruptly changed directions—as if we were in an old gangster-movie car chase. Veering away from the exit, we continued a short way, and then I saw a new sign upon a separate gate: Space and Naval Warfare Systems: Center Pacific. We entered.

It was a highly secure section of the base. The second I looked at CJ, I knew why we were there. He clearly knew that I knew and smiled. We pulled up to a small brick building, where an awkward-looking Dr. Aiken stood waiting, along with another gentleman I'd never met before.

"Hi John, I'm Jim. Nice to meet you," he called out. "I've heard quite a bit about you!"

Surprisingly, he didn't try to keep his distance. We shook hands and I was dumbfounded by what I saw. Jim was a medical doctor, scientist, and professor. More specifically, he was the primary neurologist at the Navy Marine Mammal Program, US Naval Space & Warfare Center. He had more knowledge in his head than anyone I'd ever met. His memories and emotions were overwhelmingly positive and earnest—almost like he wanted me to understand what he was about. There were no hidden agendas buried within him. I trusted him immediately. That trust only grew after he pulled me away midsentence, barking to Dr. Van Aiken, "Pete, why don't you stay here? We'll be fine. We'll meet you back up topside at 19:00."

Jim took CJ and I down to his office, where he explained what he did in more detail. He showed us two short films on his work with bottlenose dolphins and sea lions. He truly loved what he did. His main focus was trying to understand their sonar capabilities, and more broadly figure out the best, most nurturing working-conditions for various marine animals.

He got right to the point. "John, we want you to try and see if you can connect with the dolphins. We have an artificial lagoon over there, where you can wade in and meet them. I'll be with you the whole time. If you say no, I'll fully understand....but please don't say no."

I looked at CJ and he smiled. I smiled too and nodded.

We spent the next few hours in the lagoon area. It was a bit awkward at first: it was packed. Three other civilian staff members and a Navy Commander stood there, jockeying for optimum views and talking into recorders...The dolphins swam closely and then dart away, but I couldn't really sense anything, even when making a quick rub on one of their bellies. I quietly informed Jim that I couldn't really concentrate, at least not with so many people in the area. He laughed and banished them all to the hanging observation box overlooking the lagoon.

Then it happened. I was sitting on the edge of the decking surrounding the lagoon, and a female dolphin named Josephine kept coming within a few feet of me. We all saw some type of pattern developing. I moved, and so did she, each time making the same high pitched whistle as she came closer. Jim suggested he and CJ leave me completely alone, and they stepped out of the way. My feet dangled in the water, and Josephine immediately approached. She brushed by them, not once or twice but three or four times, each time stopping or slowing enough that I could reach down and touch her dorsal fin.

It was one of the strangest sensory experiences I ever had. I was able to feel emotion inside her, but it wasn't like anything I'd ever experienced previously. Josephine knew what was happening, as the moment I connected mentally with her the complex language of whistles and clicks surged forward in repetitions, faster and faster. She was clearly processing tons of emotion, with a highly-refined sense of intuition—although I didn't understand how.

It was so different than what a person felt! It was many levels faster and more interwoven: she felt several emotions in an instant, where a person might only feel one. "Feel" perhaps isn't even the right word, as it was on a completely different level than anything I'd ever felt. She tried to communicate with me, but I could only feel fragments. It was like she was writing words for me to read, but I couldn't quite see them. I felt that they were there, but had no idea what they meant. After another hour or two of trying, I felt getting exhausted; Josephine was, too—so we called it a day. After debriefing with Jim and happily accepting his offer to return, we headed back to San Diego.

Clearly, I'd taken my first step into a much deeper ocean.

19

Dawn glowed through the curtains. As always, I clumsily careened into the morning light in a panic, hurtling straight out of wild storm of images that always pursued me through the restless nights. I'd become accustomed to awaking like a man sputtering to life in an old bathtub, after falling asleep in the water. Sleep had become a feverish place, where teeming sights and flickering images jumbled themselves together—daring my subconscious to make sense of it all, or my sanity to make room.

With every passing day, I was getting better at trying to look normal. But inside I was becoming a poorly-bound encyclopedia of unfamiliar worlds, tied into knots. Nothing ever left! Not a dare, not a trauma, not even some stranger's ex-girlfriend's phone number— that was long ago cried over. None of it was mine, but nonetheless there it was. Deep in the shelving of me, there they stayed—all those pictures. I would never understand why.

Fortunately, a team of familiar faces had been assembled around me who knew me and my eccentricities. CDR Doug Lewis was the Navy Commander in charge, with CJ acting as his deputy. Two other junior Naval officers and a half dozen military and intelligence people, regularly briefed, observed all my testing. Every morning we assembled at the same time, and the routine did me good. I felt safe with them, trusting that their primary mission centered on my safety and security.

However, there were things that I could never seem to read off of Commander Lewis, which troubled me. I could see his whole life story like it was an open book: his career, his family, his highs and lows. But somehow, certain nuances of his professional life seemed shielded from me—I could barely even sense his chain of command. After the ease I'd found in accessing every other subject, it was jarring to face such an overt hole in my capabilities. The one time I absentmindedly mentioned something about it, he gently, but firmly, shut down the question with, "I'm with the good guys, John. But *stay out* of my head."

One morning I was asked to join the team for a briefing first thing after breakfast. But afterwards, CJ and I headed off in a different direction than either our normal meetings—or the hospital. When I asked him where we were going, he just smiled and implied, "wait and see." A moment later, BOOM, it came to me, a blast from the past.

We were going to meet Captain Dannels!

We drove out past some office buildings and parked. I jumped out and headed toward the closest building, but CJ gently grabbed my shoulder and spun me ninety degrees, gesturing in the proper direction. We walked about a quarter mile across a parade ground, toward a baseball diamond. I saw the silhouette of a man sitting in the bleachers by himself in his summer white uniform, eating an ice cream cone—at seven in the morning. I laughed inwardly, as I recognized him to be the legendary Captain Dannels. There was no game going on, just an empty, well-manicured field. Finishing the ice cream, he wiped off his hands and reached out to shake with a grin. There was no hesitation, he even used his left hand to grasp my forearm during the strong shake. I interpreted it as a dramatic show of respect to me, since he knew once contact was made, any secrets he had were gone.

"Hi John, I'm Jeff. Nice to finally meet you. Let's go for a walk, shall we?"

I started walking beside him. CJ fell in, too, strolling protectively a few paces behind us.

Captain Dannels thought better of it and called out over his shoulder, "Lieutenant, why don't you stay here? I think we'll be fine."

CJ obliged and began stretching instead. Off we went.

Three or four seconds down the track, Jeff turned to me and grinned.

"So? Do I check out? What are you seeing about me right now?"

My mind ran on overdrive, pictures whizzing by. He was entirely unguarded and sincere: with strong, solid memories, and clear emotions. He was of a pedigree I'd rarely known. His family was self-made financially, with an Uncle who was a US Senator from Connecticut. Jeff was third generation Navy—both his Dad and Granddad were Submarine Captains. He LOVED what he did. He'd been selected as a Rhodes Scholar right out of the Naval Academy and had been a rising Naval star ever since. Everyone knew his career pipeline would lead to him becoming the first Admiral in his family tree, and probably not the last. From morning to evening he breathed Navy. His wife always wryly referred to herself as his 'mistress,' knowing his first true love was and would always be the Navy.

He was brilliant. He devoured and processed knowledge like most men eat a hearty meal, and he loved that similarity between our personalities. He was self-confident and had every right to be. He was respected by all, both above and below him in the chain of command. He was wildly protective of me. He also knew a lot more about me than anyone I had ever met before.

"So…" he interrupted, "do I pass muster?"

"Yes, sir," I muttered.

"No 'sir' is necessary, John—you're no longer in the Navy! Jeff is fine."

He was right and had the envelope in his pocket with my official honorable discharge. He started to pull the papers out, but instead pulled his hand away with them still hidden in his pocket, and just smiled.

"You know exactly what I have, don't you?"

I laughed and admitted that I did.

He started to explain that my six-year obligation of duty had actually expired two months earlier. But by the time he'd said "six-year obligation," I understood everything. The Navy had kept me overwhelmed with work, hoping I wouldn't realize my enlistment obligation was up. (I hadn't.) They were afraid I might run from the Navy, and they didn't want to lose me, Dannels explained.

"You're not going to run, are you John? Lieutenant Kopchik is pretty fast, he'd catch you anyway." Then he yelled out, "Isn't that correct Lieutenant Kopchik?"

CJ's voice floated back immediately but muted, as though uncertain. "Yes sir, I'll always have your back. Definitely not eavesdropping though, sir—"

It was an unusual conversation we had over the next two hours. He got the truth, the whole truth, and boy did it feel good to finally share it with someone! He knew far more than I'd ever been aware of. He mentioned three events that I'd long forgotten: things that happened when I was aboard the Jacksonville that had been immediately fed back to him. I discovered that he'd known about me far earlier than my initial encounter with the Admiral, onboard JAX. I was also quite surprised to learn that CJ actually reported to Captains Dannels, but even CJ didn't know it.

Captain Dannels had set up a sort of "interested reporting protocol" regarding me—one that had been operating for years. He had essentially created dummy command structures of elaborate subterfuge for everyone that interfaced with me. They would report to an actual superior at a made up dummy command, conspicuously outside Captain Dannels' organization. That person would then report to Captain Dannels. This way, even if I'd breached my local superiors, I would only be able to see a limited sphere of where the information was headed. Finally, my blind spots relating to CDR Doug Lewis made perfect sense.

We walked around a few more minutes, with him doing most of the talking. Finally we stopped and he looked me right in the eye, saying incredulously, "You already know my whole goddamn life story, don't you?"

"Yes…" I replied robotically, automatically, almost embarrassed that I'd been peering into his memories from the moment we'd met.

"Okay, fine. Ready for a pop quiz, Calabrace?"

"Sure," I said. "Go for it."

"My sons' names?"

"Brian and Eric. Brian is a Navy pilot, Eric is a senior at Notre Dame."

"My favorite song?"

"All Day, and All of the Night, by The Kinks."

"Well, it's a classic." He paused and scratched his head. "My Mother-in-law's birthday?"

I couldn't isolate the info immediately—and stalled, "I don't know, give me a minute."

"Don't bother, I never remember it either, so I doubt you'll find it." He grinned. "Hmm, one more. What submarine did I serve as XO on, and who was the CO?"

"Glenard P. Lipscomb: SSN-685, and the CO was Caldwell. You still feel he was the most brilliant CO you've met in your career, after he taught you there's more to being a CO than just being a good boat driver."

Dannels laughed, nodding, and then we really started talking.

He knew many of the "pieces of my puzzle" that I didn't. He'd carefully reviewed every bit of the medical, psychological, psychiatric reports, all the tapes and video as they'd been taken. Although he'd read every brief and screened every test over the years, he wanted to know the mechanics of how it all worked, straight from my mouth—from my vantage point and experience of things. He was like a child in a toy store, his eyes opening wider and wider with each question answered.

For the first time in many months, I didn't just feel like a specimen in a jar, or an animal at the zoo, but like a real human being whose experiences could provide the answers that he craved. There was real empathy there. He wanted to know all the minute details and was really trying to process it. I also liked that Captain Dannels also thought that Van Aiken was an over-educated, self-promoting quack whose only skill was promoting his own agenda rather than doing what he was dictated to do. He liked Dr. Robinson from a professional perspective, but thought she was a bit of a cold fish, personally.

It was strangely difficult to vocalize *what* I saw and *when I saw it,* to him. My mouth would shoot out sentence after sentence, page after page of events, with my own simple commentary accompanying it. But for the first time, my answers and interpretations were completely unguarded and spun out clumsily, as if unsure due to the over-vulnerability. While I was in the hospital, my filters were on and my responses to questions and scenarios were guarded and only revealed partial truths—never knowingly lying—but only answering the questions asked to a certain degree. It was a subconscious protection mechanism that my brain had concocted.

With Dannels, though, it was different. Something inside of me signaled me to open the gates and let him in. I'm not sure if was intuition, his confidence and demeanor, or maybe it was just the simple words that the Admiral had given me years before…But I knew I could trust him, and so I did.

I also learned that the small team they had assembled to help support me had all been vetted by his office, even though some were not Navy. He'd sought personal assurances from each man that their primary mission was my safety and security—and *nothing* would trump that directive.

He was a bottom-line kind of man. In a nutshell, he admitted they had no more a clue medically what caused me to be the way I was than they had when they'd first started. For the most part, they'd told the intelligence people very little: other than that I was an enigma, who no one really understood. The only concrete, deterministic anomaly they'd uncovered was that serotonin and dopamine levels in my brain were off the charts. They still hadn't been able to formulate a theory on why/how I could read other people's memories or emotions, or how I was able to retain it—while others could barely store away a few birthdates. They had no idea what caused it, how it worked, nor why some people might succeed escaping the grasp of my "probing" as he called it.

He told me all he could recall about my results. During most of their assessments, I'd tested only slightly above normal in terms of IQ. I wasn't great with languages, other than English, and had poor navigation skills (I could get lost with a map in my hands). My fluid intelligence was extremely high, quantitative reasoning—normal, short-term memory—normal, visual processing—normal, auditory processing—normal. My long-term storage and retrieval were off the charts, as were my decision/reaction time speeds.

I didn't fully comprehend most of the results, but I knew that the bottom line was they were still pretty unsure about any specifics on my condition. They still hadn't even found a solution where I might sleep for more than a few hours a night…so I wasn't surprised at delays and roadblocks to comprehending what went on in my brain.

We met and talked nearly all day long, for the next ten days straight. Technically, he was debriefing me on what was inside my head, but he seemed just as fascinated on the mechanics of how the material actually got there. The talks were rarely sit-downs in conference rooms or recorded sessions, but usually long walks along the beach at Coronado. He'd moved me temporarily to his favorite San Diego hotel, Hotel Del, so we could talk more relaxed in its rooms and on the beach.

The most difficult part for me was explaining what I saw. I wasn't accustomed to talking about these things, so everything seemed terribly abstract and vague. It would be easy had it been just pictures, sounds, dates, or places—but that era had long passed. These days, I was accessing pure, unfiltered thoughts—stored in the far reaches of a person's mind—cluttered with unconscious significance, tangled in all other lifelong emotional baggage.

It was a picture, yes, but it was like a picture amid a broad surrounding gallery: one that contained every nuance of detail, every angle of the picture, and every associated emotion, whether rational or not. This stuff couldn't be captured with paint on canvas and included the full, true context of what the pictures meant to the person who'd stored them. It was like thousands of strangers' reference libraries had been quietly downloaded into my head, and all I had to do was visit the right section and checkout any information that I desired.

It was even more difficult to conjecture why languages and unfamiliar lexicons weren't presenting bigger barriers for me. I'd never understood it myself, so it seemed verbally inexplicable. Why was it that when accessed via memories, my brain could see a picture of a document, a book, or a printed word, hear a sound and know exactly the essence of what it meant? It's like it was broken down to its core—in a millionth of a second, and the simplistic core was what I saw or heard; not the document or initial dialect presented, itself. If somebody had put the same source document in front of me physically, I would've had no clue if the paper was even the right side up, and absolutely no concept of what it contained.

Finally too, I was able to see what the Navy and Intelligence people thought of me. It seems the interpretations were divided into two partisan blocks. The Intelligence people saw me as an invaluable clandestine tool that could be perfect for gathering information, but simultaneously as a wild card. They were extremely wary that I had no experience or overt training, and that I would need to be closely monitored, directed, and guided to the right path.

The Navy/Military saw me differently. I was a single rogue cell—one that wasn't part of the body-proper, a unique cell that couldn't be explained in a PowerPoint graphic slideshow. They instinctively disliked the "outlier" I represented. They didn't like that they weren't able to distill and bottle up my 'magic,' to create an actionable legion just like it. Furthermore, in one memory I'd uncovered in Dannels' head, a Three-Star Army General had concisely expressed all the hesitation the military machine might have mustered:

"He's like a single US sailor amid a battalion of French Foreign legion. He doesn't speak our language; we don't speak his. We don't understand how he works, or why…and you want me to trust him? He's not a proven asset. He's just a sub sailor: albeit one that seems to know more mind tricks than Uri Geller."

While I was in San Diego, Dannels tried to bring them around to his way of thinking. He tirelessly made the rounds through the most important and influential interested circles, acting as my number one advocate. Dannels might have been a great Navy Captain but as important—his politicking was just as well-tuned. When I'd been on the sub, my gifts had earned me the nickname "the Henry Kissinger of the Sea," but when it came to shuttle-diplomacy, I knew nothing next to Dannels. He knew exactly how to keep both sides happy. He was the type of officer who knew there was more than one way to skin a cat—so he formulated plans to cover every angle. Even his first meeting with me had been optimally planned: he knew that the common strategy of ceaselessly avoiding bodily contact with me would be a useless gesture if he hoped to eventually gain my trust. Instead, he went full throttle into the game knowing that anything in his head could potentially soon be seen. It was a ballsy move….but it worked.

Day by day, my trust in him grew. Finally, one day he mentioned why he'd come to San Diego: he was there to offer me a job. I would directly work for him even though my direct report would still be to the team and command structure already assembled under CDR Doug Lewis. We would continue to be based out of San Diego. He made it very clear that if any conflicts or reservations came up about any job, I was to call him directly. He reiterated that he felt (as did Uncle Sam) that they regarded me as a proverbial jewel in the crown of intelligence—that they'd sacrifice any mission to protect me: their irreplaceable asset.

His appeal was a personal one. "If you help us, you know LT Kopchik and I will never let you come to harm. We need you, John—now more than ever. Your country, and your friends, need your help. So what do you say?"

When I'd first been exfiltrated from my submarine life via Diego Garcia, life had been easier. My first priority had been choosing the right uniform from a very, very limited set. This, I knew nothing about.

"Clandestine Intelligence, huh? Do I have to wear a tuxedo?"

20

Nobody gave me a tuxedo, and I didn't even get to wear a gun. No Aston Martins at all!

It seemed somehow unjust. Instead, they went for the subtle route: I would blend in. We began a few days of discussions on safety and operational security procedures. Knowing that I was starting a much more dangerous and unknown career than I'd been accustomed to, I helped myself to all the operational intelligence I could find—in the experts around me. I didn't bother to ask.

The fact that nobody had intuited my growing powers to sense at a distance helped enormously, although I should qualify, *not everyone* seemed to miss it. Nobody had ever paid me quite so much attention as CJ. His initial protective instincts had eventually passed mere bounds friendship to a kinship bordering on family, but simultaneously, he'd begun to notice subtle details about me that nobody else did. He frowned disapprovingly, watching me, rocking on his heels. Knowing from ample experience the way I'd fidget while "downloading" information and subconsciously processing it, I suspect CJ might have known all along that the game had changed. But if he knew, he said nothing. I took advantage of the situation to learn all I could, hoping to be as well-prepared as possible for any scenarios where my life would be at risk in unfamiliar ways.

The first mission they thought I was suited for was in Washington, DC. I was to meet a former high-ranking KGB member named

Nikolay Yurchenko—though little was mentioned about that. Dummy structures had blocked parts of the mission from me, but I could still see most: the complications, the dangers that he might re-defect, and all the power players at play in the background. Many unknown military elements waited with bated breath to see if the nebulous rumors of "some sort of military clairvoyant nutso," might be real and might be able to glean some workable information about their notoriously unreliable Russian asset. I was simply told that he was a loosely affiliated member of the embassy staff in Washington, and they mentioned that they thought he might be somewhat unstable. They'd arrange an encounter where I could bump into him, and thereby see what was in his head. The objective stated was to know *who he met with,* rather than what he knew. From what I gathered via the brief, he was the conduit that Russian agents in the US had used to get the information back to Moscow.

My first days of preparation were terribly confusing. I'd have problems concentrating, as new people were constantly brought in to provide the briefings—but the "briefers" would bring with them emotional baggage and memories that were nearly impossible to steer clear of. My brain was no help. I'd never mastered a method to discipline my capabilities, so my mind just locked onto whatever felt strongest from moment to moment.

I had a hard time connecting my need to be prepared with my brain's hunger to feed on all the novel information buzzing through the air: strangers with strange lives and strange thoughts. The more I flexed those muscles, the more they resisted any boundaries or leashes. Guests and handlers tried to speak about mission goals, what they wanted to accomplish, or specific needs they required of me; and I would sit squirming like a toddler. I was locked in an invisible struggle of an old sailor's inner willpower to do whatever I was ordered to do, versus the strange gift now fighting for the helm—to be the master in control of a given situation. To them, it might have seemed like I wasn't paying attention; and they'd raise their eyebrows at one another uncomfortably. I tried to rein in any odd-looking external presentation; but their memories and emotions felt much stronger than any kind of abstract discussions or carefully scripted dialogues regarding the plan at hand. I saw the politics behind their silences— and my mind fixated on them immediately. I was stuck in a wild game of tug of war, where I was always the victor.

I never felt like I owed them an apology, though. It wasn't like I was missing anything...I could see the briefer's own memories of being briefed—on any given mission—by their own superiors. I comprehended their needs long before they'd uttered their first words. More importantly, I also know everything that they were being told to hide.

I was to meet Yurchenko at a place called the Au Pied de Cochon restaurant. The briefer said the French phrase with distaste—I laughed inwardly as I realized the poor woman was a lifelong vegetarian—describing a classy restaurant whose name referred to tasty pigs' feet. She frowned at my faraway look, so I forced a studious look of attentiveness, leaning forward. She continued warily. After he was seated, the plan was for me to walk by his table—I would subsequently be bumped by a planted waiter, which would push me into contact with Yurchenko. I would apologize and back off, walk away, and then be debriefed. Simple!

The backup was that if I didn't make physical contact with him initially, I would abort and head to the bar, where I'd be given a backup plan. The backup plan was already prepped, so I could readily see in my head: Yurchenko had famous love for certain Washington watering holes. I just hoped the initial idea worked—I was nervous enough, so I didn't feel comfortable improvising.

But everything about the plan worked like a charm. They'd essentially left nothing to chance, so it was hard for me to fail. I brushed up against his chair, made both physical and eye-contact with Yurchenko, apologized, and moved on. I walked right out the door, mere minutes after entering. Nonetheless, my heart felt like it was going to jump out of my skin.

It was a bit awkward for me, as I knew everything that was in his head within an instant—when I'd first spotted him upon entering the room. But I played along. He'd matched the photos they'd shown me in his brief perfectly: mid-forties, a short stocky man with a bushy moustache, thinning hair and a round face.

I certainly saw a lot, too. I almost tipped over a second time after being shoved into him; I was so preoccupied sorting through his spider web thoughts. He'd tired of the game of being a spy-handler in Rome and walked into a US Embassy to proffer services. I saw how his mind reasoned through it; he had stomach ulcers that he felt would be better treated in the US than at home. The loyalty he had towards his wife was pretty much nonexistent—he'd actually thought he might be in love with a fellow Russian colleague's wife serving in Canada: his sweet Svetlana. But she rebuffed him and now he was desolate.

His mind was very scattered, cluttered with bits and pieces of random rumors and paranoia. He seemed very impulsive: even as I'd looked at him, he didn't seem sure about his decision to defect. He considered running north to Svetlana but knew she was done with him. He'd even considered re-defecting, and considered endless strategies to convince the KGB he'd been loyal—all along. He considered his likely death in terms of "how many months?" His mind was all over the place and far more difficult to sort through than most.

Names, places, dates, times were easy. But his concepts were vague and abstract, and would jump all around the spectrum. His head was alive with pops and wisps of everything, poorly sorted and tangled together like I'd never seen before. He had memories of his earliest days in the KGB, but they too were scattered—loyalties scattered with resentment, service scattered amidst betrayals. He coveted memories of his sister and the family so proud of her pitch-perfect voice. She lived in Leningrad: protégé of the famous cellist, Daniil Shafran. Yurchenko's biggest fear about defecting was that he'd probably never see her again. She made beautiful music, and I felt its soothing vibrations as I watched him take his seat. But his mind was clearly broken. Nothing was echoing through his recent cognitive circuitry besides survival strategies.

In short, there was so much in his head that I could barely weigh what was important and what wasn't. I needed time and quiet, where I might concentrate better. But there was no time; debriefing would begin immediately. The recent memories he had were regarding a man who was a US intelligence agency employee who wanted to sell him information. He'd met with this man several times, and he was very impressed by the man's photographic memory. The man never brought notes or papers with him—everything was in his head. Yurchenko would transfer all the details into a spiral notebook that he brought to all their meetings. My brain brimmed with the information, but I carefully set it aside until I'd assembled a better composite image from which to interpret it.

The US intelligent agent had recently been telling him about an underwater cable in the Sea of Okhotsk, which was used to transmit from Russian Fleet Naval Base at Petropavlovsk to the Soviet Pacific Fleet's headquarters at Vladivostok. I really didn't know what to make of what I saw or felt, but I didn't have to—I just had to regurgitate what I saw. I could tell that Yurchenko had delivered small slivers of this information to isolated sections of intelligence, but not nearly all of it. Moreover, I could see incomplete evidence in his mind of another man, a shadow: someone buried in mystery. Yurchenko had been blocked out from the details but had suspiciously circled closer and closer to the truth—another American leak.

We left back for San Diego almost immediately, and the majority of my debriefing was done on the plane. I described what I'd seen regarding Yurchenko's early memories, but no one really seemed interested. Even his thoughts regarding defecting didn't elicit much of a response; they all knew he'd already been turned. I saw paper after paper of his in Cyrillic script and provided the detail on every page that was still in his head. A few times I caught their interest—but it seemed to quickly fade. It wasn't until about three quarters through the flight—when I mentioned the words *cable in the Sea of Okhotsk*—that I finally saw their faces light up.

One of the men onboard was a Navy Rear Admiral whose primary role was intelligence gathering. His head lit up like a Christmas tree, and I immediately knew just why. His mind was flooded with memories of a little known action—and all its sordid details: Operation Ivy Bells. I paused for a second, looking down at the papers in front of me as I honed in on his memories. In a flash of a second, it all made sense.

Operation Ivy Bells had been started in the early 1970s when the US Government learned of an undersea cable that linked two of the Soviets largest Naval Installations. This cable ran parallel to the Kuril Islands off Russia's Eastern coast, in Soviet territorial waters. The NSA—with the help of Navy divers and the modified submarine the USS Halibut—tapped the cable with a clamped-on recorder that would still allow the normal transmissions but also make a recording of everything sent. Then once a month a submarine and divers would be sent to retrieve the messages and start a new recording. Over time, the Navy and the NSA developed more sophisticated devices that lasted longer periods and tapped many other cables as well.

Now I understood why the Admiral had shown such interest, as he grilled me for the next forty-five minutes or so: he wanted to know whether details of the project had been compromised...and clearly they had.

His heart pumped harder and harder, blood pressure rising, and his voice was getting louder. Ivy Bells was a project he'd been involved with from its inception, and he felt a personal sense of shame. He cut off any other questions to me from others around the table, demanding instead to know every detail that Yurchenko knew. In the end, he knew the project was compromised but seemed surprisingly grateful to me for the information. He apologized for raising his voice and tried to explain the importance of the project in broad terms—clearly not realizing I already knew the project details in just as much detail as he did. Once again, in the corner of my eye, I felt CJ watching me, concerned.

When his interrogation had tapered out, the other men started asking questions too. In a random side note, I expressed my worries that Yurchenko seemed to be constantly considering his options for re-defecting to ensure survival. "He hasn't made up his mind yet either way, but he sure seems impulsive..."

"WHAT?!" the panicked, universal response echoed. As one body, the men cleared the table and raced off to an adjoining area to make plans and analyze the likelihood of re-defection. As it happened, we'd learn days later that he had disappeared from the same restaurant later that evening, probably right after I'd warned them of my seemingly-unsubstantiated suspicions.

I was exhausted by the time we arrived back in San Diego. I was easily convinced that we should go out and celebrate the intelligence we'd uncovered, and the miracle that we'd accomplished in terms of traceless Intel acquisition. So I did celebrate—and perhaps to excess.

Ψ

Definitely so. I awoke naked on a balcony, in the house of a stranger.

No recollections of what had happened, no baggage memories, no regrets, and looking around the empty room, no strings attached: nobody was home. I found my clothes scattered down a staircase and wondered what kind of night I'd had. But due to certain habits that had been developing, my tolerance to alcohol was at an all-time high. What should have been an earth-shattering hangover was mostly solved with some aspirins, sunglasses, and asking as few questions as possible. My friends later told me I'd climbed out a bathroom window and ran laughing in the night; nobody had been able to catch up with me before I'd found my next bar, and my former, nameless "fling friend."

The miracle of alcohol! Lately I'd found drinking to be exactly the great escape that I needed, the only flood strong enough to push away the creeping phantoms of other men's memories—memories that haunted my days and especially my nights. Creeping shadows echoed my college days, as the drinking rate increased.

However, for the first time since I'd left the Jacksonville, one special night celebrating helped me feel like I was part of a team again, rather than the specimen in a jar I'd felt in the hospital. A few days later, CJ approached with a big grin on his face, holding a commendation from SECNAV for our work with Yurchenko. I felt like life was finally getting back on track, again. I knew just what I was doing and what was expected of me. I knew how to be helpful, and I believed in my mission.

Intuitively I began to recognize a truth that I consciously resisted—that I had to get that drinking in check, before things got out of hand. Nobody said anything, and few people seemed to notice how frequent it had become, the second I was off-mission. But it didn't take too much complex analytical thinking after looking through the memories of someone like Yurchenko, to see the risks.

Unchecked impulsivity—no matter how innocuously it was packaged—was a dangerous liability, especially for somebody in my new line of work.

21

I next found myself in Egypt, which looked like every spy movie, ever—like a darker version of The Maltese Falcon. I suspect that I was sent out of random curiosity, mostly just to see exactly what somebody with my unique skillset might bring home out of the viper's den. We had a crew of ancient advisors, who scrupulously kept their distance from me. They met us at the airport and gave us a minimal Readers' Digest explanation of the contemporary Egyptian context; but I drained their minds of all the relevant info, and some messy divorces to boot. Right about the time they'd finished talking Soviet expulsions, I'd completed my analysis of their motivations for the cheating and the availability issues that had crumbled the marriages as being primarily based in childhood abandonment issues. But these aren't things you say in polite conversation, so I just looked up and smiled politely. (I'd been analyzed by helpless therapists at the hospital, and sadly for me, their lingo structures persevered in the back of my mind. They'd never known what to say about me—par for the course, for us sub sailors!)

We'd been in Egypt for three days. After being underwhelmed by our briefings, CJ turned to me while we were ferried to our accommodations. "So…? What'd you get?"

I spent the next two days explaining the complex ins and outs of Egyptian geopolitical history until he literally had to ask me to stop. "Well done, John. Now where do we start?"

I shrugged. He shrugged, too. This was going to be a strange adventure, that's all I knew.

"I'll keep you safe," he ventured. "You just do your thing."

"Oh...great."

I determined to just become a massive set of ears pointed towards the strange crowds around me, and thought it would be a great idea to scribble down notes into a notebook—whatever came to me. After the first day, even that got to be too much. I didn't need any reminders on these things that I couldn't ever forget, anyway...I'd just wait to be debriefed.

So, we walked, sat, and listened.

Everyone had their eyes on Egypt. Operatives from every nation worked under false names and false pretenses. Every morning, we set up shop in the lobby café/bar, and we'd take in the daily tide of strange characters. On the outside, most looked like characters from a 1950s movie—but from the inside I saw the cream of the crop operatives from former NATO occupations, styled with new hairdos and credentials and shipped straight to the land of the Sphinxes.

I saw them all, the eyes and ears of Latin America, of Africa, of every interest within the Arab World. I watched the surge in Asian construction companies that flooded the Egyptian metropolitan areas, and the small armies of interested negotiators with ominous briefcases that had smoothed out the works.

CJ was kind enough to help me understand the global politics behind what I was seeing. Mubarak was a strongman who had picked up the reins of state when his predecessor was gunned down, and he charted a middle path between superpowers. Domestically, things hadn't been all that much easier for the people—the transitions were tricky. Jumpy Central Security Force men believed rumors that their conscription periods might be doubled, and more than seventeen thousand rioted for days. CSF men were regularly beaten with wooden sticks by their officers, forced to act as servants, or forced to stand at attention along roadsides for hours to impress late arriving motorcades—or in some cases, Mubarak himself. Usually they were ordered to do the crushing, but now it was their turn to be crushed.

Army men and gunships began to crush the CSF protests after a few days, at the cost of a few hundred lives. Mubarak didn't seem bothered, as his allies didn't raise much protest. He'd hedged his bets that as long as he paid off inherited debts on time, nobody would bother him internationally. The locals didn't seem particularly devastated by the karmic come-uppance these shock troops had coming, either. They just kept their eyes glued to the African Cup soccer matches.

So far a number of ritzy tourist hotels and theatres had been burned down. We all sort of warily looked around at the opulent glittering staircases of our own hotels and wondered how long we had until the firebombs would be tossed near our own doors. There was no denying we were outsiders. Once again, we felt the Mos Eisley cantina vibe, but it was the upper crust version: tilted towards bigwigs traveling on company expense accounts. Curfews basically translated into universal schemes to turn all the assuredly-comped meals and expenses into a nonstop open bar, at least until the streets were clear again. The Good Life—when in Rome!

But everyone was also preoccupied with their pet projects and impatient to get to work. Britain and France were still smarting decades after the nationalization of the Suez Canal Company, licking their wounds at losses that had been spearheaded by American negotiations. The few Brits in the bar looked glum. The Soviets had initially hoped for the construction work ultimately awarded to the Asian cartel—but then found solace that the low wages awarded were even more pitiful than the rates of the local Egyptian workers. Negotiators and lobbyists sat bored on their hands, waiting for their change to shake things up. Extremely tense-looking Israelis had arrived for early preparations for a bilateral tourism deal later in the year—and seemed like they were constantly awaiting imminent disaster. An almost stereotypical assortment of portly, loud, and obnoxious Americans swarmed into Cairo, too—over their own Bilateral Investment Treaty negotiations—whose finer points were being ceaselessly sanded down.

The movers and makers of the world, we were locked into the hotel lobbies, waiting for the streets to clear. Within a few booze-filled days and nights, most of the men were purple-faced and roaring with laughter, oblivious to the turbulent world burning around them. Businessmen, intelligence men, journalists, soldiers of fortune, lobbyists, and all the lost or curious cast long shadows across each cocktail lounge in the Cairo hotels, slapping their knees and breaking the rickety chairs leaning back to laugh. Many passed the time telling war-yarns that were definitely officially non-sanctioned. I wouldn't hesitate to say I heard some monstrous stuff those days, but what did I know, and all who did know just laughed it off. All except for my somber-faced attentive friend across the table.

My traveling companion CJ was completely bewildered by the behavior surrounding us. I'd adopted a "when in Rome" attitude as I quietly sipped my imported Rum and Coke, but CJ quietly put back a tall glass of orange juice, or club soda on ice, visibly worrying that the sky was falling. He felt sober about our job here and stayed pretty quiet, and in a very out of character move, I tried to do the same. Unable to leap into the head of somebody else, my brain did some elaborate gymnastics off my cranium and deep dived into a retrospective analysis of my own mind.

How in the world did I get to this point? Normally I scrupulously avoided reflective time, seeing that it rarely did me good. Now was no better. For the first time in months, I really let my brain wander with wonder at the sheer amount of novel information I'd inputted into myself in the last few years.

I thought back, way back to Cape Cod, to beaches along Sag Harbor. Life had been so simple! I remembered the easy thrills of categorizing sea life and telling its stories, of sprinting along with Elizabeth and chambering furtively after my brothers. Where had all that life gone? I thought of the tiny racks of the Jacksonville and her cramped galley, of laughs resonating along the narrow labyrinth of pipes and electrical cables. I even thought of my hovel of an apartment at NYU, and my nocturnal werewolf's life. They were like parallel universes—passing by my mind's eye.

It wasn't just the setting differences that made life seem so vastly distanced from all previous places I'd known. It was the qualities of the people, the things that preoccupied them, and the secrets that kept them up at night. Once upon a time, my mind had latched onto the petty internal dramas of somebody like young Megan of Mineola, lovelorn and lonely Americana stuff, tired of the slim pickens of Everywhere, USA.

But magnitudes of scale now separated my present tense from those times. Even in the Navy, every person I'd met and interacted with was night and day more complex than the seemingly simple folk I'd known previously: rushing to start families, conflicted at the long inflicted separation, struggling to make ends meet at a distance, struggling to know the families they'd left back home from bits and pieces of life that showed up randomly in family gram letters—our only beacons to the bright world outside.

But even as my peers had changed and grown more and more complex, my head changed, too. There wasn't much casual peeking in with "the gift" anymore. It was full-bore periscope: locked and loaded twenty-four seven. Gone were the shakes and the wildly dilated eyes, the clumsier stages where it looked as if I was having seizures. Something enormously potent and irresistible had taken their place. An enormous, unwieldy hunger to KNOW things, all things, about all people.

I longed to access everyone, all the time, to find the building blocks at the core of them: the intensity, the intuition, the deepest core reflections of innocence from whence all their decisions were built up. I couldn't seem to keep things in stride; I dove deep every time. I wanted to know where present traits had sprung from childhood, emotional extremes, and all the tricks of their trades, all the deepest codes that guided strangers along their strange lives. The more powerful my capacity for insight became, the more my power to resist eroded—as did my already shaky capacity to act casually once I'd seen to the core of somebody. I became an x-ray machine in a business suit, sipping rum and trying to act natural.

As this phase of my being changed, so did others. My senses seemed so much more detached than during the earlier parts of my life…Sight, touch, hearing, smell, and taste stopped being interesting, or at least much less than they had been in my past.

My peers for the last few years had probably contributed something to it. It's easier to shut off the soap opera squabble of small town America when you can convince yourself that somebody's Daddy Issues or distrust of authority fell outside the scope of your own life: interesting but not vitally relevant to your own everyday functioning life. But it was different in the strange surreal world I was living in now. My world was a bizarre snowglobe of patriots and spooks, actors, and doctors blending roles in insincere shadowboxing spectacles. Everything about my world was roped off into Need To Know protocols, Eyes Only dictates, and various stages of subterfuge and shades of truth. The more cautious and jittery they became with my capacities and growing strength, the more wary I became of their capacity to panic. I knew when they panicked; I was dehumanized or worse. "The Navy doesn't like otherness," had extended far beyond one group of players—all around me were powerful and shadowy groups, who wanted to milk my skills for all they were worth and simultaneously paralyze me and bombard me with stones for fear that I was some kind of monster. Albeit their monster, doing their bidding, for now. But in the process, I was constantly presented with the manic, flitting images of the shrunken souls racing beneath the surfaces of these paranoid people. Intelligence operatives, more than anyone else, had haunted my brain, and their worst night-terrors and panic attacks came to haunt my dreams, not some nights—but *every* night.

How much was I retaining? Ninety-nine percent. There was very, very little that I was able to suppress. It forced its way into my mind and then refused to be moved or cleared away. My sense of normalcy had just entirely eroded away, and I was no longer capable of projecting a "normal" demeanor. Every aspect of every interaction was stored away. But interactions themselves were just the tip of the iceberg.

The second somebody started talking to me, parts of my brain took over the wheel, spiriting it away from my comprehending mind. It breezed right past the half-truths and persuasive speeches that strangers tend to present upon meeting other strangers, into the deeper waters, the murky depths. Rather, I'd be faced immediately with their biggest fears, their deepest longings, the guilt, their grudges, their cores. I'd have pristinely groomed church boys enter a room with smiles from ear to ear, but the first thing I saw would be the covert raid a half decade before where they'd been forced to strangle a lookout with a garrote wire: an experience they'd never be free of—nor now, would I.

The strangest thing was perhaps the sheer volume of professional/habitual data I would retain that I'd never be able to use. If the inclination ever came over me (plus the energy/ sufficient serenity to concentrate), I'm pretty sure I could have muddled my way through *using* any of the skillsets I'd started absorbing through chance contact with strangers. If only my brain had been so precise when I was in school! I saw random chefs and instantly relived their turbulent years in kitchens—moment to moment—watching every failure and success, every new revelation about ingredients and temperatures and optimal conditions. I saw every lawyer's failed bar exam, every doctor's nightmarish worst case, every politician's dirty trick. Every smallest secret of strangers' trades, codes, and the systems organizing their lives…I'd come to understand chains of command structures for every incidental character passing my way, both the role models and ghouls alike.

I knew who was having affairs and how they were hiding them, and why their marriages dissolved, and why they wouldn't just leave and start anew. I uncovered abuses, mental disorders, and imminent breakdowns—right and left. I knew all about the most traumatizing missions my secretive coworkers had been sent on, and sometimes suffered moment-by-moment nightmares that elaborated every horrible surprise they'd awaited when surveyed, stalked, ambushed, betrayed, or when ordered to betray those they'd befriended. I saw all the baggage, all the fatigue. Through their eyes I saw the schizophrenic reality of terror transferred into paranoia: a world of secret eyes, ears, and threats everywhere, behind every surface, behind every promise, behind every smile.

But every time I discovered these things, I'd be forced to make an indifferent grin while extending my hand, muttering some triviality like, "You said you visited New York, that's where I'm from!" It began to be a parody of itself—the facility with which I would see the deepest darkest loneliness residing in the core of folk playing social roles along scripts—but nobody could see me, nobody had any idea what I saw. I was a ghost, everywhere and nowhere in their eyes: as well as my own.

CJ stared straight at me when my daydreams spat me back into reality.

"Sometimes I'd really love to know what it's like inside your head, John."

Quick recovery. "Believe me, you wouldn't know where to start." I realized it wasn't a good recovery and tried again. "I certainly don't do it well." Strike two. My mind raced…

He laughed and nursed his club soda, watching me out of the corner of his eye. Every once in a while it occurred to me that CJ was one of the few people who regularly expressed interest in me, in my troubles, in my complications. He stopped seeing me as a simple asset long ago. He never assumed everything I'd been given would be easy, but he seemed to understand it as more like a burden. He saw me as more than just a camera and microphone that could record the worlds chatter. Therefore, he gave me an easy out, and changed the subject.

"Well John, I believe I understand why we were sent here—right when we were."

"I'm glad one of us understands that! I have no idea what we're doing here. I'm just here for the cheap rum. I'm minding my own business, unlike yourself," I volunteered in a comedic voice, my speech slurred by the straw between my teeth.

"Have you thought about the identities of these people around us? Perhaps the spooks back home are just hoping to get lucky, hoping that some of the folk we're bound to get marooned with during this curfew might be interesting types. I'm not much of an eavesdropper, but from the scattered snatches I've picked up by accident, I don't think that hope would be misguided."

"Are you saying you want me to stroll around at random, and hope for the best?"

"Well, I don't see what it would hurt, exactly. I wasn't given mission details any clearer than yours: we're to analyze conditions on the ground, seek out Intel on foreign interests, figure out who is who and what they're looking for in Egypt. This was General Stubblebine's idea, straight from the top: Ambient/Passive Signal Capture. He thinks you're a real boy wonder. He seems to believe you can somehow just "leach up scandals," and he always wants to test it. It does sound crazy, but I think this might be just the perfect place to start. Nobody seems to be particularly worried about protocols here, tonight." He smirked.

"Let's face it, CJ, I'm not either. I'll admit it, I had three of these JDs and Coke already."

"John, those are rum and Cokes—not the same thing. Are you sure it was only three?"

"Well I've had a few of them, yes," I hiccupped.

"Fortunately, you've got me here to look after you. I'll help you play nice. Look at that nice fellow at the bar! He looks friendly! He seems to want a friend."

I looked where CJ had subtly pointed and immediately looked away, almost laughing out loud at the supernaturally wicked, murderous glare I was getting from a barfly in the shadows. He brought a Star Wars cantina world back into mind: Sith, surely.

"No thanks, CJ. This time I'll pass."

"Fair enough. What about him?" He gestured into a corner of the room where a man dressed like a Mormon missionary played chess by himself, sipping tea.

"Well, he does look a bit kinder than Charlie Manson over there at the bar. If you buy me a coffee or two, I promise to make an effort."

"It's a deal, John. Be right back."

But CJ didn't come back—he was gone for ages. When he finally did return, he was deep in conversation with a drunken man in an elegant suit. He had no coffee. He pulled up a chair for the stranger and paused briefly to interject an introduction. "This is my new friend, Avner."

"—It's liked being locked in a panopticon, wouldn't you say?" Avner began, apropos of nothing.

"I'm sorry?"

"A panopticon. We all sit crowded into one area, where all our personal agency and actions are carefully noted by some central authority that none of us can fully see. Today I saw an otherwise everyday man making a full intelligence report into a fake cigar, with real smoke and everything. Those Russians…I don't give the KGB the credit they deserve, sometimes." He smiled as he touched his moustache.

"CJ, I told you…I needed more time to get dressed. I had a much better shirt upstairs, but he said everything was completely casual. If

I'd known I was wandering into a damn pan..opti..con, I certainly would have worn a better shirt."

Everyone laughed. "These momentous occasions do demand momentous shirts."

"Where are you from, Avner? I can't quite place your accent."

"Ah, then you are not from here…I am from Israel. My accent is a famous one, especially in this part of the world. Egypt may be an ancient confluence of traditions and cultures, but to have the accent I have, here, is to stand at a bus stop in a ghillie suit. You will be noticed, whether your gestures and intentions seem surreptitious, or not."

"See John, it's not so bad. You could've been stuck wearing a ghillie suit."

More laughs, and I did some more hiccupping.

"What will you have, Avner? Evidently I'm drinking rum and Cokes—I learned recently."

"Well if ever there was a time to try it, now seems to be the time. I'd love to join you, John-the-Shirt."

"Please do! We're sitting at the loneliest table in here, and CJ's not helping our credibility situation here by drinking club soda."

Avner was able to catch the eye of the barman, with a gesture that he'd like three more of what I was drinking. He was clearly drunk, but in the effortless gesture and micro-motions that followed, I saw the past the extremes of his behavior and intuited the smallest glimmer of reflexive exaggeration. He was a man who understood the advantages of being perceived to have his guard down, even when it wasn't fully so. Relatively drunk or not, he still seemed sharp as a tack, his eyes flicking over the room in a millisecond: assessing, appraising, and analyzing. Less than an instant later, he was fully back in character.

"So what might you fine gentlemen be doing to fill up your time, here?" Avner asked casually.

CJ cut in before I could say anything. "We're on assignment to take in the mood of American allies as the final print of the Single European Act goes down in the Hague today. We were hoping to meet with dignitaries and take formal statements to press, but instead we've only seen these walls and drinks so far. Our press passes didn't count for much—on those streets."

"Ah, that's not so bad!" Avner gestured around the room magnanimously. "There seem to be plenty of dignitaries and power-brokers here in this very hotel! It could very well be the most influential place in Egypt today, or the most insidious—take a look around! That man over there is the unclaimed bastard son of a great Caradja, which will only mean something if you know your Romanian history...He is the Egyptian ambassador's half-brother, but barely knows it himself. His Father was one of your greatest intelligence men ever, but the family ran afoul of your Hoover fellow. They hid the baby in the midst of scandal, and now he sells secrets to sheiks. The man he is eating with is his soon-to-be adopted brother, who styles himself as Count Dracula."

"I feel like I have to call bullshit on at least part of that story, or risk being called the most gullible person ever by the time you finish—" I laughed.

"No! They're strange sounding, because they are true! The real stories around here are so absurd, you only recognize fictions by their sense of reasonableness."

I paused, with a dubious look on my face. CJ leaned back in his chair, his eyes twinkling.

Avner continued. "Count Dracula there was probably sent by Caradja herself, to steer her biological son straight and offer him a living! She has regretted giving in to demands to hide the child for decades, and Count Dracula has been promised a pretty penny, and even an inheritance, to become the errand boy. But they aren't the strangest folk here, by a long shot. There, for instance—" he gestured with his cup and a slight nod towards a table, "all four of those men are Egyptian GDSSI. Now, what they're doing in here, schmoozing with foreigners while half the security state riots outside...your guess is as good as mine!" The men systematically avoided eye contact as I boozily wobbled my gaze over their table.

"And those men," Avner gestured to the opposite wall where some large men were nervously stealing glances at the GDSSI, "they're in the strange position of being paid Western agents—very hush-hush, but not hush enough—fomenting actions against several regimes who are Western pet peeves: Iraq, Libya, Syria, and more. In their own countries, they are famous for being religious zealots, extremists.

Everyone wants to play "the enemy of my enemy is my friend" card, but these men know that in this week alone, GDSSI was forced to admit to some wild allegations of torture against its own local extremists. These proxy fighters are pretty angry about that, I believe. But it's like a hydra. A few weeks ago Jordan cuts ties with the PLO, but now these folk stroll in like they own the place…But look how things are! Around here, even openly saying the words: Muslim Brotherhood—"

The room abruptly hushed, and a dozen pairs of eyes peered around suspiciously like a cartoon, seeking out the source of the taboo phrase.

For about four seconds, one could hear the crickets hidden in the woodwork, then the sound slowly recrescendoed up to normal.

His words had been carefully orchestrated to achieve a desired effect….and he was clearly pleased that it had worked. "Like I said, things are strange. But big power certainly seems to draw attention. Things are complicated for Mubarak, and he surely remembers his predecessor's death a few years ago, under very controversial conditions. These things are made worse with debts, with war-making, with secrets. Egypt's peace with my country, and yours, makes for some very unusual tensions with other players in the neighborhood—and troubles with proposed proxy wars are about to make things even worse. But like I said, a man concealed in a ghillie suit at a bus stop still doesn't blend in all that well. It's easy to spot, if you know what you're looking for."

"You may just have a point there!" I laughed. "What was it you said that you do, anyway, Avner?"

"Tractors."

Tractors?" I automatically guffawed, in spite of myself.

"I sell tractors."

"Tractors. Really?"

Tractors in Egypt?

"Something like that."

We all laughed again.

"To tractors!" I laughed. Avner and I drank our drinks down and waved at the bartender for more, while CJ quietly sipped his club soda and ordered some dinner.

"There are no secrets, friends. These days, less than ever! Why I even heard from a friend in America that Stubblebine has a new protégé and isn't just playing with spoons and walking through walls anymore, but instead he has a real life—"

"I heard an interesting thing about America, too," CJ suddenly cut in. "I heard there was a man in the Navy last year, who was selling secret information to your country! I heard they gave him a life sentence—but people thought he might have another tasking handler who went free…I heard a lot of people were pretty angry about that episode."

Avner frowned. "Well that was harsh. We're all friends here I hope, and allies, the oldest of allies. Really, is there even such thing as spying between allies? It's more like sharing at worst, warning at best. Sometimes allies give warnings! And of course I don't know if you would have any use for his information—being mere journalists, of course— but I—although being a mere tractor seller—would love to warn my allies: this information did not merely come from some lonewolf American…Rather, some friends of mine in Israel intercepted the information in a coded message from some of your friends back home, beamed straight to some very shadowy people in the USSR."

His voice steadily rose.

"As an ally, as a hardworking, freedom-loving tractor salesman, I hope you'll take those warnings seriously!"

CJ and I sat completely still, blinking and dumbfounded. Finally, without waiting for a response, Avner grabbed his hat and made to stand up.

"Well, gentlemen, it has been a wonderful night. I hope your write-up on the international mood from Egypt will be wonderful, and John, don't worry so much about the shirt, it's quite nice."

He left as abruptly as he had arrived.

"What just happened?" I mumbled.

CJ merely shrugged in horror. There was a long silence before he finally said, "What do you say we get the hell out of this country?"

"Yeah, I was hoping you'd say that."

22

After my first success, there had been fireworks. Egypt hadn't made the same splash, though I didn't fault myself—there had never seemed to be a real plan to it. A small flurry of concern had murmured through the staff, while a new parade of spooks and brass paraded through to congratulate me on my latest mission "success." The victory went down as a mixed bag, like the Ivy Bells mission. There, they'd been frustrated to learn that the wiretap had been compromised, but the additional Intel I was able to glean seemed to excite them a lot. Behind other cluttered details of heartbreak and ambition, I'd uncovered the smallest tattered hint of a bigger mystery: a leak. I couldn't get all the way at who the leak was— there'd clearly been a system distancing various links in the Intel chain, to minimize compromise risk. But I was able to see Yurchenko observing American documents, documents he couldn't have come across accidentally in Russia.

More importantly, they also seemed very interested by the Soviet military advice, which I'd seen through his eyes: for *specific routes submarines should take to avoid being detected.* So far as we'd known at the time, there was no way Soviets could know about our SOSUS hydrophone arrays. But the routes they were recommending were the only areas we'd not yet fully wired for sound. Something was moving under the radar, and everyone went into frenzy mode to find out what that was. It was only later that I realized this information had clued them into a much larger pattern of top secret information slipping into the wrong hands.

Someone was ferrying information out of my country and was doing so at a fairly high level security clearance.

My superiors seemed fascinated by that information, which wasn't surprising. Egypt and the strange rumors I'd picked up there only augmented that excitement: clearly, the leak continued. While my actionable intelligence was scattered and strange, the Egypt mission was chalked up as a success, at least on paper.

For a few weeks, I celebrated the mission's success with my friends Johnnie Walker and Jack Daniels. I did my best to relax, but there remained a creeping nervousness in the back of my mind. I'd helped my country, and perhaps that was good enough: I was doing good, using my gift for good. Wasn't that all I'd ever wanted? But more and more, the deluge of memories I'd extracted were beginning to flicker in my head. What felt at first like a leak in my mind's eye—a quick flash of Soviet gunmetal, a brief peek at some anonymous Politburo face—was seeming more and more like a stream as the days passed.

The gift began to feel more like a glitch. The longer I went without any social contact, the harder it was to subdue the flood. The only way to quash it was to drink myself into incoherence, where the images got even stranger. That is, darker.

Now, when I met a new bartender, I didn't see his wedding, but the divorce proceedings. Without meaning to, I learned which of my co-workers beat their kids, who at the grocery store had been date raped as a teen, who'd done the date raping.

Soon, I was carrying a flask around everywhere with me. But the longer I went this way, the drinking wasn't actually stopping the memories from coming, it was just blurring my eventual knowledge of them. Soon, I was having trouble deciding what a person's real memory was and what I'd imagined would be the possible memory I might see. Could I have been making these memories up? Was this gift only something I'd imagined? Had I just been getting lucky? My handlers were still probing me, trying to decide what I could and couldn't do. For so long, I'd felt like I *knew* what I knew—what I was capable of knowing—but what if I was wrong?

Ψ

It didn't take long for my keepers to decide they wanted to continue testing my skills. The moment they heard that East Germany's main man, Erich Honecker, was making an appearance in West Germany, they went mad with the thought of sorting through his mind.

What things could they strain away? What lessons, what cautionary tales? How much did he know that could hurt the US, and where was he hearing it? More importantly, what could he say about the USSR that nobody else might know?

Though they didn't say it openly, I also saw that my superiors had private worries they felt too wary to ask out loud: what did these Germans know about German nationals who'd been extracted over ratlines to the US? Was it likely that they'd give up that information abroad just to hurt the image of the West on the international stage? The ratlines had been an open secret across the intelligence communities, but nobody wanted the press to get a hold of the story and drag everything into the limelight. Cloaks and daggers belonged in the shadows, and there were many skeletons in the Americans' closet that we hoped to keep there.

So my handlers decided to see what I could learn.

It was determined that I would travel as clandestinely as possible, to reduce potential attention paid to me. Nobody wanted to telegraph punches. I would fly to France as a businessman on holiday, rove around with a camera for a few days, and then meet my assigned contacts in West Germany for final briefing just before Honecker arrived in Bonn for a "working visit," the first semi-official recognition of East Germany by a West German government that considered the East illegitimate.

It would be the same drill as with Yurchenko: get into physical contact with the target as long as necessary to get some clear reads, probe everything for information pertinent to the USA, get out, and then await debrief: archiving everything possible into meticulous notes. Simple enough.

But nobody thought of the human cost, or the sheer quantity of unfamiliar information that would be contained in this one man: how taxing it all might be on my mind. More importantly, nobody put sufficient safeguards in place.

I suppose the assumption was that in Bonn I would have the full luxury of anonymity, and in spite of my non-official cover, I'd been ensured that any risks to my person would be minimal. I was told this was the least aggressive scenario: the more isolated my travels were, the more they could insure against leaks. I would be safer.

Nobody meant to underestimate the *East German* surveillance machine.

Ψ

I arrived in my hotel room a few days early, closed the small door and placed my suitcase atop a creaky bedframe, trying to gather my thoughts.

Although I carefully avoided looking around the room, I immediately somehow felt it: a million eyes on me at once. The air crackled with the electricity of unseen equipment.

The room had been compromised—that much I knew.

I tried to present a brave face as the repercussions of that information raced through my mind, robotically strolling to the porcelain sink, washing my face and neck and slowly toweling myself dry, my ears pricking up at every last glimmer of sound.

They were there! Slight, almost imperceptible, but there.

I began to sweat but managed to control my breathing, wondering if I was alone in the room. I brainstormed unobtrusive ways to open all the likely hiding spaces: yanking open the slated closet doors to set in my suitcase, stowing my shoes in a low cabinet, hanging a spare dress shirt that needed ironing across the shower bar after pulling open the curtain.

Nobody.

I turned off the bathroom light and casually plugged in a small nightlight under the sink, my face pressed up close to the mirror to see if it was double paned.

No such luck.

But the lack of concrete evidence meant nothing; I knew I was being watched. I flicked on the television and turned the noise up, hoping the garbled voices would silence the heavy thudding of my heartbeat. The second I turned my attention back to the program, a poorly produced docudrama that kept cutting between slapstick armed robbery reenactments and a scowling host in an austere studio, I recognized the regular pulses of static interruption I'd been warned to look out for in bugged rooms. The interspersal of static gave the robberies an ethereal quality, the masked thieves garbled with a patterned thud. It was the signature signal disruption of an emitting transmitter tuned to a frequency close enough to interfere with electronics. My brain activated memories from all the intelligence-circle men's minds regularly surrounding me at work back home—and I recognized exactly how serious things had abruptly become.

The sweat became a flood, as I tried to convince myself it was coincidence. Who would bother bugging a hotel room in West Germany? Surely my handlers would have taken precautions? But as I restored my breathing to a measured rate, I realized there was no way this room was secure.

The more terrified I became, the more casual and languid I attempted to present myself and my bodily motions. I leaned back into an exaggerated yawn and in doing so noticed a long, tiny bulge running beneath the wallpaper, from the central light circuit towards some furnace pipes climbing a corner against the far wall. There was a small arc smudge where someone's sweaty thumb had recently turned the light fixture, and dust had congealed against the grease.

I massaged the flat of my back and considered what I was looking at, rolling my neck and taking in the other walls of the room. I moved over to the wall to stretch out my shins against the baseboard, and noticed a small pile of plaster dust, barely the size of a pencil eraser, piled an inch from the wall. Massaging my hands and shoulders, I slyly took in the small bump I'd never in a million years have noticed before—just off-center, on the long plaster wall.

Someone had drilled through, just hours before. Whether it was a pinhole camera, or more likely, an audio capturing device remained to be seen. *But this was real.* Someone had taken some serious pains here—someone professional.

There was a dropped ceiling in the bathroom, and I wondered how much machinery was hiding within it. Moreover, the phone, the alarm clock, the room's heater itself…

Paranoia began to set in. And no wonder! I was not James Bond. I'd signed on for a simple job—all this stuff was well beyond my pay-grade.

I panicked and decided to leave the room and clear my head. I gathered my coat and leaned into the door, gathering my breath as I made ready to face a world that I now absolutely considered hostile. But as I yanked the door open an inch and made ready to spy out one eye at a time, I felt a light impact on the side of the door.

Or rather, I felt an impact INSIDE the door.

I stopped cold.

How extreme had this become? Why would such pains have been taken? Suddenly, all thoughts of caution flew to the wind—handlers be damned! They'd tossed me into this nightmare without even checking the room.

Completely safe, they'd said. *One in a million.*

I dragged a chair over to the door and scampered up, opening it just in time to terrify some elderly Germans passing by in the hallway as I lost my balance and tumbled down. On the second time up, I scanned every crack in the wood, fingering the edges and knocking for cavities. Lo and behold, I was living in a spy movie. The door was a typical hollow door, but one section protested my fist with a low buzzing thud. I peered my nose above the top of the doorframe and saw nothing but a dusty old door with a knot of gnarled wood at the top right.

A long swipe of the finger confirmed it: the dust was dirt—it was fake. The knot, on close inspection, was nothing but a broken cork that had been shaved down to block a hole.

Obsessed, fuming with rage and simultaneously terrified, I unraveled a metal hanger and managed to fish out the cork. But something still held onto it. I tugged and twisted it until a long chain of batteries—wrapped in panty hose, all wired together— clanked out of the doorframe, one after the next. As for the cork itself, a small electronic device was implanted inside, quietly recording my life.

My breath caught in my chest as my heart stopped cold. For one wild second, I expected every other door in the hall to burst open as men with guns came rushing forth.

Keep it together, John. Just breathe…

I glanced at the smoke alarm, the air conditioning box, the bedside lamp—sure every one of them had been similarly tampered with.

I grabbed my suitcase, threw the panty hose battery chain into the trash, and stormed down the hallway. I watched every window reflection possible on my exodus, waiting for suits to charge out and grab me, or a black bag to be yanked over my head—but I'd evidently been lucky. Nobody emerged.

I stepped into a sweets shop across the street and had the owner dial a taxi, which I took to a park with a taxi kiosk alongside. Two taxi changes and a short, sporadic walk later, I stumbled into a small hostel I'd noticed by chance and reserved a bed.

The vibe was low key enough that when the desk clerk asked my name and I simply murmured, "Michael," he nodded and scratched out the letters—handing me a room key with no questions asked. I opened the door and was greeted by an ancient smell of mold and standing water that my too-exhausted mind translated as safety. My heightened senses roved the room but only picked up a mouse gorging on leftover snacks in an unemptied garbage pail.

I fell across the bed, still wearing my coat and shoes—breathing a sigh of relief and coughing in the rancid air. My suitcase was wedged between the footboard of the bed and a chair that I'd angled to lock beneath the doorknob, holding shut the door. I'd unplugged the lamps and the television and even the alarm clock, unsure if it made a difference and unwilling to overthink it. The second these haphazard precautions were taken, I fell into a deep, dreamless sleep.

The next morning I awoke to an old man singing as he staggered drunkenly home with the dawn. I thanked my lucky stars to be through the night and looked around gratefully at the filthy room that had provided my sanctuary. I hadn't tracked my movements all that well while in the taxis, instead twisting around my body to constantly check whether I was being followed. But after unpacking my maps and scanning the parks awhile, I was quickly able to piece together where I'd ended up.

The bored front desk man was easily coaxed into calling me a cab after receiving a bribe. Soon I was on my way, dropped off at a prearranged safe house that I strolled up to, unexpected.

After two knocks, the door was ripped open. Someone grabbed me by the sleeve and jerked me inside. Inside, three men in suits swam through mountains of coffee cups and old sandwich wrappers, pawing surveillance equipment or staring out window blinds with massive earphones on.

"What the hell are you doing here, Calabrace? By showing yourself here, you've put our entire operation in danger!"

I tried to rein in my anger. "Yeah, well this operation is clearly not running well, as it stands. The room you arranged for me was bugged—you know, *bugged*." I gestured wildly.

The man in charge scoffed. "Really. And how would you know that? Your decades of experience in reconnaissance?"

It only took three examples of the bugs I'd uncovered to convince them I was telling the truth. Their faces went white as I described the door.

"That shouldn't have been possible. We should have had eyes on the site the whole time—" one of them murmured, almost to himself. "Something isn't right here. I'll push the information up the pipeline and figure out what we're dealing with. What did you do, when you bailed?"

"I found somewhere unlikely. I changed cabs several times, and I was careful. But how am I supposed to survive here with surprises like that? It's a wonder I made it out in the first place."

"We'll have our best men on it, NOW. By tonight, you'll have the information we need, and you'll be on your way. By then, you can sleep in the Embassy if it would make you feel better, or in a compound, or whatever you need. Your safety is a top priority here."

"Clearly." I sighed sarcastically. "Well, what's the plan? Somehow these guys already bugged a room rented for me under a false name, supposedly under surveillance. Now I'm to liaison with them in a subtle way without fearing further for my life? What are we talking here, false noses and eyeglasses? They clearly know more than you do."

Another of the men answered with a deliberate calm, clearly worried about further setting me off. "Actually I wouldn't worry about that, specifically. The odds that they know exactly who you are—and why you're here—are infinitesimal. Far more likely, an intelligence agency noticed some subterfuge going on in the documents we furnished and decided to take a chance that you'd be an interesting lead. Personally, I wouldn't be worried."

I stared. "Well, I'm certainly happy that you're not worried, but I sure as fuck am! Tell me, where will I be effortlessly meeting this man?"

"Well that's the easy part, Calabrace. You can rest easy about any worries about vulnerability: you'll be in a castle, surrounded by the most elite soldiers West Germany can spare. You'll be on wait staff, and at any moment if you feel uncomfortable, you just walk out the door and you'll be amid a full military escort. Nothing to worry about!"

I thought about it and grunted. "That sure seems easy for you to say. It's not your neck."

Ψ

My driver, the annoyingly chipper handler from the safe house, assured me that, though they still hadn't gotten to the bottom of how (or by whom) I'd been compromised at the hotel, extra precautions were being taken to ensure that everything would run smoothly. I responded with a nod, feeling not the least bit assured. What were these precautions? Who had planned them? The same people who'd compromised me in the first place? Something had been off about this mission from the outset, but by now, the paranoia had taken total control. How could I be sure it wasn't this guy—this handler whose name I'd never even caught—who'd been surveilling me? When I looked into it, I found that I did know his name. But I didn't *know* it. It's as if I had knowledge of knowing without actually knowing.

Earlier, when I'd sifted through his memories, he seemed clean—a bit overzealous, a bit too gung ho on this mission, but genuine when he claimed not to know what had compromised me, and genuine when he said he intended to get to the bottom of it.

Nothing was coming to me now in the car: not who he was, how much he knew. For the first time in ages, I was unable to see a single memory—his or mine. How long had I been wishing for this? And now it felt not like a burden lifted, but an even greater burden.

I had to center myself, tried slowing my breath but nothing was coming.

With a graze of his steering hand, I felt I could glean it all for sure, but something kept me from it. The paranoia had gotten me completely turned around. If he *was* in on it, I was afraid to let him know I'd caught on. But then, if the handlers thought I could read their minds, why would they let me anywhere near them?

None of it made sense. I closed my eyes and tried to think of nothing as the city outside the window gave way to woolly foliage.

The grounds were an obnoxiously lush golf-course green, only a few kilometers down the Rhine from the city center, at the threshold of those famous German *hinterlands*. Distance-wise, it barely qualified as suburban, and the 19th-century revival of 15th-century architectural trills gave it an uneasily enchanted feel. Disney-on-the-Hamptons.

Beyond the stonework ramparts, the concrete drive veered left into the main entrance, a fountained turnaround worthy of royalty, while to the right, a dirt access road slithered among dense forest around to the back of the castle, where unmarked vans were being off-loaded by kitchen staff in double-breasted chef coats. I checked my waiter's bow tie in the rearview and my handler gave me one last shoulder pat.

"This is gonna be a snap," he said.

I didn't bother acknowledging him.

The kitchen itself managed to be both bustling and spotless, a peculiar nervous energy pervaded the place as sous chefs chiffonaded unidentifiable herbs at well-stocked prep stations. I sped past, trying not to be noticed, pushing through the swinging doors into the opulent dining hall, where an assortment of East German dignitaries still grumbled about having been ferried into town on half the vehicles typical for a state visit after landing a massive Soviet-made plane into the Bonn-Cologne airport. Impromptu crews, I heard, had clumped along their drive, scrubbing off the graffiti that extremist groups had scrawled: swastikas, insults, and crude cartoons. Some groups had attempted to shoot fireworks at the motorcade, throwing rotten fruit or unfurling banners jeering the East German entourage and insisting they go back home immediately. Seventeen vehicles had graced the motorcade rather than the official twenty-one, in a subtle slight that had been missed by nobody.

There, amid the center of the pack, was a tall gaunt man in hornrimmed, tortoise-shell glasses, with wispy white hair retreating over the crown of his skull away from the scowl on his face. *Honecker.*

His expression looked more like he'd been winning at a lemon eating competition than merely having a frustrating day politically. I hoisted my tray of pastries and fruit and began to mill through the room, stretching out my senses to see what I could learn, trying to focus, aware how costly a false memory could be. But the messages came clear and incontrovertible: the men were all stewing in their thoughts. Nobody was yet preoccupied with the formal festivities soon to begin.

The first thing I uncovered was that the extremist groups' messages were fraudulent. East German leaders had decided it would discredit the West if they were to gain imagery of the West clinging to far right iconography, so they'd covertly funded supremacist groups themselves from over the wall and then took a bunch of photos for propaganda purposes back home. Most wrote it off distractedly with the usual "enemy of my enemy" mentality, but several were preoccupied with the horror of enabling the same Nazi ideologies that had devastated their last few generations.

Communists funding skinheads! My God, *the games people will play for power!* I found myself thinking, dumbfounded.

A flood of images then seeped in about the Warsaw Pact meeting that had occurred shortly before, and the conflicts that had slowly begun to materialize between the agendas of the larger USSR machine under Gorbachev and those of Honecker back home. For once, the Soviets were in the midst of a surge to open up, allowing reformers, for the first time, to air their concerns without fear of major reprisal—even if their concerns went unaddressed. This was what constituted a softer, kinder Politburo, but it was exactly the opposite of what East German rulers wanted. Tensions had evidently run high, and I was able to see the terror in all of their hearts as party men had stared in horror at Honecker disdainfully announcing to Gorbachev that East

Germany had "already done all her Glasnost, there is no more need here," after being directed to change policy course to match the Soviet line.

His hubris reminded everyone of the fates of so many other haughty leaders who'd defied the party line and lived to regret it over the last few decades. They were stuck on a narrow boat with a zealot—standing up to the enormity of the Red Army, and they all squirmed in their suits at the thought of it. Honecker himself just stared ahead in a pinched sneer.

But something distracted me from the general buzz of thoughts rocketing around the room. When I looked furtively over at Honecker's section of the tables, I immediately realized with horror what it was. Leaning close to Honecker and whispering into his ear was a stocky man covered in military awards. The hair at his temples had receded and lightened with age so that the point of his widow's peak gave the sinister impression of a bird of prey rising on white wings. I recognized him with a start from the case files I'd been shown back home: Erich Mielke, head of the infamous Stasi secret police—the scourge of East Germany. He stared straight at me while whispering to Honecker, whose eyes slid onto me in a frosty glare. My blood turned to ice and my legs threatened to give out.

As I stared helplessly at the veins bulging in their necks, their knuckles whitening with rage, I was abruptly able to see a myriad of images of the typical fates of their foes: secret prisons by the score, surveillance of every detail of life, a steady noose choking away any hope of air—unless leaders in power granted the privilege of breathing. A grim series of sights stormed about in their minds. But perhaps most importantly, I was shocked to see the fantasies they were sharing, while staring at me.

First and foremost, I was clearly not a stranger to them. Nor were my abilities.

They'd both conceived elaborate visions of imprisoning me in a series of underground cells, known as the Submarine, which they'd considered ironic given my background. They'd long constructed elaborate plans of how they would use the powers of someone like me, and they'd consulted with others about the possible routes towards achieving those aims. They'd found a rising obsession with the unknown powers of fringe psychological experimentation and longed to test their theories on someone like me.

They knew about my Great Uncle—they'd known for years. They'd learned from the USSR, who hadn't hesitated to share this information. Somehow, they'd kept themselves abreast of huge swathes of my life and projects, all the while keeping the West entirely oblivious.

My work immediately shrank away to nothing: no safety, no quarter. I'd never felt so at risk, so dehumanized and vulnerable. As I stood transfixed halfway across the room, my stomach flopped over and my mouth went dry—watching Honecker raise one hand and gesture.

He gestured at me. He gestured at me to come over.

Well, this was it. The pretense of my elaborate mission and all the supposed safeguards had disintegrated the moment I'd stepped into this damn country. As my legs began to automatically stroll me towards my doom, my face turned grey and my mind played me a quiet strain of the melody from an old classical tune Gramps had loved, Berlioz's March to the Scaffold. As I approached the table, Honecker took a long drink from a goblet of ice water, and a small rivulet ran down his chin into his starched collar. He took no notice.

"The famous American, John Calabrace," he began languidly, observing me from head to foot. "I believe we can do without pretenses, shall we? I don't see any need to play spy versus spy here. It is truly a pleasure to meet someone with your unique talents."

As he spoke, Mielke's eyes burned a hole through my head, completely murderous.

"To what might we owe the pleasure of your company, all the way over here in my Germany?" He gestured around the room, claiming ownership *über alle* with a simple magical wave of his arm. "Are the depressions of Western Capitalism really so bad you've been forced to subsidize your income working as a serving boy?" He sneered.

"Something like that, yes," I stammered. "A simple businessman, working my way through Europe…" I felt my heartbeat pounding in my temples, my mouth full of a bitter copper taste as terror shook my bones.

"Please, please. Businessman? Let's not insult one another. Maybe in the GDR lines are not so clear; but you, John—you are far from a businessman, and certainly not ordinary. Still, I hope you'd be willing to share a drink with us?" He gestured politely to a chair.

I steeled my courage and thudded into the seat. At a flick of his fingers, a military aide snatched up a champagne bottle from the table behind me and poured three small flutes. Mielke refused, his arms crossed over his chest. Honecker and I watched one another to see who would drink first and slowly raised our drinks simultaneously.

"To truth," Honecker mused aloud, an improvised toast.

I raised my eyebrows and said nothing, but took a quiet sip.

"I find myself curious how your minders could be so careless with you, valuable as you are..." he began, toying with me.

I, too, wondered, though I felt disinclined to share that information with him. I squirmed instead, thinking of the ease with which they'd uncovered and appraised my visit.

"I wonder if it ever bothers you, someone who can see to the root of issues—the way you can. I wonder if you see both sides of the hypocrisy of this wall, or if you're still a true soldier, eyes glued to the flags and pageantry."

"Is that a real question, sir?" My mouth got the better of me. I reacted instinctively. "How many civilians have you ordered shot this year for attempting to cross that wall? What do your *people* think of their People's Republic? Or are there any left, between the deserters, the dead and the Hohenschönhausen?"

He wrinkled his nose with distaste. "A simple patriot, then? How disappointing. Eventually, you'll find that all the walls of the world are not as simple as they might seem. There are not purities and extremes. Rather, there is power—and the few people willing to compete for it. Surely you aren't blind to your own nation's role in that eternal struggle?"

I sat silently, staring nervously at the exits of the room, wondering to what degree the security apparatus of the GDR had already clamped down on this building. Would I even have a chance of escaping? Where were those extra security precautions when I needed them?

"For example, John, surely you've noticed that we have access to certain information about you, which you'd hoped was confidential.

That didn't come out of the blue you know; it was given to us by Americans who respects and admire our aims, above and beyond your beloved Capitalism. Furthermore, what is America even doing in Germany now? Do you seriously believe America had a tremendous problem with the imperial Nazis in the first place, besides a lack of American access to their captured bounty?"

He leaned forward, like a snake playing with a mouse.

"Tell me, what did your country do with those war spoils of WWII? How many of your beloved corporations were profiting from central roles in the brutalities and systematic slaughter, the whole time? IBM? Hugo Boss? Kodak? Ford? And how long did intervention itself take? Of course, nothing happened until it was realized that the Soviets might move into supremacy. Then suddenly—such a rush, such fervor—such PAT-RI-OTISM!! And how did you celebrate liberation, peace, and freedom?"

He licked his lips, as if already relishing going in for the kill.

"Where was that hard ideological line against Nazi excesses when you expropriated the rocket scientists, the medical advances, and whitewashed it all under Operation Paperclip, and a million identical projects? The ratlines, the Manhattan project, the endless ingenuities of your shadowy CIA? Was it all just a ruse to end your Great Depression, to jumpstart your economy with new industrial projects? War, mass mobilization, armaments, industrialization on a scale never seen, factories everywhere, and then you lasso all the Nazi brilliance and dress it up with stars and stripes. Will you whitewash it just to take it to the moon, down into your deepest oceans and throughout your intelligence agencies, as you yourselves barely survive the same witch-hunts that plague every despotism-deploring democracy?"

He was only picking up speed, but I was miles away, panicking and frantically looking for anyone who wasn't an enemy: nothing. The entire room had coalesced their attentions in our direction, so silently focused you could hear Honecker take his breath before gearing back up.

"Can your marches and parades hide the crimes of those former Nazi SS now working in Cape Canaveral today? Can you so easily obscure smudges you've hoped to remove from the history books just because it benefits you? Please, John. Power is power: You're not a sheep, and I certainly wasn't born yesterday. Those fascist police-state advocates you train at Fort Benning and export back out to terrorize the world—they never get these sort of cross-interrogations you ask of me. Will you now lecture me about hypocrisy and walls with a straight face? Do we make the dominos fall, or do you….America? For shame. At least give me the courtesy of acknowledging moral parity."

His wicked face bent into a smile, and his shoulders hunched in a slow shrug.

"We aren't so very different, after all."

All this talk was above my pay-grade. And the whole time he was speaking, I was distracted by everything that he wasn't saying, gurgling away in the deepest recesses of his brain.

I saw the desperate discussions where the USSR wanted war reparations in the fifties and tried to put the squeeze on the East Germans—after packing up and extracting tons of local factories back to Moscow. In addition to an immediate resource shortage, there were widely perceived advantages for young talented professionals who fled to the Western world, so there was a serious brain drain of professionals who might ease the burden of USSR demands. The West considered Germany one country, so East German citizens who made it had immediate right to work and rights to social benefits granted the moment they arrived. Honecker had been front and center when the buildings facing the West had their windows bricked up and barbed wire stretched down the buffer zone. When that proved insufficient to stop escapes, he'd ordered the construction of a wall, against the advice of anyone with the smallest glimmer of PR sense. It had been a propaganda disaster.

Houses were cleared away, protective boundaries ensured, and even minefields and watchtowers dotted the boundary along No Man's Land. Parents were warned that, if they tried to flee, they would be labeled "incapable of mature choices," and their children could be placed into forced adoptions by the State. Since the Second World War, nearly one thousand people had been killed at the border, and all by the order of the man glaring into my face—speaking about relativity in brutalities and democracy.

As I looked back up at the man before me, Honecker grimaced: as if it were *I* who'd been responsible for these deaths rather than him. I felt a rising wall of hate emanating off him.

But that wasn't the worst of it, not by a long shot. The worst cognitive dissonance in the room emanated not from Honecker, but from his associate Erich Mielke. This was the man who had created everyday conditions where one in seven East Germans was complicit in routine everyday spying for the Stasi: Mielke's secret police force that kept files on six million out of sixteen million East German citizens. His crews most certainly were behind the handiwork in my initial hotel room. He was the man responsible for expanding the "Special Camps," a cheerful euphemism that served to cover literal repurposing of several former Nazi death camps to continue the grisly traditions of torture and oppression of state dissidents and irritants—which he spread out into all sorts of shadow venues and black prisons to always keep local populations unaware and unsure.

After returning from many years of training with the KGB, Mielke turned the former local page boys of the KGB into an authoritarian force like the world had never seen, obsessed with audio and video surveillance everywhere, all the time. Their largest goal was to increase productivity and ensure longevity by "knowing everything, period." Mielke brought in hot air blowers to open and read mail on a mass scale in elaborate factories, before resealing it and sending it along. He opened academies to the highest realization of the arts of the Stasi: lock picking, bugging, tracking, interrogation, coercion and blackmail, violence and more. They became the masters of human intelligence, coercing lovers to spy on their spouses, bosses on their employees, neighbors against neighbors. It became mundane how regularized and depersonalized these ceaseless betrayals of necessity became. Mielke expressed it all across his face: the idea that absolute power corrupts absolutely. In a way, his powers were like a dark mirror—reflecting the worst conceivable corruption of my powers. For him, this was all a lark. A pure necessity to preserve order.

In his mind I could see all the years that things had spent going from bad to worse. It was a marvel to see someone so heinous that some observers had called his regime of terror "less free than under the Nazis." He'd taught the guards in his prisons little tricks that he reveled in for breaking the spirits of prisoners—so they'd come to develop habits like banging in the doors at all hours to disrupt sleep cycles, using alternating abrupt temperature extremes to further shock and disorient the men they'd imprisoned. They mastered the art of extending guilt-by-association, and irritants the Stasi couldn't connect to crimes were threatened with further examination of anyone connected with their family trees, or social lives. They were shamed and threatened with exposure of every last indiscretion, whether affairs, ideological unorthodoxy, conjured accusations of subversion or espionage of every stripe.

It was a wild spider's web stretched over the whole society. It wasn't that I'd never seen evil before, but simply the *relish* of it all, that bewildered and sickened me. These men considered themselves artisans of pain and fear. Beyond the slogans and ideology, there was really nothing but that. Spiders—the both of them.

I began to get really nervous as the conversation continued because I began to sense a tone of triumph in all this. Honecker was smug. He knew I was trapped; he knew it was already all over.

Surely, the whole place had been locked down. I now knew that someone within my own government had been complicit in this operation and had betrayed me before it'd even begun.

Moreover, the local intelligence operatives at the safe house hadn't heeded my concerns. Instead, they'd sent me into a wolves den unarmed, under non-official cover, relying only on the public nature of the setting to make me feel at ease. My head was spinning. I had no way out. No one to call. Had this been the plan from the start? To serve me up as a sacrifice? Or worse, a prize?

Just as the tension became too much to bear, Honecker rose and clanged a fork against his water goblet a few times. Clearing his throat, he announced he'd like to ask a few questions of his unexpected guest, in privacy.

Abruptly, and without a hint of question, everyone lurched out of their seats and cleared the room, guards and dignitaries included. Only a half dozen burly men remained, and Honecker, Mielke and Me.

Honecker's face grew darker as he began to raise up and speak in a sharper tone.

"Soon, I believe you will learn some things about the way our two countries are run. I believe the time has come to stop relying on hypocritical delineations. Today will be the start of something—"

But at that moment, there was a loud shout and the sound of breaking porcelain.

The next second, the double doors to the kitchen burst open and a flood of chefs poured into the room—all with tall hats and long, flowing aprons. There were about a dozen in all, pushing stainless steel food carts covered in long white tablecloths—topped with elaborate cake stands and steaming carafes. Honecker turned purple with rage.

"WHAT IS THE MEANING OF THIS?"

The lead chef seemed unaware of his irked host. He turned to his staff and gave a nod.

Wordlessly, they ducked into tactical positions, about half the men pulling service pistols from the back of their pants. Honecker's guards across the dining room reached for their own pistols.

"Hände über Ihren Köpfen, HANDS ABOVE YOUR HEAD" screamed the head chef, in an American accent I recognized. "NO ONE MOVE, NO ONE SPEAK, NO ONE GETS HURT."

The cooks made a beeline for me. Honecker shot a devilish look at his guards in protest, but before he could open his mouth, the tablecloths were pulled back to reveal a treasure trove of MP5's—a West German creation, and the U.S. Navy's standard issue submachine gun at the time. Honecker's guards could barely flinch; they had no hope of reacting in time. The remaining chefs fell into assault positions, training the MP5's on the stunned Germans, as Erich Mielke's hands attempted to crush the edge of the table in impotent rage.

Two men grabbed me, and the mob moved as one towards a back exit.

By the time Honecker's furious voice had exploded into the balmy afternoon, we were leaping into three identical black vans behind the complex—flying up the dirt road.

Nobody arrived in time to give chase, and not one single shot was fired in the entire extraction procedure. These were some serious professionals at work.

The lead chef took off his hat in the seat across from me, with his head facing out the window. "It appears rumors of an intelligence leak might not be as exaggerated as we thought," he said.

I knew I recognized that voice. CJ turned to face me.

"I'm glad he cleared the room when he did, John! I saw you in there sweating."

I looked at him in disbelief.

"What the hell CJ, have you been here all along?" I demanded, the adrenaline putting a hard edge on my simple frustration. "I thought you'd left me out to dry."

"Yes, well," CJ began. "You'll be happy to know there's an entire kitchen staff bound and gagged in a closet somewhere back there. We had the place the whole time."

"Bound and gagged? You're kidding, right?"

"Figuratively speaking." He gave a reassuring smirk. "The original plan was to have you in radio contact, but once the bugs in your room were discovered, we couldn't risk it—and couldn't be sure which of our communications were being monitored. So we kept your surveillance close to the vest this time. Don't worry though. You'll certainly never be taking any trips alone from here on out."

"Forgive me if I seem less than comforted," I said.

"That is, I hope you won't mind me accompanying you from now on? We'll add uncovering the spy ring attempting to compromise you into our mandate ASAP, if you buy the food and beers for the celebration tonight. We don't want to have too many cooks in the kitchen, after all."

"You can forget this *next mission* nonsense right now," I said. "I'm getting a desk job—at the beach. Better yet, I want to call the guy with the dolphins…I want the intelligence job that never involves meeting with other human beings! No captures, no imminent interrogations, and certainly no last minute intervention rescues by a bunch of *chefs*!"

CJ gave a great laugh of relief. Somewhere even farther into the hinterlands, in a vast abandoned field overrun with velvetgrass, the vehicles drove up a long ramp where they were secured into the hull of a massive Hercules C-130 cargo plane with no clear indications printed on its hull. Several commandos sprinted around yelling into walkie-talkies as the hatch closed, and just as quickly as it had started, the mission was over. Wheels up—heading home.

There were slaps on the back all around and a celebratory toast of oversweet sekt one of the recon-men produced from his van.

"Drink up," CJ said. "You can buy tomorrow. Tonight, we're drinking on the Germans' tab."

23

We'd been back in the States for one week and were no closer to figuring out what had happened. Total confusion filled my head on the plane back—so many thoughts to process—but most were just fragments that didn't connect. We'd clearly been dealing with something larger than anyone had thought.

Who had warned CJ and Dannels? Neither had been able to trace the call amid the rush.

So what *did* we know? We now knew the drunken ramblings of Avner in Egypt had been true, not ramblings at all. He may or may not been drunk, but every action and word and thought he had was planned and deliberate. Maybe they were even tied to the news we'd already gotten out of Yurchenko about networks of spies, but we hadn't put enough together to act on it.

There was indeed a rogue spy circle operating among us, forwarding information on our projects—and me. They clearly operated recklessly enough to be heard not just by their intended recipients, but at very least also by East Germany and Israel. Who knew who else had the capacity to intercept or middle-man attack those communications?

We decided that we had to act quickly. I didn't want anyone to wrap a black bag around my face. I didn't ask for this; my life didn't need any more guessing games. For God's sake, I got flustered when I had to drink Coca-Cola instead of Pepsi—I didn't need this type of stress…And I *certainly* didn't feel like involuntary relocation, interrogation, or torture, thank you very much.

It was absolutely terrifying to consider that not only did someone know that there was a new covert-services role operating internationally out of the USA, but they even knew the specifics of an experimental telepathy role and my standard operating procedure. Basically, there was a giant, flashing florescent sign with my name and capabilities on it, and a giant arrow pointing right down at me…

"What do we do? Where do we even start?" I asked.

"Well, I guess we can start with motivations. Why would somebody transmit data on you? Clearly they think that info is valuable to the USSR. Now why would that be? You're utterly un-vetted in the intelligence community. You're basically brand new! So it can't be that they think you are any sort of traditional operative with years of operations, protocols, or history to exploit. No, they clearly know that there is something special at work."

I was determined to go on holding my head despondently between my hands, so CJ just continued his line of thought without interruption.

"Now I don't know how much you know about this already, John, but there have been a lot of weird experiments over the years in the East versus West arms race, and most of it has been out of the paranoia that the other side was somehow gaining some superhuman advantages. Efforts have been made to do all kinds of unlikely things 'to keep pace' with the Soviets: mind control, astral projection, time travel…the works. Frankly in my opinion most all of it is lot of nonsense—but serious time, energy, and resources get put into these projects. It says something that nobody has yet said: "alright guys, cut the crap—from now on we only focus on real-life objectives…"

I only looked up for a moment, with the intention of rolling my eyes and gesturing the irony of delivering that particular speech to a functioning military psychic. But CJ was on a roll and wasn't derailed.

"If we haven't found a way to walk through walls, the odds that they haven't either are pretty strong. We've certainly spent the money and expended the manpower and hours. But no matter how many disappointments the Soviets might have had following up on overhyped rumors in the past, I'd still assume they wouldn't want to be responsible for missing out on an asset-exploitation scheme of the potential magnitude you represent, no matter what."

I threw up my hands in desperation. "So you think I'm like—the poster boy of a new arms race? Oh God, that is totally not what I wanted to hear..."

CJ sighed. "Honestly, I'd say it isn't unlikely. Imagine the power of that sort of rumor: that someone gleans total sum secrets just by touching someone? The security forces of the world expend a pretty sensational amount of strategy and energy trying to track down secrets. If they had a chance at such a shortcut, they'd likely do whatever it took to get it."

"Well it'd certainly be easier for them to achieve that, if a bunch of Americans were constantly trying to help them behind our backs," I said dolefully.

"Yes, it certainly would."

Ψ

"I'm glad to see you in one piece," Dannels sighed, a few days later. "I'd sure love to know what the hell we're dealing with here..."

"Well, what do we know so far? Have we been able to isolate any likely sources for a leak to the USSR?" I asked hopefully.

"We know nothing. We know jack shit. We'll be starting from an assumption that any assumptions we had already were one hundred percent wrong. This is BIG. There's absolutely no way that the level of sophistication and counterintelligence that you encountered in Bonn should have been possible, without a great deal more participation and complicity than I'd imagined possible. You were a sitting duck, and they were just waiting to nab you. For that, I feel personally responsible. I think without the quick intervention of CJ's team, you'd be brushing up on Kremlin architecture right now."

I gulped, imagining Honecker's nasty secret prison cells as I'd seen them through his eyes. "Where do we go from here? I went straight to our guys for help after finding the bugged hotel room, and they sent me right back into the den of the devil. What am I supposed to make of that?"

"John, that's not the half of it. We investigated the room, tore it apart. All those bugs, all that equipment: it wasn't Soviet style at all. Soviet stuff—you'd know it when you see it. I personally analyzed those room reports and I can say—with both regret, and certainty: those bugs were OURS, not theirs. Maybe they had help—but the bugs were ours."

The words sent a cold chill down my spine and my fingers reached automatically for my ring to steady me.

"I don't understand, why would they want to bug me abroad? I already live in a constant state of observation, and I've learned to accept that. But I've played this game my whole life—like I'm the star of some sideshow tent. For once I thought I'd been acknowledged as a positive asset to our country—everyone knows I have next to no contact with the outside world…I don't represent a threat! How is this still happening? Who is behind it?"

Dannels looked over to me pensively.

"I have no answers, yet. Perhaps some *do* see you as a threat, in spite of your services. There is no over-exaggerating the generalized military reluctance towards any 'outlier' that they cannot predict. Military embodies 'force' predicated on preconditions of control; it thrives on control. You are the strangest anomaly they've probably ever come across! What's more, you are the antidote to all those structures of secrecy that many of those men lead their lives by. Touching someone and then miraculously intuiting everything they know—represents a real threat to that type of person, and their grasp on controlling their environments. But more importantly, I believe there are multiple challenges facing us here. Clearly, we aren't just facing a force of military men, wary of someone with powers they don't fully understand. We've also got someone with access to some very covert information, someone who must be at a fairly high level—passing Intel on to the Ruskies. And this person probably isn't acting alone."

CJ waited a moment, and then spoke. "If we have a high level leak, we need to know whether this person is just a rogue with a grudge—still in process of being developed, or if we've got a full on Soviet double agent on our hands. From what I saw over there and what John has described, I don't see this as a man with a grudge passing on a few details to make a buck, to eliminate a rival, or to liquidate someone if he can't exploit him. I see a spy ring. I think it's real, and I want to seek it out—hands on."

"I wouldn't be too quick to rush into this," Dannels cautioned. "Both of you need to be acting on the assumption that you're being observed all the time and focus on situational awareness and safety as much as you can. Something doesn't add up here, that much is certain. If your instincts are correct, we still have no idea how high it goes yet, nor how well supplied they might be, or how well protected. We're going to need to have all our wits about us, to seek this one out and pull it out by the roots."

Ψ

CJ and I thought we had nothing to lose by trying to find where the leak was coming from ourselves.

It seemed oddly logical that CJ and I should seek out the origin of the leak. He was an intelligence officer trained in this kind of technique, and I was essentially an Encyclopedia Britannica of everyone I ever met. We found an abandoned office in an old building on base and set up shop. A computer, two desks, and a couple hundred file folders, with a lightbulb glowing down from an aluminum caged military fixture was our new home. All business, CJ seemed at home: a happy Spartan. I eventually had to bring in some extra lamps and a New York Mets banner to lessen the interrogation cell vibe. CJ actually smiled when he saw the banner, and then we were back to business as usual.

We were slowly attempting to form dossiers on everyone who would have access to information on me, beyond a certain generalized minimum. Theoretically, very few people would know exactly what sort of experimental capabilities I was testing: most just knew that hush-hush tests were being run under secretive conditions. When Stubblebine had initially been "encouraged" into retirement, there had been an overt reaction against any expenses that couldn't immediately demonstrate a measureable return. But military spending never remains fully-accountable for long. It was less than a few weeks before his remaining allies had managed to reinstate nearly all his projects—in more cloak and dagger circumstances, pushed more into the shadows.

He'd been under the impression that the actions taken against him were just a sign that powers-that-be were just worried that the successes pouring in would draw too much media exposure. They wanted deniability and an arms-length reporting style. An ancient military man, Stubblebine had no problem suffering a façade of prestige loss, if it meant he could consider his life's passion: the projects he'd developed over decades towards his beloved Stargate Project.

He was an odd fellow in many ways, but he truly believed in what he did. He believed that everything he did was for his country's benefit. Part of his former special access program operation was transferred into a DIA handled clone, variously called SUN STREAK or a few other permutations—but most of the rest was "deep black," officially closed. Unofficially: it was *me*, basically.

So there shouldn't have been many people who knew what was happening. Whenever there were operations planned out, I should have been able to blend in with the other non-official cover agents. Nobody should have been sticking out their necks to demand paperwork or something. My orders came from way above their pay-grade, and we kept the details murky. But somehow, somewhere, somebody had clearly gotten wind of what was going on.

Were they at the hospital or connected to somebody who was? Or was it someone who'd asked too many questions after my Navy exfiltration and had just never let it go? Maybe it was interdepartmental squabbles, where someone thought they ought to have more control over conditions on the ground, felt threatened by the unpredictable meddling-potential we represented: out here in the fringe projects? I had no idea, no leads.

So we began a vigorous campaign of brainstorming. We tacked large sheets of paper across the barren walls and scrawled all the significant possibilities where someone looking for bargaining chips might have been able to track down hints of our work. We started vetting and creating dossiers on everyone on our team, to be sure everyone checked out and that we hadn't missed some clear liability. We searched for potential conflicts of interest, for anyone who might feel slighted—or even anyone who might have somehow arranged access to our rare record-keeping system. Nothing. So far, we'd found a tight ship, with no explanation for the leaks that were starting to become floods.

Finally, CJ had an idea that held a bit more promise than what we were finding. We decided to check out computer based access queries on my name and operational records. We figured with the level of bureaucracy and secrecy at work, it probably wouldn't return much, but it might at least indicate if part of the problem in West Germany had been just a problem of complete obliviousness…What if our guys just had no idea who I was and had thus been terribly underprepared to help keep me safe?

But instead of blank screens, we got bells and whistles. *Hardly* what we were expecting.

In fact, there was no explaining *how much* my records had been accessed. Regularly, constantly, and not clustered in one region or timespan. According to the searches logs for my name, I was evidently considered the belle of the ball. But why? The people with security clearances sufficient to be accessing my most recent work would most likely be completely outside most of these records, high above anything we could access. Moreover, I should have basically gone blank, right off the records system, post-Navy—but instead the queries were continual and recent. Constant. What could they be searching for, and why?

More importantly, and much more confusingly, there was residual data & files that neither CJ nor I could access or comprehend, that implied that queries and even reports had actually begun to appear with alarming frequency *long before I'd even joined the Navy.*

Something was not right. It couldn't be right!

I reread the dates, looked helplessly at an equally perplexed CJ, and wracked my brain to understand what I saw. At first, I thought I must be bureaucratically misunderstanding something, fundamentally misunderstanding the screen, or reading it wrong. But as I stared at the dates I felt ice run through all my veins. They went back to my preteens. No, further. There had been regular reports made, from god knows where, *since my birth.* I couldn't see them, I couldn't access them, I couldn't even tell who had made them and precisely when.

But I knew all at once that my entire life had just gotten a whole lot more complicated...

"John," CJ started gravely, "I don't know what to tell you—"

But at that moment, something strange happened.

Our access disappeared, all at once. Our screen literally made a whirling sound, an hourglass appeared, and a message arose implying that the files we were seeking could not be found or accessed. Then even that disappeared—all we had was a blinking curser.

I looked at CJ, and he looked at me. After entering and reentering our credentials, we found that suddenly we had insufficient clearance to fully access the same information we'd just seen.

"And...there goes our best lead."

I covered my face, with a sigh.

Ψ

A week later, we were no closer than we'd been before. We'd hit a dead end. We were consistently running into access and clearance restrictions, which had suddenly zoomed to ten times as stringent. Ironically, having been amid the security protocols of military so long, we both knew there was little we could do at present except strategize and bring in the big guns. We visited Dannels and got his promise to look into things and do all he could.

Meanwhile, I entered an entirely new era of paranoia—overwhelmingly preoccupied with my own safety and privacy. I was therefore as suspicious as ever, when a courier knocked on my door with an extremely formal looking envelope, written in elaborate curling calligraphy.

He handed it to me and left, and I re-lowered my guard, staring down at the envelope in my hands. It was addressed to *Mr. John Calabrace*, and labelled as being from *The Future Mr. and Mrs. Matthew Riley*. The name meant nothing to me, so I looked at it in wonder for a moment before tearing it open and getting a blast from the past.

It was my Elizabeth! Elizabeth, my childhood lodestone from Cape Cod, was getting married and wanted me to come home. It would be a long engagement, but they wanted the word out—so people could free up time to attend.

I stared at the words, the names, the stamps. My brain was in a million places, and none. I thought of all the buildings I knew from those ages of my life, the wind over the dunes, of Elizabeth's laughing face, of my Mother and Father, and my brothers tumbling over the seaside.

Innocence, and simplicity.

For the millionth time, the thought harangued me that I had no idea what was real about my surveillance record, or how much those hovering questions might soon disturb the sacrosanct memories of my innocent childhood. I had no idea who would've wanted to document my life, or why. I had no idea how that could transition into someone attempting to betray me to a foreign power, someone willing to risk my life. I had no idea about anything.

Now as I thought about returning to the gentle world I grew up in, and the circles of smiling faces that constituted holidays and celebrations, I wondered how I would face that world in this state?

CJ walked in, electric and agitated as well. He was uncharacteristically preoccupied, and his normal unflappable composure seemed decidedly unsteady. His eyes were darting all over the place, his hands fidgeting.

"Are you okay?" I asked him curiously. "You don't seem quite like yourself…"

Strangely, I don't think I'd ever seen him sweat before. He seemed completely conflicted, warring internally with something.

"They are promoting me. They want me to up and move across the country." He explained the details and the opportunity offered to him, and I think I was happier than he was.

"That's wonderful, CJ! You've always wanted that gig! You'll do great!"

"They also want me to do it in three weeks."

"Oh."

"Yeah, *oh*. Who's going to look after you? Who's going to seal all these elusive leaks?"

I chose my response carefully, burying all my personal worries just under the surface.

"Dannels will. And I'll move. I'll buy a gun. I'll get a dog!" I tried to look convincing.

"I don't know if a dog is going to cut it, John."

"Please. If somebody wants to kill me, they'll still have to get past a great team here, *trained by you.* And if you hadn't noticed, I'm fairly aware of the world around me. I'm sure I'll be fine."

"Unless they improvise," he countered uncertainly.

"Yes, unless they improvise. But even then, I'll see something coming. It isn't often people dislike me. It'll stand out. I'm nice people, I'm the guy that every Mother adores—I can tell them what they want to hear"

"Well I don't like you," CJ joked sarcastically.

"Doesn't matter, because I'm getting a dog…But you should definitely take that gig, CJ."

"Yeah. I don't know."

"I don't know much of anything. But you work your ass off. That's one of the few things I *do* know. You deserve that promotion, and you and I both know you have to take it."

CJ fell quiet for a while, watching the dark street from our single grimy window. Finally his soft voice cut through the silence. "John?"

"Yeah?"

"Even if I do end up doing this thing, until we have a better idea of what you're up against—you'd better get two guns. And two dogs. And not Corgis, John—something big. And get Dannels to move you the hell out of range of these guys. You need someplace that is protectable, someplace independent. I'm not leaving these details in your hands, that's for sure."

"Oh sure, I'll get right on that. Have you got any ideas? *I am broke*, of course, they don't pay me like they pay James Bond…"

"Well, we'll see what we can do about it. Dannels will find a way; he always does."

We both sat there exhausted, staring listlessly straight ahead without an idea in the world what might come next.

"You know, this isn't really the most pressing of my problems lately, but I still feel really cheated about the whole "espionage without evening wear" thing. I was always sure such things would be provided, mandatory even. I got a wedding invite today, what am I supposed to do?"

"Shopping, John. We'll make a list. *First*, we save your skin. Then, we save the world. Last, and I mean *absolutely* last—shopping."

"This job, CJ…it's just the worst. I could've been a brilliant poker player. Think about it! Easy."

CJ laughed.

We sat drinking cold coffee dregs, watching the sunrise illuminate our messy office. It was then that I realized, with a terrible gnawing in my stomach, exactly how much I'd miss him. How much I wasn't ready for the wobbling world to spin its weird changes any faster. He represented all the stability in my life: shortly to be removed.

24

El Salvador was where everything changed, where I finally lost it. Where I knew it was over.

I'd been scrambled to El Salvador with nearly no explanation. It had been abruptly announced that I would be handled by an entirely new team "for logistical reasons beyond our control." There'd been a hostile takeover of sorts within the intelligence community power brokers—and these goons were the result. I also knew that they knew next to nothing about me, my skills, or my background. They were suits, through and through, sticking to the script—come hell or high water. Making a mental note to ask Dannels to arrange some kind of transfer ASAP once free of these autocrats, I determined to uncover their ambitions. I dove into their heads.

Most were hired help, contractors brought in to supplement a force, led by two men from Langley and one from Foggy Bottom. Even the briefers were kept intentionally unaware of their primary mission goals. I peered into one guy's head who appeared to be the chief bureaucrat of the five; and he'd been told that the goal was to "stimulate within the community a constructive discussion of American-Salvadorian issues of importance, and help to expand the lessons learned and accomplishments achieved from past missions, which will lead to an increased understanding of both nations—and their shared values." The language of suits.

I also grinned upon realizing that the State Department guy from Foggy Bottom, Daniel, was tremendously attracted to the Army Captain that would be leading the Personal Security Detail Detachment. I'm not sure why I thought it was funny, but just his memories of "my goodness, he has beautiful blue eyes," or endlessly sprinting after him at every opportunity with clingy demands, like "Captain, do you have a minute, I need to discuss some things with you…" It made me snicker every time it happened. It just seemed so out of place with the squared-away atmosphere that the suits were going after.

Ψ

It was phase one of an information campaign that skirted the letter of "counterintelligence" by happening to be focused on truths, albeit convenient ones for particular American interests. Of course, with a band of company men this eager for senior recognition, the emphasis was on *convenient* rather than truth.

We'd be members of the Socialist Party of America, men with wild eyes and olive-colored jackets who'd made our small fortunes in regional tire repair shops or criminal defense of Black Panthers and Yippies. We were here, ostensibly, to show our support and inquire about the ground situation of the Farabundo Martí, the umbrella organization consisting of five socialist bands of guerrillas, of which our primary target was the Fuerza Populares de Liberación, the FPL. Our directions were to gather information about the crimes they'd committed in the name of Communism and funnel it back to our higher-ups, preferably with documentation. That way it could be dispersed to whichever newspaper editor golfed with the bosses.

While America had droves of cameras on the ground, as well as surveillance boats and planes by the score to scoop up relevant enemy scandals, they insisted that "a slam dunk," was somewhere right around the corner.

A slam dunk would ensure that the world knew how we'd done something "really special" together in El Salvador—helping the center-right government dismantle their opposition and ending the Salvadorean Civil War, and clarifying that the USA had done very well by intervening in the small nation. With no time to lose, they decided they would send their least understood intelligence asset in to seek out and highlight that slam dunk, which they would then present to the world.

We would be stationed at a resistance camp in the hills of Chalatenango, the upshot of a long-standing deep cover assignment. One of the suits told me about the great success of their recent long distance phone call with the camp's organizer, a Colonel Fabio Ordoñez, in which the colonel had been cunningly convinced of our cover. But I could see the call in his memories. It was riddled with obvious apprehension on the part of the colonel. I had no access to the colonel's thoughts themselves—for that, I'd need to be near him— but he certainly didn't *seem* to be sold, and I had a hard time believing these suits were really so convinced they'd gotten us bulletproof cover. More likely was that they had checked off the boxes of the mission's goals to date and were basically unconcerned about the quality of their work. As it stood, a band of random American communists sounded like the most obvious cover for CIA spooks I could imagine. It looked like we weren't even that well covered.

We were going fishing, but it was unclear exactly how this was going to work. Our cover was ludicrous—these company men were expected to convince as Communists? With an American passport—fake or not—we'd be the height of suspicious, and not exactly the likeliest confidants for criminals. Even if I could glean anything with my abilities, that didn't offer much in the way of documentation. Perhaps they expected me to glean key shapes for their filing cabinets and cut keys with my mind, but that's not how the gift worked, and I thought the company had been made crystal clear on that fact.

So this was it. Pure stupidity. Not well thought-out by any stretch of the imagination but approved by some Washington Deputy Undersecretary somewhere, probably with the double intentions of justifying unjustifiable approvals given years prior and adding a neat little feather in said Undersecretary's cap when it came time for reappointments.

But with CJ in the midst of promotion halfway across the country and Dannels preoccupied with uncovering a spy ring, I had no leg to stand on in terms of negotiation or resistance. The men clearly weren't very bright, but they were used to being in charge, so they made demands because that's what they knew. Simple as that.

I missed my team more than anything, more than ever. I'd been trapped in a clown car full of company men. I had zero backup. There was not a man among them I trusted, or even one who had a moral compass—from what I could see. I remember thinking 'It's not like you can mess this up Calabrace, the plan seems to be—there is no plan, get in, get out, go home.' I'd be sent in with zero morale and zero hope of success. Great.

The whole thing was to be elaborately stage-managed, beginning with a long series of photo-ops and back-patting had been scheduled to conclude just before UN inspectors arrived to commence their work. It was a partisan ideological affair from bottom to top, to glorify certain bureaucrats above my pay-range, a quintessentially American quest for order, regularity, tradition, and shared 'Constitutional' values. I immediately approached my chain of command, doubting I was the right person for the job. I felt nervous that the gig sounded more like politicking than an intelligence gathering operation.

But they wouldn't have any of it, instead blinking while insisting the job was simple: repeating the initial mission script, verbatim. Find 'Slam Dunk' proof "that things were better today than they'd been before, that these *comunistas* were committing atrocities."

I was a bit dumbfounded. Either I didn't understand my mission, or just my bad luck. After a few more woozy answers, I got frustrated by formalities and asked them point blank if they were ordering me to fix evidence to preconceived conclusions; or was I to gather analytical intelligence that they could assess?

Without CJ or Dannels there, it was like I was talking to a brick wall. These men neither knew me nor cared what I thought. Looking through their thoughts, they didn't necessarily seem clever enough for there to be a distinction between simply rejecting the premise of my moral outrage out of hand or simply being oblivious to it. They just weren't men accustomed to complexity or excessive deliberation. I found myself wondering how they'd come here, why they'd been elevated to such responsibilities.

They all seemed to cross borders of intelligence, military and "independent contractors." Most had served in all three roles, and some for foreign governments as well. Meanwhile, they saw me as merely a malleable tool to be used and returned; and they didn't care much either to convince me of their goodwill or articulate their logic.

"Mr. Calabrace, we're not asking you to form a conclusion. We don't make foreign policy; we simply enforce it, and we amplify and leverage it. We're looking to augment the National Prestige that our persevering efforts have earned us in El Salvadorian campaigns, with a Real Slam Dunk to silence the misguided critics."

I turned to face my dear leader head on.

"With all due respect, sir, I've served as both an active duty serviceman and as part of intelligence operations. I've fought for my country, my family, my friends and our Constitution for over a decade, proudly serving alongside the greatest military men and women in the world, but I need to understand what my mission is here. It sounds like I am on a PR campaign to validate policy I don't understand or even necessarily care to, and to somehow retroactively vindicate an intervention that's a done deal. Is that the case? I'm sorry if I'm misunderstanding. I have to warn you: I'm not particularly qualified to be your concert promoter—gentlemen; I'm more of a backup vocals act."

My joke did not go over well. I received blank stares and then an icy response.

"Mr. Calabrace, you are a government employee. You are also obligated to support the exercise of American policy: however your superiors see fit to ask you to do that. That basic tenet of your employment isn't up for discussion here. We're asking you for nothing more than to help your country, in her hour of need. American policy in El Salvador is stringently anticommunist, and our policy has led us to support consistent anticommunist elements on the ground, in order to bring the anticommunist fight to the Enemy. In line with those objectives, we've asked our intelligence services to compile additional aid in emphasizing our regional successes and the excesses of our enemies. We are concerned these nuances will be maligned and downplayed by special interests within the United Nations. You are to serve your Nation's interests here by helping clarify why our interventions were necessary, and convincingly presenting a Slam Dunk success story of how our efforts culminated in a better tomorrow. Based on all the briefings we've heard describing you as the jewel in the crown of our intelligence apparatus, we know our substantial investment in your training, testing, and expenses will pay off. More importantly, you will make your country proud!"

They sat in silence a few moments as I looked straight into their faces, carefully gauging whether they were fucking with me. Nope! Unbelievable, these guys really believed the shit they were spreading. I really wanted to scream back as loud as I could "ARE YOU FUCKING KIDDING ME?" but I didn't and couldn't

"Well, Mr. Calabrace, if you don't have any more questions; you're dismissed. You'll be contacted tomorrow with travel details. Thank you for your continued service to your country."

Ψ

Four days later, our transport landed in El Salvador. I remained flabbergasted, bewildered, and evidently on the hunt for a Slam Dunk. Whatever that meant.

I was provided with a translator and a clerk, as well as an impressive protection force, and housed in a massive military base, within which I was granted next to no freedom of movement, "—for your own protection, sir."

At the camp in Chaletenango I met the colonel for only a few minutes. He had a shaved head and the potbelly-burly bicep combination of an aged strongman. He about crushed my hand with his strident grip and looked around as he spoke. "Things are going very well here," he told the translator. "We are anticipating a diplomatic phase to be initiated soon. I can not speak any more about it. Please, enjoy your stay in our camp."

In straight order, I was hustled off to a barracks, where FPL fighters mainly played cards. Ostensibly, they were merely taking a break from their long days of fighting, but I could see it in their memories: they'd been told to keep an eye on me.

The colonel himself had been warned by his superiors: "American outsiders? And they want to see how the camps work? *¡Idiota!* They are CIA."

I wasn't even sure if this was true—were we CIA? DOD? INR? Technically, the consortium of agents made it unclear what agency was pulling the strings. Still, they'd had the gist right.

When I sifted through their recollections, it became clear to me that these men were a ragged bunch. They had no documentation of *anything*, least of all any atrocities they'd committed. Some of their tactics had been as ruthless as my superiors had been selling me on—errant shootings, a scattering of executions without trial—but they were not, on the whole, given orders to execute at will, and disorganization, with its concomitant abuse of power, is the tell-tale mark of any guerilla war. Even the *American* Revolution had featured insubordinate acts of terror.

Many of the local men, I could see, had not set out to be communist freedom fighters. They'd begun, instead, in neighborhood watches and civilian coalitions formed for protection: between the government on the right and the *comunistas* on the left, they had few options for neutrality. More often than not, the Farabundo Martí had merely seemed to them like the lesser of two evils: the one least likely to murder them for a lack of proper documentation, or to cart off their young sister because they found her attractive. It isn't that there were not bad men in this camp, but among the good men, the perception was that here there were fewer of the bad. It was a depressing situation: the age-old "rock and a hard place" position for many of them. And I was certain there was very little I could learn here of any operational value.

"My friend," I called to one of the cardplayers in the soldiers' favorite English phrase. "Cómo se sale?

"I have to get out of here."

Ψ

After the failure of phase one, I wasn't interested in going on, but it wasn't up to me. From here, I was told we'd tour a series of fine estates from a heavily-armed caravan. We would basically interview rich businessmen who were thrilled with current events, to prove how great things in El Salvador had become.

But invariably, their answers and appraisals came out dark and complicated in practice. Everyone was talking non-stop 1950s themes in florid prose about our beleaguered Monroe Doctrine providing a Final Bastion against dreaded Communist Subversion, Domino Theory and Containment against infiltrations of every stripe. Nobody discussed the fact that the Wall had just fallen.

El Salvador could not have been any different from the clean, sterile, single-minded submarine where I'd learned my trade. It was pure pandemonium. Nobody could explain their goals to me without dragging Nicaragua into the discussion, and Guatemala, and Honduras, and a million contributing factors at once. Most of the fears that motivated our actions were in response to faraway events from previous decades, reheated proxy wars with all the usual suspects: Russia, China, Cuba, and Vietnam. Advisors' heads appeared no clearer than mine, and over the decades the original clarity of even their intentions had begun to unravel.

I started to get the impression that my new handlers had begun playing an extremely high stakes game of Risk, like I used to play with Nannie and Gramps. Only they were playing about 40 years of very real brinkmanship, paranoia, and proxy war. I seemed to be the only one taking it seriously. Everyone else wanted sports and cowboy movies. Everyone wanted to find that Slam Dunk, no matter the cost, the risks—or how unsound the reality was.

It was a recipe for disaster, in terms of a "hearts and minds" campaign. Short of funds, bureaucrats chose the path of least resistance: funding groups on the extreme right of the spectrum, amenable to American interests, unlikely to make a fuss doing things like nationalizing the goods we wanted. The turnover rate amid American policy advisers had become outrageous. The soldiers themselves had grown unstable. I'd been around the block a few times, spending lots of time in close quarters with soldiering men, so I knew under exactly which strains these soldiers had been operating. It was just like in Vietnam—the same morally-exhausting policies that had made burnout and post-traumatic stress endemic among their American instructors' ranks, a decade or two beforehand. I was terrified each time I dove into their thoughts, memories, and minds.

In the paranoid old mind of the bureaucrats and state-sponsored military men, I continuously uncovered an old quote by Mao about how insurgents must "swim like fish among and amid the people." The Salvadorian military must have read it somewhere: and had clearly panicked. They'd decided to respond with a ceaseless strategy of taking a military fight *to the civilians*, hoping that displacing them might disrupt the partisans' supply chains. The actual insurgents and guerillas took to the hills and waged their own terrors—and the people suffered. Civilians merely bounced back and forth helplessly, between explosions from all sides.

After my villa tours, I was sent to some small business centers in a metropolitan cluster to interview some well-to-do townspeople, who had clearly been absolutely cloistered from the events of the war. Obviously, the expectation was that I would compile a sanitized, whitewashed representation with which to cheerlead my patrons. But it seemed too much. The interview subjects were preachy and zealous and insincere, and their eyes bulged when they talked about the quiet nobility of this or that savior of the Nation, who'd rooted out this or that insidious—whatever. Even they didn't believe the words that left their mouths.

The story was always the same, always unraveling into "he started it," with an accompanying vindictive rage. There was no objectivity to be had. Moreover, I was distracted from the start by how much some of these businessmen virulently hated all the poor and remained deeply suspicious of anyone associated with them, unlike nobler businessmen I'd known back home. They were convinced the poor *brought this on themselves*, and now they must live with the consequences of THEIR actions.

I immediately thought of Gramps, but I just couldn't picture my Gramps in this context. He was an insatiable negotiator who'd been rewarded with a fair amount of wealth and success, but he had a heart and soul too—and he hated no man. Here, there was real tension, real resentment. It was us and them, black and white. It was like they taught me in nuclear physics—these were two particles: one negative and one positive that by their makeup opposed each other, on every level. The landed gentry feared they were losing their ascendency before their time. The rage was palpable and enormous. I couldn't help wondering how my Great Uncle would have dealt with such a command. Would he have just left?

It felt like grade-school, like my job was to build a pretty diorama of all the nice Salvadorians—cotton heads on bodies made of tongue depressors: stylized and sweet.

How could this be my mission? I wasn't a public relations person; I was an analyst. If they wanted PR, there were a thousand firms in every American city that would jump at the chance for a tropical vacation—even in war-torn Central America. So why send an analyst to, more or less, *fabricate* intel?

As with so many dealings in this shadowy world, I would never get a hard answer—if there was one thing the higher-ups in the intelligence community are good at, it's remaining undiscovered. MKULTRA, Operation Mockingbird, those uncovered operations vexed journalists and the public, and *when* a U.S. Agency ever admitted to an illegal operation, the message was always, "It's not like this happens every day." But with an agency that, by design and necessity, cannot be subject to public oversight, there's no guarantee. And even for the most patriotic defender of the flag, the inevitable educated guess is that these things do indeed happen all the time.

So sure, there was pressure to deliver intelligence convenient to a particular angle, and my *educated guess* was that this public relations work was not intended for public consumption but to sway centrist powers in the intelligence community who weren't so sure our involvement with El Salvador was worth continuing. All it takes is a little budget reapportionment, a revision of priorities, and the careerist intelligence bureaucrat overseeing an operation that's up for cuts might see his power slipping. It's banal and unsexy and extraordinarily petty. That is, it's office politics. The longer you last in this community, the more you realize that no one is immune: not the Justice Department, not Congress, not even the President. The horrifying part is that in some areas, office politics don't just mean missing out on promotions, or transfers to less thrilling divisions. In some bureaucracies, office politics are measured in death counts.

I kept at it, trying not to think too much about worst case scenarios. Get in, get out, go home.

I continued making the rounds, talking to wealthy housewives from the fourteen major families that had run the country since before anyone could remember—living in sprawling estates along cash crop coffee plantations—behind huge walls. Talking in abstractions about the roles of agrarian elites in international affairs and mechanistic geopolitics. Nearly all described how noble the soldiering young men were, how dutiful and honorable. They saw a tidy conflict, gushing over how they respected their Families and Values and Tradition. But what happened with the Churches here? I asked.

But they'd just stare at me blankly and ask if I'd had any cold drinks yet, maybe something to eat? Most never even left the haciendas, and the few that did had no desire to share their dark thoughts out loud, although I could see them clear as day. When I finally left in exasperation, they'd return to dusting the furniture or just ask the servants to do it, so they might sit and fan themselves by windows.

I was escorted everywhere by military escort, to carefully prescreened and sanitized locations, always listening to mad speeches while sipping tea and holding my tongue. It was like my childhood, all over again. But there was no way that this was why I was here! How was I supposed to learn anything that might help anyone—by talking to these people?

Finally, I began to develop a terrible idea. I would act on my own initiative! It was terrifying and more than a little mad, but what the hell. I had to get actionable intelligence; I had to understand the picture. I had to gauge the opinions of people who'd actually experienced the events of the last years—not as fighters, but as private citizens—or what was the point? I wanted to hear it from the ground, not from either side. So far I'd learned nothing—absolutely nothing.

So I waited and planned an escape. First thing in the morning, I knew they changed from base security watching me to an assigned protection detail. (Right before my escorts would come and drive me towards the normal daily routine of housewives and cheerleading, YAY.)

But in that window—if I managed to slip out, I could find my way to the nearby village, knock on some doors—and find some information. I managed to convince my nervous translator that this had all been agreed upon, through all the proper channels. Together, we slipped out of the base onto deserted streets.

Within ten minutes, we were in a café alongside several somber looking, gaunt men.

The second we walked in, most of the men immediately grabbed their hats and filed out the door. The bartender protested. Something I understood roughly as, "Look, get out, we don't want any trouble, America," but I gestured to relax and said I was only here for a beer. My translator began to translate, but the bartender understood me with no trouble and slid two beers down the bar with a chilly look.

The place was a hovel. Bullet holes literally indented the table legs, the wood edging dented and cracked where brawls had once disrupted the tranquility.

"Hey, would you mind if I ask you a few questions? I just don't understand anything about the war…" I began.

"I don't talk to you about nothing," the man interjected. "I don't know who you are, or why you are here; but nobody has anything to say to you about the war. Certainly not here. We mind our own business."

Even at a distance, I saw that the man wasn't as rude as he was trying to be but instead absolutely terrified. One evidently didn't stroll around here, talking about factionalism and expect to be unnoticed, or worse, unpunished. He didn't trust me and had good reason to trust no one.

In his mind, I saw an image of someone very familiar (a brother?) being dragged away in darkness: a scene of suffocating potency sitting right behind his processing mind as he spoke to me. He was not a random, disinterested stranger. He was broken, and somebody had broken him—not once—but again and again. I was too naive to consider that people might be wary of my questions, or see my role as adversarial in all this.

"I'm sorry, sir. I didn't mean to be rude, it's just that I—"

He cut me off again. "Be quiet. I run an honest business here; I don't want that compromised. If you have business with the war, or anyone involved, please find somewhere else to deal with it. We are quiet people here. We do not talk about such things."

Well, that was clear enough. I finished my beer in silence, as my useless translator sweated bullets. He didn't touch his, clearly wanting to run. He kept tapping me on the shoulder, glancing at his watch. I gulped his down as well, thanked and paid the silent bartender—and we stepped back into the bright sunshine. A man leaned against the wall outside, waiting. He waited for us to pass by in front of him, and in a quiet voice muttered in Spanish under his breath, "Hey America, you want to talk about war?"

My translator wanted to leave, quickly. He had no interest in staying, but I convinced him to help me translate. I was thrilled and saw it as a sign that what I was doing was destined.

"Yes! What can you tell me about your experience? What's happening here?"

"For my safety, I'll say nothing. You want answers, talk to your prisoners over in that base. There are many of them, full of stories. Go to the churches and see if anyone will talk. Then go to the refugee camps and ask people why they are there—not in their homes."

I pressed him with more questions, but a jeep was pulling around the bend up ahead, preceded by a large cloud of dust. The man shook his head, and his eyes darted—and he fled into a side street without looking back. I stood alone with my translator when a military jeep pulled up before me."What are you doing outside the base?" the Army Captain yelled.

"I asked my friend to show me the village, for my report," I said, gesturing at the helpless translator. "It's actually quite a scenic place."

"THERE IS A WAR GOING ON! You are not authorized to move freely, and you are certainly not authorized to leave the base without proper security escort. Sir, you will come with me, NOW." He gestured with his fingers and two men hopped down to literally place me into the jeep. My translator climbed in behind me, dejected. Two displaced soldiers clung to the jeep support structure, standing on the running boards. We sped off in an explosion of dust.

Ψ

Back at the base, after a few hours of lectures and reprimands, I was returned to my room. That evening, I bickered enough with my new

US superiors over the phone that I was finally granted rights to speak with the base prisoners: provided I always had a military escort. I hung up the phone and waited. Somehow they pushed those commands up the chain and back down to my local agents, who grumbled about the directives like the world was ending.

"I don't understand what the hell you think you'll benefit from talking to prisoners. All these men were captured after American planes spotted insurgent bases," one zealous man squawked in the background.

Ψ

I felt the prisoners before I even got to them. The guards had begun a long rambling speech that would last the entire time we toured the dungeons, but I tuned them out and prioritized my mind over my ears. I let the evil atmosphere of the place engulf me. My brain raced ahead of me down the dank corridors to gawk at the desolate souls before my eyes could get there. All around, I finally saw the parts of the story that I'd missed out on above ground, in the fancy houses and finery. Yes, some were criminals with dark pasts, but most of these people had been ravaged and shattered for simply asking questions, or raising concerns about policy.

The guards described heinous crimes in flowery ideological prose right out of a partisan guidebook. The illiterate peasants sitting before me had evidently been masterminding international subversions of the State, facilitating ceaseless foreign infiltrations of industry, as well as murdering whomever was found dead, destroying anything found broken, accounting for any hardships ever encountered.

They'd been caught in between factions, for the most part. Most were simple internally displaced people, chased back and forth by the partisan squabbles rocking the countryside. Like angry warriors the forces of revenge would wobble over the horizon on a cloud of dust. Since the civilians hadn't managed to expel or destroy the rebels on their own, the government assumed them complicit and punished them in the stead of the perpetrators, operating on the principle that mowing down easy targets would knock out at least some of the rebels' infrastructure, with the added benefit of sending them a clear message about how ruthless they were willing to be.

The paramilitaries would round up an arbitrary number and slaughter them as examples, beating and berating the rest to maintain the status quo. Some would be imprisoned, charged with whatever crimes needed a fall-guy, then executed. Some were just left to starve, or to be beaten or humiliated when bored guards needed diversion.

The prisoners looked like beaten dogs: the cagey eyes, hands raising automatically to protect the face, knees blocking the groin from kicks. They cowered upon our approach. Shame and resigned terror mingled in their faces. They'd clearly all seen death, up close and personal. Death and worse. Even their churchmen had been gunned down across the nation, after bothering the wrong people. The guards joked about it, saying the insurgents literally didn't have a prayer.

Nonetheless, the guards had completely convinced themselves of their own innate, innocent nobility in the situation. Many were not by nature terrible people, but they no longer second-guessed their orders, acting on knee-jerk reactions to commands, like frog legs zapped with an electric shock. It was Milgram experiments all over again: all the humanity of the humans crumbling beneath uniforms.

Beneath every symbolically-starched uniform and stiff military shako, these guards saw themselves as the noble protectors of justice, order, and peace. They believed in the Slam Dunk. Immediately before their eyes, they glared down on those muddy, bloody animals— clearly capable of nothing but violence, subversion, and treason. They never harbored the slightest suspicion that labels of "guilt" and "innocence" might be arbitrary, or that the designations of terrorist or subversive, insurgent or guerilla could degrade to the point of being meaninglessly applied—during the realization of daily patrol quotas. Everyone adjusted their chin straps, tightened grips on firearms, and flinched into a tighter stance of attention: "just soldiers, just following orders.'

I finally interrupted my escort's rant, growing more and more agitated by the moment. "I'd like to speak with the prisoners now," I interjected, simply.

"Are you authorized? I must warn you, I cannot be held responsible for your personal safety. I've warned you—as well as I can—about the kind of people in there."

"I appreciate your concern sir, but I'll take my chances. Could we just proceed, please?" I smiled weakly and gestured at the nearest cage door.

He smirked and opened the door, standing aside. I ducked to enter the cell, so gloomy it took my eyes a few moments to adjust. Several cringing shapes in the corner shivered, and I recognized the shapes as people. My translator reluctantly ducked into the room after me, holding a sleeve over his nose.

"Hello! I'm American. Can you tell me why you were arrested? Whose force did you fight for?" My translator rolled his eyes but dutifully translated. The guard glared at us, suspiciously, as my translator innocently shrugged.

As my eyes adjusted, I thought I saw one of the prisoners wince further at the word "American," his hands protecting his face. That surprised me!

"Do you have any complaints? Can you tell me why you are here, what you were fighting for?" I hazarded.

Nothing. Nobody said a word. Someone quietly moaned in the shadows.

The guard had had enough and babbled again about law-breakers, scum, and moral society. But as his clamor replaced my useless interrogation, my concentration finally locked back into focus. The minds of the unseen men in the room zoomed into focus, clear as day.

Most of the men were from a small town on the other side of the country, successively pushed back and forth between guerilla bands and the army. They'd had to master concealing their tiny migrant camps in tiny clusters along the riverside, but were still being regularly discovered. They'd been forced to live like guerillas, just to stay alive. Whenever patrols approached, the men took to the river, breathing through hollow reeds. They waited out the curious troops' investigations, watching in horror from beneath the water. Their few possessions would be burned or confiscated, their meager shelters demolished. They saw the rage in the eyes of the warriors as they defied a slaughter. Both sides' zealots charged them with crimes, but neither side had much evidence—however, that didn't stop either side from accusations, threats, or ultimately torture.

Worst of all were the children that they saw driven off in convoy after convoy. Children of friends, neighbors, and families: scooped up like fish in a net, packed like sardines in a metal truck and driven away to an unseen place for unknown reasons, with no explanations ever given. It sucked the life from these people, more so than the torture, humiliation, and all the basic human rights they'd already lost.

I recorded notes on their experiences: who they were, where they'd come from, the organized forces who'd pursued them, regardless of partisan affiliation. Without conscientiously deciding to, I'd begun doing exactly the opposite of my mission.

Ψ

One day my hosts proudly explained to me how ORDEN and ANSESAL had been built up under the famous Major Roberto D'Aubuisson—from next to nothing. They bursted with pride at how they'd been trained by CIA, working alongside my friends in the Green Berets and representatives of the American State Department. It didn't take long for them to display competency in the stringent anti-communist lessons they'd been so meticulously taught at the School of the Americas in Panama, and later in Fort Benning.

Although my hosts gently explained that these organizations existed "to identify and eliminate purported communists among the rural population," all I could see were the horrible realities behind those acronyms. They were Stasi-type security organizations, whose sole purpose was terror and absolute control. One in six people reported on their neighbors, families, and friends. They initiated death squads for opponents, systematic tortures, and physical destruction of every component of the opposition.

The more I lingered around the guards and soldiers, the missing figure in our geopolitical cost/benefit assessment became clear: 75,000 bodies. Many more simply disappeared, never to be seen again: a bizarre state of affairs for a country the size of Massachusetts. There really weren't that many places to go! It didn't take long to recognize the unmistakable footprints of textbook CIA counterinsurgency tactics behind those atrocities and disappearances. Someone was clearly decimating the Salvadorian civilian populations and acting with impunity. Why?

Unfortunately, with my particular gifts, nothing hidden was barred from me for long. Sooner or later I came across nearly every atrocity second-hand, through someone else's eyes. Everybody had a sliver of horror to share. The second I shared their air, all their memories became my memories, so the butchery of the last few decades progressively took firm root in my brain. Everything was jolted, everything was pushed aside. All that darkness came rushing in. Nothing pained me more than seeing the children pulled from their parents arms, pulled away from a Mother's lifeless body, a screaming baby grabbed and passed like a piece of fruit from one man to the next.

The sights would torture me....but they would never leave me—because I recognized the faces of some of the men who'd prepared them: Special Forces in Fort Bragg, NC, alongside the 82nd Airborne Division.

They were friends of mine, men who I'd joked with around the canteens and chow halls of America. I'd missed their students' handiwork—destroying 200 more displaced civilians at "El Calabozo" (The Dungeon), throwing acid atop the sad remains floating in the river.

I literally saw the prisoners' nightmares. I saw the recurring symbols that haunted them: the boots, the open cab trucks with men holding onto spindly frames rolling over the horizon, and all the specific tools preferred for psychological effect. But pushing beyond the feelings of horror, I forced myself to look deeper at the specifics. Wondering why one man who never left a fetal position was so fearfully obsessed with images of water, I probed into his recent past. I saw him suspended in a concrete pit full of water, locked within an iron cage. He was being interrogated by the same talkative guard before me now. The water was up to his jaw, and only by clutching vigilantly to the bars 24/7, could he keep his exhausted head from sinking into the water, to avoid drowning. The interrogator taunted him and kicked lightly at his already white knuckles—not enough to irreparably break his fingers, but just enough to scare him and spill a bit of blood.

But that wasn't what gave me the biggest shock. As the memories of the prisoner looped in my mind, his jailor's dialogue crescendoed into a louder pitch: threatening his family, implying they were already been held in the next cell—"wouldn't you like to save them?" I couldn't help feeling rage at the pure evil of the interrogator. He'd found family letters in the man's pockets and read them aloud in a shrill, mocking voice. As he reached the end, he pushed play on a hidden cassette player, and a shrill feminine scream ricocheted around the room. Was it really the wife's scream? The prisoner couldn't know one way or another—that part simply didn't matter. What mattered was the man I saw sitting behind the interrogator, observing the torturous affair with a bland, bored look on his face, listlessly scratching checkmarks across a page in a book labeled *Foreign Internal Defense.* He didn't seem to have a huge role, nor any particularly interesting features that drew my attention to him. No, the problem was more specific: he was wearing an American uniform.

25

I found myself confronting my superiors, not quite having thought it fully through before I began my rant. Blood rang in my ears. I didn't call CJ or Dannels first. I didn't think.

"I need to visit the migrant camps. *Now.* I know the answers we need will be there."

"What migrant camps are you referring to?" came the patient reply. I described locations and conditions and the horrors the displaced people had gone through at the hands of both sides of the conflict.

I described the rare moments of aid from guerillas, who'd once brought medicine from a nearby covert base after disease had broken out among the migrants. I mentioned moments the military had helped, when a village elder was kidnapped and implored us to encourage these situations—as policy. Mostly, I just passionately appealed for immediate intervention, thinking we could win the war of hearts and minds that I still imagined we were fighting—not grasping the full extent of cynical realpolitik wars being waged, a mere one rung above me.

"Could you describe the specifics of the region they'd been passing through when, as you described, disease struck?"

"Well of course I can, but that's not the point…if we really want to help them, what we'll have to start with is—"

Over and over my temporary mission superiors were gentle and patient with my speeches, my worries, and my naïve imploring. But as they scribbled down notes onto maps, they weren't really hearing my words—nor were they moved by my story about innocents stuck between a rock and a hard place.

They calmly explained away my shock at having seen an American officer observing interrogations and changed the subject when I continued protesting. They promised no abrupt shifts of policy, nor any surge in investigatory spending. Rather, as we spoke, they worked on triangulating bases and notating defensive capacities, scribbling plans targeting "insurgent interactivity" and movement patterns. I sensed that they felt I'd minimally served my purpose, so now I should just go away. They told me nothing of their plans. But I learned within hours—they abruptly informed me that the situation on the ground had become far too dangerous and risky, and that while I'd done a great service for my country, I was to be immediately extracted back home. I was soon to learn that once they'd roughly approximated likely locations of groups, they contacted the same shock troops whose abuses I'd just complained about, and transmitted coordinates along with requests that anyone found be neutralized. I heard the guards gossiping about it merrily in the hallway, as I was led off to pack my bags.

I never saw the faces of any of those prisoners again, except in my dreams, nor learned what eventually befell them. I spent the following months being bounced between different agencies—CIA, DOD, DOJ—rarely using my gift at all, confined to a desk as retribution for my insubordination in El Salvador. I sank into routine: get up, down a few Aspirin for the hangover, unbutton the top button of an arguably clean shirt and slide in, drive to work bleary-eyed and unthinking. At my desk, I'd approximate the look of a busy man, spending probably an hour a day in the bathrooms—anything to cut into the day. The good news was that the memories were kept mostly in check. The bad news is, it's because I spent most of my time drunk.

As the UN Truth Commissions trickled onto the television screens, it became clear that information I'd provided in El Salvador had been immediately used by covert forces to lash out at "guerillas," with a string of mission successes against "camouflaged-enemy *networks along riversides.*"

One day a memo came across my desk summarizing the specific calls. I recognized my own sentence—describing moral outrages against innocent prisoners—quoted verbatim in a report. But it had been phrased in an entirely new context: describing how *effective* the use of "caging reticent prisoners in a water well" could be on breaking down *insurgent morale* and resistance to interrogation. When I read it, I threw up.

In the blue light spewing from my television screen, I decided I was done. I had finally crossed the line. I hated myself for allowing it to happen. My life had become my worst nightmare.

Never again. Game Over.

I unplugged the phone, bolted the door, and drank until I couldn't remember.

Ψ

It had been three months since I'd stopped answering the door. At first, they never stopped coming. The assumption was always that I was just kidding around, or that it was some sort of tantrum I was going through—at worst, a ruse for a better salary.

But it was none of those things…I was *out.* Really, *I*—the very concept of me—had nearly ceased to be.

Finally, somebody managed to have me marked as on "Short Term Disability Leave." The knocks lessened to nothing. It wouldn't have mattered. Most days, I couldn't have gotten up to answer the door, even if I'd wanted to.

Alcohol had always crept along in the shadows of my life. It had always waited in the background, seductively, patiently awaiting the days after missions. It awaited the first moment when the hustle and bustle of ordered life died away, and I was on my own time. Now, it had become a way of life.

Perhaps it was because I'd abandoned everything that kept my mind busy that, after a while, even the drinking couldn't keep the memories at bay. There was no evading the images any more. The worst of them, the most painfully nausea-inducing ones—they followed me around like mosquitos, buzzing in my ears, burning my nostrils with the viscerally remembered reek of blood and terrified sweat. Imagine nightmares coming to life every waking moment and knowing that each one was a real part of someone's life. That's exactly what it was.

That evening had been no exception. I was lying on the floor in the hallway, willing the spins to slow, shaking with cold in an eightydegree balmy Coronado night. My sides felt like something was trying to supernova within me: a gnashing, turning ache. I'd tried to throw up once already but my body had refused even that; instead a pathetic foamy drool alone had quivered on my lip. I'd just sunk back on the ground to wait. I knew the way the booze would cycle on bad nights. I had ample experience.

I spent some time daydreaming about the first time I'd tried alcohol, as the walls rotated over me. I think I must have been about thirteen. My friend Michael had taken a bottle of some god awful whiskey from his Dad's living room cabinet and called me to come meet him. We went to the woods behind Nassau Hospital, where he took a gulp, and so did I. We both nearly threw up, but as teenage logic would dictate, we proceeded to drink the horrible tasting elixir till neither of us could stand. He passed out, which even I realized was not a good thing. I circled nervously around him. Ultimately, after he'd thrown up on his side awhile, I lifted him up and supported his wobbling walk until I got him back home. I rang the bell and then ran like hell for home. I walked in feeling as slick as could be, having gotten away scot-free.

But I'd never been quite the crafty type I imagined myself to be. Minutes after I got home and darted for bed, the phone broke the silence of the dark house. His Mom had called mine, and I knew I was in trouble. The next day, I discovered that evidently this was a problem above a Mom-grade lecture. She just shook her head and told me how disappointed she was; but then she ominously added, "You need to talk to *your Father* when he gets home about what happened, John." Whenever she used the word "your Father" rather than Dad, I knew it wasn't going to be good times ahead.

For the next four hours I paced, stayed up in my room, and frantically worried about what was going to happen with my Dad. I watched my Dad's Oldsmobile pull into the driveway from my bedroom window and knew it was game time. I heard the side door slam shut, as my Dad came into the house. My heart was banging through the wall by the time I heard him bellow, "JOHN! DOWN HERE, NOW."

Shaking with fright, I encountered Dad standing near the landing—his deep brown eyes staring at me. GO TO THE OFFICE NOW, he ordered, and we did. I rarely saw my Dad angry; if he was angry, there was a reason. He'd never let little things bother him, not ever. He'd survived the D-Day invasion and had metal plates in his arms and legs: he knew that annoyances in life where just that and let them pass. But now, he was clearly going to kill me.

The air in the room buzzed with the tension. For the first five minutes, he refused to say a word, only staring past me.

He finally said, "You know you could have killed yourself, or even your friend—drinking liquor like you did…You two are barely teenagers. You're lucky you didn't fall on to the train tracks, or hurt yourself in traffic coming home." He paused, letting the imagery set in. "No more of this, John. No drinking again till you are legal, understand?" "Yes," I mumbled.

"Now let's stay in here for a half hour or so, so your Mom thinks I'm giving you a big lecture."

That was it. I guess, looking back, that was basically classic for my Dad. He'd known this day would come, and although he was disappointed with my actions, he'd never let emotions overtake his perspective of reality. He got back to his work and kept funding his family. And, behind his back, I kept on drinking.

It started out nice: it helped me relax a little. I was the shy guy who became more social, the quiet guy who became the funny guy. I convinced myself that it was my own miracle cure, that I was releasing an inner me, a better me. For a while my friends would remember the funny things I'd done and said and remind me of it the next day. I felt famous, rather than faulty. My brain eventually just started accepting it as a tool, rationalizing blackouts and hangovers as the high-entry fee to *fun.*

I always wondered why I was the chosen alcoholic in the family and secretly wished it on one of my brothers, so I could be the "normal" drinker. There was never any question of just not being a drinker. How would I relax? How would I slow the images? How would I make people laugh? I couldn't imagine my life without it.

But that's the trick with most any drug, right? It comes to you in a soft-sold, friendly manner—a treat that will make the day just a bit better. But as an addict, it's never enough; you reach out for more and more and more. Your addiction grows, without a visible change. When you do finally see, it's usually a long time since it grabbed you by the balls, so now you feel you can never let go. It's like the only dependable friend remaining—since you've retreated from the real world—except now it's seamlessly transitioned into the depressant antagonist that you feel defenseless against, yet inextricably allied with. And yet with all this awareness, here I was: drunk.

I was stuck with other people's memories and emotions, but at least this made it easier to bury my own. My emotions were on lockdown, twenty-four seven. In a group of strangers, no one asked me if I was lonely. A small joke, a shared laugh, nothing bigger than that. My feelings could be kept down—chained within the dungeon of alcohol. I knew I was rotting myself from the inside out, but frankly, I didn't care.

At night, I tried to talk to the interchangeable strangers and barflies but didn't see the point in sharing half-truths, after knowing their deepest emotional purities myself. Regular people didn't say real things but hid them deep within. That much I knew. So I heard my mind crying out, "They won't believe what you are telling them anyway, so save yourself the grief and order another…and another…" I very rarely refused.

We all like to think we are different. We all think no one understands us; and to a certain extent it's true. But some, like myself, also clearly have something in our chemistry, genetics or psyche—that makes us easier targets for coping mechanisms, like addiction. The word floated in the back clouds of my mind, carefully shielded from my active mind. It emerged only in the glum moments of regret, just like I felt that night. Suddenly it was the clearest thing in the world: addiction—I was *an addict.* And it doesn't matter what it is, or how it's formed; what matters is that it *does* exist. I'd seen the pamphlets a million times: *The sooner you realize you need help, the better.* Years later my first AA sponsor would tell me, it doesn't matter how you got here, just what you are going to do, moving forward.

But I didn't have a sponsor in the early days; I had next to nobody, and even if I had, I had my own agendas, too. I was truly convinced that I needed this closed existence. I had stopped talking to everyone. I knew every scintilla of what was inside their heads, so why even bother having a conversation with them? The more I thought, the deeper I fell away from reality. I'd kick open my front door after all my drinking companions had given up for the night—scattering to stagger to their broken homes—and find the same memories of a million strangers' secrets would be waiting, crowded into the back of my skull, sloshing amid a half a gallon of a mild poison.

My head began to ache, both from the imagistic crush and from the night's dehydration alike, but fortunately I knew just the cure. I'd picked it up on the walk home, and I knew it was waiting in the fridge for precisely this moment. Ten minutes later I'd finished the forty ounce bottle. I passed out across the edge of the mattress—halfway back to the floor.

My dream recreated one particularly troubling trip, where I'd snuck away to London. The only thing I remembered about the visit—after arrival—was waking up on a dirt road about twenty miles outside of city center with no money, no passport, no wallet—and no idea what had happened the night before—the days before— or the days after. I was shivering and soaked in heavy morning dew when I blinked open my eyes, still sobbing hard in the middle of the English hinterland. Only it wasn't England, I'd fallen off the bed in my Coronado house. And it wasn't dew, either. A grown man, I'd pissed my pants in my sleep.

I'd run the laundry and cleaned up the house awhile, carefully avoiding passing any mirrors as I did so. A bright flash outside the window convinced me that a lightbulb must have blown somewhere in the room, although I feverishly hallucinated the image of a grown Bryan Walker holding a huge camera, outside the window. I groaned at the headache overtaking me, which always arrived alongside paranoia, insomnia, self-hatred. I turned off the lights, drew the curtains, and poured a bath.

Laying in state like a dead king, I subconsciously cycled through all the ritualized self-loathing procedures that alcohol uses to guarantee a lifelong parasitic host. I hated myself. I hated my life. I should exercise more. I had no willpower. I wasn't fun enough. I just wasn't interesting enough to draw in friends who'd love me like I loved them, in all their honesty and detail and complexity.

I ignored the fact that I was demanding an unfair superhuman talent out of my loved ones to insist on equivalence, but that's splitting hairs...I was down and out. I closed my eyes and let my mind wander. The water muffled the sounds of the house. All my thoughts were obscured by the dull throb of the bath water that rocked me closer and closer to sleep.

The tricky thing about the lifestyle I'd chosen was the perfect protection it provided against public intervention. Combined with my cognitive skills, I was now completely isolated and insulated from the world. That isn't to say some folk didn't try. I'd been ordered to get help before, more than once, but I always found a way to weasel my way out of *learning* anything.

I'd take the brochures, smile at the gurus, flatter their egos or puncture them at their emotional weakness...then I'd stamp my timecard and waltz out. I was a master at the game, because I knew the game board better than any competitor could.

The *glamour* of alcoholism never seemed to trouble me. The strange array of beds and bedmates, hardly even remembering names or faces of most by morning—I could imagine worse things. The cutting off of frustrated family members from your life was painful. But there, my excuse for silence had been crafted out beautifully by Uncle Sam, since I was officially a "civilian contract employee of the US Navy—working on a secret project involving advanced sonar."

The brotherhood of the Navy tried to help me, but I wasn't ready to listen. While serving onboard JAX, I remember I'd been pulled over one night for drinking and driving in Virginia Beach. When the command found out, they'd suggested I attend the Navy Alcohol Safety Action Program. Instead of listening to the messages, After first contact with the other attendees, I proceeded to read the heads of every other person in the room—fifteen men and four women. I callously surmised that they were all just a bunch of drunks, with whom I had nothing in common. So their shared program was useless to me.

The amazing power of the human mind!

I was fortunate that I never hurt or killed anyone, during those days. But like most drunks, I came close. One time we were in New London Connecticut, and I was driving my first brand new car. Two or three passengers rode with me as well, and we were all pretty drunk.

I ran into a guard rail on the on-ramp to I-95. I completely obliterated the front passenger side of the vehicle, but miraculously, no one was hurt. The police came and asked for my license and registration. When I gave them my supermarket courtesy-card instead of the requested documents, the officer got angry. I was told later in awestruck tones from my fellow drunk passengers, that what I did next seemed genius: I struck up a conversation with the officer detailing my admiration of the 75th Infantry Regiment Army Rangers Company B, which he had served under; and I represented his former company commander as my recently passed Uncle Frank. He let us go with a warning. My drinking companions were all dumbstruck. I was a hero.

But after twenty years of fighting a battle I couldn't win, I'd finally realized some moments of clarity in my battle with alcohol. It wasn't all that heroic.

One time, I agreed to attend a rehab for recovering alcoholics and addicts. Looking back, it was destined to fail from the start—because of my mentality. Although I accepted the fact that I had 'alcoholic tendencies,' I'd never accepted that I was *an alcoholic*. An alcoholic was that guy who everyone in the family tried to forget, the street guy that you threw a few dollars to—to keep him at bay. I was still working! I had a home!

I'd arrived at rehab with exactly that wrong attitude in my head. I insisted that I wasn't a common alcoholic like the rest but a very gifted man who NEEDED alcohol to control his mind from running amok. Sure I needed to control it *better*, but surely some good analysis and insight would do, in place of sobriety? I felt sure that it could all be accomplished rather easily.

I'd gone through the motions, reading the memories and emotions of everyone I talked to—from the woman at the intake desk onwards. I knew right away that she was determined to help other addicts/alcoholics, after the loss of her Mother to alcohol. I decided I wanted out of there right away, so I immediately used a similar story to hers to sidetrack her from questioning me. She never saw my subtle attack coming and left me to my own devices in no time.

I used the same playbook with counselors, therapists, psychologists, and psychiatrists. I used their own insecurities and emotional highs and lows to convince them I was defeated and hopeless. I could relate it to the deepest traumas that they'd ever suffered and explain to them how powerless I felt—just as they'd felt at those points in their lives. I could take an emotional event in their life, change the names, "one up it," and then mitigate any real obligation of emotional honesty, from me. It became more of a game than it was any form of counseling or therapy. Thus it progressively became more and more a failure for me, although in my conscious mind it was a success, because I *beat* them. I just failed to pick my battles.

Over the years I would have more than a dozen people assigned just to keep me focused on a task or mission to keep my drinking addiction from getting in the way. In a way, I guess since I knew they were there, it essentially gave me carte blanche to push boundaries further than most could. And I certainly did.

Both Dannels and CJ would periodically try and intervene to reach the sane, reasoning portions of my head. I'd usually listen and agree politely, but after that it was business as usual, and there wasn't much they could do. Every so often, after a long bender I surrendered with words that "this was it, there was going to be *a new me.*" In the early days, CJ often offered to drive me to a therapist, psychologist, or psychiatrist of my choosing when he could tell that I needed help. But I convinced him that AA would be of no use as "they don't have the mountain of issues that I do."

I went to the best DOD vetted doctors or therapists for a few visits—essentially to get a few days' or weeks' sobriety—then I'd revert back to exactly where I was before. CJ and Dannels saw it again and again with me. I thought I was fooling them, in saying that I was alright. But even without my empathic skills, they saw clearer inside me than I did.

One day, as we were walking near my house in Point Loma, watching the surf, CJ asked me if everything was alright. How I'd been doing *with the drinking*. For the first time, it occurred to me: anyone close enough to know me *knew* I was in trouble. He looked out over the water and spoke in a quiet voice, out of clear experience.

"John, You just can't do this to yourself anymore. The only one you're hurting is yourself. Even heroes have weaknesses and feel pain; that's just part of the process. All we can do is try. But sometimes, of course we bleed as well. On the inside." We'd stood quietly over the bluff, letting the words sink in.

What a treasured memory, I thought tranquilly—neglecting the moral behind the story.

But when I opened my eyes back into reality, I'd half-drowned—drunkenly slipping into sleep in a frozen bathtub. I found myself sobbing, alone in the dark.

Something had to change.

26

There's nothing like half-drowning in frozen bathtub to give you a sense of perspective. I called CJ, and he and I had the longest heart to heart we'd ever had. We covered everything—drinking, despairing, and even post-traumatic stress— albeit my strange, unique variety. In the end, he helped me with a lot of things—but more than anything he convinced me I couldn't run from my life indefinitely. Things had changed a lot in my absence. Dannels had *raised hell* when he heard what happened with my handling team; all the goons had been kicked out in no time, and heads had rolled. My trusted team returned, but they'd all been sitting on their hands while I recovered, unsure of what came next.

"We still need you, John. Work has always been where you shine the most. You need that structure…I think deep down, you need to know that you're needed. There's no better place!"

So I shit, shaved, and showered; and tried to pull myself together. "One last time," I told CJ with a warning finger in the air, "just this once—and just for you."

He grinned, and before I knew it—I was back in the game.

Ψ

The base at Tulva sat in the middle of the rubbled Bosnian road stretching from the atrocity sites at Srebrenica to those of Prijedor.

Over each site loomed the territories of opponents who'd built up conflict to increase their relative ethnic land claims: Serbia on one side, Croatia on the other. All countries involved had internalized a million insults and rationalizations and revenge mentalities for perceived grudges from the preceding decades, in World War II, and even earlier. Everyone referenced genocides and betrayals and thefts and vendettas. They'd blame *Ustaše* legacies of horror as justification for their own brutalities, or those of the *Chetniks*. There were elaborate mental gymnastics created, absolving them through the jingoistic invective of religious Patriarchs, or the imperatives of cultural and ethnic competition, the tensions of linguistic incomprehension, plus every other nationalistic and constructed division ever imagined.

It wasn't the first time; these groups had been played against each other by every occupying power in memory: the Austro-Hungarian Empire, the Ottoman Empire, the Nazis, the conflicts between Catholic and Orthodox faiths and their joined conflicts against Islam. But it was some of the ugliest conflict the world would ever see.

Even during the Bosnian War itself, the land remained a nest of foreign spies: every nation involved in peacekeeping forces, every proxy, was nestled in the shadows and crouched in opportunistic ridges, watching and calculating. Waiting, but nearly never intervening. One would be forced to wonder what exactly they were waiting for: it became some sort of spectator's coliseum, where one could watch religious minorities tossed to the lions, ethnic representatives of one region slashing at others, before the indulgent grins of comfortable world powers ready to turn their thumbs up or down only at the moment of beheadings. In between, endless carnage had stretched as far as the eye could see. The peacekeepers sandbagged themselves into bunkers and awaited the end of the war, while the intelligence services went wild playing games of cat and mouse but rarely made any of their information actionable. Nearly no mandated use of that timely information was used to aid the men with guns and mortars, barricaded outside the safe zones.

So the bloodshed crescendoed, and the foreigners sat on their hands. They reported what they saw back to London, Washington, or Moscow. Their minders filed the reports, fascinated by the ongoing conflict, but really with no reason for making the effort. Television had a field day with solemn soundtracks, but nobody stepped in between bodies and bayonets. Eventually, even the most stalwart barbarians had no more stomach for bloodlust, and the brutalities petered out.

I'd been brought in to help joint investigations planned by MI6 and executed by SAS—the legendary Special Forces Unit of the British Army. We were there to uncover exactly what had been done, and by whom. They hoped to uncover by my surreptitious means the best places where more-overt investigators might focus their tardy attentions on prosecution. Aside from a quick briefing, I'd known next to nothing about Bosnia before setting out, but my transport fixed that. The investigators' exhaustive research, fears, internalized horror and disgust were all open books to me.

I was led into a small room with a long double mirror covering one full wall, and a dim light humming over a long wooden table. Four chairs were set around it, three to be occupied and one just for ominous effect, and left tipped out at an angle. I was told to assist in binding the prisoner to the chair, so that I might achieve bodily contact unobtrusively. The first thing I noticed was the room had been set up with the exact same tactical considerations that I'd seen used by East German secret police through Mielke's eyes: the chairs would have fresh sponges lashed to their surfaces for the duration of the interrogations. I was to bind the hands of our prisoner right beneath his thighs, so all his sweat would be collected and archived in jars, which trained dogs could use to track him down in the event of an escape. I shuddered with horror at the visions swirling through my mind.

Footsteps echoed down the hall, and the doors opened. In marched several guards, a few suits, a few intelligence men, and a man in irons. From the flurry of thoughts spiraling through the air around us, I could quickly intuit the man who was before me: Milan Kovacevik. This was the wartime mayor of the town of Prijedor: a man responsible for the deaths of untold Bosnian Muslims. He snarled, as he was led to his chair.

Avoiding his eyes, I leaned in to secure the straps over his wrists, and felt his eyes burn through the side of my head as I did so. I lurched back into my seat and let the images start hurricaning through my head, as their proceedings faded into the background of my consciousness. Soon, there was nothing but a great flood, and I was faraway, swimming in scenes of Kovacevic's past.

It was like leaning into a tidal wave. I found myself immediately back in the mindset I'd found in the San Diego hospital: I retreated just as quickly as I could back into my own mind, and into any other mind in the room. Anything was better than him, better than that overwhelming darkness. It was an unrelenting chasm of despair and rage and inhumanity; and I couldn't seem to force my brain to stand alongside it, to peer directly into it. It felt like trying to stop a firehose with my thumb. I made next to no progress.

The man next to me was an SAS agent, though they'd described him as something else, something benign. At this point I didn't know why they bothered—they must have determined by this point that I wasn't easily misled. But the introductions proceeded, and formalities stretched into hours of circuitous conversational points, so I crawled into the minds and backstories of all the characters of the room, while trying to minimize Kovacevic's influence on my over-receptive brain until I could muster some sense of control and self-preservation.

The SAS agent boiled in rage, and it didn't take long to see why. His family had emigrated from Yugoslavia; and it would've been his relations who'd have borne the brunt of Kovacevic's abuses. He hoped to keep those thoughts contained to appear professional, but in reality it was all personal for him. He'd spent the night before sorting through news articles about the region, one after the other. He'd paused long and hard over headline quotations from Radovan Karadzic's famous *Directive Number 7* with his blood boiling, until his hands tore the paper in half. He'd once argued with his own Father about this man, and had minimized his potential influence: sure that he was just some fringe lunatic. At the time, Karadzic was speechmaking in the early nineties about how the Muslim birthrate was too high for Serbs and Croats to compete, and "something had to be done to protect Europe."

The SAS agent had attempted to convince his Father that Karadzic surely wasn't sincere, that somehow it was all boilerplate rhetoric. In reality, his family had emigrated just in the nick of time. Ever since, the SAS man had felt personally responsible for everyone left behind. He couldn't believe that the men who'd lived alongside him in village life for ages could just go on as if nothing had changed, planting their gardens and hanging laundry to dry as they watched every house not owned by Serbs gutted by fire. He would never have believed that white flags would be flown over the streets he'd grown up on, or that every pedestrian on the street would be made to wear white armbands to display unquestioning loyalty to the occupiers—*or else.*

Moreover, I sensed the desperation in the investigators. They'd heard rumors and hints for years, but the war torn countryside hadn't been available for searches yet. To bring anyone to justice before the international community, they would need irrefutable evidence of war crimes—tied to specific names and places. But where does one start searching in an entire country for that sort of thing? Even at the sites of abuses they knew about, what happened where? How does one prove that? It couldn't be limited to a question of hearsay, they'd need real evidence. But how?

The prisoner before them clearly thought he was already out of the woods. He knew everything—every communication, every horrible extreme made into routine policy. He knew who had shifts at which times, whom had done what to whom and where. He had a mild form of OCD, so the details obsessed him. His mind was a minefield. The more I fed on the rage in the SAS man's mind, the more my own instincts to rage were dulled and I was better able to focus my energies on unearthing all the thoughts that the prisoner was glad were safely stowed away in his mind.

More and more, his mind leapt back to three names: all concentration camps in and around Prijedor. But more than just the complexes, I began to see flash after flash of certain random buildings, dotting the complexes.

The scenes were already something out of a Hieronymus Bosch painting. I'd never encountered such horrors in my life. I found myself latching on desperately to scene s of my own childhood in flickers, just to try to hang on to some sense of self amid the horror, the ugly inhumanity, and the butchery. I found myself thinking of multiplication tables, of the cartoon adventures of Speed Racer, of anything I could use to plug out the surges of overwhelming darkness. The more I looked, the darker my own mind became.

Each horror after horror seem to eclipse the last. It left no room at all for sanity, in that cavernous, compressed dark space. It was all rationalizations and glorying in murderous gestures. With every increasingly frightful memory I swam through, after diving deep into his subconscious, I kept sensing more and more his insane core: a persistent chanting of *The Ends Justify The Means.*

He thought of nothing else: excesses didn't touch him, neither age nor infirmity were considerations. Somehow, he still considered himself a religious man, *devout* even. He saw it as a sacred calling, pleasing to heaven, that he should do the things he did. He had no regrets, why should he?

And the things he did! I saw men jogging in columns, exercised to limber them up before long sessions of beating. I saw men so emaciated they looked like tree branches catching wallpaper. I saw men dying of hunger, leaned against chain link fences, slapped and spat on and humiliated in every conceivable way. I saw men humiliated in inconceivable ways, too. And women, and children as well. Women were forced to scrub the walls of the torture rooms, with worse horrors awaiting them when left alone with soldiers in the canteen. The best thing to hope for was death. I saw murders by the score, each playing in turn through Kovacevic's eyes: in long explosions writhing through red and black.

His own mind had been fundamentally rewired and booby-trapped against reality. For each of these horrors, he'd hard-wired pleasant images to step in and obscure the horrors before him: he'd instead visualize his wife laughing on a swing, or his children smiling. He'd grin blithely into space, while deeply inhaling a handkerchief pull of perfume, ignoring the sobs and retching surrounding him. I saw the dismissive burials and the furtive forest drops, where each trench would be hastily dug and dumped full, in the darkest hours of night. Bodies in the garden, in the woods, along the roadside, behind the structures, under the structures...Dozens, hundreds of humans, disappeared into those quiet nights, never to be heard from again. Until now. Now I would speak. Now I would interrogate. Now I would—

But my moment of heroism was slowed by my human fragility. I'd never learned how to be something more than a periscope. I could

only look straight at things, and I could never really see them coming, until I'd raised up and pointed straight into something terrible. I had no filters, ever. No shades, no nuances: just the core, the deepest realization of the things madmen had wrought on the countryside.

In a way, I almost could admire that he could push the pain, suffering and depravity into the margins, and not see it—or see it, but rationalize the worst actions of what men could do to one another.

What that meant at our long rectangular table was that I'd immediately tuned out of the perfunctory conversations and drilling at the start of the interrogation the moment I'd been ordered to assist in binding the prisoner's wrists to the chair. Of course the images had flooded in, and of course I let go of the rest of the world.

Fortunately the proceedings were already intense enough that nobody noticed the slight twitching convulsions that shook my slumped body as I navigated through the million scenes at light speed, nor the gaping black wounds that were my eyes…

In fact, nobody really took much notice of me until I threw up all across the table.

Nobody seemed more surprised than me, though my associates found themselves equally curious.

"Well, mates, I think it's time for us to take a few minutes of recess. Harold, have you got a smoke? Guards, please escort Mr. Kovacevic to the holding chamber."

Everyone cleared out, without bothering me with any questions. I frantically looked around for something to clean the table, but in a few seconds a janitor pushed in a grey cart full of cleaning solvents and rags. Immune to my protests, he moved to the table and began to work, whistling as he did so. I stared at him in wonder for a moment, my head cocked to one side.

This man had no idea what was done here. He was happy as a lark. He daydreamed about eating goat meat, about pop songs by the Spice Girls, and another cleaning aide who had lustrous blonde hair and long legs. He quickly poured some sparse chemicals over the mess and wiped it up, but could barely have cleaned up two thirds of it. If you'd sat at a prisoner's height, the table would still have looked thick with sick.

I held my throbbing head and shook it violently back and forth. It felt as if it was pressurized and ready to explode. The lurch from mind to mind was just too abrupt. I still felt demons of the past prying back my eyelids from behind my shut-eyes, banging on my cranium, demanding an audience. Everyone looked up at me, or at least I thought they did. I scrolled slowly through endless scenes of atrocity, through eyes, though last words, through commands… But I felt my stomach rising again, with a threatening whale-sounding whine. I inhaled sharply and spun around, walked out into the hallway and out into the suite of offices across from the interrogation cells. The men gathered around a coffee maker, and one slapped me on the back as I walked in—smiling into my face of all greens and greys.

"Some seas are rockier than ocean waves, John. You were Navy, right? You spent most of your time floating across the world on ships! Who'd have thought you'd get green in the gills so quick out here!"

There was some scattered laughter, and I didn't bother to correct that I was a submariner. I asked to have the afternoon off, and it was granted immediately. The men shouted out that they hoped I'd feel better and to avoid cheap café's in the future. One specified that I'd better avoid a specific brothel famous for food poisoning. One said something about the terrible state of rations.

Ten minutes later and I was beyond their conversations: three quarters of the way through a quart of whiskey.

Ψ

"Calabrace?"

Without opening my eyes, I felt confident in my assessment that a murderous boa constrictor must be wrapped around my forehead, squeezing my head like grapes in a wine press. Still, the human voice seemed real. I opened one eye, then the other, and groaned.

Three men in uniforms grinned from the doorway. "Sorry to bother you, sir. You never showed up for interrogations this morning, so we were sent to make sure you were safe."

I took a step off the bed and fell backwards back into the mattress. Repressed a dry heave.

"So are you, *safe* then, sir?" a soldier asked, smirking.

"Yes, yes, just a bit under the weather is all. Give me one second," I grumbled, realizing I was only wearing socks, dirt and a hangover. The men carefully observed the ceiling and the corners of the room, ignoring my state. Three minutes later I was showered and dressed, and we rolled back over to the interrogation site.

The interrogation crew was on a lunch break around the coffee maker, swapping war stories and fishing tales. One laughed noisily as I entered and waltzed over to massage my shoulders with a mischievous grin on his face. "Good God mate, you look like hell. I hope you'll help us muster up some brilliant Intel today, to justify the bar tab I assume you're amassing."

But by this point, I didn't have to think about it. Freed from the meddling of my waking brain, my subconscious or the gift or whatever it was, "had solved for x." Knowing that we needed hard evidence, it had waited for my alcohol-induced transient amnesia to kick in, and then took over the wheel. It plowed through massive amounts of information and then casually left them front-and-center for me first thing in the morning, where they gleamed clear as day in the few seconds that I'd stood in the shower.

What flashed through my brain were the cleanup operations in painstaking detail, or rather, the holes in the cover-ups. I saw a little white house outside an enormous red complex, and watched Milan's memories of a rapid disengagement from the site. All the prisoners were thrown into trucks in the dead of night, screeching away into further barbarisms, before British observers arrived with their cameras.

But the specific details I noticed were things like the furnace assemblies, the cabinet hinges, and drawer rollers. I saw cleanup crews frantically hiding evidence of the horrible things that had occurred on this white house; but at the same time, my brain scrolled through every torturous scene that had come before in the same location. I immediately knew that their feeble cleanup efforts couldn't have possibly eradicated all that evidence.

"Luminol," I said simply. "Apply it liberally in the white house behind the complex, in Omarska camp. Start there. By the radiators, the window sills, the hinges and hardware. Everything starts there. There should be plenty."

"I don't understand, what do you—" one man began.

"Just check," I said, with finality. "I'll need some maps, lots of maps. And a red pencil."

27

The wedding had finally arrived. I hadn't had a drink in two days, in preparation for the event, and already my hands were shaking like a small tree branch in the New England fall. I was absolutely determined that Elizabeth should not have some reprise of my Sag Harbor stunt: where she'd rescued me from my inebriated mud-bath during a field trip. The idea that she should have a perfect day meant the world to me, and I couldn't bear the thought that I might disrupt from that in any way. I'd been doing everything twice—checking my shoes, carefully packing and unpacking my suit, knowing I'd have to do it all again after the car trip—but just to be sure I had every advantage going back into the dreaded public eye, where I'd be responsible to loved ones for how I behaved.

I would not drink. That was absolutely certain. It was Elizabeth's day, and she deserved the best. But like all the best laid plans, that immediately dissolved when I arrived early at the venue.

I didn't recognize anyone for a few minutes, just a blur of grey tuxes and baby blue gowns. Everyone was freshly primped and proper, in a kaleidoscope of cosmetic colors. It was warm, and my collar cut at my throat, itchy and stifling in the afternoon sun. I tried to keep my head together, asking random strangers who seemed to be associated with the wedding party if there was anything I could do to help. But everything seemed to be running fairly smoothly already, and the strangers breezed away into preparations indoors. So I stood around for a second, then a minute, and then another. I glanced over at the barman in a stiff uniform, cleaning glasses under the shade of a few trees. I stared at his bountiful wares. He grinned and me, nodding; and I could literally feel sweat spring out across my forehead. I walked into the bathroom and splashed cold water on my face, looking deep into my own eyes in the mirror.

"You know what has to happen today, John! You need to be a good boy," I spoke at my reflection, warningly. But it was an empty gesture.

Four minutes later, I strolled across the grass. Five minutes later, I finished my second JD and coke—as the barman joked that he always got the jitters at weddings, too. His head said otherwise, expressing minute frustration at impulsive wedding patrons who drink too much without tipping. I glanced at his face like he'd spoken the daggeredwords aloud, momentarily hurt, then I left a ten dollar bill in his tip jar and strutted away towards the gate.

Twenty minutes until the scheduled start of events: it seemed like more than enough time. I turned right on a street I didn't know, then turned around and tried a left for about a block and a half before I found it: a graffiti-covered liquored store, with incongruous beige blocks of paint covering up the scrawled, spray-painted words. It was glorious, like a glittering oasis in a barren desert. Into my pristine suit went three flask-sized bottles.

A homeless man insistently asked me if I had any money or alcohol as I was leaving, after watching me get rung up at the register. I looked at him like he was crazy. As he gazed at me, I realized he had recognized me from somewhere, and I quickly remembered it was a rehab I'd once attended for a day or less, total. "No, I don't have money or *booze*. It's my cousin's wedding today! I gotta go, pal…" I marched down the road, with a smile bigger than the Sun. I brushed off the pristine crease on my pants leg and felt like the most responsible man in the world. How dare a *common drunk* bother me?!

Two hours later, not so much. Everything had seemed well so far. I'd been sitting, perhaps even a little misty-eyed with sentimental nostalgia at all the changes, quietly sipping, in what I thought was a pretty subtle way from behind my sleeve (though I did spot an irate glare from the barman). But before I knew it, the ceremony was over!

Somehow, I hadn't considered what was going to happen once the passive portion of the evening passed, and we got to standing, toasting, mingling, and dancing. Intuitively, alarm bells starting quietly chiming—just before I stood up: warning that perhaps the machinery wasn't full primed for a task like 'standing up.'

But it was far worse than I could have suspected. By the time I'd strained my body an inch and a half off my chair, to move towards the group congregating in the garden pavilion beyond, I realized with horror that my legs had given up. They'd checked out for the day—called in sick. Nobody seemed to have noticed yet, so I went into evasive maneuvers. I watched the array of the elderly relatives and friends gather their purses to move from the pews, and knew I only had seconds before someone would think my behavior strange. I pushed all confused autopilot-thoughts of "angles and dangles" from my mind. I tried lifting one foot, which fortunately seemed to go fine. I tried the other, and felt myself list a little lazily to the left, my head tilting far down towards the adjacent seat than could have appeared natural.

I tried to play it off like I was clumsily looking for something lost under the seat, though I was horrified to catch sight of the barman rolling his eyes, while staring straight towards me. I managed to abruptly overcorrect, and with a sudden jolt of energy, I threw myself onto my feet. I was basically alone in the room now, and it was a good thing—as the first thing that happened was my legs failed to control my momentum. They locked straight, and I continued in my forward motion, silent, eyes wide—slamming my forehead straight into a support column in front of me. Something about the pain and shame of that moment cleared up the command controls of my body, and I managed to straighten up, bashfully, rubbing my face. This time, nobody was looking. But I hated myself and hated that I was in this state so soon. I was ashamed, already. As I emerged into the garden party where the folk circled, I knew I would regret many things before the night was through. It was a more prescient observation, than not.

I spent some time gathering myself together in the bathroom, determined that Elizabeth should remain none-the-wiser about my present sorry state. I filled an empty pint glass with water a few times and chugged it down. I washed off the very small cut on my forehead, until I thought it was barely noticeable. All the while, all I could think of was the fact that sooner or later, I would be faced with my dearest childhood friend: my favorite cousin. I would have to open my mouth at some point, and I was terrified at what the results might be.

When it actually happened, I was too far gone to be horrified, for many reasons. The drink, primarily. But who should cross my path as I rigidly staggered in the direction of my sweet cousin? Megan, the girl from Mineola, decades before. Somehow, she recognized me.

"JOHN CALABRACE?! Oh my *god*!" she screeched in a horrid Long Island dialect. She had been drinking a bit too much herself and literally jumped up and down, big hair bouncing, hands clapping as she'd happily slurred her words together. "How long has it been?!"

"Oh wow, hello Megan. It's been ages! You were just a kid when I saw you last."

"I was a kid? Look at you, Mister Submarine. I heard you went to a big shot school for nu-clear something-or-other? Your Mother was just as thrilled as could be. When I got married, I moved in right next to where she worked. We used to see each other all the time…How do you know Elizabeth? I work with her—bet you didn't know that, huh?"

"No, I had no idea! She's my cousin."

"Wow, such a small world, right?" She grinned and squeezed her shoulders together. "So tell me about your life, John! Are you married? Where are you living? Are you still serving?"

She placed an unsteady hand on my shoulder and squeezed my arm unintentionally, as if testing a tire while sleepwalking. Focusing back into the sober world for a slim moment, it became clear that Megan was no more a frequent-flier of sobriety than I was.

"Yeah, sort of. I live in California these days, working with the Navy."

"So, you're like an Admiral or something?"

"No, I'm more like…well, it's complicated."

"My husband isn't here; he never comes with me to things like this. He's busy with the union, ya know?"

"Oh." I'd be busy too, if I was him, I thought. My mind scrambled drunkenly through protocol directives, as I saw a blurry approximation of Elizabeth far off in the horizon, talking with some octogenarians. "I'm sorry about that!"

"Don't be. He's a bastard anyway. But maybe we could dance? I've been sitting by myself forever. I can't even remember what I've been drinking. I need some air, or—"

But before finishing, she arose mechanically, and then fell straight into my chest in an exact recreation of *my moves* earlier in the wedding ceremony hall. Against all the odds, I caught her. She smiled a weak smile, before hiccupping and groaning.

"On second thought, maybe not. I'm actually feeling a little wasted." She doubled over for a moment, while I looked over at Elizabeth, trying to consider what was appropriate here. When I looked back to Megan, she'd disappeared. Faintly, in the corner of my vision, I saw the barman suppressing a laugh and trying to gesture something to me; but I tuned it out, assuming he just wanted to tease me. I met the groom before reaching Elizabeth. We made our introductions and I congratulated him, told him how beautiful I thought the wedding had been, and how proud I was of Elizabeth.

"She is a wonderful woman, John. I will do anything in the world for her. It's nice to have finally met you, after all the years of hearing about you."

"I cannot tell you how glad I am to hear it. Elizabeth deserves it. She deserves it all."

He smiled at me for a moment and frowned at my shoes.

"John, did you step in something? Your pants and shoes…"

It was at that moment, that I realized that I'd missed Megan throwing up on me.

About fifteen odd minutes later, I managed to reemerge from the bathroom with the few tattered shreds of my dignity left intact. Megan had somehow contacted a cab and gotten home safe, I'd later learn, none the wiser about what had happened. Evidently, the secret would remain between the very amused barman and myself—much less amused.

On the bright side, I'd gone through such adrenaline and horror in the trial run, that I no longer feared anything about a tete-a-tete with my cousin. Scared sober maybe? The trepidation had just fled from my mind, somewhere around the time her new husband's first impression of me was colored by my tropical-cocktail-colored shoes.

"Elizabeth!"

"JOHN!" She was beside herself with happiness. "John, dance with me!" So we did.

We spent the next five minutes or so swaying on the dance floor, as she tried and failed to keep her intensely long, elegant dress off the floor. We whispered memories of days past that would never leave us and laughed like we had for decades before. Her smile was overwhelming—she was radiant with joy.

"I am so glad you're here. I'm feeling such a weird, profound feeling of completion to my life: like everyone who means the most to me is here for me, at once! I've never had that, you know? Everything is always so segmented, so broken apart and isolated. It's just insane to see everyone who matters most, from every moment of my life, in one place! Was that Megan from accounting you were talking to over there? Do you know her?"

I winced in spite of myself and tried to transform it into a smile before she noticed. In her floaty mood, it passed right over her head. "We knew each other as kids; she lived nearby."

"That's so wonderful! Tell me, John, how are you doing way over there on the California Coast? Don't you miss being closer to family? Do you have people over there? Have you got someone special? Are you ever going to move back closer to your favorite family over here?" she pleaded, smiling mischievously.

"I have pretty weird working conditions right now, to be honest. It's kind of put the rest of my life on hold, in a way: it's difficult to share much in the kind of environment I have to work in." I tried to grin but found that I said those sorts of words so rarely, my facial muscles simply hadn't compiled a contingency plan for earnest emotional discourse. My lips bent into the glummest shape imaginable and desperately tried to transition into a new expression—but to no avail.

"Oh, that's terrible! John, that's something you need to think about, sooner rather than later. Nobody in our family talks about that emotional stuff enough—petty loneliness, disappointment, isolation—that stuff adds up! There's no need for any of it...All that damn tough

New-Englander business, huh? Never forget the things you want, things that'll only happen if you make them happen. If you want friends, find them! Your work be damned. I've passed up several promotion opportunities, because happiness always trumps work." She covered her face in her hands as a photographer passed, but he pleaded with her until she straightened my suit jacket and leaned on my side with a huge picture perfect smile, then planted a wet kiss on my cheek.

"It's time for you to find a nice girl. Find people who make you feel alive, make you feel fun. You are too good to be alone. You don't want to be carrying that frown around on you, it hardly fits on your face!" She playfully caressed my face, and drew me into a long hug. She mulled something over silently, then whispered into my ear with a big smile, while waving to some folk across the garden—

"And John, you really shouldn't be drinking this much. The stuff will kill you. We've both lost people before; it's certainly not worth it."

I panicked, thinking of all the pints of water I'd had since washing the vomit off my shoes, and the two cups of coffee the indulgent barman had passed me before I sought out Elizabeth. "What do you mean, drinking too much?"

"John, really? This is me you are talking to; only bad friends avoid mentioning it. Liquor…well…let's just say it doesn't leave your skin too quickly. You do smell like bad mouthwash, but it still radiates through your pores…But that doesn't mean I don't love you, more than ever!" She gripped me tight and laughed. "I cannot tell you how strange this all is. I certainly don't feel wiser. I don't feel more capable. All these heavy rites of passage, they kind of seem like a farce. I feel as scattered and awkward as ever, like I'm still that four foot-eleven, innocent little girl in Cape Cod, with the world as my oyster—and my favorite cousin at my side. I miss that world, you know? You don't just outgrow it."

"I know exactly how you feel. I've experienced so much in the past few decades, but still feel like I've never understood life better than during those summers. But I cannot tell you how proud and thrilled I am for you and—"

"Matthew," she volunteered, long before I had time to wrack my brain for the missing name. "Yeah, I'd say we're going to have a pretty good run." She laughed. "But you'd better think about whether *you* aim to have some kids to play with mine in the next generation: our kids will want playmates. Time's a wastin', after all."

I found myself momentarily frowning, at a loss for words. Nothing could have been further from my life and thoughts at the moment than a family life. But she was grinning obliviously out over the party as time raced by, exhaling deeply, with happy tears glittering in her eyes.

"This was perfect, John. I cannot thank you enough for being here for me."

"I always will be, Elizabeth. That will never change."

And then I hiccupped; and we both laughed.

I had just enough common sense wandering out of the wedding party that I left my rental car there, and instead took a cab back to the hotel—snoring the whole way. I doubled back to get it in the morning, after a few strong coffees. I had an exorbitant ticket waiting on the windshield, but it was worth it; Elizabeth's day had not been ruined by any incidents on my account, despite Megan, and I'd gotten home safely. I'd been so exhausted from the emotional stresses of the day that I'd slept like a baby—a sleep only augmented by the booze.

I pulled into my driveway in Coronado a day and a half later in my own car, wiped out from travel and even more so from the free-floating minds crowding the air of the long, cramped flight. A car was parked before the garage, and I recognized it immediately. CJ was here! I practically ran to the door, where I saw him scribbling me a note against the rough wood.

"John! Wow—am I glad to see you! I almost drove all the way out here with them crying and barking the whole way, only to miss you! They aren't all that fond of driving, you know…"

Nothing registered in my mind. I had absolutely no idea what he was talking about. "I'm sorry, what? Who was crying?"

A grin spread across his face as he began jogging back to our cars, with an excited look on his face. "He didn't tell you? Dannels was meaning to call; he and I both went in on them. He must have gotten busy, I can never get a hold of him myself these days, with all the meetings, and—"

"CJ, what are you talking about?" I demanded, exasperated.

But just as I said it, two sets of ears rose up from the back seat of CJ's car. Two giant, playful Doberman Pinschers puppies were rolling over each other, play fighting, barking through the windows, and fogging up the glass with their breath.

"Those are for you, John. And just in time, it appears...When I showed up here, I scared off some sort of idiot who was trying to take pictures through the window. Do you know anything about that?"

The words bounced off of me, unheard. I opened the door and the two dogs bounded out and immediately pounced into my arms, knocking me clean backwards into the grass—their little nub tails wagging at light-speed. One rolled immediately to my side, licking my glasses straight off my face, while the other bounced around excitedly at my other side, whining and licking a long pink tongue into my ear.

This was something new, something entirely new. I would never be alone again.

I had a family.

28

For two weeks, I'd barely left the house. I'd hear the dogs barking on the way out the door, and suddenly nothing would be as important as playing with them. I'd rush back inside, beverage-less. It was exactly what the doctor ordered in terms of my drinking, but who could have known it would be a catalyst? So a good part of the first month of Fall went by without so much as a whiff of the real world, safely sequestered on the Coronado beach with the two Dobermans: Cash and Carrie.

CJ had managed the impossible and talked me into meeting with the intelligence intermediaries for the first time in weeks. With the amount of politics that had always been at play behind my position, it was no wonder that they were less than thrilled with me. They weren't getting a return on their investment lately. They knew it, and so did I—but frankly, it didn't bother me. I got a good amount of dressing down, before Dannels indicated with the slightest twitch of his chin that the window had closed for critique. Without me or anyone else noticing, CJ had somehow managed to subtly position himself right between me and my superiors, although off at an angle. I doubt he noticed it himself, but I appreciated the gesture. He stood at attention quietly, but succeeded in projecting the image of someone who was not to be trifled with lightly. The subject changed. We moved forward.

As always, my case officers face exterior pressures to demonstrate value and justify the resources and secrecy that all our experiments entailed. At present, the powers-that-be behind the project were shifting yet again, for the millionth time since I'd begun to work with them. Stubblebine had always been hit or miss: great when his friends had influence, and a liability when his passions led him up a tree. Recently, he'd gotten just a bit too far astray from the mainstream to please his associates, after he'd felt the need to share some of his wilder theories and pet projects with the press. Abruptly, his freereign and influence had been severely curtailed, albeit with all the sweetest of words and praise for his many years of service. The new powers-that-be pitched in to buy him a retirement speedboat. They wanted him far away from anywhere and hoped it might speed along the journey.

We'd just begun a week of new appraisals of me: "the secret toy," for the new batch of NSA/CIA/Navy Intelligence inquisitors. Everyone always reveled in the chance to familiarize themselves with my taskforce, as we were one of the most shadowy of the covert corners. The highest ranked among them still saw it as some sort of merit badge—just to be granted clearance. But it has to be said, none of this led towards me feeling more like a human, or more understood...far from it.

These folk saw me as an extremely unpredictable piece of technology whose instructions had never been printed. In that spirit, many of them came convinced they were to be the one to master me—this Trojan horse of intelligence—so their thoughts reflected that "enlightened" vantage point.

Not that they didn't try to hide it. Lord, did they ever try to hide it! There were elaborate perennial memos on security protocol to successfully isolate secrets and sensitive networks from being compromised by me: The Thing. Were we on the same side? At times, it didn't seem it. I was like the small carpenter ant eating their woodpile, and they were too busy with directives, memos, and standard operating protocols to ever notice. We'd come a long way from merely avoiding touch, but it was still the same sort of clumsy strategies at play—things I saw through immediately, but played dumb so as to save myself from unnecessary pains of adjusting to more asinine security steps.

Nothing seemed blocked from me these days. Far from slowing, my hunger for novel information had continued unabated. Drowning it all in alcohol had failed to stop the appetite, nor lessen the onslaught of images from replaying in my dreams and daydreams—it just suspended them in a distanced sort of amber wiggle before my eyes. Pulling thoughts out of air had become as effortless as looking up words in an encyclopedia. Whatever I sought floated up to me in a neat and tidy fashion: one that only increased as time perfected its learning curve. No one else knew how good I was, but I did. And in the end, that's all that mattered.

But perhaps more importantly, each night, creative parts of my brain had begun to merge old memories into the strangest dreams imaginable, as if attempting to exorcize the worst of the imagery. Opposite extremes would play against one another: the greatest extremes of joy, saddled by the most desolate shades of terror and sadness. The detestable skeletons buried in people's closets were bunched up against moments of the most pure artistic and creative joys, and true heroic virtuosity played out before dumbfounded crowds. I snored, living entire lives vicariously amid strange montages of good and evil. A strange philosophical calculus now labored day and night in my head, to approximate whether *the people* were mostly good or evil. The tabulation was slow going.

At first, it'd been an unmitigated terror. The bad was *so bad,* that I never saw much more. But lately, as my sensitivity to detail had become more regular, I began seeing all the things pushed into the shadows—the daily humanities. I saw pristine, glitteringly pure images of maternal love. I saw an old woman who spent every Saturday finding a homeless man to share soup with at the same small café, then arranging with the owner to have a daily coffee set aside for him on her tab, and she lived for the ritual. A man lived his whole life with a crippling fear of water, and yet he'd three times clambered through ice floes to rescue stray dogs who'd become trapped in the ice—smashing loose a path with his elbows—without a second thought. The airman who lost both his legs above the knee wheeled himself to the base hospital every day to cheer up the new patients, because some of them "aren't as lucky as I am" he used to think. My ability truly was a gift sometimes, and I was glad when these reminders floated in.

Ψ

The phone rang, and both dogs barked immediately. Cash's paws flew to the window sill, watching everything and everyone, even on the far perimeter, while Carrie seemed to bark, only to confirm that she agreed with his analysis. I still laughed at them as I registered the very sad voice on the other end of the line, halfway through a sob.

"John, you need to come home. Your Father...We lost your Father, John..."

The line broke into a soft wailing. I reassured her as much as I could over the line and raced to get my things together. A boy down the road was in love with the dogs, and I arranged with his parents to pay him to dog sit while I was gone. I threw everything I could think of into an old suitcase and was in the car to the airport within the hour.

But was I thinking? I knew they needed me at home. Other than that, I'd processed nothing. Certainly not that my Dad was gone.

The plane wobbled as it lifted into the air, but once it settled, the timelessness of flying set in. Memories of every plane I'd ever been crammed into flitted past my mind, as I tried to narrow in on comprehending the news I'd been given. I thought of my flight off the sub to Diego Garcia and the hops onward to San Diego. I thought of the mingled terror and excitement as I'd read the airman's thoughts at a distance for the first time and wondered if I'd ever experience such unfamiliar strangeness again. I thought of older trips, too: visiting my Grandparents as a child and the famous priest I'd met, with his sparkling ring. Whether out of superstition or purely out of habit, I still carried my identical ring, always tucked deep into the breast pocket of my jacket. It rarely struck me how little I knew about it or how strange it should be for my Great Uncle John to have had such a ring. For a while, the thought lazily circled amid images in a haze of half dreams, but before I knew it, I was asleep.

As I slept, fitful combinations of every theme jeered at the rest of my brain. Every soggy seashore mixed with the images of the wet banks of the Sumpol River, images I'd never encountered firsthand. I saw the lovely face of my curly-haired sweet cousin laughing and smiling, alongside the screams of strangers who I'd never known and never would. Every childish swimming pool blurred with my ghoulish memories of the Steinke Hood and Blow and Go! Training, and the worse memories of my trainers, who knew the worst case scenarios possible. I later learned that I'd lurched around in my sleep all flight long, dreaming of the gory end of the once S.S. Atule: decommissioned and sold to Peru in 1974. It had sunk in relatively shallow water after being rammed by a fishing trawler, but nearly everyone onboard suffered decompression issues of one form or another, and several died. I'd never even heard of the boat, but just like that, I had all the images plaguing my head, caught from the atmosphere like some impossibly-rare airborne disease.

While some friends collected comic books, I was a reluctant collector of horrors. My eyes jerked open nervously, as I realized once again where I was and where I was going. I was completely bathed in sweat. A stewardess passed and I bit my tongue. But when the second one passed, I ordered my first of several drink orders.

The rest of the trip was seen from the bottom of an alcoholic ocean, served over ice.

Ψ

How does anybody turn the doorknob of their childhood home, knowing the terrible circumstances of their visit? I was no better than most. The second I began to turn the doorknob, I wished I was literally anywhere else. But there were the sounds of familiar voices braying, and I knew I'd been spotted.

All these events, it's always the same. The first people to greet you are always the relatives you'd long forgotten: the third twice-removed half-cousin of a foster brother or someone that no one liked to begin with. They always stand near the door and pounce and say, "Oh John, I'm so sorry John. How are you taking it?!" As if there was ever a measured response.

And then it's old Aunts in flamboyant scarves and clown-layers of makeup and old neighbors wearing knit sweaters, and those big platters of every meat and cheese combination, with untouched vegetables just alongside. Wafting through all of it, though, I was cursed to know exactly what random, fleeting thoughts people might have on the day of something so grave, so personal, so intimate as family loss.

"I knew I should have worn the burgundy dress. This jacket is always itchy." Or, "How the hell do they afford this house—and yet my present for two decades has been slippers?"

Or the old neighbor who used to help Dad build overflow shelving during inventory season, who stared mesmerized at the legs of a distant cousin who'd barely passed any legal threshold of consent. Everyone had his or her own way to deal with the shocks of mortality, but I certainly wished that I didn't have to share in each unique process.

Mom was conspicuously absent, which was unlike her. Eventually I found her in the basement laundry room, folding clothes and politely wiping her eyes, immediately straightening up upon discovery.

"Oh Johnny. I'm so glad you're finally here. I'm so sorry this is all happening!" She pulled me into a long hug.

"Don't apologize to me, Mom; of course I'm here! Tell me what I can do, and I'll do it."

"Just help your Mom face the crowd, Johnny. With my boys here, I'll have the strength."

The second we passed the doorways it was the same old Mom: lively, outgoing, looking after everyone, trying to play hostess, trying to keep the reality of the events at bay. She flourished.

My brothers were less veneered. None of us had heard anything about any kind of developing illness or worries of any sort, so we were all equally shell-shocked. We sat around the couch in a glum sort of white-faced huddle, with a few wives at intervals caressing tufts of hair on their taciturn spouses. But none of us really knew how to face the situation yet…and yet here it was.

While ignoring the elephant in the room, it was interesting to take stock of all the changes that had taken place since the last full convergence of the family. We'd assuredly come together in scattered clumps now and then for holidays, but it always seemed like at least a few siblings had a scheduling conflict or a kid with the measles; we never really ever ended up in one room anymore. There we were, the same four kids, all grown and strange.

But some things had changed. Mom buzzed into the room.

"Guys, could someone grab the old bottle of Dewars out of the garage?"

I grabbed some glasses for everyone and we all began to drink. I poured myself a glass and soon another, talking about old times, life in the Navy, my new dogs. Soon, I realized a ton of time had passed, and everyone had evidently stopped drinking. I hovered on autopilot, not completely aware of time or space. But as someone stood up to stretch and mill about the front rooms, I got a clearer view of the drink situation…and my stomach fell out.

Apart from an untouched shot glass that my brother's wife had poured to play along, nobody was drinking but me. I'd finished the bottle, while they'd gotten bored or frustrated, and left.

The ceremony was nothing special, and it spat us back out into the world more confused than we'd started. The sense of abrupt finality was overwhelming. I wrapped an arm around Mom and she sat stone still, staring straight ahead. A few portly men in suits patted me on the back—the way men do—to express their profound sorrows for my profound loss. And that was it.

Some wind picked up, and a storm drove us back indoors.

The family lingered around for a few days, reminiscing and trying to distract Mom from the gravity of what was happening. It was a hopeless gesture, but that's just the way these things happen. We spent some time playing cards, looked through some photo albums, and saw a movie together. Everyone held Mom a few times as she cried, but it never happened in front of company. We put on a strong, united face together.

It wasn't long before I had occasion to repeat my drinking performance. At an outdoor restaurant, I wandered off and got drunk at the bar after using the bathroom. I took a taxi home when I realized what I'd done, and I called my brother. I told him to tell everyone that I'd felt ill, and took off early—and to make my apologies. In a terse tone, he said that they'd been looking for me for fifteen minutes. Unable to deal with that drama and my sadness at everything else, I ran out to a corner store nearby the house and picked up some more small bottles, to get me through the night.

I thought I'd played it smooth enough that assuredly nobody had noticed. But a few long hours into the next morning's events, my next youngest brother (of *Spidey-Sense* fame) pulled me aside in the kitchen. We'd always gotten along the best, and I couldn't wait to hear what new secret we might share.

"John, don't you think you could lay off the drinking, for just a few days? For Mom's sake? She's not blind. She's got enough on her plate; the last thing she needs to be is worrying about you."

My jaw hung open, perhaps for a full minute. I'd barely suspected that they'd even noticed. In the blink of an eye, I felt smaller and more worthless than I'd ever felt before. And of course, the irony was that I longed for a drink more than anything—to obliterate that void, that writhing self-loathing I felt squirming in the pit of my stomach. But instead of that or anything else, I looked him square in the eye.

"Absolutely," I simply replied.

So I did, for a few days at least. I was smashed on the flight home, though, and spent half the trip home grinding my knuckles on the toilet seat of the small airplane bathroom, retching as quietly as possible. I finished the job in the airport in California, and then forced myself to sit down and eat—and to think about everything that had just transpired. I stared at the window and forced myself to be a grownup, or at least do my best acting. I mouthed the words into my faint reflection in the window pane:

I have lost my Father. My Father is dead. My Mother is worried that I'm an alcoholic. My siblings *know* that I'm an alcoholic and resent me for hiding behind it instead of helping my Mom in her hour of need.

Finally, after beating myself up much as I knew how, I tried one more tack in the reflection.

"*I am an alcoholic*," I muttered, slowly and deliberately.

Rationalizations and extenuating circumstances rushed in to cover the words, but I forced all other thoughts from my mind and made myself stare at that sentence alone in my mind's eye.

I was an alcoholic.

Ψ

I got home and spent a great deal of time cuddled between Cash and Carrie, basking in unconditional love. They were my Velcro sidekicks. Even in the bathroom, I'd see their matching black noses pushing open the door to visit. Ecstatic to see me, they pranced around the room in wide circles before assuming the roles of much smaller dogs, trying to be lap dogs on my small recliner. I'd just sat down to try to think over all the strange mushed together thoughts when the doorbell echoed through the front hall. The dogs jumped and barked, running in manic circles.

I got up and found CJ on my front porch, grinning openly and then trying to suppress it, like he ought to be more formal.

"John Calabrace, would you be my best man? I'm getting married!"

Married. My best friend wanted to get married.

First my favorite childhood cousin, and now my best friend—both married. My brain lurched along in a spin, trying to recalibrate and take in the new information. I just nodded with a lost-looking expression that completely failed to express an inner joy that was beyond compare.

It was months before I'd admit to CJ that I'd just returned from losing my Father, the revelations about alcoholism that I felt unable to further resist, and my fear of disappointing my family. No, I'd learned my lesson, and in some oblique fashion I hoped I could make up for my family by making my best friend's day the best of his life. My baggage could wait.

And it was a beautiful wedding. A few months down the road, we found ourselves in a vineyard in the middle of nowhere, full of wineglasses, flutes, military pomp at its finest, and yes—love. I didn't drink a drop. We all lined up, and I handed CJ the ring and watched the ceremony progress in slow motion—the polar opposite of the funeral that had just uprooted my life and forced me to rebuild afresh. That was an end; this was a beginning. We all need a beginning—a new chance, a new day.

More than anything, I marveled at the thoughts. Sure, the wedding guests were interesting: the stories CJ wouldn't have wanted told, the what-ifs, the one jealous ex-boyfriend scowling in the back row. But so much more than that—the thoughts of the bride and groom: there was something wonderful about it, a glow. It was something about the way they mesmerized one another. It was a sensation unlike any I'd ever seen, something pure. They fixated on every detail of the other—preferences, dreams, memories—and stored them with a willpower I'd never imagined possible in "regular people." I finally saw something that I would classify right alongside my gift, something I'd never approached: innocent, pure, absolute love. I watched them watching each other and wished them all the world, wished I could tell them how much more that gift was than anything I had. But I knew there are worlds you can never share in words…

So I smiled, threw the rice, and watched them drive away into the dark night.

29

To ensure that I'd still be alive on his wedding day, CJ insisted I start taking my superiors more seriously. So once again, I moved amid the world of meetings and proximity protocols. A year passed like it was nothing: work meetings, sobriety meetings. The new handlers' protocol noted that I was to be handled at a distance: arm's length, no complex tasks—just tests and more tests, or the very easiest chores—but only if they could remove all potential complications. They were *company men,* the worst.

One day, my scheduled meeting was canceled, and instead Dannels walked into the room, completely out of breath.

"John, I have a lot to say, and I'm already at a loss for where to start. Bear with me here, there have been a lot of new developments. One: you're drinking too much, and it's getting noticed. Someone is painting you as that "loose lips that sink ships" guy amid the highest circles, and that needs to change. Also—"

"Well, I am an alcoholic and I'm working the road to recovery," I interjected, proudly.

He stopped, dumbfounded. "Well...there ya are, John, we've been saying that for years. Admission is the first step, and all that. I've got a number for you if you'd like it—but that business needs to get squared away, and fast." He paced to the other side of the room, glancing down a hallway, and shutting another door at the back of the hall. "But there's worse, too. Things I don't fully understand yet."

"What does that mean?" I shot back, worried by his worry.

"It means that there is no proper accounting for the wild amount of queries to your name, nor the impossibly-stretched timeframe. It means there is an entire level to this—beyond what we've been looking at. It means, John, they've been watching you since you were born."

Dannels clearly thought the world would fall out beneath me.

"Damn it Dannels, that's what CJ and I found out a year and a half ago!"

"But it's really real!"

"I KNOW. But I don't know anything else. CJ and I got blocked, right as we got there!"

"Oh, no. So you didn't see anything about watchers?"

"No..." I hesitated, "nothing like that."

"You've had more than some random aggressor, John. It's organized. There have been plants and archives and everything. Your college roommate—"

I stared at him, wild-eyed. "MARK?! You think MARK was a US spy?"

He sat down, gesturing at me to lower my voice. "It's not conjecture, John. It's substantiated. He has files, records. He made regular reports. And he wasn't the first. There were reports made in your school years: your P.E. teacher was interrogated, for Christ's sake."

"Mr. Gillen?!" I pictured the wispy old runner, who'd shocked the school by abruptly deciding to move when I was in seventh grade.

He ignored me and continued on, glancing at notes he'd tucked under his arm. "There was another kid who was shot around the foster system a bit, after fleeing your hometown. It took 'our people' a while to find him, but within ten years, I was able to see that they'd stopped and questioned him all about his childhood interaction with you, as well as a few other bystanders mentioned only in footnotes. But by far, maybe the most dramatic of all was the number of both queries and submitted reports made by another schoolmate of yours, one who seems to have made your life their life's work—"

But as he spoke, before he even got there, I had a sensation like a fog bank rising up and clearing. My brain retroactively reassembled and remembered the glimmering shadow behind a million coincidences. The prowler beyond the windows that, drunk, I'd explained away as a trick of the light. The man who'd followed me from bar to bar as the adrenaline dump eviscerated my awareness. The man who'd thrown down a gauntlet as a child and had never let it go. The man who'd tackled me and panted in my face in a horrifically combined rage and possessive desire all those years before. The lunatic. The enduring, confusing thorn in my side.

As my brain finally reached the obvious correlation that had floated just beyond a mist for years, I relived the moment years before where he'd turned around as I was entering my first Navy assignment and recalled his clumsy attempt to sabotage me even then, as I was bound to join his ship…

Bryan Walker. My God! Thinking the name, I had no idea why I hadn't seen it sooner.

"Well, John, he's actually from your home town, and—"

"Bryan! It was Walker, all along, the face beyond the window, the guy following me on the streets…"

Dannels looked crushed. "You knew?!"

"Not at all," I clarified, "not until literally this minute."

"Well that's not all, John. He may be a leak, but he isn't alone. He's protected. And it goes high. Whoever is using his services, isn't doing it out in the open. There's a lot going on here that I don't understand, but the clearances at play are outrageous. I'm doing everything I can not to raise flags just by running queries."

"Right," I replied, striding around the room in manic agitation. "This would be comical if it wasn't true. My junior high adversary has made it his life's work to stalk me for decades—aided by others even crazier than he is—towards some unknown ends. They've tracked down anyone with any knowledge of my gift or in a position to comment on my development—down to my clueless PE teacher and the schoolyard bully. Right? And then my college roommate Mark was also a—was a *plant.* He was only there to spy, not for school, not a real roommate…He wasn't there to sunbathe and fritter away the summer, but to report on…To…WHAT THE HELL DO THEY WANT, DANNELS?! When will it be enough?!"

He paused, looking just as horrified as me. "I have no idea, John. I have no answers yet. I assume it's the same thing everyone wants: they want to know what's going on in you, and how fast it's changing, and whether they can harness it to do, whatever...But there's more John. Your file isn't new. It was merged—with someone else. Your Great Uncle—Major John Grey. There's something about his covert wartime history—evidently there were some traits he'd started demonstrating that raised suspicion that the gift might be passed on, and after a few early decades of surveying your family, it was decided that—"

I felt my knees get woozy. Everything looped back through again. All the secrets, all the legends, all the rumors, all the vibes...Nothing was real, and everything was real. All my friends were suddenly potential enemies, my points of familiarity were lies—or perhaps convenient alibies for proximity and surveillance. I found myself thinking of Nannie, of the loose tiles in the bathroom.

Everything felt like it was trembling across one great wide web, intersecting every point of my life, and I was wound in the center—with my arms and legs bound tightly, staring out into the dark, blind. What was coming for me?

"*Who* decided?" I interrupted.

"His face went white. "That's the thing...it doesn't say!"

Ψ

And so began the new era of unmasked unrealities. All the same actors, all the same dates, sets, and props; and yet the underlying possibility that it had all been faked so that someone might report on whether I'd yet ripened to a point of peak exploitation, like my ancestor before me, to be harvested by whichever shadows demanded use. All I could think about was Bryan Walker: the cog in the system, the first rung on the ladder. I knew what would happen—I knew I would see that face pop up eventually in the shadows, behind a camera, behind a bush, tailing the man he thought was blackout drunk—and I feared to think the things I would do to him—if I captured him alive.

Dannels tried to bring me back down to a practical level, a purposeful and cunning level of thinking; but I was deep in the adrenaline dump.

What do I say? What do I do when I have to stroll out there and face these liars, these parasites, who want to just latch onto whole lifetimes and—

But I never got to finish my rant because someone rushed in the door, gesturing apologies. "I'm sorry, sir, it's just…the phone hasn't stopped ringing all afternoon. They've been patching calls back through, at every number…"

"Can't you just tell them that I'll call back? I'm working on something quite important, and—"

But with a flick of his eyes, the poor page clarified towards me. "I'm sorry, sir, the call wasn't for you, but for Mr. Calabrace."

"Well, who is it?" I cried, exasperated.

"It's your Mother, sir. She's quite insistent."

Ψ

Nannie was dead. At ninety years old, she had remained sharp as a tack: loving, dedicated, selfless. And now, just when I needed her more than ever, just when I needed to share this tumbling house of cards with her, she'd slipped through my fingers, too.

Mom was beside herself. Her biggest pillars in life were all out of reach: an empty nest, her mate gone, her Mother as well. Throughout the phone conversation, all she wanted to address was how proud she was of me, how much she loved me, how much she needed me to know she was always thinking of me from home, hoping that I was happy where I was, that I had a house full of love and warmth—and then she would cry, quietly, with quiet reserved dignity. I'd only hear it in her staccato breaths as she exhaled.

I promised to be home for another funeral and warned the vipers I worked for of my plans. There was an immediate clamor of protest—that I couldn't just up and take vacation every time I felt like it, but I ground my teeth and growled that I wasn't taking a vacation. One minion raised an eyebrow: and that was that. Assuredly, many formal, critical complaints were reported, as all things in my life were evidently now reported. To whomever. For whatever purposes…

I was so angry, and in so much pain, I couldn't help wanting to just regurgitate these heartless men's worst pain and horrors back on them…but I didn't.

Instead I shut my mouth and headed home.

It was an elegant affair, as funerals go. The great Christian hymns sounded over the old tree-lined graveyard, and everyone sang. A great many strangers showed up to honor the great woman, a legend across many towns. We all stood together in the green cemetery, early in the morning, with the dew still wet on the grass and the headstones. The elaborate coffin was lowered into the ground, graced with flowers, tears, and fond words of remembrance.

But as usual, none of it yet felt real. The millions of memories of my Nannie certainly didn't feel less legitimate, for her being gone. Nor the images of her glittering through her wonderful houses, or initiating me to the secrets that had since come to dominate my life. Nannie was alive in every story she'd awoken, in her shared secrecy of all my gifts, in her now lost secrets of the Great Uncle I'd never known.

I tried to pull all the threads together into one to accept the loss as a person and not simply envision the chasm I felt. Nannie, the Mother of my Mother. A girl, who lived a good long life, enjoyed love and brilliance, and passed, as all well do. But it was too tidy, too easy. Shock remained. A nice ceremony, but one that I would have to take time to process.

But as I led my Mother away from the minister, I noticed a very old man gesturing to me from beyond several rows of gravestones. She was in a daze, and at each new circle, people stopped to give hugs and kind words. She met a circle of my siblings and drew them all into a hug, so I slipped off to investigate the strange man who'd kept me locked in his line of sight, summoning feebly all the while.

Jim noticed the man too and gestured that he'd take my Mother onward. I jogged through the rows of headstones, and slowed next to him.

"I'm sorry, sir, were you gesturing for me, or—"

"She was such a beautiful young woman, your Grandmother. You should've seen her as a girl, ah!"

"Thank you, sir. Were you a friend of the family, or…"

"I'd love to share a drink with you, John Calabrace. Would you mind?"

"I'm not drinking these days, actually. However, we've got snacks and drinks set up at the house: coffee and tea, and the hard stuff if you'd like it."

"I'd prefer some privacy. Can you spare a few minutes? This will do."

"Well, I should really be with my Mother right now; honestly, she really—"

"I knew your Great Uncle, John—Major John Grey."

I almost fell over at the mention of the name. "What?! I'm sorry, who are you?"

"He saved me, John. He uncovered me, you know. Yup. I'd disguised myself for work and I'd been sent to compromise him. I assumed they'd eventually have me kidnap him. But he found me out before any of that. He found me, and warned me—that I'd been compromised by my own men, and for some reason they'd decided to do away with me."

The man paused for breath, as I stared on in shock.

"Now I was deep-cover at this point to get close to him, you understand? I'd worked my way into a position of clergy and had convinced many that I was the real deal. Not him, not for a moment. He could always sense a setup. He ferried me out. He took great personal risks to rescue an adversarial spy. He set me up with a new life. That was the kind of man your Great Uncle was. I've lived my entire life in gratitude to him."

The words washed over me pretty fruitlessly, until I made a vital connection.

"Your ring!" My hand fluttered automatically up towards my breast pocket.

"He wouldn't take anything in compensation when he paid my way and booked my passage out of the country, in his name. He arranged everything, and knew it would work in advance. He just told me to be good to my children and to find some way to make a living doing something better for the world. He was such an idealist, even then—

even after discovering that we'd been ordered to close in. I gave him the ring, that he might not forget my gratitude."

My head flickered electrically, finally connecting to a past that seemed a fairy tale.

"But do you think it was that same ring that got him killed? If they found him—"

"No, John. Your Uncle was not very vulnerable, at the peak of his powers. He would have seen just about anything coming miles away. He was too sage and cautious, too, by instinct and inclination alone. I believe he *decided* to do what he did, though I've never understood why."

I looked intently at his wrinkled, weathered face.

"What happened, exactly?"

He paused, carefully considering his words.

"I don't have those answers, only approximations. I think there was some sort of situation where he knew he had a trump card, one that would be misread by everyone closing in around him. He knew he could do great good and buy some time to mask actions of his friends by unexpectedly sacrificing himself. I suspect he allowed himself to be obliterated in his own trap, so something might happen during the distraction. He lived for that sort of selflessness—it was never even a consideration for him. But I did follow his advice, and I rebuilt a life, to make up for the one I'd wasted previously. And I've also kept an eye on you, and your life. (An old man with a clandestine past sees more than most.) I can't help but wish the same things for you, John—an exodus to a gentler life, a more peaceful life, where you might give something back, but without all the animus of "enemies" and "allies" and "subterfuge." Surely there's some plain good available to come from this," he gestured at my cranium, "from whatever family skills have been shared down the line."

"Yes, well, there are quite a few people determined that they should decide what and how I use my brain, at present," I grumbled, sadly.

"But others would love to help you align your skills with other plans, if the opportunity ever arises. If you ever find a way to be free of *them*, I will put you in contact with some people I've found in the shadows who've managed to evade the grasp and reach of militaries and spy networks. They use their skills to rebuild and to heal, never to scheme, never to entrap. When you're ready—"

But as somebody approached, I turned my head to the sound. It was just Jim. I turned back to the stranger, but he had disappeared.

"When I'm ready WHAT?!" I shouted into the trees, but nobody answered.

"Everything okay here?" Jim asked. "We're gonna take Mom back home, and make a big dinner. Are you in?"

A thousand miles from reality, I pulled myself into the present tense against all odds, if only for a second.

"Of course I'm in," I muttered, trooping towards a long train of cars, as a drizzle came in.

30

I'd never been great at making myself vulnerable. I'd never really had to observe how other people do it. Even with my brothers, it just wasn't something we did: you grinned and bore it. So far as I knew, everyone kept their guards up all the time, guarded their comportment and emotions; and yet their most intimate secrets merely melted away from their corporal form, in spite of their best efforts. That certainly wasn't a strategy I could rely on—to share my secrets with other people. So I had to learn to break it down, to temporarily pull my walls down like a draw bridge and let people in—if only for a few moments in the beginning, to test the waters.

If there were any conceivable benefits to losing so many people I cared about so strongly, then it was that I saw a distinct difference in the visceral response I felt to my own tragedies versus the reheated traumas of strangers—no matter how strong the empathy grew. I had a deep sense that as my scattered circle shrank, the core of me—whatever that was—was eroding. I only had so many intimates these days, and I couldn't spare any. No longer could I wall myself in and wait for the storms to pass. I couldn't hope that people would just stop aging, or the world would stop spinning. I swallowed my pride and my silence, and I clumsily waded into a lot of long-delayed, fragmented conversation. When I spoke to CJ later that week, he was, well, a mixture of compassion and indignation.

"John, how did you forget to tell me *that your Father had died?* I would've been there for you, man, you just needed to tell me! After all we've been through together, you forgot?"

"It just didn't seem like the time…You had your own stuff going on, and there was so much other shit happening, and—" I began, but he cut me off.

"Maybe you aren't that familiar with how this works: since you stick with the cliff notes on everyone…but people have your back. No matter what choices you make, no matter how many times you fuck up, no matter how much darkness can come into your life, there are many of us that see you as family. That will NEVER change. NEVER. That isn't a choice easily made, and it's one that is never broken. But you've got to open up, too. And now that you mention it, lately I'm hearing from Dannels that—"

I cut in, sighing, "I know, I know. My drinking is out of hand, and I should have made more of an effort earlier on, and—"

"No, John, that's not my point at all! If you had some traumatic realization that possibly half your childhood had been actually spent in a den of foreign agents, you should have let me be there for you! That's why you have a best friend: to hold you together in moments of crisis like that…"

I sat still a moment and watched him. He was dead right. I couldn't put together the words to how I'd felt, and why I'd tried to keep everyone in the dark. But of course it was there, staring me in the face. My capacity to trust had obviously taken a few punches straight to the face—that much was clear. But more importantly, it had simply never occurred to me that I had friends who would want to be there for me, or that it would mean something to them to support me. Somewhere deep amid all the self-loathing enabling the drinking, I'd allowed myself to sincerely believe I was fully isolated, ignoring all the folk who felt I were family. I didn't have any of the words to express it, but I felt a profound sense of gratefulness and relief that CJ had taken the trouble to say it all—out loud.

"All right, we clear buddy? Do you see that we care about you? Will you stop hiding yourself away in the shadows? To me and many of the others you are a whole lot more than a damn GS-13 asset. Meanwhile,

I have other important news to discuss, John. The world stops for no man, and no imminent social collapse nor conspiracy, neither."

He eyed me carefully as he poured us both some hot chocolate, though I had no idea in the world where he was going with this. He settled into the couch and sat quietly for a moment, reflecting, staring out over the window.

"The world really does never stop, John, no matter how crazy it gets. My wife and I are going to have a boy. A little baby boy. We'd like to name him after you."

"Ah, don't jinx the kid, CJ," I laughed.

Ψ

So the world pulled itself back together from the ground up, to prepare safe passage for a new life. I transformed my life, week by week, learning to erode the unnecessary walls of secrecy that I'd taken for granted as regular around all my minor life struggles with drink, with loneliness, and with the subtle self-loathing that enabled the drinking. I poured new energy and enthusiasm into connecting with my dogs, and slowly I realized that my communication with them was impossibly strong. It took me awhile to recognize an unseen expansion of the gift that I'd only glimpsed with the dolphins years before, growing quietly in the shadows this whole time. Eventually, I was able to gesture almost imperceptibly to my dynamic duo, and they'd race to respond to my unseen commands.

In every sphere, I felt myself opening, wherever possible, attempting to connect more with my human traits, beyond the hungry brain. In a sobriety support group, I reconnected with one of my favorite role models I'd ever known: an old shipmate. I'd never have guessed it, but he'd now been sober thirty-five years, and it hadn't been easy for him, either. He helped me reattach my mind to reality and respect myself. Finally, I heard someone reference an old Cherokee story that really brought it all home: a legend of two wolves. The gist was that everyone has two wolves fighting out a terrible eternal battle within them; one wolf represents everything good and pure and selfless, and the other everything dark. Which wins? The answer was ultimately whichever one gets *fed.*

And then, there was work. CJ had made me see the reality of my obligations, and Dannels had made me see the reality of betrayals that had sold me out from the start. Somewhere between the two of them, an immense fatigue had overtaken the whole prospect of the career itself. Dannels exerted every bit of leverage—and exhorted every last ally in his arsenal—to ensure that anyone within reach of me was carefully vetted and hand-picked. He signed off on every deployment plan. But the writing seemed to be on the wall the more we observed the static floating over the communication channels: someone, somewhere was wary of the slow pace of the exploitation of my gifts.

We'd also started hearing hints of people who'd rather just do away me and be done with it, file closed. They could just study the brain. Of course, that necessitated killing me; but tools took precedence, and science was meant to be cold. We could never quite track the ultimate origins of that chatter—it faded into nothing the second we shone a hard light towards it. But we didn't take the threats lightly and walked the world with our eyes wide open, taking each step carefully.

Non-retaliation became a huge theme in the way I was approaching these new threats. I saw people hoping to do me wrong, and I saw through to the misunderstandings and fear beneath. I tried to do whatever I could to diffuse them. More and more I just let it go. This became a moral quandary: my freedom to admit I could sort through all their mental baggage and unravel their cognitive knots was severely curtailed by the fact that folk see otherness as "the beast," and tend to kill it with torches and pitchforks, plowshares and swords. Even in my intelligence work, I saw misunderstandings and fear ramping up in the shadows. All my altruistic alarm bells would sound, as I wondered whether I couldn't just leave a little message somewhere that would end the squabble, and thus retune the world to harmony.

But as the thoughts passed through my mind, I recognized all the partisan minds of the military and knew the plan was doomed to failure. Outsiders' plans were never looked favorably upon, and I always knew they felt I was an outsider looking into their world.

I came to understand that the military was just like any other massive body of people. There was no unified message—just good guys and bad ones alike, folk motivated by idealism and deeply internalized distrust. Furthermore, there was no common message of salvation to be conveniently laid before the feet of combatants to diffuse conflict. If anything, I felt intensely demoralized about my role in the world and in this body of men: what good could I do? All I could do was confer a temporary advantage, and even that had to be filtered through all the typical channels and ambitions of the web of soldiers separating my unfiltered view from the final decision makers—always hidden by endless degrees of separation. I'd always been too busy with my briefings and protocols to notice it, but I still had no idea who sent my missions to my Dannels or his superiors. I didn't know if I liked them or not, whether I agreed with them or not, or whether I even trusted them. I trusted CJ and Dannels and perhaps a handful of other men I'd bonded with over the years. I suffered many more, and I was even disgusted by a fair number, after accidently accessing their past from themselves directly or their victims scattered across the globe.

Yet here I was, always jumping to the call. For the first time in my life, I found myself regularly wondering what came next.

More importantly, I found myself wondering about the strange man and his hidden band of friends, and their ideal of compassionate service—far from the world of war-making.

Could it be real? Or was it just another trick?

One day, I found myself in a small coffee shop across the street from a military base where I'd been in meetings all morning. I was reading a novel CJ had sent me to pass the long nights formerly spent drinking. While I loved the book, I'd found that Cash and Carrie had no interest in allowing me the luxury of reading at home, and every interest in sticking their snouts under the book, under my arms, or resting their heads atop the crown of my skull: like some sort of shamanistic tribal mask, one that sometimes licked your eyebrows. I nixed bedtime reading at home in favor of more playtime and training with them. But at work I found a rekindled love of reading as a solace against the stresses of my insincere, bewildering colleagues at these incessant meetings.

I found myself laughing inwardly at one of the passages in the story. As I chuckled, I noticed a blurred stranger smiling at me from my peripheral vision, watching me from a small table along the glowing window front. My blood immediately froze for fear of all the threats I'd recently been trained to be wary of; but a single glance at this man affirmed that he didn't have a trace of harshness in his body, just a jovial interest in someone's over-animated silent reactions to a great book.

"Forgive me," he laughed, turning back to his food, "I couldn't help noticing your reaction to that book. I loved it, too." He chuckled, chomping into a BLT.

I sat warily a moment, deciding whether or not I wanted to keep my guard up. But I decided—what the hell—and I let my tense shoulders fall back to a normal position.

"Not at all! I'd fallen out of the habit of reading; I wouldn't be surprised if I'm making some ridiculous faces, without realizing it." I laughed.

"Well, I won't interrupt your reading any further, I hope you enjoy it!" the man volunteered politely. He finished up his meal, still grinning, and quietly left.

As I stared at the empty chair left behind him, I found myself wishing I'd found the means to engage him in a longer conversation. Something about his face, the way he carried himself, and his confident smile, made me comfortable. Floating all around him was nothing but goodwill, easy joy, kindness, and a gentle windward spirit. I'd met one of the few, unmitigated *really good people,* yet I'd entirely missed the opportunity to make a friend. I nursed the grudge in the back of my mind until the next day, when I absentmindedly entered the same shop at the same time, once again, equally exasperated with my morning meetings. But who should I find in the same seat, but the kind-looking man watching birds out the window, while waiting for Minestrone soup to cool.

"Ah! The prodigal reader returns!" He laughed, as he glanced up and saw me lowering my briefcase with a sheepish grin.

"John," I volunteered, reaching out my hand.

"I'm David, and it's very nice to meet you, John. What is on your literary agenda for today?"

"Today? Today, I think I'll just enjoy a break from the Navy.

David laughed. "Fair enough, fair enough. I think I got lucky with coworkers: I'm the director of special projects for a small fleet of cruise ships—everyone is always in a great mood; and even when they aren't, nobody stays more than a season or two. In fact, sometimes I even long for a bit of exhausting workplace drama, if just to imply some continuity beyond the seasonal hiring practices. And you? What do you suffer through, John?"

I gestured with a thumb across the street.

"Ah! Yes, that would do it, I would imagine. But at least you'd get to see the sea! That's the number one job perk in my work—that and spending my forties dancing."

We both laughed. "I'm not much of a dancer; the arts and language always stifled me."

"Ah, believe me John, I'm not much of a dancer either. But I write the checks and pass out the bonuses for our team, so nobody dares tell me so."

We both laughed again: light, effortless, easy laughs. It was bizarre, we laughed like old friends, with the ease and comfort that I'd found with some of my oldest friends on the sub. Soon, he had to run and said he hoped we'd run into one another again, which we did. He disappeared for a few weeks of cruises, and then he sauntered in one day for his same sandwich and soup—looking exhausted but jovial as ever. We picked up right where we'd left off—and the friendship grew fast and strong. We conversed like we had all the time in the world, talking about our jobs, our friends, our families, and everything in between. And he seemed genuinely interested, too. At first, I'd been unable to suspend a faint hint of suspicion in his kindness, some sort of ulterior motive, or echoes of my sense of betrayal at Mark's evident espionage. But I could read David like an open book. There was nothing. He was just a big smile, who enjoyed my company, and was earnestly seeking to cement our friendship.

One day, he admitted that just by the nature of his travels, he had very few friends, which I found hard to believe.

"Well, I like to make conversation, sure. But when you work in a job like I do, it's hard to make long-term connections. Everyone is always in flux. Everyone feels like they're temporarily stepping out of their 'real lives.' Most of the people I work with, work for me—and it's difficult to be dating the boss. Folk come onto cruises in a state of suspended animation; it's all play-acting and Disneyland. Except for me—for me, it's real. Folk say they'll keep in touch, but I know they mean I'll maybe get a Christmas card. That's just the nature of the profession." "Well, you can rest easy, David. To this day, I've never managed to get my Christmas cards out. Believe me, I've tried. I've got stacks *half a decade old* in my kitchen, right now."

And before I knew it, for the first time in ages, I'd made a new friend. I had a friend who knew me as a sober man but also knew the circumstances behind it. David admitted he had struggled with sobriety as well; so I felt in a lot of ways we were on an even footing from the start. We bonded as thick as thieves in no time—as he filled in the cracks of CJ's burgeoning new life across the country, and the poor, overworked Admiral Dannels, behind his mountains of papers, interventions, and investigations.

Over the next year, after every mission, the first person I looked up was David, impatiently counting down the weeks before he'd be freed from a sea transit of his own to return to our familiar café life, which slowly expanded to a reconstructed social life structure, markedly devoid of alcohol. We went to movies and walked the dogs, and he eventually talked me into joining his morning jogs, which I suffered through in a constant state of panting.

But those golden days soon ground to a halt. I received ominous news that my Mother's persistent cough was in fact late-stage cancer and was taking a turn for the worse. I rushed home just in time to watch her fade away. We hugged all week, and then she was gone.

Something deep within me atrophied.

I could think of nothing but the fact that she'd been my constant support at every moment of life. Not just me, but the whole community around her. I couldn't even approach the idea that I was without parents, that I now represented the most senior generation of Calabrace.

My brothers and I didn't know where to start. There is something particular about families: social changes move in geological-time, slower. They all still seemed to perceive me as the thoughtless-drunk of years past and with all the angst and turmoil. I slipped right back into that role. In spite of CJ's insistence, I didn't call him. I didn't call Dannels. And after I left a few drunk messages on David's phone with no explanation of what I was going through, he left me a polite message in due course saying he wasn't able to return my calls. The pain of my loss of sobriety had brought back dark memories of his own; and I needed to clean up to keep our friendship intact. I was devastated.

I found myself moving like a ghost through the house I'd been raised in, peering into all the corners I remembered and living in decades long gone. I imagined the lot of us, scrambling over all the same old furniture as kids: innocent and savage, clueless, and whole. I daydreamed of all the times I'd seen my Mother provide all the answers to all the lost people her town could provide—sitting them down in the very same chair where I now found myself, desolate, crying, leaning over my drink.

As the hurt grew, I isolated more and more. I couldn't face my brothers as the funeral arrangements were arranged; too many resented my drink and my volatility—so I retreated to my old room and nursed the bottles in secret, in the dark.

Somewhere around that time, I managed to convince myself that there was nothing left—that everything worth living had been corrupted; mostly by my own doing, my selfishness, my incapacity to control my impulses and commit to a lifestyle that would please the people around me. Every brotherly intervention was shrugged off by the raincoat of my self-loathing, through which I assumed that they hated me as well and were just trying for show.

I imagined all the happy people, far away, wrapped in their successes. In my drama, I could only see them as impossibly faraway actors, in roles impossibly distanced from my reality. Married, successful, coping, happy, sustained. Somehow I convinced myself that they all felt grand, while I was just a monster, bringing everyone around me down. And as I did so, I also lunged towards other impulsive, more dramatic conclusions. I also convinced myself that there was no need to wait around for Mom's funeral to join her.

Shit-faced for the millionth time, I sat in the dark in my childhood bedroom, with a storm blowing through the tree limbs outside my window, as I composed a final note to all the friends who I'd soon free from the burden that I believed I represented. I chose a haunting old poem I'd retained from a young SAS officer while working together in Yugoslavia: The Parting Glass. I began to trace line after line onto some old stationary paper as I wept.

The Parting Glass

Of all the money that e'er I had
I've spent it in good company
And all the harm that e'er I've done
Alas it was to none but me
And all I've done for want of wit
To memory now I can't recall
So fill to me the parting glass
Good night and joy be with you all
Of all the comrades that e'er I had
They are sorry for my going away
And all the sweethearts that e'er I had
They would wish me one more day to stay
But since it falls unto my lot
That I should rise and you should not
I'll gently rise and I'll softly call
Good night and joy be with you all
A man may drink and not be drunk
A man may fight and not be slain
A man may court a pretty girl
And perhaps be welcomed back again
But since it has so ought to be
By a time to rise and a time to fall
Come fill to me the parting glass
Good night and joy be with you all
Good night and joy be with you all…

I stacked all the bottles of pills alongside my childhood photos on the nightstand and climbed into bed, staring at the rows of innocent, shining faces in the photos. Then, handful by handful, I swallowed the pills while staring out at the fuzzy moon beyond the swaying tree limbs.

31

For as long as I could remember, I'd been wandering through a snowy landscape, slowly moving through waist-high snow towards a small road that snaked over a mountain pass beyond. Frosty winds pushed at my back and blew snowflakes through my hair, hardening my eyelashes into small stalactites blinking against my cheekbones. My teeth chattered as I trudged up the pass. Blue green alpine trees drooped more than seemed possible under huge loads of snow and ice. For a long time, this world seemed timeless, and nothing changed but the wind howling steadily past.

Suddenly, the icy face of the mountain right ahead groaned and cracked, as the whole mountain face resounded with a loud boom. Birds exploded like fireworks up from the trees in flickering black curtains, and the rising dust spiraled in the wind. The snowy surface shuttered and shook as a second boom quaked the mountain range, with small avalanches coursing down through the slalom labyrinths. I looked around in horror, trying to figure out what was happening, my breath freezing in the air and tinkling as it fell to the ground in tiny ice crystals. Finally, with a third massive boom, the mountain range exploded clear away, giving way to a huge boot and a sudden flood of light.

CJ kept kicking away splinters of the door and seconds later was yelling inaudibly inches from my face, as I blinked up at him from my bed, trying to piece together what was dream and what was real. I watched him silently yell something back towards my bedroom doorway, as I recognized the silhouette of Dannels squeezing through the hole in the door. CJ shook empty pill bottles at me with a mortified expression on his face, shaking me by the shoulders yelling questions I couldn't hear as Dannels raced over and frantically placed calls from my telephone. My eyelids felt so heavy! I let them fall shut a few times, only to feel myself shaken back into the bedroom scene by CJ's huge hands. Everything felt miles away, my hearing so muffled as to be unusable, my senses numb, my arms and legs a million pounds and impossible to control. My heartbeat felt like a tiny moth, flitting beneath a single sheet of paper. I was at peace, almost gone. Without deciding for or against, I felt myself slink back into the darkness.

I awoke to a mechanized orchestra of sound and the impossibly strong smells of bleach and alcohol. I couldn't seem to open my eyes, so I just stared at the tumbled coils of eyelid veins for a while. A beep interrupted my thoughts every four seconds, and I automatically tried to sync my breathing to it—but my lungs felt heavier than usual and difficult to operate. My spinal column felt like I'd been hit by a Mack truck…and all my extremities just felt numb. My mouth was positively glued shut. I had no moisture nor control, and I felt my sharp teeth cutting into papery bone-dry lips. All of my veins, all of my nerves, my muscles, my joints that I could feel ached. Finally, mustering all my strength, I managed to yank just enough on the micro-muscles controlling my face to split the curtain of eyelids blocking my eyes from the world. A strange blur of colors melted and bent into the forms of a room full of people, and suddenly I was back in the world.

CJ stood right before me, at the side of the bed with Dannels and two of my brothers. They all looked concerned and grave, but I couldn't discern them through the fog of reverb that muffled the edges of their words. I ran out of energy and felt my eyelids slip closed. I lost consciousness for what seemed just a few minutes, before reentering the world of the living.

"Hey brother—am I ever glad to see you alive and kicking!" CJ smiled, as I blinked and turned my frozen face to him.

I tried to speak, but I felt like my throat was full of glass and glue. After a moment's coughing, I managed to speak in a voice like dead crackling leaves.

"Where am I?"

"Winthrop–University Hospital, John. You scared the crap out of us there, but looks like you'll pull through."

"CJ?!" I said, still a few steps behind on comprehending the developing world.

"Yep, it's me buddy. Dannels is here, and your brothers. Your whole family is here. They just took a gedunk-break while you were sleeping."

"I'm..." The reality of the situation set in, as I realized what they must have uncovered. "I'm so sorry...I don't...I'm a moron. I—"

"John, shut up. You just focus on getting that heartbeat evened out, and we can talk all you want about the rest—once you're feeling better."

And in time, we did. While horrified at what I had done, CJ and Dannels were talking and surprised at something else, which I picked up immediately while they were speaking in the corner. As I'd written them the words to The Parting Glass poem, something about the intensity surge of emotions had somehow...*carried.* The message had reached them both at home: intact. Line for line, verse for verse. Unsure of what it had meant, both knew that something bizarre was at work. They'd both tried to call me, and when that hadn't worked, they'd both called one another and realized that what seemed like a strange dream had become a pattern, beyond coincidence. So they called around, realized my whereabouts, and rushed to find me. Had it been another half hour, it probably would have been too late.

The strange thing is, I could barely remember having decided to do it...the wash of emotions and darkness had just felt too strong. But the capacity to transmit that sort of message must always have been there—something about the strength and intensity of that surge had uncovered another as yet unseen element to my gift: projection. I had somehow managed to project my darkest moment, my final plea, and in just the nick of time, over tremendous distance and against all odds. That, and the unflinching loyalty of my friends, had assuredly saved my life.

From the second they'd dimly realized an expansion in my powers, both had rushed to an unlikely conclusion.

"John, what I'm about to say might sound uncharacteristic for me—but I think your life might depend on it: do NOT tell anyone about this latest development. NO ONE outside the three of us, NO ONE. Too much is up in the air right now, and the stakes are stacked against you at the moment. Nobody can know. They act crazy enough—thinking you're a one-way magnet; if they think you can go remote—game over. There is no predicting what they would do," Dannels whispered.

CJ nodded his head in agreement.

"I have a feeling they'll have some questions about these medical records…" I proposed weakly.

"Well, that I can fix—we'll call it like it is. A drug overdose, plain and simple. We'll get you help, John."

CJ was more specific in his advice.

"From everything you've ever said to me, whenever you tried therapy—you always ran from it. Well if that's the case, you still need to find out what's pushing you so far out every time you go dark. You need to face your head once and for all, and find a way to deal with it head on in the future. I know a guy—my wife's brother Marcus who…"

He proceeded to tell a long story of his wife's brother, who'd attempted suicide but hesitated and had then gone up to this spartan lodge to pull himself back together. There wasn't soothing music, nor incense—no beads, candles or chanting; it wasn't that sort of place. No, he'd gone to a place more like a barren monastery. You were provided with a simple cabin: one with a bed, a blanket, a window, and a floor cushion; and all your meals were dropped off, with two knocks on the door by unseen staffers. There, you faced your demons, and yourself.

"It couldn't hurt!" CJ said, as if forgetting I'd tried to kill myself last time I was alone in an isolated room. But maybe he had a point. Maybe it was time I forced a rupture in the habits and scripted dance steps that had brought me to such a dark place.

My superiors, though—they wanted nothing of it.

"John, are you aware of how much time you've already taken off this year? I'm sorry if you've had some losses and some personal trouble, but there are certain expectations upon employment here, that..." And a predictable rant followed.

But what choice did they have? Would they requisition a new MILSPEC remote viewer? I was a rare bird, and if it took extremes to keep my sanity afloat so they could continue to exploit me, so be it!

Against the express wishes of my superiors, I made it clear that I'd be traveling off the grid for one week, in three days' time. I made lots of promises—that after that things would change, and I implied that it was vital to my psychological and professional wellbeing. Although my 'vacation' was eventually granted, no attempts were made to conceal the open hostility to my demand. The honeymoon period was over.

Two days later, I'd been trying to wrap up all my work projects to a place where they might pause until I'd returned. When I finished my work day, I felt entirely drained. I took the dogs out to some headlands near my home, where I knew nobody ever came out walking so I might allow them to run free, unleashed. I spent a good amount of time staring at the grey waves crashing against the stones below, the scenery providing a strange sense of serenity as I thought about the turbulent decade that had suddenly become the norm.

How many huge moments of my life had happened while I stood on a high bluff like this, and stared out over changing vistas? On submarine decks, on mountains, on airplanes? And on that note—what had ever become of the easy lives of Mineola, Garden City or Cape Cod? I thought of my brothers, and of my bicycle, of Woolworth's and the summers in Sag Harbor. I thought of the awkward years of school that followed and the constant battles to fit in and stay afloat—all the while feeling myself become stranger in my own eyes. I reflected on all the changes that had clung together, like a snowball rolling down a hill gaining mass and momentum, until I'd sometimes felt more like a loose brain strapped a neck thana person walking through a planet of fellow humans. I viscerally recalled the sensation of falling out of time and place and being intentionally invisible that had plagued my life at NYC. And then came the complete erosion of a self to become a cog in a wheel aboard a sub—that had ironically been the first time I'd really thrived as a man amid his surroundings. But I'd forgotten the cardinal rule: I served the machine, and the machine wouldn't take lower productivity than was possible. So they'd plucked me out and thrust me back into unfamiliar worlds and imbalance—and what had it gotten me? As close to death, as I'd ever care to be…

As I thought those words, with the wind blowing the grass down around me, a silhouette rose from the rocks, just above the cliff face. It took my eyes a second to adjust—but I knew they weren't playing tricks on me. Bryan Walker trembled before me in the half-light—with a gun aimed right at my chest.

"Surprise!" Bryan laughed nervously. "At long last—who might we have here? The great John Calabrace?! Wonderful! I hope you won't mind—I came across this gun once at your house when you were passed out and figured firearm-safety demanded that I confiscate it. 'Finders keepers,' right?"

Peripherally I scanned for the dogs, worried they might get hurt. I still remembered that this bastard was mortally afraid of dogs, and I didn't want Cash or Carrie wandering in and getting hurt by guns.

"You always knew it'd come down to this eventually, right?" he gasped, sweat pouring down his face. "Nobody disrespects a Walker like that—like you did—nobody!"

"What the hell are you even talking about? When we were kids?! Get over it, Bryan, let it go! It's been decades now!"

His eyes bulged out of his head. "Just shut up!" he screamed, approaching closer and pressing the gun against my forehead. "You shut your goddamn mouth, John! I warned you! I knew you could never handle life like I could—no breeding, no stomach for education—no eye for connections like I have—unless you could weasel them away from your betters…I've watched you, yes—you're just a drunken mess! You didn't even graduate NYU, couldn't take the pressure huh?" he spat, nervously chuckling. "I'll always do whatever it takes! And now I've made a life out of trying to figure what it is: in that fucking brain of yours—that gives you the powers that I should have—that I deserve. But at every turn, who interrupts me? YOU! Too damn tired, too frustrated, too emotional, too unpredictable—"

His eyes now nervously swiveled around with no rhyme or reason; his voice was hoarse, as if he'd finally gone out and out mad. I could barely concentrate on his lunacy-speech for fear that he might actually snap and bite me like a werewolf or simply explode. But he just kept raving, unabated.

"Finally, I decided I'd do what needed to be done for a long time…You're a freak—one that needs to be erased. I even offered up the job to foreign guns, if they could expedite the process but nothing came of it. The government was too blind to stop you, so I offered my services to every group that expressed an interest in getting rid of you! But NO, you could never just let things happen. At every turn, I'd make a plan, and who'd mess things up?! Fucking Callous Calabrace: determined to ruin my life! He'd always come away unscathed, praised and grinning. Well not this time Johnny Boy…not this time!"

"Bryan, who was it who wanted you to—"

"SHUT THE FUCK UP, JOHN!"

Sweat poured down his face. He shook all over, clearly incapable of whatever it was he planned.

"Just put the gun down, Bryan. I never did anything to you, and I never meant to—"

"You've always shit all over my life, John! Ever since I could remember, you had to flaunt your damn depravity around in front of me, teasing and toying with everyone—then walking away unscathed… They all wanted what you had, but they ignored my superiority! I had dreams! I worked hard for everything I had! Your arrogance and stupidity charmed the world—but they held me back at every turn! I could never escape your damn shadow, not once! And never once did you think of how easy it could be for us! Never once did you consider how—"

But as his voice spiraled into a shrill rage, he flailed forward and knocked me off-balance, pushing his gun arm into my chest. I tripped backwards, groaning upon impact with a root structure in the ground, whose thorns ripped through my pants. From somewhere far behind me, I heard the protective scramble of my dogs' legs through the undergrowth on the headlands and low growls rocketing towards us.

Cash burst through some shrubs and leapt into the air before me, barking up a storm. Carrie's sprinting footsteps sounded behind me—as Bryan screamed and moved his gun from me towards Cash. I threw myself forward and knocked Cash out of the way—just as a bullet whistled past, lightly grazing my arm. Bryan roared in anger, half-cringing in the presence of the dogs as he, too, lost his balance in the tangled weeds, trying to readjust for a second shot. But as one foot twisted beneath him, and an arm flew wildly across his body as he tried and failed to balance his equilibrium—some dark realization flashed through his eyes. He let himself slump to the ground just before the cliff face, and then slowly rose, with a mad euphoric grin on his face.

He laughed a depraved laugh. "I finally see it, John, I finally see how it has to happen! Of course! It's so perfect!" He took a wobbling half-step backwards.

In spite of myself, I rushed forward to help him. "Bryan, no! Whatever you think is—"

But I couldn't have predicted what happened next. His eyes locked onto mine as I tried to grab his arm and simultaneously pull away the gun he was clumsily flailing in the air. But he stared deep into my eyes with a strange cartoonish half-smile, raised my gun to his temple, and fired. The explosion ricocheted around the cliffs and awoke sea birds nesting below, who burst into flight in a noisy clamor of wings. A wash of red sprayed over me and the dogs. Bryan's broken body was propelled in a wild spin back over the cliff overhang and tipped fully out of sight, into the darkness below.

And then there was nothing but silence. Carrie and Cash continued to bark, then whined and licked at my forehead as I lay on the bluff overlooking the rocks below, cradling my bleeding arm. In one brutal instant, everything was different.

32

The dogs whined, nuzzling against my legs. I'd completely lost all track of time, staring down over the cliff. There wasn't a sound below, just the rhythmic roar of waves crashing over stones and sand. I staggered back a few steps, my eyes careening from left to right, trying to get a hold on what was happening and what I was going to do. There was no one about; the headlands were deserted. Thunder rumbled in the distance, and a breeze picked up, whisking up pollen from the plant hugging the cliff face, as lost bird feathers danced in the air. In any other circumstance, it might have been a magical atmosphere. At present, well I suppose you can guess…

Moving mechanically, I found myself back at my car, a few minutes from the cliff. I silently opened the back passenger door—on autopilot, and both Cash and Carrie hopped in. I lowered myself into the driver's seat, watching my fingertips shake atop the steering wheel. Then we all just stared at one another for a few moments, as their breath fogged up the windows. The streetlamps glare stretched through the mist, or maybe I was a little misty myself…What was I going to do?

At that moment, I realized with a start that the last thing Bryan had done with his gun was thrust it against my forehead, scratching it into my skin as he'd yelled into my face. Would that be enough to connect me with his fall? His death? Would they even find the gun, or just a body? Our lifelong animosity would surely come up…With my recent instability, wouldn't I be a perfect suspect?

I started the car with no idea where to go, suddenly counting the moments down until my capture for a crime I hadn't committed. Given the way he'd orated at me—"they'd do anything they have to remove a liability…"—I couldn't help but think they'd never get a better chance than this. I just needed to settle down and think. I needed my wits fully about me, when I had to start answering questions, which now seemed *sure* to come. But would I even get a chance? Would I even have the opportunity to defend myself, or would they just leap at the chance to frame me and kill two birds with one stone?

As panic sunk in, my hands became vices on the steering wheel. The dogs continued to whimper, and they brought me back to reality. I realized I certainly couldn't stay *here*, so I started up the engine. I needed to be somewhere quiet, somewhere where I could strategize my defense and prove my innocence publically. Somewhere I wouldn't be snatched up, unexpectedly. Suddenly, like a clear bell tolling over still water, the answer came to me.

Marcus' meditation retreat!

If ever there was a time to achieve serenity or enlightenment, this was not it. But as far as laying low…what could be better? He'd promised it was off-season and even mentioned that the groundskeeper would give me a key with no questions if I'd just mention his name. So I decided to do just that. Hoping they had an indulgent pet-policy, I wheeled the car around and moved towards an onramp on the I5. If I'd figured right, I had about six hours of driving ahead of me. I wasn't certain on my directions, but figured I'd stop closer to the foothills in Northern California. I roared into the CA night, hours before dawn would peek over the disastrous cliff face. I raced against time, towards a strange sanctuary in North Fork.

I stopped a few times for coffee, but nobody seemed to pay me any mind, just truck stop attendants in the middle of the night: the type who rarely make eye contact anyway. By the time I got to Fresno I was dead-tired but determined to get indoors, as the sky became rosy and the morning television shows started telling the nation how to think. I cringed and fled all the faster, and finally I took the sleepy country road into the hills as sunlight burst through the clouds to illuminate the never-ending dead grass, dead oak, and nearly dead cows dotting highway 41. Nothing broke up the identical scenery but the old sunbaked timber fence posts, with small glinting lines of wire connecting them, and buzzards hovering in the breeze. Evergreens finally started to multiply as we gained elevation, but that was the height of thrills the road provided. I'd almost dozed off when I approached the sign for North Fork, and my tires screeched as I just managed to wheel about and roar down the dusty road. As I passed my third roadkill deer carcass, I began to think I'd perhaps made a terrible choice. My stomach rumbled over the engine. I passed an overgrown cemetery in an old pioneer town, and decided I was definitely going to die here. But there was nowhere to go but forward, so forward I went.

In time, the landscape became rockier and the crags more defined. The trees were more triumphant than the parched oak trees and were laden with pinecones. I pulled onto a deserted road and was soon before an old rusty gate. A man was laying lime mortar along a stone wall and waved as I approached.

"A man named Marcus told me I could—"

Before I had time to explain, he cut me off and said "Yup."

He tossed me a key. "You're the last cabin, about three minutes out into the trees. Water tank is behind the main house; food is dropped off twice a day to your cabin. It's just you, me, and two other folks up now—so please bus your own dishes." And with that, he shuffled away, without a second look.

I wasn't free, but this was as probably as close to it as I could hope for. I wandered through the complex for a while ensuring that my suspicion had been right, and indeed there were no televisions in the whole camp. Honestly, it was probably all the better, in the case of a manhunt. I also didn't see any phones. I walked back through the trees and found my cabin, which was not a luxury retreat. There were four walls. One was pierced with a single window and a door. There were two cushions on the floor, about four feet wide apiece. I fluffed one up for Cash and Carrie, and they just stared at me. I fluffed up the second one and laid down myself, they both curled up under my arms, and in no time at all the walls were shaking with snores.

A whole day went by before I realized I had been pushing the incidents back home conveniently out of mind. I don't know how the normal residents of this camp would have perceived a day of silence, but I spent most of the time playing with the dogs—I barely noticed the lack of other people. But the dogs didn't sleep well after a storm kept them awake all night; so the next morning they snoozed. For the first time I could remember, I found myself in absolute silence—with no escape and no blinders. Normally I would have substituted anything: liquor, jogging through traffic, the phone or even the television blathering in the background: but this was deafening, pure, unrelenting *silence*. Deep from some manic center within me, a dull sort of worry set in, like somehow if I didn't speak to someone, I would dissolve. Even on the submarine, deep in the apotheosis of deep dark silence undersea, you were constantly in the bowels of a constantly functioning machine: one that had to turn rotors, circulate air, and fluid hydraulics, with people going about their shifts, creaks, and cracks of pressure, footsteps rushing, people laughing and yelling, etc—all the time. Here, I could have heard a leaf hit the ground. One dog slightly snored, the only respite.

As my ears adjusted, I picked up one buzzing fly in a far corner and let it out of the room through the front door. I then sat on my mat, sure I had mere minutes before madness.

But amazingly, the opposite happened. There was no social breakdown as I calmed and centered, just a paring away of distractions. Before I'd noticed what was happening, I'd begun to sink into my own mind for stimulation, rather than the unacknowledged constant opposite motion I knew well. Hours went by, and by the time the dogs woke up, I no longer noticed them; I was so entranced with all the relics trawled up by my mind, freed from my own blinders.

I raced through every scene of my life at a comet's pace, noticing peripheral details I'd never picked up and never bothered to access later. This was the first time I'd ever realized that I could access my own perceived memories the way that I did other people's; I'd simply never bothered to try. It simply would never have occurred to me to try to find some sort of internal serenity—the idea seemed kitschy and way too new-age-y. My friends would have thought I was joining a cult. Everyone but Marcus, evidently. I made a mental note: that guy seemed to know his stuff. I don't know if his goal of me uncovering lifelong sobriety would happen here, but I was definitely finding some unforeseen self-awareness.

I saw my Mother. I saw every brilliant, glittering moment I'd never considered replayable, as if suspended in crystal domes with fake snow falling—all over again. Every world was an accessible world, buried just beyond my waking life. I flew through childhood scenes— my nervous first day of school, Nannie's wobbling-and-then-broken vase. I saw a single moment in boot camp where I floundered in my long stroke—every glint in the water—and watched as the sputtering swimmer next to me was hooked, pulled out, and sent home, and it gave me just that push I needed to finish.

I smelled the smells, and all the sounds of those scenes clattered around the simple walls of my makeshift castle. I felt hyper-attenuated to the neurons firing in my brain, and I could almost feel them get excited by my newfound concentration. The sensation, if ever I could succeed in describing it, was more like unfurling wings for the first time than anything else I could imagine. I soared above scenes, above scenery, and it was all a flickering picture show, so much moving and shaking and rushing. Simultaneously, I felt every bit of air as it entered my lungs, as if I'd never managed to really breathe before. I felt entirely, utterly calm and at peace. Against all the odds.

But then something even more surreal happened. The more I thought over memories of my recent friends and allies, especially CJ and Dannels, the more I saw a strange rippling, a wobbling in the scenes. It took me a long time to comprehend what I saw, and a cold feeling descended on the images, which seemed to recede. As I locked more and more into the images and raced through the sorted playing cards like I'd mastered so long before, I began to see more and more, dissonant material entering, which I was immediately aware was wildly out of place. I worked and worked to turn a harsh whisper just below my hearing threshold, slowly managing to stretch my senses and crescendo the sound. The picture congealed as well, but it still appeared as if faraway—like I was peering through an aquarium and taking in the scene on the other side. I worked with every bit of my being to push through all the novelty and fatigue to get at this strange sight, and finally my mind clicked into gear. I realized with a start that what I saw was the present. I was remote viewing the present!

CJ stood in a room with three men in suits, and several others in uniform in an officious-looking building The complete lack of furnishings or warmth clarified that the place was military. The men looked angry. It was hard to focus as the walls kept shimmering and wobbling and my brain kept straining to slip back into my own surroundings, but I hung on. My eyes throbbed with a massive migraine, but I pushed through.

"Hyoksjhf odfko pfg!" one man yelled. I strained and convulsed, and put absolutely everything I had into purifying the communication stream just a bit more. And it worked.

"I don't know where he is. John didn't tell me anything."

"I find that very hard to believe! My Intel is that Calabrace has had a problem with Walker for years; am I mistaken in that assumption? I think it would be very easy to prove that point. Furthermore, it is in your best interests to help us as well as you can… since you're the officer charged with being his lead contact with the US Government, we might just choose to find you complicit, Commander Kopchik. We'd be well within our capacity to do so; and honestly I think we could really spin this situation however we see fit. We've told you before, Calabrace represents a liability.

"Time and time again, you've insisted we postpone decisions on his continued service, despite his ceaseless dereliction of duty and slipshod work ethic. And you!" The man gestured to Dannels, who glowered. "You've ensured us that this man wasn't just a relic of the past, that he would be accountable to standards and protocol. Do you find murder to be reasonable personal comportment?"

Dannels raised himself to his full height. "Permission to speak freely, sir?"

"Denied! Just answer the question, Admiral Dannels—" sneered a large man in a uniform.

"Regrettable. I'll speak nonetheless. I have, over several months, gathered sufficient evidence to believe there are as-yet un-presented, extenuating circumstances at play here. I believe Walker was part of a conspiracy on the life of Calabrace. And while I'm discouraged by your unwillingness to be presented this evidence, I do have ample evidence to prove it. I have approximately three hundred documents in my office, which I will present to a tribunal as soon as is possible… Sir."

A man pushed open a door and whispered something into the ear of a looming shadow alongside the superiors, who grinned as he leaned across the table. He boomed ironically, in a sad voice.

"I'm afraid your office is on fire, Dannels. Perhaps your young prodigy is more unpredictable than any of us have realized. Perhaps your constant interventions to protect him were shortsighted. Perhaps, you, too—"

With a sensation like being rendered boneless and thrown into a washing machine, I felt a strange bodily series of lurches and convulsions, as I managed to gasp and couch my way back into my present tense and my isolated surroundings. They were going after my friends! They were trying to frame the very men who had protected me! THAT would not do AT ALL.

Three minutes later, we blazed onto the country road. The silent gatekeeper scratched his head in confusion as we rocketed away from the monastery. A moment later, the key fell from the sky and clinked to the ground at his side.

33

Scenes of the road swam by, but I had my head between two worlds. At every moment I was driving, I was still seeing the faintest flickers and hearing the slightest whispers of my destination. The angry voice of some dark Deputy Undersecretary growled ferociously above all the other voices—

"If you think anyone is going anywhere before we've sorted this out, you're sorely mistaken. We will stay here. We need this squared away, once and for all. As we speak, my men are pouring over the autopsy. We will find proof that your Freakshow is responsible, and we will finally eradicate him, when we do. And you'll be next, if you continue your ridiculous loyalty—"

"Sir, I'm sure you meant to say you'll carry out a full and impartial investigation, which of course I respect, but—"

"Admiral, let me make myself perfectly clear. I have no interest in your opinion, only in the answers to my questions. Need I remind you, Dannels, to whom you're speaking? You will answer our questions, and if you think for one second that—"

"Sir, I am a United States Naval Officer. That's my core, and will always be. However, if you believe my position in this matter will play an adverse role in a full, impartial investigation, I'd be more than happy to continue my part after an immediate ADSEP," Dannels spat, disgusted.

Dannels was never one to step out of line like this. I slammed on the gas. One hundred and seventy-six miles left.

Somewhere around Palmdale, I pulled into a gas station and filled up. I walked inside to pay, when I saw an unfortunately madeup girl who looked she was in a B-Grade zombie film. I found myself staring at her face in amazement and horror. But when she saw me staring, her eyes widened. She looked back at me and then back at a TV playing above her counter of a breaking news story and screamed, *"It's HIM!"*

Two lost-looking rednecks barreled towards me, and I sprinted in shock back towards the car. The men slowed to a stop, when two furiously barking Dobermans arose over the window sills of my car. I managed to leap over the hood to the driver's side, slide in, and blast out of the station back towards the highway. The rest of the drive was a blur, adrenaline drowning out details.

I slowed to the gate and the Marine manning the base perimeter asked politely for identification. Realizing abruptly that I would never again be able to blithely hand someone my ID card, I felt sweat bead on my forehead.

"I'm terribly sorry for this," I muttered, grasping around in the dark.

"For what? I missed that sir, say again?" he apologized, leaning over the sill to hear me better.

"This," I muttered, blasting through the turn-style and the gate. The windshield immediately shattered into a sea of spider web cracks, but in the rear view mirror I could see the bewildered guard grabbing his hat and gun and trying to shove out of his door to shoot at me, as he sounded the alarm behind him.

For forty seconds, I sped along on instinct alone, towards the area I'd seen in the projected vision. As I checked details mentally between the two worlds, I could tell I was mostly in the right place, a feeling that was verified as I screeched to a halt next to CJ's car. I threw open my door and stuffed my dogs into CJ's car, hoping they'd be safer there than in mine. Around the corner of a far wall, I started seeing the long wobbling lines of laser sights and knew I had to hurry. Right as I saw the first responders burst from behind the wall, I was inside the building. I made it through two hallways before meeting my first man with a gun, who's first shot flew high, and I managed to rush through one more set of doors. Thereafter, a loud voice boomed, "SIR STOP IMMEDIATELY, OR I WILL SHOOT!"

I slowed and saw three guards leveling pistols at me, with a conference room alongside that I recognized from the vision.

"Stop sir, *do not move.* I will take you down, if you give me any reason to," The burly guard warned.

"I understand, I understand. I just need to see the men in that meeting," I yelled.

"John?!" I heard CJ's voice from the beyond the door. The walkie-talkies crackled to life, and the guards were asked whether they'd apprehended an intruder. They barked that they'd controlled the situation but immediately protested when asked to escort their charge into the meeting. After a moment's reluctance, I was patted down, and then led into the room.

"Well isn't this a surprise?! The sailor of the hour! We've been wasting our whole evening looking for you, Calabrace! Sit!" barked a man bathed in shadows, as another man pushed me into a metal chair.

"My apologies, sir. If someone tried to kill you, you would have probably run for your life as well."

The man leaned forward, exposing a cruel, wind-broken face in the gloom of the bureaucratic barren conference room. "It seems it was you who tried to kill someone, Calabrace. And you did a bang up job at it. We found traces of your DNA on the weapon, not far from the victim. We know you were there."

"Sir, I never said I wasn't! I was there walking my dogs, when that lunatic Walker pulled a gun on me. Bryan shot himself!"

"Well, not according to this report, Calabrace…" the shadowy man replied. "It implies that the single bullet through this man's head was fired by a disgruntled former classmate, one who'd held a grudge for years, and that man was *you.*"

Dannels jumped in. "As I said before, sir, I can prove that these allegations don't tell the whole story. Given time, I can reconstruct the research that has mysteriously," he said as he eyed the dark man on the right, "been *lost.* But as I've said, I wish to level a formal protest here and furthermore declare a charge of open conspiracy against an official agent of the United States government, and a patriot."

"That information seems to be missing, Admiral. Surely you don't expect a tribunal to wait around and—"

"*Sir*, none of this will be necessary. Please call in anyone who you'd wish to witness my confession," I replied calmly.

CJ looked at me like I'd lost my mind, but I tuned it all out, quietly closing my eyes and gripping on to the metal arms of the chair. Struggling to retain my fear and nausea, I sat serenely and breathed deeply. The highest echelons of interested parties filtered quietly into the room, buzzing their discontent at the unorthodox scene unfolding around me, just as I reached my most strenuous height of projection. I felt my eyes and gums bleed, as my hands clenched tighter and tighter, focusing on all the information and all of their minds. I saw all the evidence, all the secrets, all the pathways, all the noise and silence—but deep within myself I found a deadly, silent calm.

I watched heat rise off my body as the men looked around in shock, wondering what they'd just witnessed. Then, one after the other, their heads twitched and cringed. Their mouths fell open and their eyes dilated, like mine had so many years before.

"WHAT THE HELL IS THIS?!"

"JESUS, IT'S IN MY MIND!"

"GUATEMALA?!"

I had locked and loaded. It was like I was in a warehouse of all their memories. I had every image, sound, feeling, and passion flawlessly indexed in my head. I then placed them like an artist dabs paint to a canvas, knowing the full impact that each thought or picture would have on each man.

It took a lifetime to develop, but in a mere second, it was done.

It was like a game of cards where I doled out hands so they each held a wild card, with their colleagues' worst secrets. Every person was momentarily possessed with a magnitude of information that none could have ever experienced before. Two men retched horribly in a corner. Several shivered. Nobody made eye contact, all kept their eyes on the floor.

"Sir…" the guard kneeling over me muttered, giving up on trying to rise me back up, "I have information in my head that I…It's fucked up man…I don't know how it got there, but—"

"So do I," chimed in one voice, and then another.

"WHAT THE HELL IS THIS?! THIS IS YOU, CALABRACE, SOME TRICK..." the same voice protested again from a corner, terrified, with his voice warbling.

I slowly rose. I felt the two guards point their guns at me from behind, but I steadily ignored them.

"In your heads, you will find all the evidence collected by Admiral Dannels, and so rudely destroyed by...well, that information is also in your heads. Several of you were chosen, yes chosen, to host some very sensitive information—so that you might fully understand the nihilism of secrecy. There is no such thing. Now, if you please," I apologized to the guards but stepped away from them.

They stood there with their mouths open, but I knew they wouldn't shoot me on their own initiative. They had too many other thoughts in their minds to even think about me. The room was silent, besides two men crying quietly in the shadows.

"I have given you a glimpse into what it is to see the essence of people around you—in their full and constant complexity. It doesn't make either of us damaged goods; it doesn't make us a risk. It certainly shouldn't lead you to the convenient path of framing innocents as liabilities. I never asked to be in this world of secrets. You brought me here; you grew me. Frankly, I have no desire to live in your world anymore."

One of the men started fussing, "I don't have to listen to this, I don't have to—"

But his commanding officer grabbed his jacket and said, "Stand down and shut your mouth. I have some very troubling information about you in my mind...Information that I'd very much like to have rigorously disproven, before you leave my sight. Is that clear?"

An impatient hulk far behind the desk cracked his knuckles. "I'd like to take stock of what we're dealing with here. Am I correct in assuming that many, if not all of you, are receiving highly classified information via some form of telepathic communication?!"

There was a murmur, as I quietly approached. "Sir, I'm so sorry! I didn't see you back there, you must have come in late. I missed you!" Within an instant, I'd transferred a small encyclopedia into his mind. His eyes bulged and he groaned as he relived experiences of some less savory expeditions long reclaimed by the shadows of history. Feeling a bit cocky, I chose a Greatest Hits collection of sordid secrets that would have horrified anyone; and I gave an equal inoculation to everyone in the room of the horrors, mistakes, and failed plans that most had hoped would never see the light of day again.

I stood up and paced the room, staring into their eyes as they cringed away from me. "I'm sorry if this bothers you. I just wanted you to know a tiny taste of what I'm capable of. Sometimes, I don't even know…If anything, it is a testament to how devoted I've been to my job, to my country, and to you—sirs, that I've kept my sanity, with the things I've seen."

The quietly-crying officers in the shadows had been joined by a third, and together, they rocked back and forth, wailing in horror at the limited sights they'd seen.

"Among the images, I'm hoping right about now you're all accessing the full, unfiltered last hours of Bryan Walker, including a last minute meeting he had with several of you—shortly before meeting his untimely end. Take some time to sort through the details, and do with them as you see fit. However, let me assure you, in addition to that incidental data, the complete historical files on each of you here today, and some of your less-favorably remembered operations, chronological data, names, places, and contacts have all been remotely stored for safe-keeping. Think Operation Cyclone, 1980 Turkish coup d'état, funneling money to the Solidarnosc activists in Poland. And we certainly can't forget the overthrow the Sandinista government of Nicaragua…"

A shadow stood in the darkness, and everyone immediately changed their bearings. He evidently interrupted with some standing. "What is the point you're trying to make, Calabrace?"

"Simple, sir. I've only taken measures to 'protect' this information, as insurance for my own safety. My family has been unfortunately over-interfered with, in a manner unbecoming of this great country, for generations. This has to stop. I want out, and I believe my record will show that I am both innocent and trustworthy. I deserve to retire and be left in peace. If not, I will do what I must, to find peace. Perhaps this information would better serve the nation, if taken public?"

The assembled Intelligence crowd gasped in horror, then immediately began clamoring to know where the information was hidden.

CJ stood up and bellowed, "Well for one, those missions are in my head, sir. All the minute details and everything. It's horrific. It's almost like they were planted there by someone," he said, repressing a grin as he looked at me.

Dannels chimed in, "It's all in my head too. I'm not sure how, but I know more about these missions now, than I was ever made aware of—even acting as the Armed Forces chief liaison with Congress."

Five or six other voices piped up with the same observation, from around the room.

"I also saw Walker try to kill Calabrace here, before dying at his own hand," the guard muttered in an embarrassed voice, frowning as his partner shoved him reprovingly.

Once they'd all realized that I had progressed to the point of being able to copy images, timelines, and the complete emotional experiences of humans into others this way, they demanded to know how many others knew. They clearly wanted to mop up—it, me, whatever.

"C'mon Calabrace, these are serious National Security issues. Tell us who knows! Take us to the secrets…Then let's just put this all behind us, shall we? Learn from our mistakes? We can make this all go away, okay?"

I looked into the faces bathed in shadow and simply stated with the slightest grin, "I'm sorry sir, I don't recall off the top of my head… but I can assure you the information is safe and secure. Nor do I recall doing anything wrong, at any point. Correct me if I'm wrong. If you lie, we'll share it with the rest of class here. No games, General… I'm tired of games."

By now, they all knew they had been played. There were some very long, frustrated faces around the corners of the room. But they also finally understood that I was too valuable to let go, while I understood myself that I would never return to business as usual.

A Three Star in the room spoke first. "We need you, and you clearly know that. If you want to go public, we prefer that you don't… because it will put you and your family in imminent danger from every other intelligence agency in the world. But we won't try and stop you." He stood up, and spoke sincerely, albeit awkwardly. "We'd rather work with you than against you, John. We can work a plan that brings us both on the same side. I have thousands of men and women suffering from trauma, post-traumatic stress, brain injuries and worse. I believe you could give them hope and give them a second life—with talents like you've just shown us. I believe there is a role for you doing something more challenging, something more personally rewarding. What do you say? Give us a chance…You know every word I just said is the god honest truth."

"Well, sir, as I'm sure you've all seen by now, certain of you were involved in a certain conspiracy with the recently deceased to discredit and sabotage me. Some even helped feed my info to the Russians!"

The General nodded gravely and snapped his fingers. All the men stepped away from three men in a corner, now known to be the culprits, already sobbing and shaking together in a line. They were led from the room by the dazed guards.

"Thank you, sir. I would also need to have full control over the workings of *my organization*, and of course, all charges dropped— for any actions carried out in defense of my friends here—as well as your assurance that their career pipelines will not show so much as a blemish…"

"Done." The General nodded, with another senior member of the group adding, "We agree. Anything else? Let's end this today."

"I'll also need a water bowl, if we're going to be here a while. I have two dogs out in a car that really need me now," I added sheepishly.

JOHN TOLLIVER

EPILOGUE

It took a few weeks to realize it was all over. The rush, the terror, the entire era: just like that. It was like a massive wave toppling over an unprotected harbor had suddenly pulled back and dissipated back into the sea. I was free. No more surprises, no more surveillance, no more threats.

I spent what felt like a few millennia figuring out where I was at, watching the door open and close as everyone who cared about me came by to check in. They'd knock and open the door, and open it smiling, play with the dogs, prep food and hot drinks, and wait for me to slowly tune in to reality as it unfolded.

But fortunately, this didn't last forever. Like any spring thaw, I slowly began to readjust and pushed a bright smile to the surface as I realized everything was fine.

David and I became closer, after things started to settle to a normal pace in Coronado. He'd followed a lifelong dream to settle down and open a restaurant, and now every afternoon he'd come by and check on me, to see how I was doing. He and I regularly walked down the coast-side along the Silver Strand Blvd with the dogs, watching the Navy vessels pull in.

It took time, but eventually I began to feel like a person again—like the long hunt had abated, and I could come back into the open. The dogs leaped about as happy as ever, oblivious to the previous tension and growing serenity alike—just thrilled to be alive. For once, I felt the same way. The prospect of a new decade loomed before me—one where I'd finally have to decide for myself the way my life progressed. It'd been such a long time since I'd had that kind of control that I barely knew where to start. I could blame myself, my government, or world politics for my isolation; or I could choose to look forward…

I chose the latter.

Over our long walks, David had started asking probing questions about my past: about the university life I'd run away from, about my childhood dreams, about everything that had come before the strange day I'd decided to join the Navy. It was odd, because everything before had come to feel like a completely separate life—equal and distinct. The language, the customs, and the expectations of that military pace of life had completely subordinated everything that had come before it; and now I was left with the daunting task of welding the two ungainly halves together. And stone sober, to boot. It was a new world.

I started with my brothers. In a long series of weekend trips, we slowly rebuilt the effortless trust and confidence of our childhoods—especially Richard and I. It was slow going for some of them—my life had just been too far from their traditional white picket fence, one-point-five child, two-car garage existence. I spent time, played with their kids, and finally had long talks with their spouses and friends—long evenings, again—stone sober. For so long, I'd fled from Everywhere, USA, into anything but. But now I was determined to stitch back together all my relationships into something more than a simple safety net: instead I kept adding, kept packing down those relationships until I'd formed a new bedrock, something lasting. My life began to take shape atop it: structures built atop a new stability.

David and I went Christmas shopping and bought stuff for all my nieces and nephews and all of his—both thrilled to have a friend during the nightmarish crush in the stores. We bought a ship in a bottle for CJ's son, who lived for anything related to the ocean—just like his Father. David grabbed me a ridiculous onesie for Elizabeth's as yet unborn daughter—with huge lettering I LOVE MY UNCLE BEST. (Babies don't care for the semantics of first cousin once-removed… I figured it would work.) I sent a polite Christmas card to poor old Megan and her thankless husband: with me and all my dogs smiling before the broad shores of San Diego. Carrie wore a Santa hat, and Cash gnawed on a large plush candy cane. These are the things you do, I suppose—to be a good person? I was determined to do whatever it took.

Around those days, I also forced myself to let go of a search that had begun to obsess me, searching for my old college roommate Mark. The more I thought about it, the more I finally realized that neither of us would have been able to fully articulate the strangeness of those years—and we'd both lived our own lies around each other, our own betrayals and secretive, cloistered lives. So I did my best to subconsciously wish him well and washed him completely free from my mind.

When David had a networking meeting in NYC, I took the opportunity for an extra trip. He showed me around his old stomping grounds near Wappinger Creek, and I met his wonderful Mother: a warm librarian at one of the oldest libraries in the country, and his Father—an amateur theatre director. As we wandered around the ancient Grinnell Library where she worked, I gushed and gushed about History for the first time in ages—drawing on long dormant memories from my NYU days, talking about printing presses in the nineteenth century, waterwheels, and attacks on bastions of lost Loyalists in the eighteenth century…

"You should be teaching, John!" she laughed. "We could use a few folk with long memories like yourself, these days!"

David picked up the chant. For the next few days, he harped on the idea of a new hobby, a new vocation to fill up my time.

"Why don't you give school another shot? You've got nothing but time…and you could use something to concentrate on, as you get things together. What do you think?" Seeing the hesitation and conflict in my eyes, he wavered and looked away to regain his courage. Grinning, he muttered with renewed energy, "Well, sleep on it, at least. It couldn't hurt!"

In NYC, David went to his meetings, and I decided to look up an old friend, one I'd almost forgotten. Sober, I could barely find my way, and the alley surprised me as I'd half passed it. I turned inside and looked at the familiar bricks, the fire escapes, the old trash cans and boxes in the cold light of day. It hardly looked like the same place, but sure enough…I recognized the doorframe from the assault that I'd witnessed decades before. Before I had time to reconsider, I forced my legs forward, reached up, and knocked on the door. A few seconds went by, and a dog barked inside. I heard chains moving, and a bolt slid out; then the same familiar face peered out into the dim light of the alley. It took a second, but he recognized my face, and his own transformed in a flash.

"Why, look what the cat dragged in!" the man laughed merrily, "I do believe I know you, son!"

"John! I don't believe we ever shared names…But I'm John. John Calabrace."

"I'm Michael, John. So pleased to have met you, formally now—and practically, then. Thanks, again. I don't imagine I was doing so hot that evening, way back when…"

"No problem! As luck would have it, neither was I!"

We both laughed. We drank coffee inside for hours. Eventually we made our way to a nearby café for a late lunch, with Michael of course refusing the second I politely offered to push his wheelchair.

"As I recall, last time you dragged me somewhere, it was none too pleasant," he laughed.

We sat together for hours, discussing our strange lives since we'd seen each other last. It seemed that he'd made quite a habit of intervening in unfair fights. One of the times he'd intervened, he'd gotten some press and achieved some local celebrity. Amidst all the flashbulbs and interviews, he'd met a man starting work on a project to control artificial structures with brain power—theoretically including limbs—who asked him if he'd be interested in helping with the project. Over the years, Michael watched in awe as that research moved out of the theoretical plane, towards reality. Finally, during a visit to the main project site at Duke University, friends had introduced him to another shy researcher—evidently visiting from across the country—who was nonchalantly walking on a pair of artificial, mechanical legs.

The doctor was a climber from California, who had lost both his legs to a double amputation after disastrous frostbite. Seeing past the apparent loss, he'd immediately engineered made-to-purpose legs to get back to his climbing obsession: sometimes fitting wedged slim "feet" to fit in thin rock crevices inaccessible to "normal" climbers' feet, or raked ones to move more easily across loose snow.

The veteran and the engineer had become fast friends, and now Michael was thrilled to announce that within two weeks, the rest of his visits to the Duke University experimental trials would be on his own two feet, albeit mechanical ones. He was thrilled. By the end of our meal, his infectious enthusiasm had warmed me to the core, and I remembered something I'd barely acknowledged—there was work to be done.

I abruptly remembered the man in the cemetery, whose ring was in my jacket. I remembered his vague murmurs about helping people, and I knew *this* was my shot at doing something like Michael was getting—enabling the kind of help he deserved. I knew that there had to be people all over in Michael's position, people who gave all they could, without question, but got banged up in the process. That was what I wanted to do: find a way to help those people. In the back of my head, I made a note to myself that sooner or later, I'd have to find a way to make that dream a reality. And I knew the first step was reconnecting with the mysterious man I'd last seen at a funeral.

Michael and I wrapped up our visit and exchanged contact info, promising to stay in touch. As I gave him the vague outline of my life moving in a new direction, I found myself wanting to find a way to help the men who'd given all they could, like he had, and then similarly been left in the shadowy alleys of the world.

"Heck, go ask them! Look at me, I'm happy as a clam; don't ask me! Go ask them! I guarantee if you go and visit Walter Reed, you'll find the men who did all they could and are suffering more than they bargained for. Go talk to them, and they'll help you find out what needs to be done!"

Just like that, I had my decade worked out. Through the interventions of my friends in the military, I'd soon begun a project of regularly working alongside post-traumatic stress veterans in Walter Reed, creating experimental therapy projects to help with recovery and reintegration. As they rebuilt, I felt myself doing the same. I'd found my purpose.

Thanks to David's encouragement, I simultaneously returned to school and before too long was fighting to defend my dissertation, as Nannie had always wanted. My brothers were both dumbfounded and thrilled, and three cheered me on as I became an official PhD. CJ and

Dannels could never quit conspiring to bring me back under the wing of the military establishment, reminding me that "retirement isn't real." So eventually, I even got into the habit of doing sporadic mediation work for Navy and Defense industries, doing conflict resolution (such as only I could). Few could know exactly how I was so capable, but for the first time in years my old submarine nickname reemerged, and I was hailed anew as "the Henry Kissinger of the Sea!"

Before I knew what was happening, I'd emerged from the dark spell of my life, as an out and out *Good Person.* Everything I did got to be so darn good-hearted and wholesome, it almost made me sick—John Calabrace had become an innocent boy again: Johnny the Dreamer.

I wrote a letter to my old sobriety counselor—who'd fought so hard and long without thanks, and finally I gave all the thanks he was due. I wrote to my Sea-Dad Rusty, who'd tried as often as possible to lead me ashore from the stormiest seas, and thanked him too. Eventually, every remaining tangled knot had been sorted out. I was a new man, the man I'd been, and the child as well: all in one. I had a family; I had laid out roots.

More than ever before, I felt surrounded in warmth and love.

And so one stormy afternoon, I found my way back to the small icy cemetery where so many familiar family souls slept, ready to say my finally scattered thanks. I stood over the row of graves for a long time, reading the names aloud and tracing my fingers over the words as I laid down flowers, setting down the heavy load I'd wrapped my overcoat around and an armful of flowers.

Staff Sergeant Frederick Calabrace. I touched the simple scrollwork and imagined my Father, working late into the night in his study to provide for the family all those years. I laid my hand on the gravestone, and wished he could see me now…

Nancy Gray Calabrace, the sweetest Mother anyone could ask for. Mom had waited hand and foot on my Father when his heart had begun acting up, and when she lost him she'd moved right in to help her Mother, never pausing for a moment. After Nannie had passed on, Mom hadn't been long herself, as if knowing she'd run out of people to care for. I laid a large stack of roses on her grave and knew somehow she was smiling at me, wherever she was.

Finally I passed to *Nancy Gray*, who lived to ninety-plus, sharp as a tack to the very end. A fresh rose was already lying on her grave! My head swiveled into the darkness.

"I told you, son, they never made another woman so kind," a gentle voice muttered behind me. I spun around, my heart pounding. In the shadows behind me, the old man I'd seen so long before was leaning on a cane.

"You! I didn't know if I'd ever see you again!"

"Ah, that's fine, that's fine. Time doesn't move so fast when you're my age. I've been patient. And you've been busy! I've seen some big changes in your life, John Calabrace."

Well, all the surveillance in my life hadn't disappeared completely.

"Yes, there's been some of that. I hope you approve of all you've seen," I laughed.

"Indeed, I do, John. But I do wonder whether you've thought about what I've said, about some friends of mine? Friends like yourself, friends with abilities that might seem unusual, at least to the outsiders. As it so happens, you've already met with an associate of one of our people, a doctor in California, who—"

"Ah! The man who helped Michael?" I burst out, thrilled.

"Quite so, John! Well done. We've been doing all that we can to change the expectations of—"

But I cut him off, before he had any need to make further explanations.

"I'M IN!" I boomed.

Snow fell on the stones around us, and he smiled down warmly at the line of names.

"You know, they'd all be so very proud of this boy who grew into such a man, John. Your Mother, you Father, your Grandmother, and—"

But I'd already knelt down to the ground, and was fumbling with my jacket—an innocent smile playing over my face, reflecting off a glazed surface sheltered within the fabric. My friend peered quizzically over my shoulder, confounded as to what could so preoccupy me in such a solemn moment. His eyebrows leaped up as I tore away the jacket, and gleaming marble shone in the chilly air. I leaned the plaque against the base of Nannie's gravestone with reverence and slowly rose back to my feet.

He looked at me for a moment quietly, and in a voice of warm satisfaction read the script off the new stone monument, finally secure where it had always belonged…

Major John Grey: He Gave All He Could.

Rest in Peace, Now and Forevermore…

He smiled, and clasped my shoulder. "Well, shall we begin, John Calabrace?"

The trees glittered overhead, and the dancing lamplight sparkled over the gate. All was right in the world. We stomped our feet through the ice and stepped into a brighter future.

www.ingramcontent.com/pod-product-compliance
Lightning Source LLC
Chambersburg PA
CBHW020932310726
48980CB00007B/741/J

* 9 7 8 0 6 9 2 7 7 2 7 0 6 *